the AMERICAN WAR

The American War

Published by:
Two Peas Publishing
PO Box 1193
Franklin, TN U.S.A.

Also by Don Meyer

The Sheriff Thomas Monason Trilogy
Winter Ghost
McKenzie affair
Uncle Denny

Jennifer's Plan
... the only thing sweeter than revenge is retribution.

The Protected Will Never Know
-A Vietnam memoir

www.dpmeyer.com

the AMERICAN WAR

DON MEYER

two
peas
publishing

FRANKLIN, TENNESSEE

The War Remnants Museum in Ho Chi Minh City (formerly Saigon) is a memorial museum for what is referred to in Vietnam as *The American War*.

ONE

The explosion of the first mortar round, hitting right inside the compound, shattered the quiet of the night. Before anyone had a chance to react, several other rounds smashed into the earth throwing dirt and debris about. The cries of pain permeated the air as the defenders scrambled for cover.

Artillery shells and small arms fire followed the barrage of explosions. Dead and wounded soldiers were strewn about the camp as the shelling continued without a break in the dark of night. Structures, defenses and the supply depot were all quickly destroyed in the continuing barrage.

An American Special Forces soldier tried to get his bearings inside one of the defensive holes as dust and debris flew around him through the air. He felt a hand grab his shoulder in the flying dust.

"You okay?"

"Yeah, just…"

Lying next to him in the hole, another American Forces soldier, a sergeant, stopped long enough to take a breath. The sergeant swallowed hard, trying to moisten the dust gathering inside his mouth before speaking.

"You still got that radio from yesterday's patrol?"

Another round hit close to their hole, sending more debris and dust into the air. They shielded themselves from the fallout, and then slowly rose back up.

"I said you still got that radio from patrol yesterday?"

"Yes. Yeah, it's right here, still on my gear."

The sergeant nodded, pointing toward the instrument.

"Right now, I don't know what works and what doesn't. Looks like they've hit everything in camp. Don't know how many, if any, radios are left working. Guard that thing with your life. Got any extra batteries with you?"

The sergeant watched him nod in the affirmative.

"Always carry one extra on patrol."

The sergeant nodded and placed his hand on the radio man's shoulder.

"Well son, start working through the frequencies, see if you can make contact with anyone and advise we need Medevac choppers in here right now... we got wounded everywhere."

The sergeant grabbed the man's shoulder again.

"Looks like you in trouble, get the hell out of this hole, make your way inward, but start calling now."

The sergeant was up and out of the hole before he could respond, but he did anyway.

"I'm on it."

The shaken, dust covered radio operator, repeated the call signs, waiting for a reply. Allowing himself a moment to survey the scene, he looked over his bunker just as another shell hit, sending dust and debris hurtling his way. A moment later he gathered himself into a sitting position, looking desperately for the handset to the radio.

Two men jumped into the hole beside him, neither of which spoke English. He thought at least one was Vietnamese, but the other was probably one of the Chinese Nung soldiers supporting the camp. Nodding to acknowledge their presence, he went back to looking for the handset. The two men watched his frantic search intently, until he finally pulled the radio out from under the dust and debris, and yanked on the cord until it became taught. Looking at the man next to him, the Chinese Nung fighter, he tugged again at the cord to let the man know he was kneeling the handset. Bowing, the soldier rose up to let the cord pull free. Small arms fire intensified and the two soldiers directed their attention to returning the fire.

The completely rattled American Forces soldier brushed off the radio and used his fatigue shirttail to clean up the handset before trying to reach the Medevac helicopter. A shell exploded outside the hole and the Chinese Nung soldier slipped back, his face now missing. The Vietnamese soldier screamed and vacated the hole. Before the radioman could react, the sergeant was back in the hole yelling.

"What's the status on those Medevacs?"

Noticing the radioman staring at the dead soldier, he got between the two.

"Forget about him, do your job. Get those birds in here. We got wounded all over the fuckin' place."

Just as quickly, the sergeant was gone again. Another round hit close sending dust and debris into the hole covering him. He repeated the call signs, waiting for an answer. Finally the whirl of helicopter blades buffeting the air could be heard over the explosions and confirmation of their arrival crackled over his radio.

Hearing a series of explosions close by, he looked up to see that the wire had been breeched, men... soldiers... their soldiers were coming through the breech. Remembering what the sergeant had said, he crawled out of the hole dragging the radio, his rifle and a bandolier of ammo.

Looking around first, he headed toward a group of soldiers preparing to load the wounded in the hovering helicopter. Just as he approached, a volley of bullets smashed into the side of

the Medevac, causing it to waver, but the bird stood fast, until
they loaded the last man on. In a stinging cloud of dust the helicopter was gone.

Bullets danced around his feet, as he made his way to
another potential shelter. Climbing inside the new hole, he was
greeted by another group of Chinese Nung Troops. As before,
they nodded his presence, but continued pouring fire into the
moving wave. One of these soldiers tapped him on the shoulder
and pointed toward the rear, deeper into the camp. Looking
to where he was pointing, he nodded and quickly evacuated
the hole. Running low he made his way over to a bunker and
slipped inside, but found he could not get any radio reception,
so immediately crawled back out.

Looking around, just as another round hit near him, followed by automatic weapons fire, he hit the ground and
crawled into another hole. He could see the hole he had left and
the men standing outside of it, apparently in hand-to-hand combat. Sliding down into the new hole, he started calling and was
greeted this time by an Air Commando Pilot who confirmed
that more birds were on the way.

In what seemed like forever, the sun finally started to rise
in the sky and light moved over the besieged camp. Heavy firing continued throughout the compound. Piercing screams
from wounded men could be heard over the noise of the explosions and intense rapid small arms fire.

The sound of approaching aircraft and helicopter blades
buffeting the air brought some relief. Keeping the handset next
to his right ear, he held tightly to the .45 pistol in his left hand.
Funny, he thought, I don't remember how I got this pistol or
where. His M16 was still strapped across his left shoulder and
the bandolier of ammo was strapped across his chest as well.

Someone jumping into the hole beside him brought a quick
reaction and when the dust settled the .45 was pointed in the
sergeant's face.

"Hold on son, I'm one of the good guys."

Slowly the sergeant pushed the gun down. Before he could say anything else, the radio man raised his hand.

"Right, same place as earlier. Don't know how many. Take what you can. Right. Yes. Roger."

"Sarge, that's the birds coming in. We should let them know so they can get the wounded ready. Said they can't stay on the ground too long. What's the status out there?"

The sergeant sat back against the dirt wall. The sweat on his face mixed with the layers of dust forming a rather grotesque expression.

"Vietnamese soldiers have been hit pretty hard. Chinese guys held back the breech, killing most of the invaders... half the enemy killed in hand-to-hand. Lost a few of their own. Last I hear, we got two KIA, don't know how many wounded yet. Haven't accounted for everybody in this shit. Camp's torn to shreds. Once we get the wounded out, we're going to pull back to the north wall see if we can shore up a more compact defensive position. We're spread too thin to guard this whole compound. I think Intel was a little short on their estimates, there's a lot of those little fuckers out there. Regulars, none of that guerilla bullshit, these are hard-core soldiers, the real thing. Looks like they aim to take this camp one way or another."

Traffic on the radio interrupted their conversation.

"Sarge, they're coming in, maybe we better..."

The sergeant nodded and stood up, pulled himself out of the hole, and motioned for the radioman to join him.

The noise of planes and helicopter blades buffeting the air overtook the sound of gunfire. Gunships and A-IEs strafed enemy positions outside the camp, pouring on a heavy barrage of firepower, at the very least keeping the enemy's head down for the time being.

"Sarge, said they'll be bringing in supplies later. Medical, ammo, maybe some chow, as soon as they can clear. Probably in drops, the runways too tore up to land anything. Hopefully hit the target, but we should be prepared to go fetch anything falls short."

The sergeant nodded. The first of the Medevac helicopters landed, wounded men were quickly loaded on board, the chopper taking off almost as soon as it landed. Another bird was right behind it.

In the daylight, the destruction became clear. Bodies were strewn about the camp. No attempt was made to recover those, the focus was squarely on the wounded. With the weather ever threatening, wounded out and resupply in was the priority. Sporadic gunfire could be heard over the roar of engines as planes continued to strafe the outer defenses, along with the circling gunships. The noise was deafening. However, all appeared to be stabilizing inside the camp. The sergeant was busy giving orders on shoring up the defenses, in preparation for another attack.

Standing off to the side, the radio clutched firmly in his hand, the handset tucked under his right ear, the .45 still tightly gripped in his left, the urge to take a leak suddenly overcame him. Looking first to where the latrines used to be, he decided it really didn't matter and stepped behind the bunker and let it flow.

The radio crackled, the first of the resupply was on its way in. He looked for the sergeant, finally getting his attention and updated him on the arrival of supplies. The sergeant began gathering troops to get ready to unload and secure that precious cargo.

In the midst of all the deafening noise all seemed eerily quiet. Hopefully they would have time to rebuild their defenses and prepare for the next attack, which they knew would be coming sooner rather than later. The rest of the day dictated that immediate need.

Located in Thua Thien Province of I Corps near the Laotian border, the A Shau Valley is a slit in the mountains, a valley thirty miles or so long, filled with elephant grass as tall as the people trying to walk through it. The natural formation protected by a rim of triple layered canopied jungle. Sitting forty-five miles west of Hue, the remote western edge sits on the Laotian border. Listed as Enemy Base Area 611, the valley has long acted as a main entry point of the Ho Chi Minh Trial into South Vietnam and a strategic NVA operations area. The North Vietnamese used the area as a conduit for bringing in supplies and troops as well as a communications route for the North Vietnamese Army and Viet Cong operating in and around I Corps in the north.

In the spring of 1966, the A Shau Special Forces Camp at the south end of the valley was just five miles from the border with Laos. A barbed wire and earthen walled triangular shaped fortress about 200 yards long, it included an airstrip of about 2,300 feet comprised of a pierced steel planking base, just outside the perimeter of the camp.

This outpost was astride the route to Hue and Da Nang and was a clog in the NVA offensive strategy. Disrupting a major infiltration route adjacent to the Ho Chi Minh Trail, the camp served as a thorn in the side of the enemy's plans. Deep in Viet Cong controlled territory, the camp's role was to monitor traffic coming down that trail on the Laotian border.

Defending the camp were ten American Special Forces soldiers and 210 South Vietnamese Civilian Irregular Defense Group (CIDG) soldiers, supported by Air Commando units equipped with A-1 Skyradiers and AC-47 "Spooky" gunships. Patrols were run out of the camp to conduct search and destroy missions, occasionally running into Viet Cong resistance. Initially a rather routine mission, but all that changed in early March, 1966.

Reports of a large scale NVA buildup in the valley, consisting of four battalions, among them the 6th and 8th from the North Vietnamese 325th Division with the express purpose of taking the camp, put everyone on notice. Two days before the attack, the camp was reinforced with seven more American Advisers, interpreters and a MIKE force of 149 Chinese Nung soldiers. The camp was immediately put on alert in preparation for the impending attack.

The North Vietnamese Army came into the A Shau with the sole intention of ridding the valley of the American Special Forces camp and reopen those infiltration routes, desperately needed to move men and supplies into South Vietnam. The camp needed to go and the NVA would stop at nothing short of accomplishing that task.

Shortly after midnight on the second day, the raining down of mortar shells slamming into the compound once again shattered the quiet of the night. Unlike the night before, these rounds had found their range hitting with deadly accuracy. Following closely behind of the marching shells, a torrent of machine gun, RPG shells and small arms fire ripped through the fortifications.

The Sarge and the radio man were instantly awake, not that they were ever really asleep, and crouched lower in their hole as the rounds smashed into the compound. The other two men in the hole with them, Chinese Nung soldiers, were up and ready. After about an hour of probing the mortars stopped and small arms fire continued strafing the camp.

"Soldier, you better call in and tell them we're under full

scale attack and we could use all the help we can get."

As he repeated the call sign, waiting for an answer, one of the other men tapped the sergeant on the shoulder and pointed. The Sarge looked across the compound to where the man was pointing.

"Shit they breeched the south wall. They're already through the barbed wire. This is going to get real ugly real quick. What are you hearing?"

The firing inside the camp intensified as the defenders tried to block the enemy from further infiltration into the compound. A defensive position of Chinese Nung soldiers rose up from the east and provided covering fire as the others retreated further back to the north wall, the south wall now fully breached and being used by the enemy to attack the inside of the camp.

Heavy fighting continued until daybreak, but the cloud cover was still too thick to bring in any air support. The defenders continued their retreat to the north wall, eventually giving up the east side of the camp.

During a scamper to a new position, a recoilless rifle shell exploded next to the sergeant and the radioman, sending them both crashing to the ground. Picked up and dragged by the Nung soldiers, the radioman broke away and rushed back for the radio, which was now in two pieces. Grabbing everything he could see, he beat it back to the new hole. The Nung soldiers provided covering fire as he dived back into the hole.

Sarge was braced against the inside wall, a large patch of red covering his chest.

"Sarge?"

"Never mind that. Can you get that thing to work again?"

"Don't know?"

"Don't know won't cut it. Yes or no?"

Looking at the pieces in his hands, he realized that the battery case had separated from the radio. The bad news was the battery was missing. He looked up at the Sarge who was investigating the hole in his left shoulder, the burning piece of shrapnel still lodged under the shoulder bone. Without hesitating he pulled the hot metal out and threw it to the ground.

"Fuck it."

A Nung soldier wrapped a bandage around the wound. Sarge nodded and turned to the radioman.

"Well?"

"The good news is I can put it back together."

"The bad?"

"The battery is missing. Must have fallen out when it came apart."

"And?"

"Well, we have two options. Crawl back and get the missing battery, or continue moving back and hope we can find one in the resupply cargo."

"The resupply will belong to them shortly. Not a good choice. So I guess it's plan A."

Before the sergeant could react, the radioman was out of the hole crawling to where they went down. Sarge yelled from the hole.

"Stay flat, don't stand up. They will put covering fire down for you."

The radioman crawled on elbows and knees, dragging the .45 with him. Sure that he was in the area where they went down, he felt around in the dust and debris for the battery. Crawling a little further away from the hole he found it, next to the body of a dead mangled Vietnamese soldier. The crumpled body had actually protected the battery from any further damage.

Turning, he raised the battery in the air and started to crawl back to the hole, the battery in his right hand the .45 in the left. The Nung soldiers continued their covering fire. He could hear the bullets zinging over him. The crawl was slow and dusty in the churned up dirt. Finally he slid back into the hole. Two of the soldiers patted him on the back. Sarge nodded.

"Well."

"Couple of minutes."

Sarge nodded.

By the time he got back on the air, strikes were being provided by Air Command and per Sarge's instruction, a napalm drop was requested for the south wall.

"Sarge, they want to know if we need another supply drop."

"Negative. They'd get it, but we're running low on everything. Request evacuation. Tell them the gooks have breached the south wall and our friends here say they are at the east wall… his people are pulling back. We'll try to regroup by the north wall… bring those birds in over there."

The radioman relayed the requests.

"Said they'd forward it and get back to us. Can we hold for now?"

Sarge stared at the radioman, grimaced and smiled.

"That's just great. Tell them they got an hour, maybe two, then send body bags, because we won't be here."

The radioman sat silent, handset in his right hand the .45 in his left. Finally he passed on the message. He did not receive a reply.

The sergeant tapped his rifle on the radio to get his attention.

"We need to get out of here, get back toward the wall."

He tapped the Nung soldier closest to him. Waving his hand in the air he pointed, the Nung soldier nodded his acknowledgement and spoke to his men. Laying down a covering fire he motioned and the Sarge and his radioman exited the hole, moving fast and low across the compound. Bullets bounced around them. The four Nung soldiers were walking backwards, firing as they went. Finally they all reached a bunker and slid inside. The radioman stayed outside. The sergeant looked out questioning.

"Sorry Sarge, radio won't work inside."

The Sarge disappeared back inside but was back out in a moment with two Nung soldiers. Together they went around the bunker, reaching the backside just as a rocket propelled grenade exploded beside them. Damn, someone had a bead on them. Firing came from the opening of the bunker and they saw two enemy soldiers fall, one carrying the rocket launcher, apparently heading for the bunker.

"Jesus they're that fucking close, right inside the compound."

The Sarge looked at the Nung soldier who swept his arm in a let's go motion. Again they all moved out further toward the north wall.

Finally the call came that the decision was made to evacuate all personnel from the camp.

The last move had connected them up with another American advisor and one of the interpreters, so they could finally communicate.

"Anybody seen the LT?"

"Yeah, he was on the second chopper. Alive when he left, but…"

Sarge nodded.

"Who's running things?"

"Until we hear different, you are."

Sarge looked at the advisor, and quickly nodded. He directed the interpreter to tell the Nung soldier to have his people destroy all the equipment and give the order to start gathering for lift out. The Nung soldier nodded and started barking orders in Chinese to his men.

"How long we got?"

The sergeant looked at the advisor, the interpreter and the ranking Nung who had joined them.

"Couple of hours tops. According to my guy." He pointed to the radioman. "Said they are bringing a dozen or so Sikorskys to lift, but they can only land two maybe three in this area. It'll get more and more intense as the defenses diminish. Might need to execute the escape plan. Not everyone will get out by chopper."

The Nung soldier spoke and the interpreter translated.

"Said he'll keep his men back, they'll leave through the escape route. He also said to watch out for the Vietnamese, they won't stay so easy. He also said...well you get the idea."

Sarge nodded.

"Soldier what's... shit, what's your fucking name anyway?"

"Aldrich, Alan Aldrich."

"Alan? Listen up. This is going to get pretty dicey. We need to be on the first birds that land. You understand?"

Alan Aldrich nodded in the affirmative.

"Use whatever excuse you need, but make sure you and I are in the ready to get on the first or second birds, after that... well just make sure, okay?"

Alan Aldrich nodded again.

Sarge turned to the advisor and the interpreter.

"That goes for you two as well and anybody else you see. Be the first group. You understand."

The advisor looked at him questioning. Sarge let out a sigh, grimacing as he did.

"It's simple arithmetic. We won't be able to lift everyone out, a good number of those left will have to use the escape plan. Hope the NVA only want the camp, won't chase them. Either way the scramble will get ugly... at least among a certain group. Our Chinese friends will be long gone before they even know they left. I've seen it before. Just be ready."

More soldiers poured into their area as they prepared for the evacuation. However the enemy wasn't letting up, pushing even harder into the last secure area on the north wall.

The roar of helicopter blades was heard overhead. Gunships were laying down a heavy covering fire. The first two Sikorskys landed quickly loading troops and pulling out just as fast. A barrage of machine gun fire pelted the birds as they sat there. The next two landed and as they pulled out anti aircraft fire hit one of the birds. It disappeared in a cloud of smoke.

Sarge, the advisor, the interpreter and Alan Aldrich had been caught in the opposite side of the evacuating helicopters and now had to make their way across through the mob to try and get on one. Suddenly fire erupted around them, each man turned and returned fire. The two Nung soldiers that had been with them did so as well, finally quelling the onslaught. But now it was too late to try to get to the choppers that were being mobbed by the other soldiers.

"Alan, I have an idea."

Alan Aldrich sat next to the Sarge, the advisor close as well.

"See those two gunships circling. Put a call in, say we need an extraction, four Americans one hundred feet from the evacuation point. Got a place to land."

Sarge pointed to a break in the fortification.

"We can get to there and he can pick us up."

Alan nodded and made the call.

"Affirmative Sarge, be here in one zero mikes."

"Than we better move."

Sarge attempted to stand, but slipped, back, his right foot covered in blood. The advisor and the interpreter supported him as they made their way to the pick up point. As the Huey swooped in, it was pelted with heavy small arms fire, but held its ground. Several NVA soldiers had made their way around the compound and were preparing to enter through the very breach that the Americans were attempting to escape from.

The Huey held fast, the door gunner pouring out the covering fire. The other door gunner came across and was using his M16 to provide additional cover fire.

The four Americans reached the helicopter and pushed the sergeant on board. As the advisor climbed in a barrage of small arms fire exploded all around them, hitting the advisor in both legs and the interpreter in the back as they fell into the chopper, the other door gunner quickly pulling them on board.

Just about the time Alan Aldrich thought he had made it, he felt the pain in his arm, his leg and finally his hand. Standing sideways probably saved his life as the bullets tore into his right side. Had he been straight they would have hit him center chest in the groin and the fatty part of his leg.

Using his left side, and not letting go of the .45, he pulled himself into the chopper. The PRC 25 radio, known to the men as a Prick 25, that radio that had been his life line through all this, slipped from his bloody hand and dropped to the ground as the Huey lifted off. The door gunner screaming insanely as he poured out the rounds, firing at the ground below.

"Mother fuckers."

The door gunner continued his heavy firing until they were airborne and pulling away.

Alan Aldrich reached over to the sergeant.

"We made it."

Sarge nodded.

The Huey banked and turned sharply for one more pass, the door gunners on both sides giving it all they had, before pulling up and heading out of the besieged camp.

Explosions rocked the camp as the equipment and weapons were destroyed, taking quite a few of the enemy soldiers with it. Using that as a diversion, the Nung soldiers made their way to the escape route out of the camp and headed for the rendezvous point. When the last of the Vietnamese realized no more helicopters were coming, they quickly followed along. Evacuation helicopters were already hovering when the soldiers got to the pick up point.

This time the evacuation was orderly as the Nung soldiers provided cover while the Vietnamese were lifted out. The last group of Nung soldiers out dropped a handful of white phosphorous grenades as the Huey lifted off covering their exit.

Back at the camp, the NVA quickly moved in to fortify their freshly captured compound and reinforce their position with antiaircraft guns and ground artillery.

The camp was theirs now, but more importantly they owned the A Shau Valley completely, having driven out the last remaining resistance from their valley.

TWO

Another cloud of dust rose high in the air as the next cadre of cavalry rode into camp. Soldiers in full cavalry regalia, mounted on some of the finest horses to be seen. Truly a spectacular sight, these soldiers on their mounts prancing into camp. Never mind the dust they churned up as they passed by, they were the elite, the fighting force most coveted. The men watched as the cavalry passed keeping their attention as another group of soldiers came marching into camp close behind the horse soldiers.

Men came from all over, mostly from the northern states. They came from the Army of the Potomac, the Army of West Virginia and as far south as Louisiana from the ill-fated Red River Campaign. Now they were all together and they still kept coming. They had come by train, by march, on horseback and by directive, gathered in a field, encamped just south of Harper's Ferry, near Halltown.

Soldiers milled about, gathering together, not sure where they belonged just yet. Some were exhausted from the march to get here. They nodded to fellow soldiers as they set up their positions, erecting another tent, and another and another. Trips down to the bank of the river provided relief from the heat and dust swirling about them.

Most of the men understood they would be moving out in a day or two, and waited patiently for confirmation of their final attachments and assignments, happy to be at rest for the moment. As more soldiers and cavalry poured into camp a feeling of uneasiness fell over the men, wondering just how big this gathering would be and more importantly the size of the battle which they were surely about to enter.

The soldiers that arrived had set up their tents in the usual grid pattern. Officer tents, or quarters, were aligned in the front of the new street with the regular soldiers along the lines a unit would form. However, with all the men now arriving that pattern started to become strained with tents being set up anywhere they could be. Most of these tents consisted of a wedge, a six-foot length of canvas draped over horizontal poles placed side by side.

The Quartermaster wagons continued to stream in, carrying the supplies needed to sustain an army of this size. The wagons pulled in next to the hospital facilities, to the mess tents, to the supply and storage facilities. The wagons to be used for ambulances, ferrying soldiers from the battlefield to the hospital facilities, pulled in and parked.

More wagons rolled in carrying the hay and grain for these horses, many more of which were corralled outside of camp, horses for the cavalry, horses for the artillery, horses to pull the cannon, horses for replacement and of course horses to pull all these wagons. The parade was continuous, so much so that except for the dust they churned up, they would not have been noticed.

An army doesn't move without the quartermaster corps, manned by people that are often forgotten. Cooks, clerks, mechanics, laborers, quartermaster people, commissaries, provost-marshals, provost judges, wagon masters, agents, teamsters, scouts and a host of others needed to man all these wagons and supplies.

Of late, Negroes—freedmen—have been used where possible to fill some of these jobs. An army marching was always followed by a steady train of wagons loaded with the necessities of war, which included great stores of food and forage for the animals, medical supplies and weapons and ammunition. As the war progressed, a great mass of freed Negroes had joined that train as well.

The dust continued to rise in the air as another group of soldiers marched in and another unit of cavalry rode into camp followed by ever more wagons. Even though most of the soldiers knew, or at least believed they would be moving in a day or two, the process of setting up a new camp was in full swing. All of this would be taken down packed up and moved again as soon as the orders came down. But for now the business of creating a camp for this large number of officers, soldiers, cavalry, animals and support cadre was the job facing the quartermaster.

Those soldiers that had arrived already milled outside their tents, watching the activity around them, knowing in the morning they would be drilling as usual. Soldiers of one unit were butted up against the other units in their regiment. The early arrivals had the opportunity to get set up and have this time to reflect. However the later arrivals had to search for places to pitch their tents and join with their regiments or brigades.

No one who saw the massive amount of men, cavalry, horses, wagons and continuous flow throughout the day, could believe this was anything less than a major undertaking. While officers, from the platoon right up through the regiment and brigade were either mum, or not informed yet on this campaign, it didn't take much to realize something big was in the wind.

On the southern end of camp, regiments of the same brigade, who had set up earlier in the day milled about each others "street" trying to make their own sense of all this activity.

Brigadier General James B. Ricketts commanded the Third Division, now part of Horatio Wright's VI Corps, his second was Colonel J. Warren Keifer, comprised of First Brigade, commanded by Colonel William Emerson, which included 14th New Jersey, 106th New York, 151st New York, 184th New York, 87th Pennsylvania and the 10th Vermont.

Second Brigade, was commanded by Colonel William Ball, and included 6th Maryland, 9th New York, 110th Ohio, 122nd Ohio, 126th Ohio, 67th Pennsylvania and 138th Pennsylvania. Third Division had been moved from the Army of the Potomac III Corps to this new Middle Military Division.

Two men from different regiments looked across at each other and nodded. A commotion off in the distance caught both of their attention. Somebody, certainly someone important, had arrived in camp. Several officers were making their way to a large tent set up in the middle of camp, the headquarters area. Without speaking and still quite a distance away from each other both men had the same thought.

All movement came to a halt. The camp stood quiet, the dust swirling around as a lone rider rode up to that headquarters tent. In a moment everything went back to normal.

Horses carrying riders continued their journey, horses pulling artillery started back up, men marching continued their quick step and the hustle and bustle of erecting tents overtook the noise. The dust continued to swirl heavily through the air.

The two men went back to their normal activities, talking to the men around them. All of them wondering who had rode into camp just now and what it all meant, what it all would mean and where were they going, especially with an army of this size.

To the southwest of the Federal encampment, the Confederates waited, confident that the Shenandoah Valley still belonged to them. A foray into the valley by the Yankees a few months earlier had been completely repulsed by the Rebels and they had no fear of any other attempts to enter the valley by the Federals, they would easily put down any such incursion, as they had before.

Besides, the Confederates had driven the Yankees from the valley once before back in 1862 when Stonewall Jackson rampaged through the valley destroying the Federal forces, driving them out and claiming the valley for the Confederates.

Why would it be any different this time?

Three

Sam Kensington sat up with a start, his body covered in sweat, breathing heavily. Looking around the room, he tried to orient himself to the surroundings. He was lying on a bunk. Lopes was on his right and as he panned around he could see other men standing or sitting on their bunks. He continued his turn until his eyes fell upon Wilson, sitting on the bunk next to him on the left, cleaning his weapon for the hundredth time.

Wilson, Big Stick as he was called, always said you can let your dick rot and fall off, but if your weapon fails you, you won't need your dick anyway. He looked blacker than usual. Kensington tried to focus tighter. Of course being in the hot blazing sun day after day puts a tan on everyone, black or white. He heard Wilson speak.

"Having that dream again, Four Seven?"

"Huh? Yeah. You know? Same shit. Can't seem to shake it. Thought maybe we have a break, relax a little, maybe I'd get some real sleep."

"You smoking that cheap shit again?"

"Huh? No. I don't smoke that crap. Leave that for the pot-heads. That righteous group, you know?"

"Maybe you should lay off that rotgut all you rednecks drink."

"Redneck? Who the fuck you calling a redneck?"

"Slowdown Four Seven. I just meant that stuff you call booze all you red neck white guys seem to drink."

"I ain't no redneck."

Wilson looked up and stared him down hard before smiling. "You white?"

"Huh? Yeah, I'm white. Well a little darker, but I can show you white."

"So you say you're white?"

"Yes."

"Then you're a redneck. All y'all white mother fucker's rednecks to me. You all look alike."

Kensington looked over at his friend and cohort.

"Yeah, that's what we say about all you black dudes. You all look the same to us."

Wilson reached over and stuck out his hand. They did an abbreviated version of the black dap handshake, the one reserved for whites.

"But it don't mean nothing."

"You got that right. But it don't mean nothing."

Kensington wiped his hand across his face, looking around the room once more. The room was a hub of activity. He leaned over to Wilson.

"So, Stick have you heard anything yet?"

Wilson shook his head no. Kensington nodded.

"What's your gut say? Think it's on?"

Wilson nodded yes. Kensington sat silent. Wilson went back to cleaning his weapon.

"Hey, Four Seven answer me this. Where were you this time?"

"Say what?"

"The dream. Where were you this time?"

Kensington wiped his hand across his face again and pulled himself up in the bunk resting his back against the wall.

"Not sure, some sort of base camp, lot of troops massing, foot soldiers, you know infantry, cavalry, artillery and the like. Looked like we were getting ready to march somewhere. Lot of brass around a big tent in the middle of the camp near head-quarters, lot of animated conversation going on."

"So you still fighting two wars, one in your head and one here in reality."

"Look Stick, I gotta tell you, its pretty god damn real in my dream, feels like I'm right there. I can taste the dust that's swirling in the air, even smell all the horses moving about."

Wilson nodded. He leaned in closer.

"You still think you're back there?"

Kensington turned and looked at his friend leaning in closer.

"That's what it looks like. Has to be the Civil War, the uniforms, the gear we have and those ancient weapons, looks like a musket. Like to have that."

He pointed to Wilson's M16.

"Sure do some damage with that."

Wilson nodded looking at his gun all cleaned up.

"Well answer me this Four Seven, you north or south?"

"Based on the blue coats we are all wearing, I'd say Federal."

"Federal?"

Kensington looked at Wilson, nodding.

"Yeah, that's what they keep calling us, Federals."

Wilson remained silent, Kensington continued.

"You know, blue coats, I gotta believe Union forces, so north."

Wilson nodded, pointing to Kensington.

"Don't figure man. If I didn't know you like I do, I'd put you up for a fucking psych eval. But I've seen you in action man. We fought together... one jungle shit hole after another.

We've walked so many patrols together... I know you've got it together. This shit makes you dream about all kinds of things."

Wilson looked around the tent, leaning in closer.

"I know guys dream about being back in the world, dream about the day they be getting out of here, even about being back home with mom's apple pie. Others dream they in hell, get all religious and shit... Me, I dream about pussy and how I can get me some, but being in another war, that's pretty fucked up."

Kensington looked over, about to speak, but Wilson continued.

"Maybe you should dry out for awhile, you know lay off. Hey that pussy we got a couple of weeks back, that do anything to you?"

Kensington stared at Wilson.

"No. My dick's fine. No oozing or dripping. She was clean, same as yours."

They both sat silent for a moment. Wilson reassembled his weapon.

"Look Stick, I appreciate you keeping this on the QT, especially since as you say, its pretty fucked up. Hell, I don't know what it is."

Wilson nodded. He reached over and touched his friend's arm.

"Listen, I know a brother over in supply, says the XO is a Civil War nut, knows all about it, relives the battles and shit like that. Maybe you go talk to him find out where you are, you know, then maybe you can make some sense as to why you dream about that shit?"

Kensington nodded as he looked over at Wilson.

"Sure that would go over... shit, you're serious about that?"

Wilson waved his hand in the air.

"It's a thought. You do whatever the fuck you want."

"How do you know?"

"I know a brother."

"Of course you do. Is there any place you don't know a brother?"

Wilson smiled a wide grin exposing a full mouth of bright white teeth.

"Us brothers got to keep each other informed, so you white redneck mother fuckers don't try to get over on us massah suh."

"You gonna start that shit again?"

Before either of them could say anything more, the platoon sergeant barged in motioning everyone together.

"Listen up."

All talking in the room stopped as the men gathered around a center bunk, standing, leaning and sitting on that bunk.

First squad was currently configured with only six men. At the top was Harold "Don't call me Harry mother fucker" Wilson, otherwise known as Big Stick, as in walk softly and… along with Albert Samuel "Sam" Kensington, otherwise known as Four Seven.

The other men were Arturo "Lopes" Lopez, a Puerto Rican from New York, two white southern rednecks, Jimmy "Whitey" Whitehead and John "Big John" Smith. To finish up the squad was Raphael "Smooth" Johnson, the only other brother in the squad.

Stick named the new guys, it was what he did. Actual names were forgotten so as not to get too attached, "handles" allowed some distance, or so it was thought. Wilson especially liked calling a southern white guy "Whitey," who either was in on the joke or simply didn't get it, more probably the latter. Wilson had time on all of these guys and a month and change on Kensington, which made him the senior and for that, respected.

Wilson and Kensington stood leaning against a support

pole. Whitey and Big John sat on Big John's rack. Lopes and Johnson stood off to the side.

"First off, I brought you two more cherries to fill the squad."

"Great, now I can pass on this fuckin' radio."

"Negative Whitey. I need experience right now. Give it up when we get back. No one gives up anything right now. Understand?"

Owen Hubbard, the platoon sergeant, had been in the 'Nam almost a year, earned his stripes in the field, not like the "Shake & Bakes" that come out of NCO school as instant sergeants and for that he was respected. The men listened.

"I thought I'd brief you guys first. Second squad is still out on patrol, third is on detail, but you guys will be point on this operation."

"So you give us FNGs?"

Sergeant Hubbard looked at Johnson, always with the mouth.

"Look Johnson, you only got two fucking new guys, I gave four to second squad and five to third squad. Too many guys rotating, sick wounded, what have you. The platoon is pretty thin. It was the best I could do to get this many anyhow."

The sergeant paused, looking at the squad, he rested his eyes on Wilson who had stood quietly so far, but he knew would chime in soon enough.

"Besides I got you guys another brother, even up the odds a bit."

He saw Wilson smile.

"Okay, where was I? Yeah, no changes right now. Take these two under your wings and get their shit straight."

The two new guys stood where they entered not sure what to do next. The sergeant turned and motioned for them to move over by the rest of the men. Slowly they did, still not sure where to stand. Smooth gave the black dap handshake to the new brother. Kensington nodded to the new white guy.

"Okay, here's what we're gonna do. Wilson and Kensington, I want you two to hump an M79 along with your rifles, carry both. Whitey you pack a .45 as well. One hand on the handset, one hand firing, you understand?"

Whitey nodded. Sarge pointed at Wilson.

"Wilson, you still got that .45?"

Wilson nodded.

"And I'm keeping it."

Sergeant nodded.

"Didn't figure anything to the contrary."

Wilson smiled. The sergeant looked at the others, pointing.

"Big John, I want you to hump an M16 with the M60. Just in case that fucking thing jams up, I want you armed. I'm gonna have the new big strapping white guy hump an M60 as well and you are all gonna carry extra M60 ammo and M79 rounds. Everybody double up on weapons. Johnson, the new black guy is with you."

The men sat in silence waiting for the Sarge to continue. He looked around the group, nodding.

"To help with the load, for now we'll only be carrying a day to a day and a half rations. We'll be re-supplied every other day, but a full canteen compliment. We'll be getting support from a Huey company assigned to this mission exclusively. They'll provide transport, cover and re-supply."

"Oh, and if anyone has any of those one shot wonders LAWS rockets, turn them in, carry extra M79 rounds instead."

"One shot wonders?"

Wilson answered without moving.

"Yeah, you get one shot and you wonder if it will work."

Sarge nodded, pointing at Wilson.

"One last thing, before I take questions. No pot, no booze

and no pussy from here on out. No one gets stoned, drunk or develops a case of rot dick. I catch anyone they'll walk point the whole time. I don't care if you're hung over, out of focus or your dick is about to explode. No sick bay, no excuse, no bullshit. We should be leaving in a day or so, so nothing from here on out. Do I make myself clear?"

The nods were slow in coming, but the message was received.

"Okay then, questions?"

Sarge looked directly at Wilson, but it was Johnson who asked.

"So where we going?"

Sarge looked over at Johnson, the new brother standing stiff as a board next to him.

"We're going back into the A Shau Valley. In a day or two we'll be transported by deuce and a halfs, trucked to a firebase, staging area for transport by Huey. You'll get further details as they become available."

"Back to the A Shau? Didn't we do this before? Who's fucking idea was that?"

"See these stripes Johnson, there's only three. Don't have access to what they are thinking, only tells me what to do. I follow orders just like you."

Wilson stepped away from the pole looking directly at Sergeant Hubbard. Kensington watched him.

"I know a brother was in the valley in '68, said a lot of good men got killed and wounded, including some of you white folk, then we gave it all back, just left. We gonna do that again? Shit if we're gonna give it back, why not just let them keep it in the first place? What you think about that?"

Sarge looked at Wilson, then glanced at the others knowing they needed an answer.

"Well if I had an opinion, which I don't and if asked, I wouldn't give one... but, here's what I know about '68."

Sergeant Owen Hubbard wiped his shirtsleeve across his face, removing the sweat gathered there. Swallowing hard, he pulled his canteen and took a long sip of water.

"In the spring of '68 we choppered back into the A Shau Valley again to disrupt the flow of men and supplies from the north into South Vietnam in a drive labeled Operation Delaware. Built a bunch of firebases for support and to interdict enemy routes of withdrawal and infiltration. B-52s bombed the Valley for five days before troops were moved into place. Once again we occupied the airstrip at the Special Forces Camp we lost in '66 and began to rebuild the strip and camp. Several patrols into and around the camp led to the capture of a large quantity of supplies, weapons, ammunition, trucks, bulldozers, explosives, rice and other food supplies including farm animals. After a successful sweep of the area and total destruction of the enemy's supplies, orders were given about a month later to pull out of the valley once again."

"And?"

"And what?"

Sarge looked over at Wilson, but he noticed everyone else's eyes were on him as well.

"Look, all I know is that there have been reports of a large buildup of North Vietnamese forces in the A Shau around Base Area 611, which straddles the Laotian border just north of the valley and south of the Da Drong River. Most of this base area is thought to be in Laos, encompassing Route 922. Several infiltration points that have been inactive since the '68 incursion are now active again, being cleared and maintained by an NVA engineering force. Route 922 from South Vietnam into Laos along with a heavy concentration of anti aircraft guns along with a heavy flow of trucks coming in has made someone's asshole pucker up."

Sarge paused, as he looked around the men, he realized he still had their full attention.

"Further reports said several regiments of NVA, including the 6th and 9th were reported to be entering the valley at will working their way east to meet up with the 812th and eventually meet up with the 4th and 5th regiments that had escaped the valley back into Laos after the '68 drive. Without any resistance the force would continue to grow stronger."

Wilson nodded.

"So we're the resistance?"

Sarge looked at Wilson, again wiping his face with his sleeve.

"Not exactly. We're the clean up. The jarheads already did a sweep pushing and chasing those little fuckers back into Laos. Quite a few kills and captured a bunch of supplies. However, once they pulled out those little bastards started moving back in. That's where we come in. They won't be expecting a second mission to follow up that earlier push, or so the theory goes."

Sarge looked at Wilson, but he raised his hand in the air before Wilson could ask, Sarge continued.

"Yeah, Wilson, I know what you gonna ask. Listen, I got contacts too. A buddy of mine from back in the world works in G2, gave me all the Intel he had. Said he heard my unit was going back into the valley, thought it would be the right neighborly thing to do. Of course it cost me a case of single malt scotch, but what the hell?"

Pausing, Sarge motioned for someone to come into the tent. A clerk dressed in starched fatigues entered handing the Sarge a package and left just as quickly. Sarge held the package.

"Now you know as much as I do. Wilson, I'm sure you can check with a brother and fill in the blanks if need be, but basically the bottom line is we are going into the A Shau Valley to finish what the Marines started, what happens after that I just don't know."

Sarge removed a bottle of that single malt from the package.

"But, in the meantime, I though we could have a little drink to… well to whatever."

He unscrewed the cap and took a healthy swig before passing the bottle to Wilson. Wilson followed suit, handing the bottle to Kensington and so on.

As Sarge started to leave, he turned back and pointed to Wilson.

"By the way Wilson, you're squad leader now, Jones won't be coming back, he got reassigned, but I'm sure you knew that already."

Wilson nodded. Kensington punched him on the arm.

Four

Walking through the "street" between tents soldiers mingled with the men from the other regiments tented next to them. The two men who made eye contact before met up at the back end of the street, near an opening. Nodding once again they stepped closer.

"Where you from?"

Looking over at the man speaking, the soldier nodded and pointed to the rest of the men around him.

"10th Vermont."

Looking at the rest of the troops gathered the speaker nodded.

"Assigned yet?"

"Not sure, but we've been with First Brigade, Third Division III Corps, Army of the Potomac last couple of months."

The two men stood silent, watching the men milling around them, the sun baking through the dust.

"How about you?"

"87th Pennsylvania."

"With us still?"

"I 'speck."

The soldier nodded.

"Maybe we're still with this division as before. After Monocacy, we stayed in camp until we were marched here. Told to set up. Said we'd get orders soon. Then you guys came in. What about you?"

Pennsylvania nodded.

"Same. After Monocacy, we went back to camp with the Army of the Potomac, III Corps, but two days ago, we started our march here."

They both stood silent. Finally the speaker pointed.

"Sure a lot of men coming in. Looks like cavalry and artillery been arriving all day long. What you figure we're up against?"

"Don't know, but it looks like we're massing for a major push somewhere and soon."

They both stood silent again. Two other soldiers joined then. They each nodded their hellos.

"Either of you fellows know where we're going?"

Vermont and Pennsylvania both looked at the man asking, shaking their heads no.

"Sorry, 14th New Jersey."

The man stuck out his hand. The other men shook hands.

"Said to set up over here by you men. Either of you know who we're assigned to yet?"

Both men shook their heads no.

"Followed those guys in." He pointed to the latest group of cavalry marching through camp. "Sure do kick up the dust. Where you boys from?"

"87th Pennsylvania."

"10th Vermont."

The man nodded.

"Thought we'd be staying with the Army of the Potomac, this close to Virginia, but fellers I talked to on the way in said no. In fact some of them boys are joining us. What do you figure we're in for?"

Neither man answered.

"I guess we'll know soon enough. Nice talking to you boys. I better get set up."

The two men watched as he walked away and joined another group of men milling about. They stood like that for a spell. Finally Vermont turned and walked away. Pennsylvania did the same, each joining the rest of their units.

Although a good distance apart, the two men watched as another group of soldiers came into camp, followed by an artillery unit, which was followed by another unit of cavalry. The camp was growing bigger.

As the day wore on, the dust seemed to obscure the other side of the camp. The activity that so overwhelmed the camp earlier was now just a memory forgotten by the steady arrival of troops, cavalry and artillery still pouring into the camp. Tents had been erected everywhere. What once was a straight line of units became a more hodge podge of setups as the new arrivals looked for spaces to pitch the tents.

It was an astounding sight, all these men and horses and cannon finding areas to establish, regroup their unit into their area. The 10th Vermont and 87th Pennsylvania had arrived early enough to establish their unit area while there was still room to set up orderly. They also happened to set up next to each other. The units arriving later had to make do with what they could find, scattering around them best they could.

The roar of wagons arriving followed by a new cloud of dust flying in the air, signaled the arrival of additional Quartermaster. Those wagons carried food, supplies of all kinds, uniforms, equipment and above all, ammunition. The horses strained against the weight of these wagons as they rumbled into camp.

"Hey Vermont."

Looking over at the man speaking, he nodded pointing.

"Looks like they're moving in the Quartermaster regiment."

Stopping, the men turned and faced each other.

"Vermont, the name's Nathan DeLacroix."

"DeLacroix?"

Smiling, the 87th Pennsylvanian shook his head.

"From Louisiana originally, folks settled..."

"Louisiana? You're a southerner?"

Waving his hand in the air, DeLacroix stopped him.

"Hold on Vermont. I said I was from Louisiana. Folks relocated up north back in the thirties, set up a trade business. All I've ever known is Pennsylvania. You got a name Vermont?"

"Kensington, Samuel Kensington."

The two men shook hands.

"Well Kensington, Samuel Kensington, what you think about this?"

Samuel Kensington looked at the man standing next to him and then back over the camp.

"When we joined the Army of the Potomac, it was already there. Not like this. Looks like we're building a new army and a right big one at that."

DeLacroix nodded.

"Sure thing."

The two men stood silent watching the camp swell as more wagons of the Quartermaster rolled in.

"Well Samuel, I can say this. When we left Monocacy, I thought the only campaign we were headed for was Richmond, go up against Lee and his Army of Virginia but this isn't the way to Richmond. Where you think we're going?"

Samuel Kensington looked at his new friend, waiting a bit, before speaking.

"Sergeant Major told us earlier that our brigade, which I believe also includes you boys, are still attached to Ricketts' Third Division, for sure, but now we're attached to Horatio Wright's VI Corps."

DeLacroix nodded. Samuel Kensington continued.

"Word has it that this new army is massing for a move into the Shenandoah Valley in Virginia."

"Thought we were in Virginia already?"

Samuel Kensington shrugged his shoulders.

"Could be. All that marching, not sure where exactly we are."

DeLacroix nodded.

 **Five**

His eyes opened wide, but the room was still dark. Sam Kensington sat up, dropping his feet to the ground. The sweat covered his whole body, soaking the brand new olive drab army boxers he had requisitioned that day to sleep in, procured from supply for this purpose only. He was desperate for a full night's sleep and had decided to remove his uniform completely against his better judgment.

Slipping his feet into the jungle boots at the side of the bed, he stood and walked outside the tent. Wilson was outside.

"You got a date?"

Kensington looked over at him, then looked down at his get up.

"Huh? No. Needed to take a leak."

"Well, I'd put something on before I strayed too far. Mortar round comes in, you might be stuck in your skivvies and boots. Look pretty stupid."

Kensington nodded, but didn't move, taking in the cool night air, his skin becoming clammy from the perspiration turning cold. Wilson offered his pack of smokes. Kensington took one and leaned in to get a light from Wilson's lighter.

Pulling heavily on the cigarette, Kensington let out a sigh with the smoke.

"What'd you say about the XO? He knows this Civil War shit?"

"That's what the brother told me. Into all the battles and shit. Big buff. You know how you white guys get caught up in that shit."

Kensington looked at Wilson, but just nodded, not willing to engage him this time.

"Maybe I should talk to him later, before we truck out of here."

Wilson nodded.

"Here."

Kensington looked over. Wilson pushed a pint of whiskey toward him.

"Take a sip or two, help you sleep."

"Sarge said."

"Damn Four Seven, I know what Sarge said. We ain't going on a drunk, just some sipping whiskey. Help us sleep."

Kensington nodded as he unscrewed the cap. Tilting the bottle to his lips he took a two-chug drink. Sucking his lips back he said in a choked whisper.

"Not bad. Where'd you get that?"

Wilson looked at him, but just smiled.

"Yeah, you know a brother."

Kensington started to go back inside.

"Hey, I thought you had to take a leak?"

"I lost interest."

Kensington disappeared back inside the tent. He made his way back to the bunk, falling onto the top, boots still on and mercifully fell asleep. He slept soundly until he felt the poking.

"Hey, Four Seven get up. Let's get us some breakfast, while we still can. Be C-rats soon enough."

Kensington looked up to see Wilson standing over him,

dressed and ready.

"Yeah, give me a minute. Sure be nice to take a shower."

"After breakfast. They got some 55s set up."

Kensington nodded. He remembered seeing the 55-gallon drums set up with a pull chain behind the tents. Hopefully there would still be water in them by the time they got there.

They walked together over to the mess tent, entering and getting into the line. Looking around they wound up sitting next to the two new guys that Sarge had brought in yesterday. The new guys sheepishly acknowledged their presence. Kensington spoke first.

"Enjoy this stuff while you can. We hit the bush, its C-rats from there on out."

"C-rats?"

Kensington looked at the new white guy.

"C-rations, you know that canned shit we get to eat in the field. It's pretty bad stuff, but after a while… well, you'll know soon enough."

The new white guy nodded. The new black guy sat silent.

"Sarge said to watch you guys and learn, the two old timers."

Before the new white guy could finish, Wilson slammed his fist on the table.

"Old Timers, who the fuck?"

"Slow down Stick, he meant most experienced."

Kensington took a bite as he patted Wilson's arm.

"Four Seven, you the white guy in this bunch, I'll let you straighten out this fucking new white guy."

Kensington continued to eat, while the two new guys sat motionless, finally finishing his mouthful.

"Listen, Stick here is the best at what he does, it would be in your best interest to watch and pay attention. For that matter just watch the rest of the guys in the squad. Watch and learn. We're here to take care of each other. Remember that. No bullshit in the bush. You got attitudes or opinions, about anything, stick them up your ass. In the bush there's no room for any of that bullshit. You understand? You fuck up out there, your body goes home in a bag."

The two new guys nodded yes.

Kensington pointed as he continued.

"Look we've all been through it. Just follow our lead. Don't try to be no fucking hero, just take care of business. You watch his back and he'll watch yours and we'll watch both of your asses."

Wilson leaned in to speak softly.

"You listen to what he says, might keep you alive."

The new black guy spoke softly.

"Stick, how did?"

Kensington raised his hand in the air.

"I got this one."

Wilson sat back in his chair staring at the two new guys.

"I'm sure you boys have heard the expression, walk softly but carry a big stick?"

The two new guys sat stone-faced. Kensington shook his head.

"Jesus, they're brain dead too. Listen up. It's an expression, you know, like you can be a bad ass but not show it, just let people believe that you can."

Wilson raised his hand shaking his head.

"Listen up you dumb fucks. When you're in the bush, you need to be as quiet as possible. You walk softly, quietly, you know? But if you do come across something you need to be carrying. In our case usually an M16, that you can flip to auto and put a hurt on someone. You understand?"

The two new guys nodded in unison. Wilson looked at Kensington. Kensington knew what was coming next.

"You see. You treat your weapon right and it will take care of you. Because if you don't and you need it, it won't be there. You treat it better than your own dick. Cause it don't matter if you dick falls off, as long as you got your weapon. If you don't, you won't need your dick anyway."

The two new guys sat motionless waiting. Kensington kept eating. He had been through this speech before.

"Besides walking softly and carrying my weapon into battle is not why they call me the Big Stick."

Kensington finished his bite and waited. It took a minute but the new guys finally got it. Kensington shook his head. The new black guy smiled and reached across slapping fists with Wilson. The new white guy sat back in his chair, arms across his chest.

"So why do they call you Four Seven."

Kensington smiled.

"That's a long story for another time."

While he finished his breakfast he thought back to the first time he met Wilson and how he got his name.

Just like the new guys, he arrived cold and was thrust into the squad. Wilson greeted him first and looked him over.

"First thing you want to do man is get them dog tags off your neck. Don't want to be ringing no bell when you walk through the bush. Pull them off the chain, put them in your pocket or ruck."

Sam Kensington removed the chain from around his neck and dropped the tags on the bed. Wilson immediately grabbed them up.

"Albert Kensington."

"I prefer Sam."

"Albert Kensington."

"I said I prefer Sam."

Wilson looked at him for a moment.

"So your initials are AK?"

Kensington looked at the man holding his tags.

"Yeah, but I go by the name Sam Kensington, so actually."

"No, actually your initials are AK?"

Kensington looked over at Wilson, not quite sure what he was getting at.

"O positive, that's good, case I need blood and Catholic. Won't hold that against you."

Kensington nodded. Wilson put the tags back on the bed.

"Do you know what an AK is?"

Kensington looked over, nodding.

"Yeah, an AK-47 rifle is the rifle of choice for the enemy."

"Enemy? Every motherfucker over here is the enemy. I'm talking about the gooks, the VC, the NVA. It's their rifle. You get it now?"

When Sam Kensington didn't respond right away, Wilson continued.

"Your initials dude. I can't call you AK and we don't use names, you know… so from now on you're Four Seven. That works."

Kensington stood there as Wilson walked away. He retrieved his tags off the bed looking at them, never noticing the initials, never really caring what was on the tags until now. Once Wilson decided that was his handle, it stuck.

Wilson was still staring at the two new guys.

"I'm not ready to name you guys yet. Don't even want to know your fucking name either. For now you're the new black guy and you're the new white guy. Now go, you're dismissed."

Kensington watched as the two new guys left the table. Wilson leaned over, closer.

"Still thinking about talking to the XO today?"

Six

Standing in the middle of the compound, Sam Kensington looked around the mass of tents and Quonset huts erected as the headquarters group. Fresh from a 55 gallon drum shower and wearing a set of clean jungle fatigues from the laundry pool, he walked to the center hut.

Inside he was greeted by another spit and polish clerk, in his neatly pressed jungle fatigues and shined boots.

Jesus, we're in the middle of a jungle and this guy is sharper than if we were stateside, he thought, as he looked the clerk over.

The clerk returned the stare, barely hiding his contempt for this disheveled man in front of him.

"I said, can I help you?"

Sam Kensington broke his stare and looked at the clerk.

"Huh? Yeah. I need to see the XO."

"And what business do you have with the executive officer?"

Sam Kensington looked at the clerk, his contempt growing. He took a breath before answering.

"It's a private matter, if you don't mind?"

The clerk leaned back, taking in another look at the man

before him.

"Well as you can imagine, the exec is quite busy and can't be bothered right now. Why don't you come back later, maybe I can work something out then?"

Sam Kensington stood still, a smile coming over his face, masking his urge to deck this smart mouthed clerk, right here and now. Slowly backing away he spoke softly, almost too soft for the clerk to hear.

"Yeah, why don't I do that?"

Before the clerk could respond, he was back outside. Hunching his shoulders the clerk went back to his desk.

Sam Kensington walked a ways away from that center hut, stopping the first man passing by, obviously another clerk.

"Hey, where can I find the XO?"

The clerk stopped and turned.

"The XO? Yeah. Yeah, he should be in that hut right there. Lieutenant Orville Smith. Military Academy dude, but down to earth. Call him "O" or LT Smith, doesn't fancy Orville too much, you know."

With that the clerk was gone, Kensington still nodding.

He looked at the hut the clerk had just pointed out, two over from the one he had went in. Nodding to himself, Kensington trekked over to that hut and promptly walked in.

A clerk didn't meet him this time, but rather a hub of activity. Waiting a moment to gather in the mood of the room he approached the first man he saw.

"Excuse me, but I'm looking for a LT Smith?"

"Well son, you've found him. Lieutenant Orville Smith at your service."

The man stuck out his hand and Sam shook it.

"So, what can I do for you?"

"LT, I wonder if I might have a word with you in private?"

Lieutenant Orville Smith looked at the man before him for a minute, then looked around the room.

"Sure I could use a break. Let's step outside, grab a smoke."

Kensington nodded. The two men walked out into the afternoon sun then stepped to the side of the hut for a bit of shade. The Lieutenant offered Kensington a smoke from the pack, which Sam accepted. Holding the lighter for Sam first, they both lit their cigarettes. Sam used his cigarette to point to nowhere in particular.

"Don't seem as hard to get to you as that clerk in there indicated."

"Clerk? What clerk? What are you talking about?"

Kensington looked directly at the Lieutenant.

"When I went in that hut to ask to see you, some goddamn REMF gave me the third degree…"

"REMF?"

"Yeah, you know Rear Echelon Mother Fucker."

"Yeah, I know what it means."

The two men stood silent. Finally Kensington waved his hand in the air.

"Sorry sir. Just can't understand them sometimes, you know, its just…"

The lieutenant stopped him.

"Anyway?"

"Yeah, anyway, I heard that you were some kind of Civil War buff?"

The lieutenant smiled, relaxing a bit, taking a pull on his cigarette.

"Yeah, rumor has it. I did a piece at the academy and since then I've been know as that Civil War expert."

Sam Kensington hesitated, maybe this wasn't such a good idea. He was about to leave, but the lieutenant continued, waving the cigarette in the air.

"But, interestingly I do know quite a bit about that war. As I researched that piece I became more involved with the aspects of that conflict and did quite a bit of research. Why."

The lieutenant stopped, looking at the man before him.

"But, you didn't come here to ask me that."

Sam Kensington nodded, but didn't speak. The lieutenant nodded as well and spoke softer.

"Why don't you just tell me what you need?"

The two men stood silent. Sam finished his smoke and field stripped the butt, scattering it to the wind.

"Well it's like this."

Kensington wiped his brow on his sleeve. He looked around the area, but only the two of them were there and no one was within hearing distance. He continued.

"I've been having these dreams, these dreams where... that I... where I'm in some sort of... I'm not sure how to say this."

Kensington stood quietly. The lieutenant waited.

"I've had a few before... but last couple of nights... they've been so vivid, like I'm there. It appears I'm in some sort of base camp and we're massing for some kind of assault and... well, it seems so fucking real."

The lieutenant nodded and waited, but when Sam didn't continue, he spoke up.

"And what? You think these dreams have something to do with the Civil War?"

Kensington nodded, waving his hand in the air for effect.

"Yeah, I'm pretty sure."

"Can you tell where you're at, or where you think you're at, or maybe who you're with?"

Kensington shifted his weight, looking at the Lieutenant and then looking away.

"What do you mean?"

The Lieutenant took a pull on his cigarette.

"You know, the area the camp is set up in, something like that. Or maybe you can tell me the names of the people, officers around you, like that."

Kensington nodded.

"Well last night's dream, I still don't know where... but I found out that my unit, I believe we're the 10th Vermont and another unit the 87th Pennsylvania are tented together as part of a larger... a fellow I've been talking to... and we know we're still attached to Ricketts' Third Division, but now we've been told that we're assigned to Horatio Wright's VI corps... no longer with the Army of the Potomac, fresh from Monocacy... something like that... if that means anything."

The lieutenant nodded, a smile coming across his face.

"Really? You sure its Ricketts' Division?"

Kensington nodded.

"That's what I remember."

The Lieutenant nodded.

"And you think, now attached to Wright's VI Corps?"

Kensington nodded, his sprits lifting, hopefully.

"Yeah, I mean yes sir. Any of that shit mean anything?"

The lieutenant removed the pack of smokes from inside his uniform, offering one to Sam and taking one himself. Again he lit both cigarettes, taking a long pull before speaking.

"Well, if you're with Ricketts, I would have said Army of the Potomac, but that would have been with III Corps, but you said you've been attached to Wright's VI Corps... that leads me to believe you've already been moved and you're about to be part of the Shenandoah Valley Campaign of 1864."

"The what?"

The lieutenant took another pull on his cigarette, using it as a pointer as he spoke.

"I'd might need to follow up on this some more, but I believe that if you're with the VI... and that you're with Ricketts... that corps and the XIX Corps were assembled to march into the Shenandoah Valley toward..."

Sam Kensington raised his hand in the air, stopping the LT.

"Sorry sir, I'm still not following. Who's Ricketts?"

The Lieutenant smiled.

"Of course. Let me explain. Ricketts would be Brigadier General James B. Ricketts, commander of the Third division."

Kensington waited, shaking his head, a look of confusion on his face. Noticing, the Lieutenant took a deep breath before continuing.

"Well, in the early months of 1864, the Shenandoah Valley in Virginia hardly saw any Federal troops. The few that were there, were stationed up north defending against any potential attacks on the capitol in Washington. The Confederates had a free run through the valley for supplies and troop movement and a direct route to Lee's forces. As part of an overall plan to push General Robert E. Lee into a defensive position around Richmond, Lieutenant General Ulysses S. Grant chose to move decisively to end the Confederate threat in the lower Shenandoah Valley, thereby depriving the Confederate army of the Shenandoah Valley's abundant essential supplies of food and forage."

LT Smith took another pull on his cigarette. Sam stood stone faced.

"So, Lieutenant General Grant sent the VI and XIX Corps to the Valley, including two cavalry divisions, further consolidating various military districts of the region into this new Middle Military District camped at Harper's Ferry, a massive formation of Federals second only to the Army of the Potomac."

The Lieutenant took another pull on his cigarette Sam Kensington did the same, listening attentively, trying to understand any of this shit.

"After that formation, Major General Phillip "Little Phil" Sheridan, who had been the cavalry commander of the Army of the Potomac, was selected and given command of all these forces of the Middle Military District, which Little Phil eventually called the Army of the Shenandoah. His primary mission was to route Confederate Lieutenant General Jubal A. Early out of the Valley to the south and if the Confederates crossed into Maryland, he was to block their return. Second, he was to destroy all supplies in the Shenandoah Valley, which could not be consumed by his own army, thereby cutting off this vital support to General Robert E. Lee's Army of Virginia."

Another pull, but as he released the smoke, the lieutenant looked around and pointed the cigarette into the air for effect.

"Basically, with Lieutenant General Grant backing Lee into defensive positions around Richmond and Petersburg, Grant intended to keep Lee from sending reinforcements to Lieutenant General Jubal A. Early, commander of the Valley forces, while Sheridan was pushing him out of the valley and to further prevent Early from supplying Lee from the valley harvests. It was to be a massive campaign. Some still contend it was a turning point of that war."

The two men stood silent, finally Kensington finished his cigarette and again field stripped the butt, letting the particles drift into the air. He then looked directly at Lieutenant Orville Smith.

"Begging your pardon sir, but what the fuck does any of that mean?"

Orville Smith smiled.

"Sorry, I got carried away there. Basically, from what you told me, you know, about what units you're with, it appears your dreams place you in the camp prior to that campaign. That much I can tell you. Somehow you're dreaming about that specific campaign. But beyond that I really don't know what drives those dreams. Did you consider seeing…"?

Sam Kensington raised his hand in the air.

"Don't go there. The only reason I'm even speaking to you is because I thought if I knew where I was at or what I was doing, I might be able to make some sense of it. Some sense of why the fuck I'm dreaming about some other fucking war when I'm right in the middle of this fucking war."

The lieutenant nodded.

"Sure, I understand. Any thoughts why? You have kin might have fought in that war? Something like that?"

Sam Kensington shrugged his shoulders.

"Really don't know."

"Well you think you're with the 10th Vermont, you from that area?"

"No, Illinois, just outside of Chicago."

"Kin from Vermont?"

Kensington shrugged his shoulders again.

"Don't know that either."

Again the two men stood silent. Finally the lieutenant spoke.

"Tell you what, let me try to do some research on that campaign and if you have any more dreams, you know... I mean, any more details, before we pull out, you come talk to me again. Maybe with more details we can... you know, maybe figure something more out. Right now all I can tell you is that you're in camp, part of a new Army configuration massing for a new campaign into the Shenandoah Valley in 1864."

Kensington looked at Orville Smith.

"Between us of course."

Kensington nodded.

"So run that by me again, what's about to happen?"

The Lieutenant smiled.

"Sure. The Shenandoah Valley was a major Confederate stronghold that provided a supply route to Lee, that Grant was trying to crush. So basically, Grant wanted to control the valley to stop the flow of men and supplies to the enemy he was trying to defeat. Moving a large army into the valley was his way of disrupting that flow and routing the enemy from that valley."

Lieutenant Orville Smith reached for his smokes, offering one to Sam again, but he passed. The lieutenant lit his cigarette about to continue, but Sam stopped him.

"Sorry sir, I still don't get it. Somehow I thought if I knew where I was or what I was doing, I could make some sense of it all. You know, why I would be dreaming about that. But…"

The two men stood in silence for a long time. The lieutenant finished his cigarette and dropped his butt to the ground.

"Soldier."

"Kensington, Sam Kensington, sir."

"Sam, you're probably right. There could be a connection… some trigger that puts you there. How about if you come see me tomorrow, whether you dream about this again, or not, you come talk to me anyway? I'm going to look into that campaign some more and see if there is anything else pertinent that might help."

Kensington nodded.

"Sure, why not. You gotta admit though it is pretty fucked up. My buddy dreams about pussy, me I'm dreaming about some other war."

Orville Smith smiled.

"Okay, I'll give it to ya. It is pretty fucked up."

The two men smiled.

"Listen Sam, let me look into this some more, see if I can give you something else to work with, you know, maybe… well maybe there's something."

Kensington nodded.

"Sir, these dreams are so vivid… I can taste the dust and heat, smell the horses… It's like I'm there, not some abstract thing, where I'm in some void."

"I understand. Do you dream when you're in the field, or just here?"

Kensington looked at the Lieutenant and smiled.

"Hell, I don't sleep when I'm in the field, so I don't have a chance to dream."

Chuckling, Kensington continued.

"Sorry. Mostly when I'm in. I still sleep lightly, but the dreams come then, usually."

"You think maybe it's the heat of battle triggers the dream?"

Kensington looked at the Lieutenant.

"No, actually I don't. Don't seem to dream at all, but when I'm relaxed, maybe rested, they seem to overwhelm me. Stick... my buddy, we've pulled a lot of patrols together, been through some shit, you know, didn't dream any thing, but lately... Well last week or so, I had a couple... then last couple of nights they've been so..."

Kensington stood silent. The Lieutenant leaned in.

"Something out in the field maybe triggered anything? You know particularly bad, you know, I mean, anything might have got into your subconscious, that kind of thing?"

Kensington shook his head no.

"They're all bad, nothing like that."

Kensington perked up, pointing at the Lieutenant.

"Okay, tell me this. Why the Civil War, why not any past wars? Why am I dreaming about a build up for some obscure battle that was fought one hundred years ago? Why then? Why that?"

The Lieutenant looked at Sam for a long moment.

"I'm not sure I'm qualified to answer that question and since you don't want to... Well, let's just focus on what... well what we know and what we can ascertain from that. As I said, let me do some research into that campaign and see if there is something that might be causing... well, why you're so focused on that particular event."

Kensington nodded.

"Thanks LT. Appreciate you listening, maybe give me some answers. Something I can work with to stop this shit. Don't know what else to say."

Lieutenant Orville Smith reached out and shook Sam's hand.

"No problem, Sam. Kind of interesting, give me something to think about besides this bullshit here. Let's stay in touch, okay?"

Kensington walked away, waving as he left. Lieutenant Orville Smith watched shaking his head. Before he could give it any more thought, another soldier called for him, finding him on the side of the Quonset hut he motioned for him. The lieutenant went back inside the hut as Kensington disappeared across the compound.

Sam Kensington sat by a row of sandbags off to the side of the compound, trying to sort this shit out. If his dreams were about that other war, what did it all mean? For that matter, what did it all matter? He watched other soldiers milling about the camp, wondering what the hell his next dream would bring... Ah fuck it, he thought, who cares what his dreams meant. The only thing he needed to focus on was where they were going and what they would do when they got there. Who gives a shit what that other war was doing or was about to do.

Dreams were bullshit. Maybe the XO was right, maybe he had kin in that war and they were... or are... fuck! Maybe now that he knew where he was, he wouldn't dream anymore. Although knowing where didn't seem to answer the question yet. Probably didn't need to see the XO anymore, he had what he needed, some idea of what was going on and the like.

Slowly rising from his make shift seat, he made his way back to his own tent, taking his time getting there. At least he could tell Wilson what he knew, where the XO thought he was. He owed him that much, no Wilson deserved that much. Well, at least he knew where now, but still had no fucking idea of the why.

Stepping into the tent, the afternoon heat inside was stifling. The tent looked empty. Almost everyone was probably outside getting some fresh air. Lopes lay sprawled on his bunk, obviously asleep, the sweat beading on his forehead. Big John sat on his bunk writing a letter. Sam Kensington sat down beside him.

"Hey, Big John."

"Hey."

"Where is everyone?"

Big John stopped his writing and looked at Kensington.

"Stick took the two FNGs on an ambush for the night, along with Smooth and Whitey with the radio."

"An ambush? With the new guys? Why?"

Big John shrugged his shoulders.

"Sarge came by, asked if we needed anything and Stick said yeah. That he needed to break these new guys in, on account of where we're going. Said he wanted to take them out get their feet wet, you know. Said he wanted to take Smooth and Whitey with the radio along."

Sam Kensington nodded.

"Say when they'd be back in?"

"Tomorrow late. In the morning Stick's gonna take them on patrol first."

Kensington patted Big John on the shoulder.

"Well if anybody can show them the ropes, it's Stick."

"Fuckin' A."

Kensington left Big John, who quickly went back to his letter writing. Sitting on his own bunk, he thought this out. At least he could wait until tomorrow to tell Wilson the conversation he had with the XO. Maybe they should meet again and he'd know more by the time he saw Wilson.

Seven

"Yeah, so what's in the Shenandoah Valley that's so important?"

Nathan DeLacroix stood facing the interior of the camp, waving the dust from his face as the horses pulled another battery of artillery into the camp. Samuel Kensington stood alongside him, watching and waving as well.

"Confederates."

DeLacroix nodded.

The two men finally turned away from the dust and walked back into their street. DeLacroix pointed.

"Quartermaster wagons unloading supplies. You have everything you need? I heard we could get anything we needed, replace anything might be torn up or beat up, fresh uniforms, and plenty of ammo."

Samuel Kensington nodded.

"Did that already earlier. Sergeant Major had us in formation early this morning, right after drill. Marched us right over to the quartermaster and got everything we needed. Got me a new haversack, my old one had a bullet hole in it... with clean utensils."

DeLacroix nodded.

"Got you a new bread bag huh? You get any of that embalmed beef? Heard we might get some. I'll stick to the salt horse. Salted meat for me, no canned beef."

Kensington nodded.

"Drew ammo for those new rifles. Even got a new uniform. Damn these wool blouses are hot in this summer heat."

DeLacroix nodded and smiled.

"They sure are. You been to Robber's Row yet? Hear a whole new set of Sutler's wagons came in this morning. Anything you could want. That is you got the money."

Nodding, he turned to face DeLacroix.

"Hey, I see you carry a pistol."

Samuel Kensington looked down at the revolver in his belt.

"Yeah, it's the new Colt Army. Picked up a bunch of paper cartridges, so I don't have to load my own powder and ball."

"Why you want to carry a revolver for, awful heavy with everything else we need to carry?"

Pulling the revolver out of his waistband, he held it in the air.

"It's my good luck charm. I've had it since Cold Harbor. Don't mind the weight. Comes in handy when I don't have time to reload the musket."

DeLacroix took the weapon and looked it over.

"Still, once we get more of the Spencer Repeater Rifles, don't see the need to lug this thing into battle."

Samuel Kensington took the pistol from DeLacroix, sticking it back into his waistband.

"All the same, I'll hang onto it for now."

DeLacroix nodded.

"So Vermont, you got any more drilling this afternoon? We got the afternoon off, back at it in the morning. Our Lieutenant said with all the arrivals still coming in, we should lay low and stay out of the way, something like that."

Kensington shook his head no.

"Good, than let's find us something to do, get out of this dust. I know a guy running a Faro game in his tent, has some Bark Juice, you know, good ole home grown we can sip on. You got any money left?"

Kensington pulled some crushed bills and a couple of gold coins from his pocket.

"Will any of this do?"

DeLacroix smiled.

"That will do right fine."

The two men walked to DeLacroix's street and disappeared into a tent on the left.

Inside, several men were gathered around a felt cloth covered with a suit of cards, spades to be specific, the ace through the king arranged in two lines, with the seven set off to the side. Coins mostly, some currency and other items were placed upon those painted cards, while the man behind the cloth turned a card, to whoops and yells and sighs of anguish.

DeLacroix nodded to the man turning the card.

"Well Vermont, here's the squarest game of Faro you'll find in camp, Joe Buxton deals a straight hand, you win or lose. No horseplay here."

Nathan nodded to the dealer.

"Joe."

"Nathan."

"Where's that home grown you always talking about?"

Joe Buxton pointed to the rear of the tent. Nathan DeLacroix retrieved the jug, pulled the cork, took a swig and handed the jug to Samuel Kensington, who did the same.

"Got room for two more?"

Buxton pointed and a couple of men spread further apart, so they could squeeze in.

"Vermont, you know how the game is played?"

Kensington nodded.

"Played my share of Faro when we were back in Washington, but spent more time upstairs getting a horizontal pleasure. Felt my money was better spent there, than on the turn of a card."

Nathan DeLacroix let out a gregarious laugh, eventually the others joined in. Joe Buxton pointed to the painted cloth.

"There's no upstairs here. Put your money down and I assure you, one of us will get a pleasure out of this."

DeLacroix laughed again as he slapped Kensington on the back.

"Where's that jug? We got maybe one, maybe two days here, let's enjoy what we got."

"Amen brother."

The jug passed among the men. The turn of a card signaled another round of yells and sighs as money left the cloth and new bets were placed, each of the players waiting anxiously for the next turn of a card.

Early evening found the two men, slightly inebriated and looking for food. The Negroes had the cooking pots going, as the men made their way over and got a plate of hot beans, some beef and a cup of hot coffee.

Sitting on a log by the side of the campfire, DeLacroix savored his meal.

"Won't be long before we're back on hardtack and salt pork."

Kensington nodded.

"As long as we get our coffee. I'm carrying an extra bag of beans to crush as we go. Got to have my grounds for coffee in the morning. Only thing makes all this tolerable."

DeLacroix nodded between bites.

After their meal, the two men handed their tin plates to two Negro ladies charged with cleaning up.

Slowly walking back to their respective streets, the two men bid each other good by.

"Take care, Vermont."

"You too, Pennsylvania."

The sun was setting in the west casting an eerie glow through all the dust still swirling in the air. No units had arrived in camp in the last couple of hours, but the activity was still feverish.

The Army of the Shenandoah was formed, all that was left was organizing the Brigades and Regiments to stand ready when the order came in the next day or two.

Eight

Big John and Lopes sat on their bunks, as Sam Kensington rose up, wiping the sleep from his eyes. Lopes nodded, Big John was otherwise engaged. Sam nodded back to Lopes.

"What was that shit we drank last night anyway?"

Lopes smiled and pointed to Big John.

"Big John, you tell him."

Big John smiled and looked over at Sam.

"Just some moonshine, a feller I know over in headquarters makes up, when he can't get the real stuff. Gets his ingredients from the medical guys, a little alcohol, a little of this and a little of that."

Sam Kensington nodded.

"How much did I lose to you two fuckers playing three handed Tonk last night?"

"Lose?"

Lopes pointed to Sam wagging his finger.

"Hell, you won almost every hand. You were on fire mother fucker. I quit before you won my balls."

Big John nodded.

"Yeah, took all my spending money. Now I have to wait to

the next payday, buy me some stuff."

Sam Kensington moved his eyes from man to man.

"Really? Don't remember."

Lopes shook his head. Big John waved his hand in the air. Kensington swung his legs off the bunk.

"You guys eat? I'm gonna get some chow."

Both of the other men shook their head yes. Kensington nodded.

"Well, see you later then. Hopefully there'll by water left, get me a 55 shower when I get back."

Kensington walked out of the tent into the morning sun and heat, the noise and activity of the camp greeting him as well. A helicopter took off in the distance, the roar of the blades popping in the wind.

Inside the mess tent, he got in line with everybody else and filled a tin plate with pancakes and bacon. Stopping for a cup of coffee first, he made his way over to an open table. Before he could take his first bite, another man sat down across the table from him. He looked up to see Lieutenant Orville Smith sitting there.

"Slumming, sir?"

The lieutenant smiled as he sipped his coffee.

"No finished, just finishing my coffee. Thought maybe we could talk a bit."

Kensington looked at the Lieutenant. He obviously looked excited.

"Mind if I finish my breakfast first?"

"No. Not at all. I have some more information. Did you have another dream?"

Sam stopped mid bite, trying to remember, but his head was still a bit foggy. He continued his chewing before speaking.

"Not sure, sir. Head's a little fuzzy. Had some rotgut last night, still trying to get the cobwebs free. Let me get some coffee down, maybe that will clear things up."

The lieutenant sat in silence while Sam finished his breakfast. At one point the Lieutenant refilled both of their cups. A spit and polish clerk came over to the table, by the look on his face, obviously wondering what the hell the XO was doing sitting with this disheveled grunt. The Lieutenant noticed the clerk's demeanor and quickly dismissed him.

"Son, you have something for me?"

"No... I mean yes. Captain asked me to give you these papers."

The Lieutenant took the envelope from the spit and polish clerk and set them on the table without opening them. The clerk looked on, fully expecting the Lieutenant to review what was in there and give him further instructions. The Lieutenant noticed the clerk's impatience.

"I'll deal with those later. Right now I have some very important logistical information to discuss with this soldier. The information gathered in the field is invaluable to our mission. Everything can't be assumed from someone sitting on their ass at some desk in the rear. He has been out on patrol and I asked him to meet me here to tell me what he has found out. So now if you will excuse us, we have important business to discuss."

The lieutenant waved his hand in the air and the clerk slinked away. Kensington looked at him as he sipped his coffee.

"Jesus sir, don't know if there is enough room to lift my feet that high. Bullshit is pretty deep right about now."

The lieutenant smiled.

"Goddamn REMFs."

Sam smiled and raised his cup to the Lieutenant.

"Fuckin' A."

Kensington finished his breakfast and the two men walked outside to the side of the mess tent. The Lieutenant offered Sam a cigarette, which Sam accepted. Lighting both, the Lieutenant waited as they each took a pull.

"Anything, Sam?"

"No, not really. We're still in camp, nothing new. What about you?"

The lieutenant took another pull, letting the smoke drift from his mouth.

"Well, I wasn't able to do much more research. Really don't have anything here. Talked to another officer last night, he's also into the Civil War, had to do a lot of that at the academy."

Kensington raised his head staring at the XO.

"It's okay, I didn't say anything about you. I just told him, I had been thinking about that campaign, kind of comparing notes sort of thing and did he remember anything specific about it. That's all. But all he could remember was that it was a big drive to rid the valley of the confederate stronghold and disrupt the flow of men and supplies. Pretty much like I already told you. But at least he confirmed what I thought was happening."

The two men stood silently. Finally the Lieutenant spoke softly.

"Sam, I do have one thought to give you. I wonder if you're just dreaming about being in that camp at that time, or will you be going into battle, I mean in your dream? If it's just a question of the camp, maybe it's some sort of mind thing remembering about that camp from some studies or reading about that campaign, or something like that."

Kensington looked at the XO, not sure what he meant.

"I mean, maybe you studied about that gathering or had to do a paper on it and the fact that you're under some pressure... well, maybe that has something."

Kensington shrugged his shoulders.

"No idea. Don't remember anything like that. And if I'm not?"

Lieutenant Orville Smith stood silent for a moment, waving his cigarette for emphasis.

"Well, if it as simple as that I wouldn't give it any further thought."

Again he stood silent. Sam waited.

"But, and this is a big but, if you do go into the battle as well it could mean you are reliving some experience and maybe you should talk to..."

Kensington turned and looked hard at the XO.

"Sir, we said."

The Lieutenant raised his hand in the air.

"I'm only saying. But let's get back. I'm still pretty certain and my buddy concurs, that the events we discussed still puts you in position for the Shenandoah Valley Campaign of 1864. The why, I don't know, at least not yet."

The two men stood silent for a long time.

"Look Sam. I told you what I know about the events as you described them and I hope that helps you to understand why you are having these dreams, but beyond that, all I can give you is more information."

Kensington nodded. The Lieutenant continued.

"As you know we're probably moving out tomorrow, next day at the latest, so we won't have a chance to get together, but if you want, make notes if your dreams progress, you know into battle and we can talk next stand down. I'll be glad to analyze anything you might come up with and maybe we can work through this."

Sam Kensington nodded, turning to face away for a moment.

"Sir, I do appreciate you taking the time to listen and maybe give me some insight into what the fuck this is all about. Maybe now that I understand what's happening or about to happen, I can, you know? At least now, I have an idea of where I am, which should help me to understand what might happen next. It's something anyway."

The XO patted Sam on the shoulder.

"Well you take care son, be careful out there."

"Sure thing, sir. Thanks."

Sam Kensington waved goodbye to Lieutenant Orville Smith as he walked away. Digesting their conversations of the last few days, he tried to make some sense of the dreams, but nothing came to him. They were dreams, nothing more.

A 55 gallon drum shower later Sam Kensington was standing by his bunk, putting on a fresh set of jungle fatigues when Wilson and the others walked in. Nodding to each other, Wilson dropped his gear next to his bunk.

Smooth was with the two new guys, while Whitey dropped his gear on the floor next to his bunk and dropped down on the bed. The two new guys left Smooth and dropped their gear at their bunks.

Wilson stripped off his shirt, sitting on the bunk he unlaced his boots.

"Need to get me one of those 55 gallon soaks, be right back."

With that, he was gone. Smooth came over.

"Everything okay. Heard you had to meet with the XO?"

Kensington looked at Smooth.

"Huh? Yeah, just talked about a couple of things. Wanted to know what we were finding on our patrols, you know, like that."

Smooth nodded.

"Not looking to pull you?"

"What? Me, no. Said he wasn't getting a true picture from the desk jockeys, wanted an actual field update."

Smooth stuck out his hand, they did the white version of the black dap.

"Good, can't be losing nobody else right now, especially not you."

"How'd the new guys do?"

Smooth turned to look at the two new guys now sprawled on their bunks.

"Not bad. Need some seasoning, but they look like they be okay."

The two men did the white version of the black dap again.

"But it don't mean nothing."

"But it don't mean nothing."

As Smooth walked away, Wilson walked in wet and naked with only his boots on.

"You got a date?"

Wilson looked at Kensington.

"Not yet. Didn't bring the clean stuff. Didn't want to put this shit back on. Only option."

Kensington nodded as Wilson dressed.

"When you're done, let's grab a smoke."

Wilson nodded.

"Smooth says the new guys did okay out there."

Wilson nodded again.

"What made you decide to pull an ambush voluntarily?"

Wilson tucked his pant legs into his boots as he tightened the laces.

"Thought it might be better to train these guys before we get out there. See how they react on an ambush, you know spend a night in the bush."

"Then a patrol this morning?"

"Nah. Just a long way back. Wanted to see how they do. Need some work, but not bad. Remind me of you when you come in. Second day, we went on patrol together. Liked you from the start."

"I had a good teacher."

"Fuckin' A."

Wilson laced his other boot. Leaving the shirt open and loose he stood up.

"Shall we get that smoke?"

The two men walked out of the tent and continued across the compound toward the sandbags Sam had sat on yesterday.

Pulling and lighting up a couple of cigarettes, they each took a pull letting the smoke drift out before speaking.

"Drank some of Big John's rotgut last night. Apparently I cleaned out Lopes and Big John playing three handed Tonk."

Wilson nodded, letting Sam take his time to tell him.

"Spoke to the XO yesterday about... you know."

Wilson took another pull, letting the smoke drift out slowly.

"He's pretty sure it's the Civil War too. Even thinks he knows the place and time, like that."

Wilson took another pull, this time blowing the smoke into the air.

"Here's what he thinks. Based on the unit I'm with and the commanders in charge."

"And who might that be?"

Kensington looked at Wilson.

"Well, I'm with the 10th Vermont, we're tented next to the 87th Pennsylvania, assigned to Brigadier General James B. Ricketts' Third Division and we've just been attached to Horatio Wrights VI Corps."

"Who?"

"Never mind. Apparently in that war, officers are in the field with the men, not back in the rear."

"Amen brother."

Wilson stuck out his hand and the two men did the white version of the black dap. Kensington waved his cigarette in the air.

"Anyway, what it all means, or at least what he thinks it means, is that I'm part of a great army that is massing for an assault into the Shenandoah Valley in the summer of 1864."

"Where?"

"The Shenandoah Valley Campaign of 1864. The plan is to march into the valley to rid it of the Confederate stronghold there and to stop the flow of men and supplies into and out of the valley, especially to help Grant put pressure on Lee in Richmond, or something like that."

"Say what?"

Kensington sighed, taking another pull on his cigarette.

"It is a new army led by Major General Phil Sheridan, Little Phil..."

"So you're with the guy that burned Atlanta?"

"Huh? No. That was Sherman, this is Sheridan."

"All you white mother fuckers the same to me."

"Do you want to hear this or not?"

Wilson waved his hand in the air.

"Yeah, go ahead. Skip the people shit, too fucking confusing."

"Yeah, to me too."

Kensington took the final pull on his cigarette, field stripping the butt and letting the particles blow in the wind.

"Anyway, this new army is being put together with several parts, infantry, cavalry and artillery to march into the Shenandoah Valley to drive the Confederates out, disrupt the flow of men and destroy or confiscate the supplies the valley has. Basically kick some ass and take their stuff."

Wilson smiled a wide grin, almost to the point of pissing Sam off.

"Hey, it's what the XO told me, I don't know if it's true or not or what the fuck it means. You're the one told me go talk to him. Shit, I was hoping if I know where I'm at I'd maybe figure out why I'm having these fucking dreams..."

Wilson raised his hand in the air.

"Hold on Four Seven. Hold on."

Kensington paused. Wilson offered him another smoke, lighting it for him and then one for himself. A long pull and the quick release of smoke, Wilson waved his hand in the air.

"Just say what you just did slowly one more time."

Kensington waited, not sure if he wanted to continue this conversation.

"Go ahead. Once more slowly."

"I said, according to the XO, it appears I am part of a force that is massing to go into the Shenandoah Valley."

Wilson raised his hand stopping him.

"And what are you doing now?"

"I'm trying to tell you."

Wilson waved his hand.

"No, right now. You and I and all these other mother fuckers here. What are we doing right now?"

Kensington stared at his friend, not getting what Wilson wanted. The smile grew wider showing pearly white teeth against Wilson's sun darkened face.

"Think about this. Why are we here? Why are all these other guys here? What are we about to do? What did Sarge say yesterday?"

Wilson used his hand to coax Sam along, while Sam spoke.

"We are massing for an assault into the A Shau Valley..."

Kensington raised his eyebrows, pointing at Wilson.

"Fuck me."

Wilson continued.

"And?"

"So we can stop the flow of NVA from moving troops and supplies."

Kensington shook his head.

"No fucking way."

Wilson put his hand on Kensington's shoulder.

"So tell me what the XO said again."

Kensington looked at his good friend and buddy.

"No, fuck me, fuck me."

"No, Four Seven, one more time."

Sam Kensington shook his head as he spoke.

"Grant sent a large force into a Confederate held valley to

stop the flow of men and supplies from that valley."

"There you go."

Wilson stood back taking a long pull on his cigarette, letting Sam digest all that.

"And I'm part of that force that is massing to go into that valley, to, you know?"

Wilson waved his hand in the air.

"Okay, Four Seven, what's the next part?'

Kensington looked at Wilson, still shaking his head.

"Fuck me."

"Continue."

"Stick, this is really fucked up."

"You got that right."

"Here we are massing a large force to send into the A Shau Valley to stop the flow of NVA troops and supplies from getting into or out of that valley."

The two men stood silent. Wilson finished his cigarette and flipped the butt away, while Kensington field stripped his butt. Wilson put his hand on Sam's shoulder.

"Well Four Seven there's your answer."

"What's my answer?"

"You're in some kind of fucking parallel war."

"A what?'

"Don't you see Four Seven, your dreams are mirroring what we are doing. I don't know nothing about the Civil War or why you're in that camp or whatever, but it seems that since it's the same as today, you must have had kin or something come back to rattle your feathers. You got kin?"

"Don't know. The XO asked me the same thing."

"Well, it must have worked out, because you're here."

Wilson let go with a hearty laugh, so infectious that Kensington joined in.

"So Four Seven, don't need to think about it no more. We solved your problem. If you still dream about that other war, it's just because of this war."

Kensington nodded.

"Maybe you're right. Maybe it's that simple."

"Of course I'm right. And it is that simple. Next time you dream, you compare it to what we are doing and just remember, it's really this time, not that time. Why you got to go to the Civil War for answers is still pretty fucked up, but now we know it don't mean nothing."

"But it don't mean nothing."

The two men did the white version of the black dap handshake.

"But it don't mean nothing."

"But it don't mean nothing."

"How about we go get some chow, like to get a good meal."

"You heard something?"

Wilson nodded.

"Brother told me we're being trucked out tomorrow. Deuce and half's be here in the morning. Might get one more night at the fire base, but then our cavalry arrives and we mount the Huey's to go back into the A Shau."

Kensington nodded.

"Just like there."

"Do what?"

Kensington looked at Wilson.

"I said, just like there. Cavalry's been arriving for the last two days. Horses really churn up the dust."

Wilson smiled slapping Sam on the shoulder.

"See, just like I said same there as it is here. Except our horses got blades and fly us away, but they do churn up the dust as well."

Kensington smiled.

"So we're going tomorrow?"

"That's what I heard."

Kensington nodded.

"Yeah, XO thought the same thing."

The two men walked silently towards the mess tent, Sam deep in his thoughts, Wilson with the smile of satisfaction for having solved his friends' fucked up dreams.

Nine

The orders had come around 1:00 am, men stirred from solemn sleep to prepare to move out. The sound of tents being taken down, the smell of fresh boiling coffee, men stretching and moaning about the hour. It was time to go, break camp and march into the night.

Gear was strewn about as the soldiers prepared to pack up. In addition to each man's weapon, ball cartridges, powder and lead, every soldier carried the rest of their equipment on their person. A haversack, suspended from a shoulder strap, with usually three days rations, eating utensils, a three pint canteen, blanket folded and tied to string over their shoulder, shelter tent half, personal items and some extra clothing.

Dressed in a forage cap and Union blues, each soldier loaded all this gear onto his person, by way of cotton or canvas straps or hung off the belt, prior to moving out.

It was not uncommon to find several discarded items left when the men moved out, items they determined was not important or would unnecessarily add to their load. What may have seemed important to them while in camp, no longer mattered once they had to load up and carry all that on their person.

Along with the musket and the aforementioned ammunition, it was extremely rare for an infantryman to carry a pistol as well, the added weight alone, coupled with the extra cartridges, made that decision easy.

Word had passed down that several of the units were being outfitted with the new Spencer repeater rifles and some of the soldiers had been directed to draw cartridges for that weapon as well, so they would be ready to switch out their rifles without having to wait for that new ammo.

The fires and lanterns burning gave the camp a display of shadows as men moved about striking tents and loading up. Wagons were parked near the Quartermaster tents, which men were breaking down, while others were loading up the supplies and forage. Sutler's wagons were making ready to move. Horses nayed in the distance as they were harnessed up to artillery pieces, cannon and wagons. The dark of night only served to mask the chaos of a camp being deconstructed.

It had been a couple of hours since the call, Samuel Kensington stood at the ready with the rest of the 10th Vermont. Fully packed and strapped up were the men closest to him, the men he would normally bivouac with. Right next to him stood Everett Fremont and Jethro Longworth. To the side stood Alfred Lanning, Reginald Harrington, Edgar Fairchild, Rufus Merriweather and Edward Hutchens. Men he had come to know well, men he could count on and they him. And certainly nearby would be Pierre LaSalle better known as Frenchy. These were the men he knew best, the men he would go into battle with side by side.

The 87th Pennsylvania lined up next to them. The last of the campfires were burning themselves out, the aroma of fresh brewed coffee still permeating the air.

Shifting his weight to adjust the various items strapped on or hanging from his shoulders, Samuel Kensington thought about his decision to carry the revolver in his waistband, along with the paper cartridges he had gotten from Quartermaster. The musket stood tall on his left side. He further wondered when they would get their Spencer repeater rifles and how much weight that would add.

Slowly the line started. It wasn't long before his group moved. He looked back watching the 87th Pennsylvania shift into position behind the last of his unit. With the sun rising in the sky, he knew they were marching into the Virginia night to get this started.

Brigadier General James B. Ricketts' Third Division, which included Samuel Kensington's 10th Vermont and Nathan DeLacroix's 87th Pennsylvania, trailing behind Brigadier General George W. Getty's three brigades, crossed the Opequon Creek around 7:00am. Closely behind these units, Major General Horatio G. Wright's Artillery Brigade and the First Division commanded by Brigadier General David A. Russell moved forward. A couple of miles down, Major General William H. Emory's two XIX Corps Divisions rested in the lowlands, waiting while the wagons and Russell's Division passed.

Moving an army of this size and scope was a monumental task and necessitated a constant amount of strategic planning. Off to the side watching as the Army of the Shenandoah passed, waited the hundreds of men that belonged to every army to provide support, the cooks, the officer's servants, hospital staff, Quartermaster people, sick and infirmed, the usual freeloaders and the ever growing populace of Negroes that had become part of the Federal Army.

Once across the Opequon, Ricketts' two brigades further lengthened the ever growing front. Colonel J. Warren Keifer's brigade created the Third division's right front. The formation stood in position by 9:00 am, just two hours after crossing Opequon Creek. Sending his skirmishers out, Ricketts probed, while the other divisions and brigades got into position as support for him.

Waiting for them on the other side was Major General Stephen Dodson Ramseur's Division, attached to Second Corps of the Confederate Army of the Valley, commanded by Lieutenant General Jubal A. Early.

Probing by Ricketts' skirmishers added the sounds of musket fire to the Confederate cannon fire. The VI Corps artillery rolling into position returned the cannon fire. Once all the divisions were in place the signal was sounded to move forward. Generals Ricketts and Getty started their advance.

Ten

Sam Kensington woke with a start, sweat covering his whole body. Wilson was sitting on his bunk next to him, staring.

"Damn Four Seven, you sure do fidget a lot when you're in the dream."

Kensington nodded, wiping his hand across his face.

"You ready for some chow? Heard the deuce and a half's will be here around ten. Maybe we get breakfast one last time?"

Sam nodded, swinging his legs out of the bunk and sitting up. Wilson stood and walked over to Smooth's bunk.

"Smooth, you want to join us for chow?"

Smooth looked at Wilson and then at Kensington.

"Yeah, but I better get these FNGs ready. Maybe meet up with you later."

The two black men slapped hands. Kensington was standing behind Wilson. Smooth watched the two men walk out.

In line at the mess tent, Wilson piled on the flapjacks, sausage and bacon. The brother serving watched until Wilson raised his hand.

"Going back to the bush, need my nourishment."

The brother serving nodded. Pointing behind him, Wilson

continued.

"Same goes for my man."

Sam Kensington watched as the server loaded his tin plate. He nodded his appreciation. They found a table near the side and sat down. Eating first, the two men sat silent. When Wilson finished he pushed the plate away and downed one of the two glasses of orange juice he had. He waited. Finally Sam finished, sipping his coffee.

"So Four Seven?"

Kensington looked at Wilson, waving his hand in the air.

"We broke camp and crossed some creek, moving into formation."

"And?"

"That's it really. We're moving out."

Wilson nodded, Sam sipped his coffee. The two men left the mess tent and slowly walked back to their tent, grabbing a smoke along the way.

While Wilson cleaned his weapon, Sam continued working on his ruck. Wilson looked over.

"Hey Four Seven, that new?"

"Yeah. The old one had a busted strap, couldn't fix no more. Figured as long as we are in camp, I'd get me a new one, start over."

Wilson nodded, watching. Sam was pulling stuff off the old ruck and attaching that to the new getup. Each canteen hung with a D-ring, carrying nine still he disbursed them around the outside. C-rats, M16 magazines, an M79 "thumper," rounds for that, poncho and poncho liner and some personal items still lay strewn on the bunk, while Sam continued putting his new rig together.

"How you carrying this thing?"

Wilson looked up at Sam holding the M79 grenade launcher.

"Across the top, got me a strap to hold it in place."

"What about your machete?"

"Still get to it. Stuck down from behind my neck. Thumper still in reach."

Kensington nodded, looking at the back of the ruck, the area that lies against his back. A freshly flattened C-ration box braced for support to prevent the cans inside from grinding into his back. The machete stuck down inside the two pieces of box.

"Yeah that could work. Quick release?"

Wilson nodded.

"How many cans you carrying?"

Wilson looked up pointing to his ruck on the ground.

"Got me two days chow, couple cans peaches. Got to have my peaches. Dumped the crackers and that white bread shit. Couple of maggots and brains, pork shit, but no ham and mother-fuckers. Save that for you redneck mother fuckers."

Sam looked at him. Wilson shrugged.

"Sounds right. Got me two days, a couple of apricots and no crackers. Spaghetti, you know, as you said, maggots and brains and some pork. I'm not sure I believe we'll get resupply every two days. Hell the last time we were out we were lucky to get supplied every three days, sometimes four, and that one time we only got ammo. Took another day for them to send out the C-rats."

Wilson looked back up, smiling.

"Yeah, we had to eat that gook shit. Some wild potatoes and those fried bananas."

"Don't forget those mangos we found."

"Yeah, had the runs for a whole fucking day."

Sam Kensington pointed, laughing. Wilson waved him off. He continued to pack his ruck. Wilson finished cleaning his M16 and laid the piece on his bunk.

"Here."

Kensington looked up and over at Wilson. Stick was holding a .45 automatic and two magazines. He reached for the pistol.

"What's this for?"

"Thumper's no good close up. In case your sixteen jams up. Give you something until you can clear it."

Kensington set the gun and magazines on the bunk.

"What about you?"

Wilson waved his hand in the air.

"Still got mine. Had a brother over in... you know get me another. The A Shau is a bad place. Shit, if Sarge thinks we need two guns... anyway thought we should be prepared, you know."

Sam nodded.

"Feel like some fucking bandito, carrying all these guns at the same time. Maybe I should strap some M60 machine gun ammo belts across my chest, you take some pictures."

Wilson looked at his friend and smiled.

"Yeah, I'll get the whiskey and women."

They reached across Sam's bunk and slapped hands, not the usual, but enough.

Sam finished packing his ruck and set it on the floor next to his bunk. Sitting down in front of the ruck, he slipped his arms into the straps and stood up shifting his weight to feel the load. The ruck sat nicely on his shoulders, high on his back, the aluminum frame resting on the small of his back. Wilson came around lifting the ruck slightly as Sam adjusted the straps. Sam nodded and Wilson let go.

"Feels okay."

Wilson nodded. He pulled the cross strap tighter, then went around back and tested the M79 Thumper strapped there. Sam reached around to pull the thumper free. He handed it back to Wilson who strapped it back in.

Sam turned as Wilson picked up Sam's M16 from the bunk

handing it to him.

"Try it now."

Sam held onto the M16 as he reached back and removed the thumper, slinging the sixteen over his shoulder.

"Yeah, that works."

Again, Wilson put the thumper back into the strap.

"What you thinking about that?"

Wilson pointed to the .45 automatic pistol lying on the bunk.

"How do you carry yours?"

"I have a shoulder holster."

"How the fuck did you get that?"

"A brother got it for me."

Sam nodded.

"Of course he did."

Wilson pointed.

"Maybe we can do something with your ruck?"

Sam looked down to where Wilson was pointing, but Wilson stepped back.

"Be back in five."

Kensington watched Wilson walk out of the tent. Slowly he lowered himself down and let the ruck drop to the floor behind him. Removing his arms from the straps he stood back up and sat on his bunk.

Not too bad, he thought, he'd carried heavier. He lay back on the bunk resting, almost about to close his eyes when Wilson came charging back in.

"Here, use this."

"Where the fuck did you get that so fast. Who is this brother you know?"

Wilson smiled, handing Kensington the shoulder holster.

"Some officer just lost his."

"You stole this?"

"Hell no. But supply is going to be one short for now."

Kensington nodded as he tried on the holster. Wilson

helped him adjust it.

"Keep it loose, so your ruck fits under. You right or left?"

"Both."

"Fuckin' A."

Sam got back on the floor with the holster on and slipped back into his ruck. With Wilson offering a hand, he raised up. Together they worked on the straps until neither of the straps bothered the other. Wilson stuck the .45 into the holster. He handed Sam the M16 and his steel pot, which Sam put on.

"Where's my camera? Don't you look the fuckin' poster child for this man's army?"

Kensington set the M16 on his bunk, removing and dropping the steel pot helmut on the bunk as well. Dropping back down to the floor, he slipped back out of the ruck, but keeping the shoulder holster with the .45 inside he sat back down on his bunk. He slapped hands with Wilson, doing the white version of the black dap handshake this time.

"But, it don't mean nothing."

"But it don't mean nothing."

An hour later they were all standing just inside the gate as the two and one half ton trucks, "deuce and a halfs," pulled up. As each truck filled up, they moved forward and that truck pulled away. Once all the trucks were loaded, the convoy left the camp heading for the designated firebase for the night.

First Squad was on the same truck. Wilson and Kensington continued their usual banter, while Whitey adjusted his radio to battalion frequency. Big John leaned back, the M60 machine gun resting in his lap. Lopes and Smooth sat across from each other each with a new guy on their side. The other two squads were in the trucks behind them.

Sarge said they would get one more hot meal at the firebase, so don't use up their rations. Hot meal on a firebase meant out of containers served first come first served and if you were lucky that shit was still hot by the time you got your turn.

The trucks bounced down the road, passing through a village or two, or makeshift housing for the locals along the route. The road was built by Army engineers and didn't take into account what might be or might have been in the way, pushing forward. The villagers had rebuilt or settled right up against the road as if it wasn't there. Trucks roaring through momentarily interrupted their existence, but otherwise were ignored.

The villagers had been warned that any livestock on or crossing the road would be killed, run over or what ever it took to get by, because the trucks would not stop for any reason, so as not to be sitting ducks in a possible ambush. There had been some close calls with water buffalo on the road, but they always managed to get out of the way in time.

The trucks picked up speed as they left the gate and would be rolling down the road at a good clip. Villagers learned to move out of their way and not to try to engage the occupants. Usually they just stood and watched as the trucks rolled by.

Wilson leaned back, his back bouncing against the brace on the back of the deuce and a half. Kensington watched him for a moment, leaning forward, bracing his feet from the bouncing that the truck was doing on this makeshift road. The others mostly did the same. The trucks continued on toward the firebase.

Shortly after nineteen hundred, Kensington and Wilson were sitting outside the bunker at the firebase, grabbing a smoke.

"What you think that was we just ate?"

Kensington shook his head.

"Damned if I know? It was thick and cold. Some kind of

processed shit."

Wilson pointed to the perimeter of the firebase.

"Hueys be here first thing in the morning. We be leaving early back to the A Shau. Smooth said he heard chow was from five to six. Want everybody on the line by oh seven hundred for lift off."

Kensington nodded. The two men sat silent for a bit. Wilson spoke as he looked out on the perimeter.

"Four Seven, you know I never get in nobody's business?"

Kensington looked over at Wilson, waiting.

"But I gotta ask. Those dreams, been heavy lately. Okay we're here, but out there?"

Wilson paused, Kensington waited.

"Been wondering if they are going to continue when we're out there, you know back in the bush?"

Kensington took a moment before answering.

"Well Stick, haven't had the dreams before once we're out. Can't say for sure, but I feel when we're back in it, I won't have time to relax, get any real sleep, you know? Don't know why they're so heavy now, maybe it's like you said getting ready for this, might have triggered something."

The two men sat silent. Wilson lit another cigarette, pulling heavily and exhaling a steady stream of blue smoke. Kensington spoke softly.

"Stick, you know I got my shit together."

"Ain't never thought otherwise Four Seven, ain't never thought otherwise. I just wondering, with all we'll have to deal with in that fucking valley, I hope you don't have to deal with that other bullshit same time. That's all."

"Understand. Appreciate the thought."

Kensington pulled a smoke from his pack and lit it, exhaling heavily.

"You know I've had the dreams before this, seem to go away as soon as we were out, didn't think about them until recently.

These last few days, most we've been in, too much time to relax. I'll be fine out there. Besides I don't sleep in the bush no way."

Wilson nodded, pulling on his cigarette, exhaling the blue smoke into the air.

"Yeah, you and me both. Be no sleeping in the bush. Jungle eat you up and spit you back out, you fuck up out there."

Wilson turned facing Kensington.

"Tell you what Four Seven, I see you twitch, I'll wake you up."

"Huh?"

"Seems like every time you dream the dream, you start to twitch in your sleep. You make one twitch, even if it's just to fart, I'll rouse your ass. How'll that be?"

"It's a deal. You do that, I'd be most appreciative."

The two men did the white version of the black dap handshake.

"But it don't mean nothing."

"But it don't mean nothing."

They sat silent for a long time. Finally they both rose up standing, stretching.

"Well Four Seven, sure wish I had me a nip, help me sleep, but we finished that back at camp."

Kensington smiled, reaching inside his jungle fatigue shirt.

"Try this."

He handed a small container to Wilson.

"What's this?"

"Some of Big John's rotgut. He had to get rid of what was left. Smooth and Lopes got some too, but he and Whitey probably drank the rest before we left camp."

Wilson nodded tilting the container to his lips, taking a chug. Sucking back his lips, he spoke hoarsely.

"Jesus, what is that shit?"

"Some redneck homegrown."

Wilson nodded.

"Amen."

The two men went back inside their bunker, Wilson still trying to clear his throat. Kensington took the last sip and tossed the container in the bunker's gathering trash pile. Smooth, Lopes, Whitey and the black new guy were playing Tonk, asked if they wanted to join in, but both men declined.

Wilson checked the watch schedule, asking each guy if they knew when they were up and if they had any questions. The black and the white new guys looked like they did, but didn't want to admit that, so they just nodded, they understood. Kensington watched the black new guy, while the white new guy listened in. Smooth had taken the two FNGs under his wing.

Kensington crawled into his bed roll inside the bunker back corner, set up next to Wilson, wondering what this night would bring, Big John's rotgut burning his stomach. He watched Wilson talk to each man separately, making sure they understood their assignment. He lit a cigarette and tried to let his mind wander, trying what Wilson had told him. Just keep thinking about pussy until you fall asleep. He smiled at the memory.

Wilson sat down on the bedroll next to him.

"Four Seven?"

Kensington raised his hand in the air.

"I know. Now let me be, I'm thinking about pussy like you said."

Wilson smiled and sat back against the dirt wall, looking at the schedule.

Sam looked over, then turned back staring at the ceiling. He ground his cigarette on the floor and let himself drift, the vision starting to form. He smiled as he faded away.

Eleven

The line moved slowly, advancing under heavy Confederate artillery fire, cannon shot bouncing and exploding all around them. The terrain offering no help as the rugged ground caused further delay. Navigating the rough terrain while cannon shot fell all around, jolted the soldiers every movement.

Jethro Longworth was on Samuel Kensington's left and Everett Fremont was on his right. He could see Alfred Lanning and Edgar Fairchild further left and he was sure the others were moving forward in the dense smoke created by the Confederate cannon shot and musketry fire. The soldiers on either side of them trudged forward with him in line with every step.

A cannon shot exploded right in front of their advance, men fell from the fragments all about them. A soldier cried out.

"The commander has fallen."

Major Edward Dillingham, commander of the 10th Vermont lay mortally wounded from a piece of that shell. Two other men behind him lay dead as well. Men on either side lay wounded or dead from the continuous onslaught of cannon shot. Shell fragments flew by and dissected trees and still they pressed forward.

Longworth, Fremont, Kensington, Lanning, Fairchild and several other 10th Vermont soldiers slid into a hollow, protected for a time by the churned up terrain. Catching a much-needed breath, they paused before climbing out. Slowly, they struggled to gain ground, pushing forward under the heavy onslaught.

Approaching a hill, the Federals pressed forward, facing a furious volley of musketry from Ramseur's Virginians and North Carolinians. Pressing on, the Federals routed the Confederate position, but again were met with cannon shot, from Confederate Colonel William Nelson's artillery batteries.

Samuel Kensington and Everett Fremont veered left just as a cannon shot hit in front of them. A soldier unknown to them, stood for a moment mortally wounded with shell fragments in his chest, before dropping to the ground, Jethro Longworth immediately took his position, keeping the line, as they continued forward.

Samuel Kensington watched as a line of blue clad soldiers from what he believed to be the 87th Pennsylvania on their flank continue forward toward one of those Confederate batteries, braving the cannon shot being leveled at them. He could see that the unit was scattered and broken.

Men continued to drop, others screamed in pain as a shell fragment or Minie ball struck their bodies. The smoke from the powder blurred everything, even the sun, the density preventing them from seeing in front of their advance.

Dropping into a ravine the forward advance was slowed even further. Fighting to scramble up the far side, they were met with a volley from the right flank leaving them exposed. Fortunately, a return volley from a Federal unit armed with Spencer repeaters drove the Rebels from that position and the blue clad soldiers continued their advance.

Samuel reloaded his musket, wishing he had one of those Spenser repeater rifles already. He ran his hand over the butt of the revolver tucked into his waistband, knowing that was there if needed. So far it had been a dash, fire, reload, a dash, reload and fire exercise. It was during a reload that that unknown soldier took the shell fragment in the chest. Kensington remembered the look on that soldier's face as he held his ramming rod in the Musket when the fragment tore into his chest, a look of "huh" more than anything else crossed the man's face. Samuel did not see the man drop as he turned away and continued his advance.

Everett Fremont stood next to Samuel Kensington, sweat running through the dirt on his face, breathing hard as they readied for the next movement. Jethro Longworth stood off to the side of both men. A volley of musketry passed across above them, while they were still below ground. Men just reaching the top of the ravine dropped and fell into the depression struck by those Rebel Minie balls.

The soldiers regrouped and continued forward, marching, crawling scrapping toward Ramseur's front. Crossing open fields now, they endured continuous artillery barrage never wavering, still driving forward. Lines of Federals, sweating in the heavy blue clad uniforms, turned the landscape into a moving sea of blue water.

Fremont, Kensington and Longworth along with Alfred Lanning and Edgar Fairchild and the rest of the men from the 10th Vermont, continued to move the line forward, while men dropped all around them, the cannon shot tearing through their ranks.

A shell burst to their right sending fragments into the air. Samuel Kensington felt a tug at his haversack, turning to look, he saw Fremont pull the hot metal from the pack and patted out the fire it caused. His haversack was torn open and the contents lay on the ground, but it had buffered the impact and kept the fragment from hitting him. He picked up what he could, stuffing the spilled contents into pockets and his waistband. The two men nodded to each other.

A moment later three soldiers on their far left fell, wounded from another cannon shot, this time Fremont caught a piece in his tent roll, leaving a blackened smoking spot, that was quickly patted out. Again the two men nodded. New soldiers joined the line replacing those that fell and the advance continued. Finally Ramseur's line broke and fell back, allowing the Federals to stop and rest for a brief respite.

Samuel Kensington, Everett Fremont, Jethro Longworth, as well as Alfred Lanning and Edgar Faichild, joined up with those new soldiers along the line. Soon thereafter, Reginald Harrington, Rufus Meriweather and Edward Hutchens joined them. As usual no one knew where Frenchy was. Together they piled fence rails and fallen trees along the front for protection. They stood defense holding a line, while other units continued the advance now routing the last of the Confederates on the flanks.

As Samuel Kensington removed his gear, he looked at the hole in his haversack. He would need a new haversack, but he hoped he could get by with this one for now. Working to patch the tear, he pulled out his housewife. Everett Fremont sat down beside him.

"You really think you can sew that up, with just your housewife kit?"

"I have to do something."

Fremont nodded.

Satisfied with his handy work, Kensington checked and cleaned his musket, Everett sitting beside him, was doing the same with his musket.

"Did you see that soldier go down?"

Samuel Kensington looked at his fellow soldier.

"No, I turned when his face contorted. He was in the middle of a reload. I don't think he had time to understand what had just happened. Hope so anyway."

Everett Fremont pointed.

"That was pretty intense what we went through out there. Surprised we made it. Very few others did. The 10th took a licking out there. Heard the commander went down straight off."

Samuel looked at him.

"Yeah, heard that too."

The two men sat in silence cleaning their muskets. Finally Samuel spoke to no one in particular.

"Thought we were suppose to have those Spencer's by now?"

Another soldier just to the right of the two men, answered.

"We do. Can't you tell?"

All three men chuckled. Fremont pointed to Samuel.

"I see you still carry that revolver, what for?"

"It's my good luck charm. Didn't need to use it this time, mostly we were facing the cannon shot, but it's come in handy before."

The third man chimed in.

"Well we ever do get those Spencer's, you can forget that thing."

Samuel looked at him a moment before speaking.

"Nope. No matter, I'll hang onto it, don't mind the weight, use to it by now."

"Suit yourself."

"Who?"

"Alfred Nichols at your service. We moved up when you boys started dropping off. Had us join you on the line. Don't know who's left. Officers and I think our sergeant fell as well. Not sure who's in charge anymore. You boys know?"

Kensington nodded and pointed at Everett.

"Everett Fremont and I'm Samuel Kensington. No, sure don't."

Nichols nodded.

"Well, I 'speck someone will step up say he's in charge. Any idea how long we'll be here?"

Kensington and Fremont both nodded no.

"Well then, I'm going to get me some shuteye. Didn't get much chance last night. Talk to you boys later."

The two men nodded and remained silent, sitting back enjoying their momentary respite from battle. Lanning moved in next to them, nodding before lying back against the ground.

"The others?"

Lanning looked up at Fremont.

"I saw Fairchild and Meriweather behind me. Hutchens I believe is over there. Think Harrington is with him. Don't know about Frenchy."

Fremont nodded. Lanning fell back against the dirt, his musket clutched firmly in his hands, his eyes closed.

Twelve

Stepping into the dark, Sam Kensington left the bunker, enjoying the crisp cool air of the early morning. His guard shift had been the one before and he hadn't gone back to sleep. Smooth was there, pulling the last shift. The two men nodded as Sam stepped off to the side. Using his hands to cup the lighter, he lit a cigarette, pulling heavily and letting the smoke drift out.

In the distance the sun was rising in the sky, casting an eerie glow over the A Shau Valley. Somewhere in that valley several units of the NVA were doing whatever it is they do, not realizing all hell was about to be brought down on them. Well, let them enjoy the moment he thought sarcastically and allowed himself a chuckle.

Although he sensed him before he saw him, he was still surprised to see Wilson standing next to him.

"Hey."

"Hey."

Sam offered him his pack of smokes, but Wilson declined, showing he already had one lit. He nodded, putting the pack back in his jungle fatigue shirt.

"You up for some chow?"

"Don't know if they're serving yet."

Sam Kensington turned his wrist to look at his watch.

"Another twenty or so."

Wilson nodded and sat down next to him.

"What's the latest Four Seven?"

Kensington sat silent for a moment taking the last pull on his cigarette.

"We're definitely in battle. Marching on some line toward a Confederate position, you know like that."

"And?"

"And what? I had another dream that's all."

"You know what I mean. Anything we can relate too?"

Kensington smiled waving his hand in the air.

"Well I suspect, that soon we'll be in the valley advancing on some gook position, marching over some jungle terrain and like that, so yeah, it's relative I suppose."

Wilson nodded.

"Still don't get it Four Seven, why you're dreaming about this other war, a war that you barely know anything about. You must have had kin or something make you go back, but why the Civil War, why not some current war, you know like the big one, WW deuce? Seems like that be more appropriate."

Sam nodded.

"Wish I knew, Stick. Wish I knew. Thought maybe the XO might have some answers. All he knew was that it was a battle in a valley, a hundred years ago. You might have the best answer, some parallel war shit kind of thing."

Wilson nodded.

"Let's eat."

"You sure you want to eat that container shit again."

"Be first in line, get the good stuff."

Sam nodded. Wilson helped him up. The two men walked to the staging area. The sun was up in the sky lighting the firebase. The popping of rotor blades broke the silence as helicopters started arriving. They had heard several arrive last night, but now more were coming. Sarge had said last night that the lift was going to be big, everybody going to their LZs all at once, landing in mass.

Wilson, Kensington and Smooth, whose guard shift was over and had joined in, walked to the chow area, being the first three in line. Powdered eggs, rubber bacon and congealed potatoes made for an appealing breakfast, coupled with luke warm coffee that could have been used for helicopter blade lubricant rounded off the last hot meal.

The three men sat and ate their meal in silence. Smooth and Kensington actually drank the black coffee, but Wilson poured his out. Afterward, they scraped the metal-pocketed plate, swooshed it in the water for rinsing and stuck them on the discard pile, to be washed and used again. Smooth left them to go hit the latrine.

"You ever burn shit Four Seven?"

"Fuckin' A. You?"

"Fuckin' A."

They walked silently back toward the bunker. Sam stopped and turned.

"Might not be a bad idea, take one last dump sitting before we head out and I have to shit in a hole."

Wilson kept walking with his hand in the air.

Standing on the line by the Hueys, with their gear and weapons, they waited for the word. Hueys were lined up on both sides of the tarmac and men were standing on both sides of each Huey waiting.

Wilson, Kensington, Lopes, Whitey and the new white guy would be on the first bird. Smooth, Big John, the new black guy and the lieutenant and his radioman would be on the second bird and so on.

Wilson's squad would be on the ground first, with the lieutenant, who would join up with second squad once everybody was on the ground. Sarge would be traveling with third squad. First squad would be point, second in the middle and third squad would bring up the rear. So far, they were still designated to operate in platoon strength.

With Wilson the new squad leader, Kensington and Smooth would be walking point, alternating the slack position, until the two new guys got more time in the bush. Third squad with Sarge would pull rear guard as the platoon moved. All this had been drilled into the men over the last twenty-four hours. The veterans knew what to do, the drilling was for the eleven new guys that joined the platoon.

The blades began to turn as the helicopters started their engines. The noise and dust swirling in the air became overwhelming. The men mounted up, pulling their ruck sacks on, securing their steel pots on their heads and readying their weapons—locked and loaded.

The Hueys were at full throttle, the signal was given to load up. The new white guy was instructed to get in first, sit in the middle, while Lopes and Whitey sat on the left side their feet hanging above the slick. Wilson and Kensington stood on the slick on the right side and let their ass drop to the metal floor, leaning back letting the weight of the ruck rest on that floor holding them in place. Wilson turned and saw that Lopes and Whitey were on, then he looked at the new white guy, he could see the apprehension on his face. Wilson winked and gave a thumbs up. Facing the door gunner he waved his hand in the air, with his index finger raised. The door gunner nodded. The

Huey rocked as it slowly lifted off the tarmac into the air, gaining elevation as it climbed into the sky.

Wilson stuck his fist out, Kensington hit it with his fist.

The Huey continued to climb, started a forward motion, then waited as the others pulled in behind him, carrying the rest of first squad, second squad and third squads, six birds in all carrying their platoon. The formation started forward, crossing the valley in the south, then using the terrain as a cover, turned north along the Laotian Border toward their designated LZ.

Fighter jets had bombed the area followed by an artillery barrage, followed by helicopter rockets into the area to prep it for landing. Cobra gun ships escorted the lead Hueys into the LZ, providing cover fire as each bird landed.

Staying at full throttle, the Huey hovered inches from the ground as the men disembarked. Wilson and Kensington off to the right, Lopes and Whitey off to the left. Wilson waited and reached out to the new white guy pulling him free of the bird. The door gunner nodded and the Huey was back in the air, a second Huey coming down right on the spot the first had occupied a moment ago. The rest of first squad and the lieutenant were on the ground.

Spreading out and providing a defensive perimeter around the LZ, the soldiers dropped their rucks and readied their weapons. Once the platoon was in, they moved off the LZ and took up a defensive position to the west along the Laotian border in the Northern A Shau Valley. The immediate plan was to get away from the LZ and continue moving throughout the day in a Reconnaissance in Force, or RIF operation.

Smooth took point first, Kensington walked slack, leading the squad and the platoon further away from the LZ into the jungle. After a couple of hours, the men broke for chow, setting up guard positions on the left, right front and rear of the platoon.

"Stick you want me to take the next point?"

"Smooth, you good or you need a break?"

Smooth looked at Wilson, then at Kensington.

"Four Seven, you ready? I'm getting ripped to shit in this elephant grass, could use a break let somebody else cut for awhile, I'll do slack."

Wilson looked at Kensington, who nodded.

"Yeah, I'm good."

The lieutenant came over.

"Who's up?"

Wilson pointed to Kensington.

"Good job, Smooth. Sam here's the path."

The lieutenant knelt down next to Kensington, showing him the map covered in plastic that he marked with a grease pencil. Sam nodded he understood.

"Don't know what the terrain is like up ahead but I'd like to cover a lot more ground by night fall. Suppose to be here in the morning, so if we can get another couple of hours in before we set up, that would be outstanding."

Sam looked at Wilson and smiled.

"Assuming we don't run into those fellows not real happy we're in their backyard."

The lieutenant smiled.

"Of course."

The lieutenant walked away to his radioman and got on the horn. Wilson sat next to Kensington, Smooth moved in as well.

"Lotta jungle to cut through. Pretty slow going. Been trying to stay high, don't want to dip down too far, get caught low."

Wilson and Kensington nodded they understood. Smooth nodded back.

"What you think Four Seven, we make that much ground like he wants?"

"I think Smooth is right. Pretty thick shit going through and I agree we need to stay high. You know we're still carrying full loads, start feeling it as the day goes on. I'll do what I can."

"Roger that Four Seven."

The word spread to saddle up, get ready to move out. Kensington followed Smooth's lead, breaking through the dense jungle vegetation slowly, staying high on the ridge. After another two hours, the signal came up to hold up. Sam stopped in place, waiting. In a minute the word was to go.

A half hour later they came upon a flat area, with some clearing. Sam stopped the platoon, looking for a long time to see any movement or signs of activity. Finally he motioned to have the lieutenant come up. Wilson joined them.

"Sir, looks like a good area to stop maybe set up for the night, good spot for an NDP. You can see across the opening. We can set up in here deep, put out defenses for the night and watch for movement. But it looks pretty old. Hasn't been much activity here in quite a while."

He waited for the lieutenant to digest the idea. Finally he nodded yes.

"Yeah. Wilson you pull your men back. I'll have second squad do a recon of the area before we get too comfortable. Pass the word, no hot Cs yet, no cooking. Keep it very quiet until we recon the area, maybe until we set up our NDP, maybe an ambush site."

The lieutenant left. Kensington dropped his ruck, but kept his focus on the front open area. The new black guy and Smooth came up branching off to the sides, setting up to keep a one-eighty on the open area. Wilson tapped Kensington on the helmut.

"I'll be back in five mikes."

Sam nodded. He pointed to Smooth who nodded back. Where Smooth had set up created a blind spot. Smooth moved back further to see around some elephant grass. He popped his fingers, the new black guy looked over, Sam pointed to where Smooth was, the new black guy nodded.

Wilson came back with Big John and the M60 machine gun. He set up next to Kensington. The new white guy was behind him. Wilson pointed and the new white guy took Sam's position. Wilson motioned for Sam to follow him back.

Sarge, the lieutenant and Bob Grite, the second squad leader were together waiting. The five men sat down while the lieutenant spoke.

"Having flat ground for the night is encouraging, but I don't want us to be lulled in to anything just because. Bob, I want your squad to do a recon around the perimeter, before we get too comfortable. I believe Kensington is right, there hasn't been any activity here in awhile, but we know they are all around this valley, don't know if they might decide to come this way tonight just to fuck with us. Have to know we landed and might be moving around in here."

"Roger, Sir."

"Sarge, you take third squad back a bit, see what's defensible for the night, before we tighten up the perimeter."

Owen Hubbard nodded.

"I think we should set up two ambush sites tonight, here and here."

The lieutenant pointed to his map.

"Take them from second and third squad. I want one behind us and one to the left up above. We can guard the lower from the perimeter, set up a defense line, two rows of claymores."

Bob Grite, Sergeant Owen Hubbard and Wilson all nodded.

"Wilson keep your men in, you got point again tomorrow, but have your squad set up a full front defensive position, watching that opening. Kensington may be right that there hasn't been any recent activity, but anybody walks into that opening, I want them to know we're here now, you understand?"

Wilson nodded.

"Kensington, you went off course back there."

"Sir, I wanted to stay high…"

"Let me finish. I think you moved us further north, we should be going due west, which still works, but we may have to make up some ground tomorrow to get back on course."

Before Kensington could answer, the lieutenant raised his hand.

"Hold on. I know we need to stay high. You and Smooth did a good job of keeping us from dropping down, short of walking along the ridge. And God knows this shit isn't easy to cut through. All I'm saying is we veered off course a bit. Just keep that in mind. That's all I'm saying."

Kensington nodded.

"Got it, Sir."

"Okay then, we all have our assignments. Pass the word, no cooking until we can recon the area, just break in place, put out your defensive positions and hold until Grite gets back with second squad. Is that understood?"

Everyone nodded yes. The lieutenant nodded back.

"Good. Let's go."

Wilson and Kensington went back to their squad's location. Wilson told Lopes and Whitey what was going on and instructed them to relieve Smooth and Big John, leave the new guys in place.

Wilson sat back against his ruck and lit a cigarette. Kensington did the same. As the two men sat silent enjoying their cigarette, Big John and Smooth, came back in.

"What's up?"

Wilson looked at Smooth, motioning for him to sit down. Big John sat next to him.

"We're going to hold in place for now. Second's doing a recon of the perimeter, third is going back a ways to get a bead on a defensive position, we're setting the front. If all looks good, we'll be setting up here for the night. Smooth recon the opening, see what we need to catch anything walking through and stop anything that might think they can walk through."

Smooth smiled.

"Nobody walking in my front door."

"Big John, you and the new white guy both have 60s, so position those to fire one eighty across that opening. Anything hits the trip flare, you paint them with those 60s."

Big John nodded.

"Roger that."

"LT wants two ambush teams tonight, one in back and one up high, but we get to stay in, cause we got point again tomorrow."

Smooth nodded. Wilson looked at Kensington, who waved his hand in the air.

"For now, you take five, Four Seven and I will relieve the other two in a bit, leave the new guys out, you two can pick them up later."

Kensington finished his cigarette and stood up. Wilson nodded and joined him. The two men walked out relieving Whitey and Lopes.

Second squad's recon was negative, so the rest of the platoon prepared to set up for the NDP. The two ambush teams left to acquire their position. Wilson's squad set up their front defensive position, putting out trip flares and claymores. Big John worked out two spots to lie the M60 machine guns for the one eighty fire across the opening. If anybody appeared there, they would be in for a world of hurt.

Smooth and Kensington took the first watch manning the 60s and the clackers for the claymores, since they had point the next day, they would then be able to get a full night's sleep. Wilson relieved Kensington with the new black guy, Lopes would be next with the new white guy, then Big John and Whitey would take the final watch.

Sam Kensington pulled the poncho liner over his head to ward off the mosquitoes and settled in for the night. Cutting through the jungle all-day and carrying all this shit had strained his muscles and tired him out. Hopefully it would help him get right to sleep.

Pussy, he thought, just keep thinking about pussy. He felt his eyes grow heavy and in the next instant he was fast asleep.

Thirteen

Sam Kensington woke just before daylight. Wilson was still asleep next to him, as was Lopes and the two new guys. Smooth was sitting up against his ruck. They nodded to each other. Having been first watch they got to sleep though the night, which Sam actually did. And as far as he could remember, no dream.

He rose up and knelt down by Smooth.

"Sure like to get some coffee on."

Smooth nodded. Sam checked his watch.

"Damn it's only five, won't be light for another hour. You ready to cut some more jungle?"

Smooth just smiled. Sam nodded as he walked back to his ruck. Placing the poncho liner over his head to mask the light, he lit a cigarette, pulling deep and letting the smoke drift out.

In what seemed like forever, the sun finally came up. By then the rest of the guys were awake and waiting to put coffee on. Wilson sat against his ruck running his hand over his face and through his hair, shaking off the sleep.

"Four Seven?"

"No."

"Fuckin' A."

"Wilson."

Sarge was standing near their set up, motioning.

"LT wants to see us."

Wilson nodded, standing and lighting a cigarette. Sam watched him leave, readying a punched out C-rat can, placing piece of a heat tab in the void, filling the canteen cup half full with fresh water, he used a cigarette to ignite the flame. Coffee would be ready in moments.

As Sam was taking the first sips of the hot brew, Wilson came back.

"Listen up. LT wants to run a couple of patrols before we move out, so we're gonna be here a bit longer. Get some chow in you, after… Smooth, you and Lopes relieve Whitey and Big John out there, so they can eat."

Wilson checked his watch.

"In about a half hour, I'm gonna take the two new guys, Four Seven and Whitey with his radio, out for a quick look see up ahead, past the opening. Like to know what's there before we walk into it."

Wilson lit and pulled on another cigarette.

"Any questions?"

The two new guys sat stone faced.

"All right then, eat drink and be merry."

Kensington finished his coffee and opened a can of pork stuff, which he heated on the C-rat, can fire. Wilson sat back down.

"Even that shit we had at the firebase is looking better already."

"Fuckin' A."

"How we going?"

Wilson looked at Sam, pointing.

"I'm point, put the two new guys in the middle, Whitey in

the middle of them, you bring up the rear."

Kensington nodded.

Standing at the defensive position, where Lopes and Smooth had manned the guns, they prepared to move out.

"You disarm the trips and claymores?"

Smooth nodded. Wilson saw the claymores sitting by the 60s. He nodded back.

"Let's go."

They kept to the brush, what there was of it, and crossed the opening quickly, traveling with only weapons they could maneuver easily. Wilson breeched the overgrowth and stopped, waiting until everyone was in the cover.

"Looks like you were right. Nobody been here in awhile."

Kensington nodded.

Wilson rose up using his hand to signal to move. He took them on a zigzag pattern through the jungle growth. After forty-five minutes, he stopped the group. Reaching for the handset on Whitey's radio he called in. Nothing to report, he was coming back.

"Four Seven, take us back."

Sam nodded starting the trek back. He skirted around the trail they had just cut, ever watchful for anything that might have slipped in behind them. In a half hour they were back inside the perimeter.

"Stick, ground looks passable above where we went through, I'll take us out that way."

Wilson nodded.

"Go see the LT, tell him what you said."

An hour later everyone was packed up and ready to move out. Kensington went wide around the opening, hitting the overgrowth he had scouted earlier, just above where they had patrolled. Cutting through the elephant grass and weeds he cut a path due west, as the LT had instructed.

Two hours later they reached a plateau on high ground that looked like it would be defensible enough to take a break. He motioned the LT up and pointed to the area. The LT ordered everyone to stop in place and put out defensive positions while he sent a squad out to recon the area.

The recon reported the area was clear. Again it looked like no activity had been there in quite awhile. The platoon moved onto the plateau, to rest and broke for chow.

"Kensington."

"Yes sir."

"Good job, we're right on course. I'm going to send a patrol out forward to the right to see what's up ahead, but you keep us left."

"Roger that."

The lieutenant walked away and Wilson came over.

"Area looks pretty old. Either we're off track or we're about to walk into something. Looks like we're crossing, more like a flanking movement."

"Stick, I believe you're right. But remember right now we're the blocking force, anything comes our way."

Wilson nodded. Whitey spoke up.

"Been hearing a lot of traffic on the horn. Couple of units making contact one of them hills over there."

Whitey pointed to the south.

"I 'speck, they get those little fuckers on the run, we just might be in the thick of it pretty soon."

Wilson and Kensington nodded.

The first round exploded about twenty-five meters outside the perimeter, the next round within ten meters as the mortars were being walked into their defensive position.

The next round exploded on top of Wilson, Kensington and Whitey right in front of them, but the blast went sideways, no shrapnel came their way. The next round hit behind them. Three more rounds exploded inside the perimeter. Screams of pain were heard about the chaos, dust swirled in the air, hot pieces of shrapnel were flying everywhere.

Sergeant Owen Hubbard was at Wilson's location, pointing. "You boys feel like a little hike?"

Kensington nodded, Wilson was already standing, Whitey was up with the radio strapped on his shoulders, and two guys from second squad were right behind the sergeant.

Before anyone could say another word, the sergeant was leading the way out of the perimeter into the bush, breaking through the jungle grass and overgrowth.

They approached a small opening, Sarge stopped, raising his hand. A puff of smoke could be seen across the field. The pop of another round going airborne sounded. The Sarge motioned and the men fanned out creating a semi circle around the sighting. One of the men from second squad carried a 60 and he set up directly across.

The sound of another round "popping" from the tube was heard. The Sarge lowered his hand and each man opened up with his weapon into the area of the smoke. A scream and yelling came from the area, while bullets rained down on that location. In a moment the firing stopped, the Sarge keeping his hand in the air.

Pointing, he waved his hand to the left. Wilson and Kensington made their way around. The Sarge did the same on the right, Whitey stayed with the M60 gunner in front. Sarge and the other guy from second squad worked right. Together the two teams moved in flanking the location they had just put heavy fire on.

Wilson motioned and Kensington crawled in beside him.

Pointing, Wilson waved his hand, Sam understood. Slowly they approached the area from the left. They could see the Sarge and the other guy doing the same on the right. The two teams broke through the jungle overgrowth simultaneously, standing in the now abandoned area.

A mortar tube was still smoking in the middle, NVA gear was everywhere, and most importantly there was a large amount of blood on the ground, but no bodies.

Wilson picked up a pith helmut.

"NVA. Regular army mother fuckers."

The others nodded.

"Looks like we got some of them."

Sarge nodded.

"For a fact."

"Sarge, should we go after them?"

The sergeant looked at the guy from second squad, thinking for a moment.

"Sure like to, but our element of surprise is gone now. We better get back, just regroup for now."

Although every man standing there wanted to go after the fleeing NVA, they knew Sarge was right. Smart play was to go back. The four men filed out of the area back into the opening. Wilson pulled the pin, let the spoon fly and dropped a grenade down the mortar tube.

"Fire in the hole."

The grenade and tube exploded, destroying it. Wilson kept the pith helmut he found. They met up with the 60 gunner and Whitey before heading back to the perimeter. Whitey called in that they were approaching. Smooth stood up and waved them in, keeping his M16 pointed behind them in case one of those little fuckers decided to follow.

Sarge made a report to the lieutenant. Wilson stood off to the side, nodding. The guy from second squad nodded and they all dispersed. Lieutenant said they had two wounded and a Medevac was on the way, they were going to bring it in right here, so button everything up.

Kensington was already packed, his weapon cleared and reloaded. He had used up a magazine and a half in the barrage of fire. Wilson stood beside him.

"Knew those little bastards had to be around."

Kensington nodded, pointing.

"Heard two guys from third got hit."

Wilson nodded.

"Yeah, two of the new guys in that squad, wrong place, you know?"

Kensington nodded, selecting a cigarette from his pack and offering one to Wilson, who took it and waited while he lit both cigarettes.

"So Four Seven, what you make of that round explode right in front of us, but go another way, pretty fucking weird man."

Kensington looked at Wilson, not sure what he meant.

"Rounds hitting everywhere. What you mean?"

Wilson pointed.

"Look around, you see the blast area, mother fucker went right around us, how you figure that?"

Kensington looked where Wilson was pointing and he could see the concussion from the round, tore up both sides of where they had been with no visible front debris, more like a V shaped explosion.

"Hey, defective round, we got lucky."

Wilson shook his head.

"Whitey, what you think, we get lucky?"

Whitey looked up from his radio at where Wilson was pointing.

"Every day in the bush is lucky, no big deal. When your time is up in the A Shau, your time is up."

Smooth chimed in.

"Yea, though I walk through the valley of death, I fear no evil because I am the evilest son-of-a-bitch in the valley."

Kensington smiled, even Wilson cracked a smile.

"You mother fuckers philosophers now, maybe I get that shit engraved on my lighter."

Kensington patted Wilson on the back.

"Hey, chalk it up to one for the good guys."

Wilson smiled waving his hand in the air.

"Still, I ain't never seen no round do that, break sideways."

Wilson waved his hands in the air in a V shape. Kensington nodded, Smooth waved his hands in the air and Whitey belched.

"Damn, that fuckin' pork stuff trying to come back up."

All four men chuckled.

The sound of an arriving Huey buffeted the air. Men scrambled to tie their gear down. The Huey followed the smoke in sitting at full throttle as the two wounded men were loaded on, their gear tossed in as well, a box of ammo was thrown off the bird as it lifted off back into the sky.

Once the Medevac was gone the lieutenant motioned to the box of ammo.

"Anybody needs, get it, the rest you hump."

Big John grabbed several boxes and passed them around. Wilson, Kensington and Whitey reloaded their spent magazines.

Within the hour, they were packed up and on the move. Kensington led them through the ambush site, the mortar tube sat there, blown apart. Blood and equipment lay scattered on the ground. He continued through a ravine, ever mindful of the eminent presence of more NVA in the area. Now that they had made contact, more could and would be expected.

Sam brought the platoon to a halt and motioned for the LT to come up. The LT, Sarge and Wilson joined him there. He pointed to a rise on top a ridge that he thought might be a good location for an NDP. The LT agreed and Sarge volunteered to lead a patrol to recon the area first.

Sarge was back forty-five minutes later. The area looked clear. They went up and over and all around the rise, no signs of activity, but a trail lower down had been used recently. Might be a good place to set an ambush.

They made their way onto the rise, quietly setting up. No cooking tonight. The LT agreed with the Sarge and set up an ambush across the lower trail. He also sent out two ambush sites, one off the backside and one off the front. Since they had the high ground, the only concern was the NVA walking in and he wanted to hit them, before they got to the perimeter.

A stronger defensive position was established on the weak side. Trip flares were set followed by claymores as they secured the Night Defensive Position and settled in for the evening.

Wilson sat close to Kensington.

"You and me got the late watch tonight. Smooth be walking point tomorrow."

Kensington nodded.

"How late?"

"Midnight 'till two."

"My favorite, middle of the night."

"Hey Four Seven, we ain't had to pull a 'bush yet, be up all night then."

Kensington nodded.

"Fuckin' A."

Wilson slid back against his ruck, laying his M16 next to him. He pulled the forty-five from the holster. Kensington watched.

"Stick, we did good today."

"Fuckin' A."

"Thought about that shell. You know weird shit happens out here, but that's…"

"That's what I'm saying."

"Anyway see you at midnight."

"Roger that."

Fourteen

Smooth tapped Wilson first, then Kensington.

"You're up."

Wilson sat up, sliding his hand across his face to wipe the sleep away. Kensington rolled over and looked up.

"Damn, wake me when it's over."

"Let's go Four Seven."

The two men grabbed their weapons and steel pots and made their way to the position. Shivering in the cool midnight air they had each grabbed their poncho liner as well.

"Sure could use some hot coffee."

Wilson nodded, he sat by the M60 on the left while Kensington took the right. Each gun pointed outward at a forty-five degree angle. The detonators for the claymores were in between the two guns.

"Smooth says it's been quiet so far."

Kensington nodded, huddling under his poncho liner.

"You okay?"

"Yeah, nothing, been sleeping okay, at least until tonight. Barely closed my eyes. LT say what we're doing later today?"

Wilson shook his head no.

They finished their shift and went back for a couple more hours of sleep.

Just as Sam took his first sip of coffee, Sarge came over to their setup.

"Listen up."

Smooth, Whitey, Big John and the two new guys gathered around Wilson and Kensington. Lopes was out on watch.

"LT said we're going to spend the day here, run patrols and wait for some resupply. Maybe we'll move out later in the day, but we could be spending another night here. Just in case, dig in, fortify your defensive position."

Sarge looked around at each of the men.

"Look we know they're out there and after yesterday's contact, be alert. Wilson, put a team together and take them out to the front off the rise. Go out about an hour, sweep around and come back in. I got second heading due south and sweeping around out there. Third is going north, do the same. I got a three man team heading back a ways, make sure no one following us."

Sarge paused and looked around the men again.

"Any questions?"

There were none.

"Good. Wilson, prepare to move out in an hour."

Wilson nodded. Sarge left as quickly as he had come.

"Me, Four Seven, Whitey on the radio, the new black guy and Smooth will go out. Big John, you and Lopes stay back with the 60s and keep the new white guy with you, maybe start digging in a bit. I want to travel light. Get some chow, hot coffee, be ready…"

Wilson looked at his watch.

"In three zero mikes."

The men drifted away, back to what they were doing before Sarge had come crashing in. Wilson sat next to Kensington, who lit a smoke and yawned. He watched as Wilson opened a can of peaches.

"That breakfast?"

Wilson paused between bites.

"It's all I got left. Ate that other shit last night."

Kensington stood next to Wilson while the other men passed the two M60 machine guns.

"Claymores in?"

Big John nodded.

"Trip flares?"

"Disarmed for now."

Wilson nodded.

"Smooth you take point, Four Seven will bring up the rear. New black guy you follow Smooth walk slack, Whitey, you in the middle, then me and Four Seven bringing up the rear."

The men nodded. They had done this before and understood the formation. Smooth led them off the plateau, down into the jungle, snaking his way through the overgrowth. Fifteen minutes out he picked up a trail. Motioning Wilson up, he pointed.

"They've been here recently. Head that way, see what's over there."

Smooth nodded.

The team inched up a slight rise and made their way through thick underbrush. Smooth stopped, motioning Wilson up again. He pointed.

In an opening just ahead of them they could see two maybe three NVA soldiers, standing. A fourth appeared. Wilson motioned to the men behind him to spread out, form a line. Using his hand he directed the men into position. Holding his hand in the air in a closed fist he waited.

A fifth NVA soldier joined the others and as they started to walk into the opening, Wilson lowered his hand.

"Now."

All five in Wilson's team fired at once, dropping the first three men and hitting the other two as they tried to head back into cover. A moment later a volley of AK47 fire came from behind the brush where the NVA soldiers were standing.

Wilson's men returned fire. Bullets flew back and forth furiously until Wilson raised his hand and his men stopped firing. All was quiet. He motioned and Smooth worked his way around the left side. Pointing, Kensington nodded and worked his way around the right. Wilson held up his hand and the two men stopped.

Nodding to Whitey and the new black guy, the three of them put another burst into the brush, but were not met with return fire. He nodded and Smooth and Kensington moved closer. Smooth reached the area first, on slightly higher ground. He peered down and raised his hand in the air. Kensington moved closer coming straight in. He walked to the opening where the dead soldiers lay and motioned.

Wilson, Whitey and the new black guy moved forward, meeting up with Smooth and Kensington. The three dead NVA soldiers lay in the opening, hit several times. The other soldiers that tried to get away were just inside that opening. Several blood spots on the ground suggested others might have been wounded. But most telling was the mortar tube lying on the ground along with a couple of rocket launchers and two AK47 rifles.

"Let's get this stuff and get back. New guy search the bodies, collect everything they have."

The new guy looked at Wilson with an expression of complete shock on his face.

"Hey, we've all had to do it. Let's go, we need to get out of here in two mikes."

As the new black guy went through the pockets of the dead soldiers, Kensington strapped the two AK47s across his shoulder and picked up one of the rocket launchers Whitey picked up the base of the mortar tube. Wilson got the tube and the other rocket launcher.

"Hey, you finished?"

The new black guy looked up from the body he was searching.

"Almost, one more."

Wilson nodded keeping his eye on the man.

"What's your name new guy?"

"Darnell Smith."

"Well from now on Darnell Smith, you're Body Man."

Darnell Smith nodded.

"Let's go, let's go. Smooth, take us back the long way."

Smooth nodded.

The team snaked its way around the other side of where they had come, ever watchful for movement or signs of previous activity. Finally they made their way back into the perimeter, passing Big John and the new white guy sitting by the guns. Lopes was behind them, taking his turn with the shovel, straight into the center of the perimeter, where they dropped the captured weapons.

Sarge and the LT came over looking at the weapons on the ground. Wilson had called in saying they had made contact and had five killed and some weapons.

"Sir, no doubt they were heading our way with that tube. Don't know how many got away, but sure enough blood to suggest we hit a couple of those that di di maued. But they know we're here, that's for damn sure."

The lieutenant nodded.

"Uniforms, Pith helmets, NVA regulars for sure."

The lieutenant looked at Wilson, nodding that he understood.

"Resupply should be here within the hour, with C-rats and ammo, once we load up, we'll get the hell out of here. How's it look up ahead, see anything we can get to before night fall?"

"Didn't go that far, sir. Ran into those fuckers first. Thought it best to pick up the weapons and head back, let you know what we found."

"Yeah, makes sense."

They all stood silent. Finally Sarge spoke up.

"LT, maybe it's best we stay here, have gunships do a dance around our perimeter, dig in for the night, maybe run patrols out later deeper, see what's out there, set up a 'bush or two tonight, revaluate in the morning. We got a good perimeter on the high ground, make for a good LZ too, get resupply in. Battalion said they would send replacements for the two we lost. Might be a good play we stay right here another night."

The lieutenant nodded.

"Makes sense. Let me clear it with the CO. Wilson you up for another run out there, get further, see what's up ahead, before we move out?"

"Affirmative, sir."

"Prepare to move out in an hour. Sergeant, run two more patrols up and down and maybe we should set up a listening post behind us, case they try to work around behind us."

The sergeant nodded.

"Sir, we got an LP out about fifty meters on our rear already."

"Right, good. All right, let's go."

The lieutenant turned to his RTO monitoring the radio.

"Get me the CO on the horn and find out the status of that resupply."

"Sir, they're really in the shit further south, trying to take some hill."

The lieutenant, Sarge and Wilson looked at the lieutenant's RTO.

"Whitey said earlier that something heavy was happening south."

Sarge and the Lieutenant looked at Wilson. Wilson looked at the sergeant hoping he would pick up his lead. Sarge nodded.

"LT, maybe we should start working south for a bit, in case we have to intercept, you know?"

The lieutenant nodded.

"I'll check with the CO. Wilson you start out west, work your way around and head in from the south. Let me know what's out there."

"Roger that."

"Son, what's the word on that resupply?"

Sarge and Wilson stepped away as the lieutenant took the handset from his RTO.

"Stick, try to go as wide as you can. We already know those little fuckers are here, but we need an escape route. Once we start moving we need to evade as best we can. If we need to take them on, let's do it now, while we're setup. See if you can draw them out, put some gunships on their ass, bring in some artillery, open our path."

"Understand, Sarge. How far you want me to go?"

Sarge looked at his watch.

"We still got five hours of daylight. No more that two out, two back in, less if you can, but make a wide sweep, okay?"

Wilson nodded.

"Got it."

Wilson left and went back to his men, explaining the latest plan. Doing another patrol wasn't their first choice, but it was probably better than moving with full rucks.

Again Wilson had his men in the opening, ready to move out.

"Four Seven, Smooth, who wants point?"

Smooth stepped forward.

"I already know the way."

"Same formation, Four Seven?"

Kensington raised his hand in the air, letting the others pass him by.

Smooth led them through the same path they used the first time, veering slightly until they reached the dead NVA soldiers. Flies were starting to make a home on the sun-bloated skin. Stepping around them, Smooth followed the path those soldiers had probably taken, until he stepped off back into the overgrowth. Trail walking was a dangerous sport in the jungles of Vietnam and was to be avoided at all costs.

They came upon a rise that led to another plateau, not as big as the one they had set on but workable for an NDP, if needed. Reaching the outskirts of the plateau, Smooth stopped and crouched down. Wilson joined him and looked out as Smooth pointed. There was a well-worn trail across the plateau, which had been used very recently.

"Think it was them or somebody new?"

Smooth shrugged his shoulders.

"Hard to say. We followed the same course. Could have been them."

Wilson moved forward staying low. The dirt was churned up as if there had been a lot of activity recently.

"Let's go around."

Smooth nodded and led the team around the plateau on the upper side. They picked up the trail on the other side, which led back into the jungle. Wilson motioned forward and they paralleled the trail for a distance. Finally, Smooth stopped again and Wilson joined him.

"Trail goes off that way. "

Smooth pointed, Wilson nodded.

"Okay, Whitey, call it in. We followed the trail to..."

Wilson looked at his map and gave Whitey the coordinates.

"Smooth, how about we circle back? We been out hour forty-five. Let's do a wide sweep back this way, see if anything else out here?"

Smooth nodded.

Sweeping around, they came upon a rise where they could see the plateau they had passed in the distance. Smooth kept working them further out until he cut back in toward the position.

Walking past Big John, Lopes and the new white guy, they came back in exhausted from humping through the intense heat, the tall elephant grass and heavy jungle overgrowth, and dropped down at their rucks. Wilson dropped his steel pot and walked to the center where the LT was. Sarge joined him.

"Followed a trail past where we greased those NVA this morning until it veered off in this direction."

Wilson pointed to his map.

"Gave the coordinates to the CO, after Whitey called it in."

Wilson nodded.

"There's a plateau here, might be a good spot for a new NDP, but we noticed that on the way back we could see it from a rise, might be a problem. Found nothing on the way back. Just more fucking jungle."

The lieutenant looked at Wilson's, then his map, noting the areas Wilson pointed out. Sarge tapped Wilson's map.

"What about out here after the trail turns, anything of interest?"

Wilson shook his head no.

"Just more jungle. We cut for three zero mikes, but then gave up and turned. You still figure we spend the night here?"

The lieutenant looked up from his map.

"Yeah. Might as well, they'd know we're there as much as they'd know we're here. Resupply came in, we got more C-rats and more ammo, so have your team load up."

Wilson nodded.

The lieutenant motioned and Bob Grite, second squad leader joined them.

"Wilson, I want you to fortify your front, dig in set defensible positions, you need to make a stand. Grite, take a team out this way and set up an LP, hell make it an ambush you got the opportunity. Sergeant, have third squad send a team out, relieve the LP and move further away set up an ambush out there. Also fortify our weak side more, have the men dig in, man it with two man teams, here and here."

The lieutenant looked around the position.

"Let's bring it in more, tighten it up. With the teams out, we don't need this much space. I want a tight NDP, dug and fortified. We got two hours daylight left, let's get to work."

Grite, Sarge and Wilson nodded. They broke up and each man went to their place.

Wilson explained the plan and walked out to the front position.

"Let's bring this in a bit and dig a hole right here, mount the 60s in either direction, get a one eighty fire. We get to stay in tonight but we have to fortify this area. Put two sets trip out, one long, one short, claymores in between. Make them think they get past one, they in, then we blow the second line."

Wilson stood looking the area over.

"As you were. Put one 60 here directed straight on and the other 60 over there crossing. Dig two holes. First line of claymores detonate from here, the second in the other hole and put one more line right here. Set them one eighty."

Wilson looked over the area again, and nodded yes.

"We're doing two, two man teams through the night, one in this hole the other over there."

Looking at the men along side him he pointed.

"Two on, two off, then back on. Smooth, you and Body Man do eight to ten this hole, Big John, you and Whitey do that hole, Four Seven and I will do ten to midnight this hole, Lopes, you and the new white guy do that, that hole, then back on midnight to oh three hundred, then we do oh three hundred to daylight. Long night, nobody sleep much."

Everyone looked at Wilson.

"Listen we know they here. We know they be bringing in mortars. Dig deep, get ready to cover, pack and store your gear. Bring it in tight, not more than a meter from the holes. Let's put the thumpers in the holes. You hear something, you put some of those rounds out there first. Don't fire the 60s until you have to. Don't be giving your position up, else they put a rocket up your ass. Keep the thumpers popping. They trip the flares blow the claymores and wait. Don't fire until you have to. Understand?"

Nodding they understood, the men waited, but Wilson was finished. They disbursed back to their rucks following his instructions. The men had loaded up on ammo and C-rats from the day's resupply. They took turns eating and digging, setting up for the night.

The sun began to set in the distance, light faded, but they were ready. Everyone sat on alert at the holes until eight o'clock when the watches started.

Wilson sat against his ruck, the forty-five in his hand, trying to catch some shuteye. Kensington sat next to him, the M16 firmly in his grip, also up against his ruck. Lopes and the new white guy sat across from them, pretty much in the same layout. Wilson looked over the other men.

"Hey, new white guy. What's your name?"

"Louis Humphries."

Wilson nodded.

"You be Hump from now on. Now get some sleep."

The new white guy nodded.

Kensington whispered.

"Named the new guys?"

"Thought it was about time."

The men fell silent, trying to catch a little shuteye before their shift.

The tapping came too quick. Kensington opened his eyes, not sure he had slept yet. Wilson stirred next to him. Lopes and Hump were already up, moving toward their hole. Wilson and Kensington moved into the hole in front. The other four men took their spots next to their rucks for some shuteye.

"Damn Stick, that was fast. Don't think I even slept."

Wilson nodded.

"That's the plan."

The two hours crawled by, neither man speaking, just watching intently in front of their position.

Wilson pointed to his watch, Kensington nodded and waited while he got the others back up. Silently they switched positions, Kensington falling back against his ruck, Wilson doing the same. Lopes and Hump were back as well and looked fast asleep already. Sam's eyes fluttered once but then closed tight as he drifted off.

Fifteen

After a long sleepless night, the brigades of Brigadier General Ricketts were instructed to shift further west, the soldiers continually moving to set up on the left front of Confederate Major General Dodson Ramseur's division. Although taking most of the long night to accomplish, the troops were finally in place, forming the blue line. Ricketts attacked Ramseur's line with his two brigades.

Samuel Kensington and Everett Fremont stood at the ready, behind the vedettes, those mounted sentinels in advance of the pickets. Moving the line en echelon from right to left, the blue clad soldiers marched forward toward the Rebel line.

Samuel Kensington waited as the line beside him started to move. Fremont stood next to him, watching and waiting as well.

"You ready?"

"Are you?"

"Wish I had some coffee first."

"Sure enough."

"Hey Kensington?"

"Yeah?"

"Think them boys be waiting for us, we go after that

cannon?"

Kensington nodded yes, pointing to the rear.

"Looks like our boys going to put cannon shell on the crest before we get there, keep those Rebels heads down until we start the climb."

Aligned to the left of the rear force, much like steps, they moved forward. The skirmishers kept a volley of Minie balls toward the Rebels that were met and returned by Ramseur's sharpshooters. The attack had begun.

Fremont and Kensington surged forward, shouting their arrival to the Confederates. Lanning and Fairchild were beside them, with Harrington and Meriweather further down. Edward Hutchens was just above them.

Minie balls whizzed by as they started their climb. Men dropped on either side of them, hit and sliding back down the small hill. New soldiers filled in the voids. Lanning and Fairchild closed the gap between the other four men abreast of each other. Harrington and Meriweather moved further to the right, navigating some trees and a rock. On the other side they all met up, continuing their line movement.

They surged forward, firing and climbing. Stopping to reload, a wave of soldiers passed and fired, stopping again while the next set of reloaded soldiers passed them and fired.

Hitting the heights first, driving toward the Rebel cannon, Kensington fired his musket toward the men manning the nearest cannon. A Rebel soldier had a bead on him and fired, but was hit first sending his shot skyward. Seeing two other Rebels come out from behind the cannon, he pulled his pistol and took aim, but before he could fire, those two gray clad soldiers turned and ran toward the rear, away from the cannon.

Moving forward, revolver in hand, Kensington stood behind the captured cannon, Freemont right beside him, watching as the rest of the Rebels that could flee did so in quick step. Lanning and Fairchild were on the other side of the barrel, gaining a position from which to fire, but those gray coats that could, continued their exodus from the position. The wounded and dead stayed where they were. As the rest of the blue clad soldiers came over the hill, they eventually overran the Confederate position, capturing several cannon.

Amidst the Confederate gear and several dead or wounded Rebel soldiers Kensington stood next to that same captured cannon, as Fremont, Lanning, Fairchild and other soldiers looked at the ground for souvenirs. Fremont pointed at him.

"Hey Kensington, you planning on taking that cannon with you?"

"Yup. Sowed up my haversack just so I could put this in, should be no problem now."

Fremont smiled.

"Need help loading it in?"

"Huh? No, I got this."

Fremont nodded.

"Just the same, I might need you to help me load one for myself."

Kensington waved his hand in the air, nodding yes.

He watched as Fremont and others probed the ground for anything of use. On the littered ground lay several Rebels, some obviously dead, but a few wounded, now being checked and tended to by Federal men. Nodding to no one in particular, he put the revolver back into his waistband. Once again, he had not needed to fire it, but it was always at the ready.

As the Federals started collecting the artillery and removing it from the earthworks, he watched as an officer, a general, came upon the crest on horseback.

Quite excited, his horse spinning in his hands, he yelled out, asking what the men were doing, why were they not fighting. Before anyone could respond, their own General Ricketts rode up and confronted that other general, explaining that his brave men had just captured the Rebel cannon position and were enjoying the spoils of their victory. More importantly, he would take charge from here. The other general looked at the goings on around the captured cannon, gave a half hearted nod to Ricketts and quickly rode off.

Fremont stood next to Kensington, Lanning and Fairchild stood to the side. Harrington, Meriweather and Edward Hutchens joined them, as did several other soldiers as they all waited for further instructions.

Their General was livid at the other general's words and was still very animated sitting astride his mount. Brigadier General James Ricketts watched intently as that other general disappeared from the crest, before turning to an officer near him, barking orders. Taking one last look, the general rode off.

The captured cannon was to be stripped from the crest and moved to Federal lines. The position was to be held from a counter attack until the removal could be achieved.

Edward Hutchens gathered the men, Lanning, Meriweather, Harrington, Fairchild, Fremont and Kensington close together. Fremont and Kensington both looked for Longworth, who they hadn't seen in awhile.

"Lieutenant wants us to move to the back behind the cannon post a guard until they can get these out of here. Those men over there will join us on the flank. We got most of the 10th here and them boys from the 151st New York, going to stay with us, until the cannon gone."

Fremont pointed and the others looked to where he was pointing. Jethro Longworth was coming toward them, a bit ruffled and dirty.

"What happened to you? You were right next to us."

Longworth stopped, set his musket on the ground, removed his forage cap and wiped his brow. He pulled the strap from his shoulder to show them the torn material.

"Minie ball hit me, think it was only a ricochet though, didn't hit that hard, knocked me backwards, back down the hill.

Lost my footing and rolled end over end. Got caught up with some of those boys from the 151st New York, we went around the cannon, chased those Rebels back down the other side."

"And?"

"And nothing. Said you boys were over here and that I maybe should rejoin you."

Longworth stood there brushing himself off. He was covered in dust and debris. When it was apparent he would say no more, Hutchens continued.

"As I was telling them we're going to post a guard until they can get the cannon off."

Longworth nodded. Hutchens motioned and the men moved toward the other side, the back side away from the cannon.

"Here, this should be good."

Kensington and Fremont dropped their gear, as did Lanning and Fairchild next to them. Harrington and Meriweather did so a ways away. Longworth joined those two, as did Hutchens.

Samuel sat against a tree, putting his musket in his lap. Freemont and Lanning took up a firing position, Fairchild sat down next to him.

"Think we got time for a little shuteye?"

Samuel looked at Freemont, who nodded.

"Yeah, we got this, anything starts you'll be the first to know."

He nodded, waving his hand at Fairchild, who nodded back.

He ran his hand over the pistol butt in his waistband, letting the musket slip from his grip, but still close to his leg. Fremont came over and knelt down next to him.

"Saw you pull that thing. Looked like you were finally going to get to use it?"

"Everett, that Rebel had me in his sights. Don't know why he waited to fire. Had he not been hit, causing the shot to fire wildly... well I don't know. Might have got him first."

Fremont smiled.

"Who do you think shot him?"

Samuel looked up from half closed eyes.

"You did that?"

Fremont shook his head yes.

"Well, I fired his way. Several others did too, one of us got him that's for sure."

Nodding, Samuel saluted his friend.

"Much obliged. Mind if I get some shuteye?"

"Not at all. I'll get you in fifteen, might like to get some myself."

"Fair enough."

Slowly his eyes closed and before he could adjust he dozed off, his hands dropping to his sides.

He felt a tapping...

Sixteen

The tapping grew harder, until finally Sam opened his eyes.

"Four Seven, you're up."

Kensington looked at Smooth, now stepping away and settling up against his ruck. Wilson was sitting up next to him. "Let's go."

Kensington picked up his weapon and steel pot, following Wilson to the hole. Body Man was waiting for their relief. Nodding, the men exchanged places. Lopes and Hump had already relieved Whitey and Big John.

"Hey Stick, you think this through before you set these shifts?"

Wilson looked at Sam, smiling.

"Yeah."

"Then how come we get the shit shift?"

Wilson nodded and pointed to Sam.

"Keep you from dreaming, you don't get no sleep."

"Didn't work."

"What?"

Sam waved his hand in the air.

"No big deal. Not sure if it is anything."

Wilson nodded. They sat silent for a bit. Finally Wilson waved his hand in the air.

"And?"

Kensington looked up, then over at Wilson.

"Okay."

Looking around, Sam got deep in the hole, covering his hands, he lit a cigarette, taking a couple of quick pulls, releasing the smoke into his hands, before putting the butt out.

"Okay, it was pretty quick. Did we even sleep?"

Not waiting for an answer he continued.

"In the middle of the night we started a march… pretty sophisticated stuff, all lined up in step like formation, fully loaded gear, moving forward in ranks, no cover, cannon shell exploding all around, theirs and ours…"

Wilson waved his hand in the air.

"How about the short version?"

Kensington smiled, continuing.

"Yeah, right. Anyway, looks like we captured this hill or crest or something that had several Confederate cannons. But then this general rode up…"

"General? There ain't no fucking generals in the field. They be back in the air-conditioned Quonset huts, sipping single malt, talking about how they gonna sacrifice us for some meaningless piece of real estate. Shit."

Kensington sat silent for a moment, waiting to see if Wilson was going to continue.

"Anyway, this general rode up all pissed off about something, but then our general, Ricketts, rode up."

Sam waited to see if Wilson would go off on that statement, two generals in the field, but when he didn't, he continued.

"And told this other general to leave us alone. Anyway, we captured a bunch of cannon from the Confederates that the regiment was going to bring back to our lines or something."

Sam paused. Wilson waited.

"Anyway, it ended quickly, that 's all I remember before Smooth woke me up."

The two men sat silent. Wilson took his turn going deep in the hole for a couple of quick pulls on a smoke.

The rest of their watch dragged on. Neither man spoke much. As the sun broke they sat huddled in the hole looking out into the jungle. It was much harder to see things as the dark of night faded into daylight.

"What you think about the latest dream? Mean anything?"

Sam looked over at Wilson, shaking his head no.

"Not much. We took some hill, captured some cannon. Too quick really. Don't know if it has any bearing. Certainly not anything we're doing. Might have been a flash, piece of something that might have been more, if it wasn't so quick. One thing though, a Rebel had a bead on me, but didn't take the shot, like he froze, then took one himself. Don't know if that means anything."

Wilson nodded. They sat silent until Smooth relieved them.

"Sure glad to see you. Need some fucking coffee."

"Roger that, Four Seven. Told Hump to get some chow, relieve me in an hour, like that."

Wilson nodded.

The two men left the hole and gathered at their rucks. Sam put coffee on and used his P38 to open a can of C-rats. Wilson watched as he navigated the P38 around the can, pulling the lid off.

"Pork stuff."

Wilson returned from his meeting with the lieutenant and Sarge.

"LT wants to run a couple of more patrols before we leave. Grite's taking a team from second squad out to the south. Sarge is taking a team from third squad to the rear. The two ambushes are in, didn't see or hear anything last night. Quiet so far."

Kensington nodded.

"What about us?"

"We sit for now."

Sam sipped his coffee. Whitey waved his hand in the air getting their attention.

"Lotta shit to the south. Still trying to take some hill over there. Been in contact with a large element of NVA they think. Colonel flying around in his bird directing the assault."

Wilson pointed at Sam.

"See Four Seven. I told you ain't no generals in the field. Hell, ain't nobody but lieutenants out here and the CO. All them higher ranking officers well hidden from battle. Generals in the field, shit."

Kensington smiled at Wilson's rant, but he had to agree with him. He'd never seen an officer ranked higher than a captain, the company commander, ever in the field, didn't really think about it either.

"I got to go relieve Big John, but I'm telling you heavy shit to the south. Just listen to the horn, it's non stop."

Wilson and Kensington watched as Whitey left, his radio next to his ruck.

"Hump, you monitor that for now. Let me know you hear anything I should know."

The new white guy looked at Wilson for a moment, but reached over and then grabbed the radio from Whitey's ruck, pulling the prick 25 next to him.

"Sure thing Stick, I'll let you know I hear anything."

Wilson nodded. Sam finished his coffee and used a drop of water to rinse out the cup before putting it back into his canteen case. Wilson sat down next to him.

"Think it's time we got out of here. Been here way too long. Just a matter of time before we get hit. Those little fuckers are on the move out there. Lot of tracks yesterday. Might be a supply route, have something to do with that shit that's going on over at that hill, that's taking all the shit."

Wilson pointed toward the south. Helicopters were flying around in the distance, the sound of artillery was audible from that direction as well. A soldier from second squad walked over.

"Wilson, patrols are coming back in, LT wants you over there."

Wilson nodded. He stood patting Kensington on the shoulder.

"Get them packing up. Lopes, you relieve Smooth when you're ready. Big John, you do the same."

Both men nodded. Wilson left. Sam stood and rolled up his poncho liner, tucking it back onto his ruck, closing things up and strapping them down. The thumpers were still at the holes, he would load that when they broke down the defensive hole.

Wilson was back almost as quickly as he left.

"Patrols said there was beaucoup tracks out there, especially to the south, must have been running supplies and men right past us last night. Probably needed over there, left us alone. LT wants us to move out in three zero mikes. Four Seven you got point, besides you know the way now."

Wilson smiled showing those white teeth. Kensington nodded.

"Sure thing. Listen Stick, I'll get the holes broken down while you pack up."

"Already packed."

Kensington looked at Wilson's gear and saw that he had already packed everything up. He nodded.

"I'll let those guys know anyway."

As Kensington approached the nearest hole all hell broke loose. AK47 fire was streaming across their defensive position. Sam dived into the make shift hole, getting into firing position. He and Lopes put out a volley of return fire with their weapons. Sam nodded and Lopes manned the 60, while Sam put out several M79 rounds, exploding rapidly around their position, Lopes continued the barrage from the 60. They both stopped and waited.

"Whitey, you okay over there."

"Fuckin' A. Wilson's here with me. Following your lead. He has the 60 and I'm putting thumpers out."

They all waited, but no more fire was coming. Finally Wilson spoke up.

"Have that new white guy come up with Whitey's radio and get Smooth, Lopes you stay in that hole, Whitey will stay here and we'll go take a look see."

"Negative, Wilson. As you were men."

Sarge was at the hole with Kensington, pointing.

"Wilson I got a team making it's way around, cut them off they try to escape, you stand fast, in case they come back."

"Roger that."

Sam could hear the disappointment in Wilson's voice. Hell they shot at us, we should be the ones go get them.

The radio buzzed, the patrol was coming back in straight at them. Wilson came over sending the new white guy to the hole he had just left. Bob Grite led the team.

"All clear Sarge. They di di maued out of here, some blood, but nothing else, they grabbed gear and bodies. Lot of tracks. Probably heard us, wanted to harass us a bit, maybe keep us in place until they passed. Anyway, that's what I figure."

Sarge nodded, he looked at Wilson, who nodded as well.

"Yeah, sounds right."

The men stood silent for a moment, finally Sarge spoke.

"Alright let's saddle up and get the fuck out of here. I believe we've overstayed our welcome."

"Roger that."

Sarge and Bob Grite's team left the hole. Wilson nodded.

"Okay let's get everything packed up."

The claymores were lying by the hole and the trip flares had been disarmed and were there as well. Each man grabbed his piece. Lopes pulled the 60 from its placement. Sam grabbed his thumper.

Sam Kensington led the platoon through the jungle and over-growth, following the trail they had made the day before. The lieutenant had instructed him to stay the course to the west, but with all the recent NVA activity, he told Sam to also look for trails and signs of recent activity and use his judgment as to how to swing.

Keeping the spacing between men a little longer than usual the line stretched quite a ways back. Sarge was bringing up the rear. Sam stopped, and knelt down the weight of his ruck shifting on his back. Humping through this shit was hard enough, but carrying all this weight as well in this heat wore one out. Holding his hand in the air to stop, he motioned for Wilson to come up.

"What you see, Four Seven?"

Kensington pointed. A well used trail was just in front of him crisscrossing their route. Wilson nodded, but Sam stopped him and pointed to the trail. Wilson saw it, he turned talking to the man behind him, Body Man, the new black guy.

"Get the LT up here, he needs to see this."

The two men waited while the lieutenant made his way up. "What's up?"

Wilson pointed to the trail. The lieutenant nodded, but Wilson pointed again just as Sam had. Finally the lieutenant saw it.

"Bicycle tracks?"

Wilson nodded.

"Fuckin' A. That and beaucoup tracks everywhere. Means

they're bringing in heavy supplies, probably bigger ammo, maybe rounds for the rocket launchers, shit like that."

The lieutenant nodded, turning to Body Man behind him.

"Have Whitey bring his radio up."

The lieutenant called the information in to the CO. Handing the handset back to Whitey he turned to Sam.

"Kensington, which way you want to go?"

Sam looked at the lieutenant, then at Wilson, pointing.

"Looked like the best route would be right through there. Cross over there and make our way through those trees."

The lieutenant looked where Sam was pointing, but Wilson kept his gaze on Kensington, he knew what Sam was getting at.

"But that would put us at the base of that ridge over there."

The lieutenant could barely see where Sam was referring to.

"I suspect, it might be better we go up, approach that rise from the top. Put us a half a klick off course, but I'd sure like to have the high ground. We go that way around, maybe two klicks off course and we'd be dropping down. Don't know what's around that rise over there either."

Kensington paused. He looked at Wilson, who nodded his approval.

"Your call sir, but I had my druthers it would be go high. Afternoon heat, carrying all this shit, it's gonna be slow going."

The lieutenant nodded.

"Makes sense. Mind if I get the sergeant up here, see what he thinks?"

Kensington nodded.

"Roger that sir."

The lieutenant turned talking to Body Man and Whitey behind him.

"Pass the word, break in place, put out defensive positions. Have the sergeant come up here."

The sound of rucks and men dropping filled the air. Sam and Wilson dropped theirs and knelt clear of the weight. Finally,

Sarge made his way to them. Whitey and Body Man fell back to give him room. The lieutenant brought the sergeant up to speed on Sam's plan. Sarge nodded, pointing in both directions.

"Kensington, what are you saying? You thinking of swinging around and climbing that ridge, go that way from here? What about that flat over there? We'd have to cross it?"

Sam waved his hand in the air.

"Not necessarily. If we stay high we can keep sweeping around, maybe half a klick or so, keep high and deep. If we need too, we can use that opening to set up an NDP."

The sergeant nodded, thinking about what Sam said.

"Makes sense, sir. Out of our way, but I agree with Wilson, lot of activity lately and those bike tracks, we might come across more of these. Lot of shit happening south of here, probably bringing men and supplies in from Laos for support."

Wilson nodded.

"That's what I've been saying."

Sarge nodded pointing to the rise.

"What you boys think? Pretty tough jungle to get through. Might be the right way to go, but it's going to be tough."

The sergeant looked at his watch.

"Three maybe four hours we'll have to set up our NDP. If we don't make it to the flat area or don't find anything else to use, could be a long night."

The four men remained silent. Finally Sam interjected.

"We'll make it. Long as we don't hit anything, we'll get through that shit."

Wilson nodded.

"Fuckin' A."

"Sergeant?"

"Right LT, we better get moving. Kensington, good luck."

The lieutenant and the sergeant were gone after giving the order to saddle up. Wilson stuck out his fist, he and Kensington did the white version of the black dap handshake.

"But it don't mean nothing."

"But it don't mean nothing."

Sam Kensington moved the line forward. Dropping down slightly, he angled the movement sideways up the rise, so that they wouldn't have to climb straight up with the gear late in the day. Cutting through thick jungle vegetation, he maneuvered the line onto the rise, rising a bit before leveling, he kept them moving. Shortly after seventeen hundred hours they reached the flat land.

Stopping and looking, he motioned for the lieutenant to come up. Assessing the area, the lieutenant ordered a break in place. He further ordered Bob Grite to take second squad and do a recon around the area. They waited while the patrol checked all the way around and down the other side. The patrol crossed over the top and dropped down the other side. Finally at five forty-five they reported back that the area was clear. Some tracks and recent activity, but all looked quiet for now.

The platoon moved into the flat area to establish their NDP, digging in, setting trip flares and claymores, the soldiers went about the work of securing their perimeter.

The lieutenant sent out two ambushes, one across the trail, ready to hit anything that might try to use it during the night, and the other on the high point of the rise. Sarge took the team up there and Bob Grite took his team to the trail. The perimeter was tight, each man no more than five meters apart.

Wilson checked the set up and detailed the watch. Kensington had the midnight to two, Wilson would be after him. They ate chow, smoked and finished their coffee quickly before night set in.

"Hey Four Seven, good job. Thought you might have mountain goat blood in you. That was some fucking climb and at that pace."

"Wanted to give us enough time for setup and chow before dark."

Wilson nodded.

"You planning on dreaming tonight?"

"Hope not."

"Gave you middle shift, break up your sleep."

"You're too kind to me."

Wilson smiled.

"Fuckin' A."

Once again Smooth was tapping him on the shoulder.

"Four Seven, you're up."

Kensington sat up, rubbing the sleep from his eyes. He looked at Smooth and nodded. Struggling to get up, he grabbed his gear and made his way to the hole. Setting up, getting comfortable, he looked out into the night, letting his eyes adjust to the darkness in front of him.

He didn't remember dreaming. Hell, he didn't remember sleeping. Well, so far so good.

Whitey was monitoring the horn, nodding and pointing.

"I'm telling you, there's some heavy shit going down over there."

Wilson, Kensington and Smooth, drinking their morning coffee, looked to where he was pointing.

"Some fucking hill they're trying to take."

The men could see helicopters circling in the distance. Gunships could be heard firing.

"Wouldn't be surprised we get ordered to go there, help out."

The other men looked at Whitey, but he remained silent. Wilson motioned.

"You hear anything like that?"

"Nothing yet, but we ain't doing much here. Figures, they'd move us there or at least toward the fighting."

The men sat silently enjoying their coffee.

"Wilson? Hey, Wilson?"

It was a guy from second squad walking up to where they were set up.

"Yeah, who wants to know?"

"Hey, the LT wants to see you, sent me to gather you up."

With that the man turned and walked back to where he came from. Wilson rose slowly, stretching.

"Probably more patrols, shit like that. Back to work. Pack up, clean up, be ready."

Kensington nodded, Smooth raised his hand in the air, as did Whitey. The others did likewise.

The lieutenant, Sarge and Bob Grite were gathered around a map when Wilson joined then. They nodded their hellos. Wilson stood off to the side, not able to get closer. Finally, the lieutenant stepped back and pointed.

"Sarge thinks that would be the best way to get there."

"Get where?"

Pointing to the map, the lieutenant continued.

"Hill 900 to the south of Dong Ap Bia. We've been ordered to get there fast and provide strike and support from the south, shore up the attack on hill 937 there."

Wilson nodded, as did Bob Grite. Sarge took the map and used his finger to outline a possible path.

"I make it to be about three to three and a half klicks, no more than four klicks from here. We'll have to cover some tough terrain, probably some NVA along the way. We already crossed over one of their routes."

The sergeant paused, keeping his finger on the map.

"Bob, you or Wilson see any different?"

The two men looked at the map where Sarge was pointing, studying the grids.

"That's a lot of up and down, through some heavy jungle shit, be hard to cut and hump with full rucks, make any real distance. How long we got to get there?"

The lieutenant looked at Wilson and for no particular reason pointed to his RTO.

"Orders said immediately. What you think immediately means?"

Wilson smiled, not quite sure what the lieutenant meant. Sarge cut in.

"Well LT, based on the contours and terrain we've been through so far, I'd say day or two is as immediate as we can get. But if we make contact, we could be held up indefinitely. What are they saying is the time frame for us to get there?"

The lieutenant remained silent for a moment, the other three watched and waited. Finally he folded his arms across his chest.

"Orders said to be on the move by late morning."

"That gives us two hours to pack up, get chow and get moving."

The lieutenant looked at the sergeant and nodded.

"Wilson, you boys still good for point?"

Wilson nodded. The sergeant looked at the map.

"Sir, I think a straight line might bunch us up, waiting while the point cuts."

Pausing, he pointed at Bob Grite.

"Bob, how about you and me spread this out as far as we can, might leave some gaps we need to tighten up along the way, but otherwise we'll be crawling up each other's ass."

Grite nodded, Wilson looked in as the sergeant pointed to the map.

"When we're climbing, we'll tighten it up and when we're dropping back down we'll spread it out."

Grite and Wilson nodded. The lieutenant looked on, finally nodding.

"Fine, sergeant, fine. But make sure you can regroup quickly, we hit anything. I don't want men spread out can't join back up."

"No sweat."

Wilson turned to Bob Grite.

"I got two good men be doing the point, Four Seven and Smooth. I'll have them tandem, you know double point, wide slack, put the new black guy in between, keep it on the sway. Four Seven got us here yesterday, he'll get us there."

The men stood in silence waiting for Wilson to continue.

"I'll keep Lopes at the rear of my squad, make sure we stay in contact with Grite's squad behind us, maybe you do the same with Sarge? Keep the drag short."

Grite nodded, as did the sergeant. They stood waiting for the lieutenant to interject, but when he didn't, they started to disburse. The lieutenant spoke up.

"One last thing. The report mentioned that the NVA been running in and out of Laos, bringing supplies and fresh troops in. We already suspected that earlier."

The lieutenant paused, then looked at each of them.

"I'm sure we'll run into one or more of those supply routes on the way there. Be alert, be ready. I don't want the platoon spread too wide… I want… I imagine we will most likely walk into a moving force, but if we hit something pulling defense, protecting those running, then… well… look, just be sure we can bring this back together without confusion, or worse, get severed."

Sarge nodded, pointing to Wilson and Grite.

"Sir, you don't have to worry about these two guys. Anybody can make this work, it's them."

"No doubt sergeant, but… no doubt. Thank you, men."

The three men nodded. Sarge patted Wilson on the back.

"You keep us moving, Grite will keep it tight and I'll bring up the rear."

"Roger that."

Wilson brought the rest of his squad up to speed, detailing their plans.

"I knew it. I knew we was going there."

The others looked at Whitey.

Wilson outlined his idea in the dirt, as Kensington and Smooth looked on.

"What you think. Can we do that?"

Smooth pointed to the ground.

"Sure thing Stick, but that's lot of ground to cover, through this shit and you know we're gonna hit something. How long you say we got?"

"Immediately, whatever that means."

Smooth nodded, Kensington stayed silent.

"Four Seven, you the mountain goat. What you say?"

"I agree with Smooth. Pretty thick shit to cut through and I'm with him, we're gonna hit something. What's up with this spread out formation?"

"Sarge believes it will be slow going and he wants to make sure we're not up each other's ass, that's all."

Smooth and Kensington nodded. Sam pointed to the ground.

"So where are we going?"

"Some fucking hill called Dong Ap Bia, 937 meters high. But we're actually heading to hill 900, south of that crest, that's our destination. About three, four klicks from here."

Seventeen

Dong Ap Bia is one of the many jungle shrouded mountains of South Vietnam, this one slightly over a mile from the Laotian border, rising from the floor of the A Shau Valley. A solitary massif, it dominates the northern valley rising to 937 meters. Flowing down from this main peak are a series of ridges and fingers, one of the largest extending southeast to a height of 900 meters, another reaching south to 916 meters. The entire range is composed of rugged, uninviting wilderness blanketed in double and triple canopy jungle, dense thickets of bamboo and waist high elephant grass, in most cases taller than the men walking through it.

Just a week earlier, Hill 937 was little more than a few lines on a map, its brown contours meaningless, but for the NVA on Dong Ap Bia, the mountain is too valuable to give up.

Dug in deep and securely sheltered in the caves of this mountain, especially from airstrikes and gunships, the NVA was also protected by heavily jungled ridges leading to the southwest and northwest, providing routes of concealed infiltration. The 29th NVA regiment, fresh from North Vietnam, had built their base camp at the top of this massif.

Two miles away sat the Laotian border, which allowed them the freedom to bring men, ammo, more guns and supplies in and out as necessary. Armed with the AK47 assault rifles, rocket-propelled grenade launchers and machine guns of varying types and sizes, they were prepared to defend this fortification at all costs, not ready to evade this time. Whatever force was coming, they were prepared to meet them head on.

Sam Kensington stood at the ready, ruck secured on his back, thumper strapped in, the forty-five tucked into his left side, steel pot sitting on his head turned backwards. He waited for the others to saddle up.

Smooth stood next to him, the new black guy off to the other side. Wilson approached them.

"Okay, you got the course?"

Both men nodded. Wilson gestured with his hand.

"Okay, keep working around until we can turn south. Shouldn't be more'n half a klick, maybe only four hundred meters."

Kensington nodded, the M16 in his left hand and the machete in his right. He tapped the machete to his steel pot and started forward. Smooth fell in behind and just to the left, putting the new black guy to their right. Basically they were cutting a two man path, allowing the men behind to file into two positions rather than a single file approach.

Wilson followed Kensington, Big John followed Smooth and so on, the others falling into place. Bob Grite kept his squad back, watching Lopes move into one of the slots before starting forward.

Sam kept moving forward, gradually turning to the south as instructed. Hitting an open area, he stopped the platoon.

Wilson came up and joined him. Kensington pointed, Wilson nodded.

The whole area was filled with tracks, both men and bicycle tracks. A lot of activity had gone through here and very recently. Not wanting to cross the open area, they both looked to each side, but neither side offered a passage.

"Pass the word back. We have to check it out first, before we can continue. I'm taking a team do a little recon to the other side."

The lieutenant came up, stopping next to Wilson, who pointed.

"Sir, I think we should check it out first."

The lieutenant looked at both sides of the open area, and quickly came to the same conclusion as Wilson and Kensington. They couldn't go that way.

"How do you want to do this?"

"Sir, I thought I'd take Whitey with the radio, Smooth and the new black guy, rifle team, circle around and see what's over there."

The lieutenant nodded, turning to the man behind him.

"Pass the word, rest in place. Let Sarge know what we're doing, put out a rear position."

In a moment Wilson's team was out of their rucks and ready to go. Sam watched as they made their way around the open area, staying covered as best they could.

Twenty minutes later they were back, walking through the open area, up to where the lieutenant and Kensington were waiting.

"All clear. Activity just cuts through nothing either side or down. We should be able to walk right through."

The lieutenant nodded.

"Pass the word, moving out in five."

The lieutenant left and Wilson sat down next to Kensington.

"Looks the same up ahead, more jungle shit, bamboo,

elephant grass. Thought I saw another opening up ahead. May have to do this all day, hell all the way. We're walking through their routes. Gonna hit them sooner or later. Keep your eyes open for movement. Don't think we'll hit anything entrenched until we get closer."

Kensington nodded and stuck out his hand. They did the dap handshake.

"But it don't mean nothing."

"But it don't mean nothing."

Sam hit the next opening, but there were no signs of activity, just an open area. He guided the platoon around the open area as best he could, finally reaching the other side. The over growth was so thick that he was sure no one had been through here. Checking his course, he veered to the right and entered the thick jungle, cutting as he went. Smooth was right above him doing the same.

At the next opening, now due south, again the signs of activity were evident throughout the opening. He stopped the platoon and was just about to call Wilson up when he heard voices. Waving to stay quiet, he motioned for Wilson to come up and pointed to where he thought he had heard something.

Wilson sat next to Sam listening intently. Finally, he heard it too. There were definitely voices and they were getting closer. Motioning to spread the word back, he brought up Big John with the 60 and pulled his thumper from the back of his ruck before dropping it. Sam already had his in his hand, pulling the forty-five from the shoulder holster. Smooth moved to the side, the new black guy joined him just to his left. The men waited. The voices grew stronger. They were close.

Suddenly, the first man appeared in his khaki uniform and pith helmut, definitely NVA soldiers entering the opening. One, then another, then another, carrying their AK47s at their sides, one man carrying a rocket launcher across his shoulders. They looked dirty, as if they had just come from battle, which may have lead to their nonchalant attitude, as they walked through the jungle, following a well defined path.

When the number grew to a dozen, Wilson signaled. Kensington and Wilson let go with the thumpers first, dropping rounds into the middle of the group. Smooth and the new black guy let loose with their sixteens and Big John opened up with the 60.

Several NVA dropped to the ground, but others scampered for cover and another group that was just hitting the opening opened up returning fire. The firing was intense for a few seconds, then suddenly stopped. Wilson gave the signal to cease fire. They waited.

When he was sure the NVA were gone, Wilson motioned for those with him to move out. Kensington, Smooth, the new black guy and Whitey with the radio followed him into the opening, making their way to the remaining bodies lying on the ground.

Stepping into the area the NVA had come from they ventured down the trail a bit. A significant amount of blood was on the trail and brushed against the elephant grass. They followed the trail a bit, but turned back. The rest of the NVA had gotten away, with whatever wounded they could take.

By the time they got back the Lieutenant was waiting for them. Sarge had even come up to find out what happened. Wilson explained that they had heard voices coming and decided to hold a reception for those boys.

Sarge said it first.

"Sir, it's getting late, maybe we should look for a spot to set up our NDP, maybe get resupply in the morning before we move out. We got maybe two hours more."

The lieutenant nodded.

"Kensington, see if you can find us something in the next hour or so. Take it slow, but see what you can find. We're heading due south now, gone maybe a klick or so, not much. Think we can get another half klick in before we break."

"Not sure sir, we haven't covered much ground yet, real slow going. And... well...you know?"

"What? Say what you're thinking."

Wilson interrupted before Sam could finish.

"Sir, we're all thinking the same thing. They know we're moving now, crossed their path, this far south. They know what we be doing. Might be better we find something quick, in case they be coming back or be looking for us now."

The lieutenant looked at Wilson, but Sarge interjected.

"Wilson's right, sir. We should be thinking about what's coming."

The lieutenant raised his hand in the air.

"I have an idea for tonight. Been thinking about it all day."

They all waited.

"Kensington, how much further can we get before we have to call it?"

Sam looked out to where they had to go and pointed.

"Well sir, that's hard to say. If it's the same shit, then not far, but we do need to get away from here."

"Of course. Sergeant?"

"I agree. Not much further, but definitely away from here. What did you have in mind?"

The lieutenant looked at the men and raising his hand in the air spoke freely.

"It's just a thought, but I didn't think we'd be able to set up a platoon size NDP tonight, so I had the idea that each squad set up ambush style. You know we'll go high and low, fade back, like we been doing, but separate positions."

The lieutenant waited for the negative reaction he expected, but it didn't come. Sarge smiled.

"Shit, that just might work. Wilson?"

"Ain't no different we pull a 'bush outside the NDP. What the fuck, why not."

Bob Grite chimed in.

"That way they won't catch us one place. One gets hit, the others sit tight catch them coming in or trying to get away. Either way we can put the hurt on anybody comes too close. You know they'll be looking for us, won't expect to be spread out like that. Why the fuck not?"

The lieutenant nodded.

"Sam, find us someplace to set up. No more that an hour out, give us time to stage this."

"Roger, sir."

Fifty-five minutes out, Kensington found just the spot. A slight ridge on the left, deep jungle to the rear and a plateau to the right, two high grounds and a cover.

The lieutenant and the sergeant mapped out the formation in the dirt as Wilson and Grite looked on.

"Okay the two high spots can fire up, down or ahead, but not back. The rear can fire forward, but not up, straight fire up anything they want to the rear. Everybody got that?"

Sarge, Wilson and Grite nodded.

"I want the squad on the plateau to dig in and face forward, but keep a watch to the rear down the slope on the other side. The squad on the rise should face forward as well, but watch the down slope on the other side. Both of these positions have direct fire to the bottom, case they walk through."

Wilson and Grite nodded. Sarge waited. The lieutenant erased the markings in the dirt with his boot. Starting over he slashed at the dirt.

"Sergeant, your squad is to face the rear, wait for somebody to come up on us. But… but you have to watch either side as well. This way they could walk right up on us and we'd still have the edge. They'd be expecting or at least looking for one position, not three. Let's use that to our advantage. Any questions?"

Wilson, Grite and Sarge nodded no.

"Okay then, let's get this set up. Grite, I'm still with you."

The men broke up and went back to their squads.

Wilson explained the plans to his men. They were the squad on the plateau. Open, but time to dig in, set up defensible positions. His men made their way up the rise to the top of the plateau, surveying the area and deciding on positions.

"No different than any 'bush. Don't fire across, second squad on that rise. And don't fire behind, third be back there. Your area is straight ahead or straight down. But behind us down the slope is fair game. If they were to come it would be from there, try to walk up on us, figure we set up in a regular NDP, maybe probe the perimeter, but we don't have one. Set claymores, but no trip flares. Mortars still possible. Probe the center, which there isn't one. This could work, stay alert."

Wilson looked out over the plateau, pointing.

"I want three holes, one front, one forty-five this side and one down slope. Don't worry about the rear, third squad back there. One man per hole watch. Two hours on, two off, through the night. Lopes, you, Big John and the new black guy first. Big John put the 60 in the forty-five hole, swing both ways. Four Seven's and my thumper be in the other two holes. Hump, Smooth and me got second shift. Hump, give your 60 to Big John when he comes off, keep it fluid. Then Four Seven, Whitey and me will do third shift. Then we do it again."

"Fuck, Stick, you're pulling two shifts?"

Wilson looked at Smooth.

"We're one short to make this work."

Lopes raised his hand in the air.

"Hey, I'll pull an extra hour first shift, then you only have to pull three hours, not a double."

Wilson nodded.

"That work. You okay with that?"

"Fuckin' A, Stick. Been taking it easy all day, making sure the guy behind me stays close, no big deal."

Wilson nodded.

"That's it then. Get some chow, coffee, grab a smoke, grab your dick and rest up. It's gonna be a long night."

Sam Kensington felt the tapping on his boot. It was the new black guy.

"Four Seven, you're up."

"Yeah, okay."

Sam sat up wiping his hand across his face. The new black guy crawled up to his ruck, covering himself with the poncho liner. Sam crawled the few feet to the hole. He wondered which hole Wilson was in.

Looking out into the night he waited for his eyes to adjust. He was in the hole on the down slope. Shadows and movement as the breeze moved the grass back and forth caught his attention, but all appeared quiet.

He looked at his watch, apparently Wilson was determined to keep him on midnights to prevent him from getting any continuous sleep. Well so far it was working, he didn't have time to dream, or sleep yet. The two hour shift dragged on without incident. Finally he evacuated the hole, tapped the next guy and crawled up to his ruck. Sleep took awhile to come.

Sam Kensington woke with a start, sitting up quickly, looking around. Smooth was up and about. Others were either up already or still on watch. He looked at his watch, just after six. He swiped his hand across his face.

Wilson came back into the area, walking straight toward him, motioning for anyone else around to gather up.

"LT's taking shit, says we're moving too slow. Need to be there now, so we're going to saddle up early and move, take resupply later in the day. Wants us moving in the next three zero mikes. Pack it up, grab some coffee, a smoke, whatever you need to get going and be ready. I'll get the guys in the holes."

Wilson was gone as fast as he had come.

Sam poured water into the canteen cup, lighting a heat tap in his cooking C-rat can, letting the water warm, pouring a pack of instant coffee into the now boiling water. Slowly sipping the warm liquid, he put out the fire and let the cooking can cool.

Rolling up his poncho and poncho liner, he packed those back on his ruck. Feeling the can to make sure it was cool enough first, he packed that away. Checking his sleeping area for anything else, he went back to sipping the hot liquid.

Wilson came back with the others, handing Sam his thumper, which Sam took and strapped to the back of his ruck. Wilson went over to his own gear and in what seemed like an instant, he was packed and ready.

"Smooth, you and Four Seven up for another day?"

Both men nodded.

"How you figure we do that?"

Kensington started to speak, but Smooth interrupted him.

"Same as before, we cut two paths, keep things spread out. Don't think it will be any different out there."

Smooth pointed toward where they would be going.

"Anyway, we can pick up the pace?"

Kensington and Smooth looked at Wilson, then at each other, both answering.

"Long as we don't walk into nobody."

Wilson nodded. Kensington continued.

"We still got what, a couple of klicks to go, then a hill to recon and climb. At least another day, maybe two, but we hit the shit, might not move at all."

Whitey interrupted.

"Heard Bravo Company got lifted to that other hill. How come we don't get the Hueys? We gotta walk through this shit to get there. What the fuck?"

Wilson, Kensington, Smooth and the others looked at him. Wilson smiled.

"Want the official or want me to bullshit you?"

Whitey smiled.

"Which ever one I'll believe."

"Well, the LT said they were going to the hill on the other side, further away from where they were at, but we're heading straight to the hill we need to be on. Besides we ain't been in no area we could get lifted out of."

They all sat silent, finally Whitey nodded.

"That the bullshit version or the official?"

"Both."

Whitey nodded again.

"Well, it's all bullshit to me."

"What you hearing today?"

Whitey looked at Wilson first then the rest of the squad that had gathered.

"Well they're still in the shit. Looks like they hit a large NVA force that won't quit and run. Staying put and fighting back. Sounds like the whole force is there or heading to that hill. You've heard the gunships pounding the top. Somebody's serious about taking that hill. Just as serious as the gooks are about keeping it."

Wilson nodded, pointing.

"Okay, let's get this packed up and get ready to move. Whitey call over to second squad and let the LT know we're coming off the plateau, meet in the front where the jungle comes back together."

Whitey nodded and started running through the call signs.

Fifteen minutes later, the lieutenant, Sarge, Bob Grite and Wilson were gathered at the front of the platoon, rehashing the plan. The lieutenant pointed to the map.

"Wilson, tell your men to take it easy cutting. As we get closer we're sure to run into some of them heading to or leaving the hills. I was told this morning that we would probably run across NVA reinforcements heading to the hill they're trying to take. Might hit some leaving with wounded back to their sanctuary in Laos. Either way, there's a good chance we'll run into something."

The lieutenant paused.

"But, there will probably be some reinforced or defensive positions set up to protect those coming and going. I gotta believe we'll run into some of those. If we do, they won't hit and run and that could bog us down. We'll need to break through those. So Wilson, tell your men, they hit anything looks like it might be a defensive position, pull back and I'll have artillery or gunships or both put the hurt on them. Try not to engage unless necessary. You understand? We need to keep moving, even if we have to go around."

Wilson nodded, Bob Grite pointed to the map in the lieutenant's hand.

"Sir, maybe if we shifted left a bit, we might be able to sweep around. Might take longer, you know cover a little more ground, but it would give us the edge, we run into those little fuckers."

The lieutenant looked at where Grite was pointing. Wilson leaned in closer to see and Sarge looked over the lieutenant's shoulder.

"Sergeant, any thoughts?"

"I see where Bob is going with that theory, but it could add another klick to our path, might cost us another day. Not sure we, I mean you have that option."

The lieutenant nodded. Wilson stood back. Bob Grite waited.

"Sir, I think Bob is right. I hear what Sarge is saying, but my men been cutting pretty good. I think we stay on course we'll be okay. Ain't no question we're gonna run into them, question is where and when."

The lieutenant looked up, first at Wilson, then Bob Grite, then at the sergeant.

"Gentlemen, I think for now we keep moving forward as planned, see what's up ahead. Terrain starts to work against us we'll follow Bob's advice. That work for everyone?"

The three others nodded.

"Alright, then, let's saddle up and move out."

Thirty-five minutes out as the platoon kept up it's snaking movement, second squad swung a little wide and stumbled into a recently vacated defensive position. Stopping the platoon, Bob Grite wanted to run a quick patrol to see where the trail went. The lieutenant agreed and he took a team away from the position into the jungle. The platoon rested in place.

Moments later, all hell broke loose. AK47 fire could be distinguished from the return M16 fire as the team engaged in a fire fight. Sarge immediately put together a team to go help out and was on the way toward their position. The remaining soldiers tightened up and setup a defensive position. Kensington and Smooth pulled back, setting up next to Wilson and Big John with the 60 pointing forward.

A volley of bullets skimmed over their heads and cut the

trees and elephant grass all around them. Wilson held up his hand and motioned. He and Sam put out several M79 rounds first, but they were met with another volley. He lowered his hand. Big John cut loose with the 60 pouring rounds into the jungle in front of them. The shooting stopped.

Waiting to make sure the enemy had left, everyone stayed low and focused on the jungle in front of them. Finally, Wilson pointed and Whitey, Sam and Smooth joined him as they made their way forward to the point of contact. Again they were met with a blood trail and some pieces of equipment.

"Fuck they were right here. Wonder if they were waiting or were moving in?"

Wilson looked at Smooth.

"Let's go."

The men headed back to their position.

"Stay alert."

Big John kept the 60 pointed forward toward the jungle. Kensington, Smooth and the new black guy kept their weapons forward as well. Sam had the thumper beside him. The new white guy sat next to Big John ready to feed belted rounds, his 60 beside him, in case they needed to swap out. Wilson stayed behind them, waiting to hear from the lieutenant. Whitey spoke up.

"Second has two guys hit. They're bringing them back here, gonna bring a Medevac in to get them. Sarge says to lock it down for now."

Wilson nodded, pointing.

"Let's clean this up, setup better."

The men shifted and moved into place in a defensive position rather than the make shift position they set up in.

"Stick, LT wants to know if there's anything forward they can bring a bird in."

"Negative, Whitey."

Whitey relayed the message back to the lieutenant.

"Sarge says they got something where he's at, get a bird in there. LT wants us to pack up and move his location, secure the LZ."

Wilson nodded.

"You heard the man, let's go."

Everyone grabbed their gear and prepared to move toward the sergeant's location. Slowly everyone moved into place. The two wounded men from second squad were in the middle, one against a tree, the other laying flat on the ground, while the medic tended to them.

Wilson moved his squad into position, filling in a perimeter around the area. The opening was tight, but a bird could get in. The wounded men's gear was placed next to them to load on the bird as well.

The buffeting of the blades against the sky signaled the Medevac helicopter was coming in. The ground churned up dust and debris as the Huey angled in for a landing.

Suddenly a volley of bullets struck the bird, rocking it in place, but the pilot held fast, waiting until the wounded men were loaded before taking off as fast as he had come. The men on the ground returned fire around the perimeter, but no further shots came in. The shooters had hit and run.

The signal was given to saddle up, prepare to move out. Kensington led them back to where they had been, but drifting slightly left as Grite had suggested earlier, at least for a stretch to sweep around where they had made contact.

Sam hit another open area and stopped, motioning for Wilson to come up. Not only were there fresh tracks, but dust was still swirling in the air.

"Damn Four Seven, fuckers were just here. Can't tell which way they headed. Maybe it's those we ran into earlier?"

Kensington nodded, pointing across the open area to the right. Wilson saw and signaled for the lieutenant to come up. As the lieutenant approached, Wilson motioned for silence.

Pointing, Wilson directed the lieutenant's view toward the right side of the opening. Finally he saw it.

"A bunker?"

Wilson nodded. Kensington pointed further right to another bunker. The lieutenant reached for Whitey.

"Have Grite and the sergeant come up. Sam, let's pull back a little."

The three men slid back into the jungle away from the opening. Grite joined them, with the sergeant right behind him.

"What's up?"

"Sam spotted two bunkers just to the right of the opening. Tracks so fresh, there's still dust in the air. Might be the ones we ran into earlier, but maybe not."

Sarge looked at Wilson, then the lieutenant.

"How do you want to play this sir?"

"My first thought was to bring arty or gunships, but they'd hear it and di di mau before that did anything."

"Want me to take a team and sweep around, maybe catch them?"

"No, Bob, you're down two already. Sarge, I thought you and Wilson could put a team together, go check it out."

Both men nodded.

Wilson got Smooth and Kensington, Whitey with the radio and joined Sarge with four men from third squad. The rest of the platoon set up in a defensive perimeter.

Smooth led the way, walking point around the right side of the opening toward the bunkers. Sarge brought up the rear, with his men. As Smooth moved into place just right of the first bunker, Kensington moved in beside him, Wilson slid in on his left. The three men looked at the bunker, but couldn't ascertain any movement. Sarge put his men to the rear, watching their backs.

Just as Kensington and Smooth were about to move closer, a barrage of AK47 fire erupted from that first bunker, spraying the ground and foliage all around them, dirt and debris flying into the air as the bullets bit into the ground. In an instant the three men returned fire. Wilson and Kensington fired off their thumpers at the bunker, explosion after explosion as the shells made direct hits, raking the bunker. In a moment all firing stopped.

Wilson pointed and Smooth and Kensington moved to their sides angling around the bunker, moving closer. Smooth was there first, signaling the all clear. Kensington came in from the other side and Wilson moved forward. Sarge and his men joined them.

Two bodies lay mangled in the first bunker, NVA uniforms, pith helmets to the side and a significant blood trail leading away from the hole. Some gear remained, including a destroyed AK47, pitted by the M79 rounds, exploding inside the bunker.

Sarge led his men to the other bunker, but it was vacated, no blood or equipment.

"Must have pulled out when we hit the first bunker."

"Lotta blood here, Sarge. Maybe we should pursue, finish the job."

The sergeant thought about that for a moment, but shook his head no.

"No, can't. No time. We gotta keep moving. Whitey call it in."

"Already on it, Sarge."

Back inside the perimeter, Wilson grabbed Kensington's shoulder and pulled Smooth over talking in a whisper.

"What the fuck was that?"

Kensington shook his head, not understanding the question.

"Smooth, you saw it, what you think?"

Smooth smiled, his teeth showing through the dark dust covered face.

"Damned if I know?"

Kensington looked at both men.

"Still don't know what you're talking about?"

Wilson let go of his friend, putting his arm around him and Smooth walking them a ways away from the other men.

"They had us dead to right, right in the line of fire. Even mother fucking new guys don't miss that close, that open. How come none of us got hit?"

Smooth shook his head. Kensington looked at both men.

"I mean they fired what fifty, a hundred rounds right at us. You got any marks?"

Smooth shook his head no.

"You?"

Kensington shook his head no.

"Me neither."

The three men stood silent for a moment.

"Just like that shell blew sideways."

Wilson looked directly at Kensington.

"Something weird here. Maybe something to do with those dreams?"

"What dreams?"

Wilson and Kensington both looked at Smooth.

"Four Seven dreaming he back in the Civil War, fighting Confederates. One war's not enough for him."

"Say what?"

Wilson looked at Kensington, but Sam waved his hand in the air.

"Don't know what to make of it, but I keep having these dreams I'm with some outfit back in the Civil War. That's why I went to see the XO, back in camp. He's some kind of Civil War nut. Anyway, he was able to figure out where I was at and what was about to happen, like that."

"Four Seven's in some parallel war, some fucking thing like that."

Kensington looked at Wilson before continuing.

"Anyway, that's all I know. Stick has been putting me on shitty shifts so I wouldn't sleep. Don't sleep. Don't dream."

Smooth shook his head.

"So what? You think that had something to do with what just happened?"

Kensington shrugged his shoulders. Wilson pointed.

"You were there both times. Shell exploding sideways missing all three of us. Now being shot at point blank, in the open, nothing. Something's fucked up for sure. That's what I'm saying."

Smooth stuck out his hand. Kensington did the dap with him.

"But it don't mean nothing."

"But it don't mean nothing."

Smooth turned to Wilson and they did their full black dap handshake repeating the refrain.

Sarge passed by.

"LT says to saddle up, we're moving out. Got a lot of ground to cover yet today."

The men went back to their rucks. Wilson and Kensington strapped in their thumpers. Sliding in and rising up, the men got into position. Wilson pointed and Sam led the way, Smooth on his left. They started cutting up and around where they saw the bunkers, avoiding the open area altogether.

An hour and a half later they reached an area Sam thought would be a good spot for an NDP. The afternoon was late and if they wanted to set up, grab some chow and such, this might just have to do.

The lieutenant and Sarge came up and sat down next to Kensington and Wilson.

"Thought this might be a good spot set up our NDP?"

The lieutenant nodded.

"Let me call it in, see what the CO says. I think we're still about a klick maybe a klick and a half away. Might want us to keep going."

"Just a klick sir."

Sarge pointed.

"You can see the hills over there. Should be there by late morning, get an early start."

The lieutenant nodded.

"Hell, we've paid our dues today. Fuck it. Sarge, take a team out, recon all the way around. Looks high enough to defend well enough. Let me know what you find, before I make my decision."

"Roger that, sir."

Wilson and Kensington pulled back into the jungle, as the lieutenant and the sergeant left.

"Four Seven, didn't mean to, you know… let Smooth know what."

Kensington raised his hand in the air.

"It's okay."

"Besides Smooth's cool, he'll keep it to himself."

"Really, it's okay."

The two men sat without speaking. Smooth joined them.

"LT gonna let us set up here?"

"Sending Sarge out with a team, recon. Then he'll decide."

Smooth nodded.

"So Four Seven, where you at?"

"Huh?'

"You know, the Civil War, where you at?"

"The Shenandoah Valley."

"The what?"

"Shenandoah Valley, it's in Virginia, some kind of Confederate stronghold."

Smooth nodded and looked over at Wilson before looking back at Sam.

"That mean something?"

"Don't know. At least not yet."

Smooth nodded.

"You got kin fought there or something?"

"That's what everybody keeps asking, but I truly don't know."

Smooth nodded, looking over at Wilson, before patting Kensington on the leg as he left.

"I told you he's cool."

Sam nodded, letting his head fall back against his ruck.

Before he had a chance to get into it, the patrol returned and said it looked clear. The lieutenant decided to set up their NDP as Sam had suggested. Wilson set the watch schedule, again putting Sam on midnight.

Eighteen

In the morning, they prepared to move out early as the lieutenant had directed. Kensington would still walk the point, but straight line this time. Wilson was behind him at slack and Smooth behind him this time. They left just after oh seven hundred.

Once again Sam reached an open area, but before he could call anyone up, AK47 fire ripped across towards him. Dropping to the ground and lying behind his ruck, he could see the NVA soldiers across the opening, set up behind some rocks to create a makeshift defense. Wilson finally crawled up next to him and Sam pointed. Together they fired their thumpers, scattering the NVA across the way.

Waiting for a bit to ensure the enemy had left, a second barrage of AK47 fire came from the right side. Either the NVA soldiers had moved their position or another group of soldiers were setup there.

The rest of the platoon returned fire as Wilson and Kensington concentrated on the position in front of them. Again, the firing stopped just as quickly. This time voices and commotion could be heard from the side position as the NVA soldiers scrambled to move out.

Wilson and Kensington pulled back to where the platoon had set up a defensive position, waiting for another attack, but none came. Finally, Sarge called everyone together.

"I think we caught them moving this time. Probably had to hold us in place while they passed. Don't think they want to engage us right now. Need to feed the hill, or take the wounded out."

The men sat silent waiting for him to continue.

"Sam, what's it look like up ahead? Can we go around, still get through?"

Kensington nodded.

"I think so. Before I ducked for cover, I saw a little ridge. I was thinking of climbing, take us around where they were."

"Sir?"

The lieutenant looked at the sergeant, but pulled out and reviewed his map before answering.

"We're almost there, probably why we ran into them. Yeah, let's get moving, follow that ridge, but come back down quick. Okay saddle up, let's go."

Kensington was back on the path, climbing the ridge he had spotted. Once on top, he could see the trail they had followed up. He continued for a ways before dropping down. The word came up for him to halt. Wilson joined him with Whitey and the radio.

"We're here at the base of Hill 900, other platoons arriving, I think the other companies as well. Orders are to wait until everyone gets in place."

Whitey interrupted.

"LT confirms to hold for now."

Sam dropped his ruck, as did Wilson. Big John came up and set his 60 facing outward. Whitey sat next to Wilson, the radio squawking constantly.

"What they saying?"

"Nothing much. Everyone wants to know where everyone is. Looks like we're going to move into place in force set up a perimeter together."

Wilson nodded.

"I'm going to talk to the LT. You all know what to do."

As quickly as he left, Wilson was back.

"We're here, set up an NDP for the night, tomorrow we start probing this mother fucker. The rest is moving in around the base, our spot is right here. Just know there's friendlys everywhere around us. Don't get trigger happy. Each platoon is going to set up blocking positions. Anybody comes down off the hill is going to run into one of us. Same as anybody tries to get in gonna have to deal with one of us."

Wilson set the watch and assigned the squad to their position. The rest of the platoon set up for the night, as did the other platoons now in position.

Shortly after dusk, one of the other platoons was hit. An intense fire fight broke out, but was short lived. Seconds later another position was hit with heavy firing.

Wilson tapped Kensington on the shoulder.

"Mother fuckers trying to find a way out."

Kensington nodded. Moments later it was their turn. A small force walked into their trip flare and the new white guy on watch blew the claymore, sending screaming men into the dark. For good measure he put a couple of thumper rounds out.

"Probing us. Looking for a way out."

Kensington nodded. No one was sleeping tonight.

The rest of the night was the same, occasional probes as the NVA tried to find a way out. Just hours earlier, this had been an open highway to Laos for them to bring men and supplies in and take the wounded out, but now it was sealed up tight.

As Sam had thought, no one slept much during the night. The morning was no better. Each of the units was going to run patrols into the hill, find a way to the top to control this ridge of the mountain.

Wilson had said, "Not only were they not getting out, but we 're going to let them know we are here in force."

The rest of the day was spent probing up the hill, testing their fortifications. Time after time contact was made and the terrain added to the aborted efforts to secure Hill 900. The NVA efforts to get in and out of the hill fortifications added to the assaults. Until now, the contact had only been skirmishes, but since they had reached the hill, they were encountering heavy opposition.

Wilson, Kensington, Smooth, Whitey, with the radio and the new black guy were running a patrol around the side when they hit several NVA coming off the hill, apparently with wounded.

The two NVA soldiers leading the group opened up on Wilson's team.

"Smooth, to your right."

Smooth hit the ground and fired into the direction Wilson had shouted. Kensington put out a thumper round. Wilson did the same. The new black guy opened up with his sixteen. Amid screams and confusion, the NVA soldiers attempted to escape, but Wilson's team was upon them and captured four soldiers, all wounded. Whitey called it in and another team close by joined them to remove the prisoners.

Smooth stood next to Kensington as the men were gathered up.

"Luck still holding?"

Kensington looked at Smooth, then Wilson, who stood smiling near by.

"Fuckin' A."

Wilson led another patrol that afternoon, with the same team. A squad from one of the other platoons came into heavy contact on the far side of the hill. Wilson was directed to move toward their position to offer assistance, but by the time they made it over there, the contact had broken off.

The squad had two killed and three wounded during the intense fire fight. Wilson's team helped evacuate the dead and wounded to a spot where a bird could be brought in.

Just as the Medevac came in and hovered for a pickup, a burst of AK47 fire smashed against the left side rocking the bird in place. The pilot held fast as the men were loaded onto the Huey. In an instant the bird was airborne.

Wilson's team fired in the direction of the assault, putting some thumper rounds in the general area, but there was no return fire. The NVA either had left or had done a hit and run on an easy target.

Sam led the team and the rest of that squad back to the area at the base of the hill. Once there, they disbursed back to their own areas. Bob Grite was coming in with his team at the same time. Sarge and the lieutenant were waiting. Bob Grite went first.

"No doubt they are all over this fucking hill. We crossed paths a couple of times, but just fired back and forth, let 'em know we're here. They did the same."

Wilson, Sarge and the lieutenant waited, but Bob said no more. Wilson pointed.

"We went all over that area, up and over. Made contact this morning, got some, you know about that. Nothing this afternoon, until we were ordered to help out that other squad. Little mother fuckers fired at the Medevac, but he got off. Clear on the way back."

The lieutenant nodded.

"Our orders are to get to the top as fast as we can. Nobody has been able to get very far. Not us or anybody else. Gotta believe the higher we go the more entrenched they'll be."

The rest of the men stood silent, waiting for the lieutenant to continue.

"It's getting late, we need to move our NDP over there."

The lieutenant pointed to a small rise just above the base of the hill.

"We better set up some ambushes for the night."

He looked directly at Wilson, who nodded.

"Sarge, you and Bob... you and Bob."

He paused looking at the area they would be moving to, staring as the others waited.

"Sergeant, that rise doesn't give us much cover, falling away from the side of the hill like that. In fact it puts us in a vulnerable position. They could just climb down and turn it into a shooting gallery."

Again they waited as the lieutenant looked around.

"There. We're going to move there. It's behind the rise and further up the hill. That will give us more cover."

The three others looked to where the lieutenant was pointing. Sarge nodded, as did Bob Grite. Wilson pointed.

"How about I set my ambush just above you, that way they try to get close, we cut them off?"

The lieutenant nodded.

"Fine. Fine. Sergeant, why don't you take a team just to the left of the position. That way, you and Wilson will cover both flanks? Bob, you set up inside cover front and back. Have your squad and whatever is left inside provide three sixty defense, but leave the two flanks open. Let the ambushes cover. Leave an opening, in case they need to get back in, we come under heavy attack."

Wilson, Sarge and Bob Grite nodded. The lieutenant waved his hand in the air.

"Saddle up, lets move into position, then send the ambushes out."

Wilson sat next to Kensington, pulling hard on his cigarette.

"We get to pull a 'bush tonight."

Kensington nodded.

"Up there, after the platoon moves into position for the night. Right flank, in case they try to climb down on us."

Kensington nodded again. Wilson finished his cigarette.

"Sarge has the left flank. Grite is going to secure the NDP."

Smooth came over and sat next to them.

"Who's going out tonight?"

Wilson pointed.

"Us three, the new white guy, Hump. He can switch his 60 for the new black guy's sixteen. Whitey on the radio."

"The usual?"

"Yeah."

Smooth lit a cigarette, offering the pack to Wilson and Kensington, who both declined.

"Heard second platoon is running a night patrol around the side of this fucking hill."

Wilson nodded.

"Whitey says they're getting their asses kicked on the big hill, trying to take it. Lot of guys getting shot to pieces and shit. Even some of you white guys."

Kensington nodded. Smooth smiled.

"Don't look like we're getting up any easier over here."

Smooth finished his cigarette.

"I'd better get ready."

With that he was gone leaving only Wilson and Kensington, who had been silent up to this point.

"What're you hearing?"

Wilson blinked his eyes and pulled a cigarette from the pack, lighting it amidst a cloud of smoke.

"Not much more'n I told you already. They trying to take the big hill, while we are trying to secure this one and Bravo Company on that other hill."

Wilson took a long pull on his cigarette.

"Idea is to keep the routes closed so they can't reinforce or bring supplies and ammo in, like that."

Kensington nodded.

Wilson directed his team into position at the ambush site, digging into the soft ground, to give them a defensive hole to operate from. Smooth and Kensington took the left side, while Hump and Whitey took the right side. Wilson hung in the middle ready to go either direction.

As dark set in, each man took his spot. Sleep would be cat naps only, two men on the look out at all times, rotating every hour.

Somewhere around one am the sound of a mortar tube broke the silence. In an instant the first round hit just outside of the perimeter Grite and the lieutenant had set up. The cry of incoming stirred everyone into position.

Wilson tried to gauge where it had come from and elected to put out a couple of thumper rounds. The popping of the tube sounded as more rounds were sent into the perimeter, this time hitting inside the defense.

About the time Wilson decided to take his team toward the sound a burst of AK47 fire buffeted his position. An instant later another burst of AK47 fire hit Sarge's position. The NVA knew exactly where they were at and were coming to get them.

An RPG round whizzed past them, exploding just beyond their position. Wilson waved both hands in the air and Kensington and Smooth moved to either side, crawling from the original position. Wilson moved forward, keeping Smooth and Kensington in a line with him moving forward.

The second RPG round whizzed past and exploded quite a ways back. Hump and Whitey stayed just behind and in between Wilson, Smooth and Kensington.

Smooth and Kensington continued their crawl forward, Wilson still in the middle. The sound of the Rocket Propelled Grenade Launcher was right in front of them as the third round was fired. Wilson signaled.

Smooth, Kensington and Wilson laid flat as Hump and Whitey rose to one knee. Together they all fired at once, lighting up the area in front of them. The sounds of screams and the thud of bodies falling and men running became evident. The men stopped their fire and crawled further up.

Again, Wilson gave the signal and they fired in tandem, this time working the area in front of them from left to right. No response this time, but they could hear Sarge's position taking heavy fire. Slowly they moved forward, finally reaching the area the attack had come from.

A lot of blood, but no bodies or weapons were left behind. The trail they used to retreat was on a line with Sarge's position. The heavy fire at Sarge's position was probably from the NVA soldiers they had just routed, moving away, they had now run into the sergeant's ambush.

Whitey called the perimeter and was informed they were okay, no one seriously hit, but a couple of shrapnel cuts. Wilson had him ask if he should help out Sarge's location. They waited. Finally the lieutenant said no, just to go back to their ambush site, but reset as best they could. Whitey raised his hand keeping Wilson close.

"Sarge got two men hit, maybe three. He needs to go back in, needs to get a bird out, pick up the wounded. Lieutenant says to bring it back in, they're going to try to get a bird in outside the perimeter in the flat area we crossed before setting up there."

Wilson nodded.

"Let's go. Stop and pick up anything we left behind, then head on in. Whitey, let them know we'll be there in twenty."

Whitey nodded and called it in.

Slowly they made their way back to the ambush site and gathered up anything left when they had moved out. Just as slowly they made their way back to the perimeter and walked back inside.

Bob Grite already had a team out securing an LZ for the Medevac that was on the way. The sound of blades buffeting the air filled the dark night. The ground was turned up sending debris and dust into the air as the Huey slowly made its way into the makeshift LZ, spotlights illuminating the ground.

While at full hover, the wounded men were loaded on and the bird was airborne back into the night. Grite brought his team back into the perimeter. It was just after three.

The lieutenant called everyone over.

"Look, it's the middle of the night. It's another three hours 'till daylight, so here's what we're gonna do."

He waved his hand in the air as he spoke.

"We're gonna turn this into an ambush site. They already know we're here. Bring it in, tighten up this perimeter and bring the gear into the middle. I want two man posts the rest of the night."

The lieutenant paused.

"In the morning, we'll find a new location. Get organized then."

The lieutenant paused again, then turned to the sergeant.

"How many?"

"We lost six, so far, couple of others questionable, but still here for now."

The lieutenant nodded.

"I'll get replacements in the morning."

Sarge nodded.

"That's it. Let's go get this tightened up."

Kensington sat against his ruck. Smooth sat by his. The two new guys, Hump and Body Man were by theirs. Big John and Whitey leaned in. Wilson knelt in the middle of the squad.

"Same drill, two on, two off. Four Seven, you and me, over there. Smooth, you and Body Man over there. Lopes, you and Hump relieve us in an hour and a half and Whitey, you and Big John relieve them same time. Understood?"

The rest of the night passed quietly. No further contact was made. Sarge summed it up with "they needed to get out and we were in the way."

In the morning, Kensington lit a fire under his coffee. Striking up a smoke as he waited, Wilson came over and sat down beside him.

"How you doing?"

Sam looked at Wilson letting the smoke expel from his mouth.

"Fine. You ain't' letting me sleep none, so I ain't been dreaming any either."

"Good. That's my plan. Keep you sharp."

"Sharp? How the fuck can I be sharp, I don't get no sleep?"

Wilson smiled. Smooth sat down beside them.

"Same shit today?"

Wilson nodded yes. "Same shit."

Smooth lit a cigarette, letting the smoke drift from his lips.

"How soon we moving out?"

Wilson shrugged his shoulders.

"Haven't heard nothing yet."

Smooth took a pull from his cigarette. Kensington took a sip of his fresh heated coffee. Wilson took the cup and took a sip, handing it back to Sam. The three men sat silent. Whitey came over dragging his radio with him.

"Just heard we're gonna make another stab at getting up this fucking hill."

Wilson nodded. Smooth and Kensington looked up. Whitey walked away.

By late morning, Kensington and Smooth had put together a team of Lopes, Whitey on the radio, Body Man and Hump to go on patrol. Wilson would be staying back this time to meet with the lieutenant and Sarge. Another team from Bob Grite's squad would be going the other way. The idea this time was to scout out areas where the platoon could move to advance from and make their way further up the hill. Orders had been received to get off the base and start making their way to the top.

Smooth walked point this time, Lopes behind him, at slack, Hump next, Whitey, Body Man and Sam brought up the rear. He wound them around several rises, making his way toward the center, gradually climbing. Tall, thick elephant grass, bamboo fields and dense jungle terrain kept the pace to a crawl. Finally, Smooth reached a plateau that looked like a good spot to set up an NDP. Smooth stopped the team, while Kensington came up to join him. Smooth pointed.

"We should be able to get what's left of the platoon on here for the night. Set a 'bush there and there."

Kensington nodded.

"That should work. Whitey, call it in, tell the LT what we found. How does he want to proceed?"

Back in the perimeter, Smooth and Kensington briefed the lieutenant and Sarge on what they found. Sam noticed Wilson wasn't around, but let it go until he got back to the squad.

"Hey, Big John, where's Wilson?"

Big John pointed to an open area that wasn't there before.

"He and Grite and a few men are cutting an LZ for resupply. Might be getting a couple of fucking new guys as replacements. We're down seven. Have to send another guy in with the resupply bird. Doc said he took shrapnel when the perimeter got hit and he can't stop the bleeding, cut's too deep."

The buffeting of the air by the blades of the resupply Huey signaled the arrival of the birds. A gunship and a second Huey hovered as the first landed, pushing boxes of C-rats and ammo off. Just as quickly it was up and away, as the second bird came in, carrying two new guys. The wounded man was loaded on board and as it began its lift off it was struck by a large round, rocking the ship as black smoke drifted from the engine compartment. The bird sputtered and rocked, but before it could get lift it crashed to the ground hitting hard into the jungle not far from the LZ.

Sarge grabbed everyone around him and made for the Huey's location. AK47 fire blazed across the makeshift LZ scattering the men there. The gunship was on it in an instant providing cover as the men got off the LZ.

A team headed in the direction of where the fire came from, while Sarge and his men worked their way toward the downed Huey. Kensington and Wilson joined up with Sarge, while Smooth and Lopes took off with the team after the shooters.

Taking only a few minutes to reach the crashed bird, the men fanned around providing security, while Sarge looked inside. The wounded man was okay still lying on the metal bed of the Huey, where he had been placed. The door gunner on the right was sprawled outside laying face down. Sarge checked but he was dead. Whatever had hit the bird had hit him as well. The other door gunner was helping get the pilot and peter pilot out of the Huey. They both appeared to be okay, except for obvious cuts and bruises.

Sarge gathered the wounded together away from the Huey, did a quick check confirming everyone could walk. He had the two biggest guys carry the deceased door gunner and had Kensington lead them out away from the crashed bird.

Back at the makeshift LZ, a Medevac was already on the

way. He gathered the men to wait. The Huey was in and out, as the gunship provided support in the direction the firing had come from.

A Chinook "shit hook" was hovering where the downed Huey sat, with a gun ship on either side. Two men repelled down to the disabled bird attaching a harness to the stricken helicopter. Slowly the downed Huey lifted off the ground and was airborne swinging in the air below the shit hook, the two men on the inside of the bird had their rifles at the ready on either side. In a moment, all the birds were gone and the air was quiet.

Sarge pushed the men back into the perimeter, told them the show was over, to go get C-rats and ammo from the resupply and be prepared to move out in three zero mikes. Finished, he went over to speak to the lieutenant.

Smooth led the platoon up to that plateau he had found earlier, then watched and waited as the men moved into position. Serious gun fire and explosions could be heard off to the west of their position. Smooth looked for Whitey.

"What are you hearing?"

Whitey sat down heavily against his ruck, keeping the handset close to his ear.

"A company over to the west of us is engaged with a fortified NVA unit, trying to get up that hill."

Smooth nodded.

"Also heard another two birds been shot down trying to bring resupply in. Said it sounded like gook fifty-ones firing at them."

The men stood silent, acknowledging the impact of that statement.

"Listen up."

Wilson came into the center of their squad.

"We'll be pulling another 'bush tonight right where Smooth thought. Grite's taking a team out to the other spot."

The squad looked at Wilson waiting, but he said no more.

This time Wilson took Big John with the 60 out with him. Kensington, Smooth, Lopes and Whitey on the radio, made up the rest of the team, leaving the two new guys behind.

Smooth took them into the area he had thought would be a good spot to set up an ambush for the night. They could see the rest of the platoon on the plateau, now dug in for the night.

Wilson set the positions and set up between Lopes and Kensington. They had grabbed some chow before they left the perimeter and with daylight fading, a final smoke was in order.

The night passed quietly, at least for them. Fire fights and explosions were going on all around them as other units either made contact or had NVA soldiers breech their setups.

Shortly after midnight, Wilson and Kensington set up watch together. The night was silent, too silent.

"Stick, I don't like this, it's too fucking quiet. We've been hit every night so far."

Wilson looked out in front of him, then up above.

"Night ain't over yet."

"Fuckin' A."

Their shift and the rest of the night passed without incident.

Kensington was heating his coffee and pulling on a cigarette, when Wilson came over, dropping heavily to his ruck.

"LT says we're running more patrols today, probing this mother fucker. Says we have to get to the top now, support those guys getting shot to pieces on the big hill."

Sam looked at Wilson, but couldn't read him.

"Hey, we've must have put the hurt on them some. Cut off their routes, picked them apart so far."

Wilson nodded.

"Fuckin' A."

Kensington handed him his coffee cup, Wilson took a sip, handing it back.

"LT wants us to work around the edge, make our way through the side. Pretty thick fucking jungle over there. Spend all our time cutting. Middle is too steep to go up, have to find another way around. Company on the other side, has the same problem. Cutting through that shit is slow. Suspect once we get higher we'll hit fortified positions. Gotta believe they're entrenched further up."

Wilson sat silent, Sam nodded, again handing his cup to Wilson, but he declined. Sam put out his cigarette, finishing his coffee.

"How soon we going out?"

"Ten to twenty."

Wilson stood up motioning to the other squad members.

"Listen up."

The morning patrol went rather smoothly. They cut a path around and actually gained some elevation. By the afternoon, several units had made contact, one platoon reaching a fortified position, which they had backed off of and called in the gunships.

Smooth took them on a round about route over and down before starting a climb to the side of the hill, gradually making his way toward another plateau. As they approached, Smooth stopped the team, motioning for everyone to come up. As they gathered in line looking out, they saw what Smooth had seen.

An NVA unit was set up on the plateau, but it appeared to have not dug in, just massing and resting. Wilson had Whitey call in the coordinates and slowly moved everyone back.

"Let them put the hurt on them. We'll wait here in case anyone comes our way."

In a moment, the first artillery round hit and scattered the NVA soldiers for cover. As Wilson thought, a group headed their way and were immediately cut to pieces by Wilson's squad. North Vietnamese Soldiers were scattering everywhere, trying to get off the plateau. Several more rounds hit, tearing the plateau to rubble, dust and debris flying through the air.

Wilson's squad held fast, ducking from all the debris flying through the air. Once the rounds stopped, several NVA soldiers ventured back onto the plateau, recovering wounded and scattered equipment. Wilson had moved his men back into position and let loose with another barrage, cutting those left standing to pieces.

Their victory was short lived as several bursts of AK47 fire came at them from the right. Lopes and Hump spun and turned, returning the fire in that direction. Wilson and Smooth fell back circling toward that position and when they were close, they let loose with their own barrage of fire, quieting that position.

Wilson signaled and everyone held in place waiting for a renewed attack, but none came. Figuring the NVA soldiers had left, they slowly ventured onto the plateau.

A wounded NVA soldier lay writhing on the ground. Equipment, weapons and ammunition lay scattered around the area, too much for them to recover and carry back.

"What about him?"

Wilson looked at Whitey.

"Let him be. Grab what we can and let's get the fuck out of here."

The men gathered what equipment and weapons they could gather and stacked the ammo in a pile. Smooth tied a grenade to the pile and pulled the pin.

"Go. Go."

The team hightailed it off the plateau just as the grenade blew, detonating some if not all of the ammo. Heavily laden with the weapons and equipment, Smooth led them back to their perimeter. The lieutenant met them when they entered.

"Now."

The lieutenant pointed to his RTO.

"I've ordered another artillery strike on that position, just waiting for you to get back in."

Wilson nodded, his team dropped the captured gear and weapons in the center by the lieutenant.

"I've also got a bird coming out to pick up this stuff, bring more ammo for us, some C-rats, get a quick resupply."

The lieutenant walked away. Wilson's team went back to their rucks.

"Stick, any word on where we're heading tonight?"

Wilson looked at Kensington.

"Nope. Probably right here again. Probably pull another 'bush."

Sam nodded, Smooth did the same. Suddenly the lieutenant was standing there.

"Wilson, anything beyond that area you saw could be an NDP?"

"No, sir. Once we saw them we stopped looking, but Smooth might remember something."

The lieutenant looked at Smooth.

"Anything?"

Smooth shook his head no.

"Sorry sir. Stick is right. Once we found them we stopped looking. But what I do remember was it was straight up, pretty thick and I'm sure they're waiting for us to try it."

The lieutenant kept looking at Smooth, but thinking. Wilson interrupted.

"Sir, you figure we stay here another night? Pull another push?"

The lieutenant finally looked at Wilson.

"Yeah, that's the current plan, but Sarge thinks we should set up as three ambushes like we did before, get out of the perimeter setup. Might be better to defend that way."

Wilson nodded.

"Sounds right."

The lieutenant looked at Wilson, then up the hill.

"Tomorrow we're going up. We're gonna have arty walk from your contact point all the way to the top, followed by gunships. Maybe we keep their heads down, we can gain some ground."

"Sir?"

"Smooth, I know what you're gonna say. The jungle is pretty thick and it's gonna be tough cutting, but we got arty clearing and some napalm, burn this shit out."

Smooth nodded.

"Good job today, men."

The lieutenant walked away.

Wilson set the shifts and just as daylight was fading a new enemy moved in. The rain. It had been raining lightly off and on the last few days, but nothing like this. The downpour started and just didn't stop.

Early the next morning, the lieutenant gave the order to move out. The rain slowed the gunships, but artillery was putting on a show.

Kensington climbed halfway up the hill before stopping, coming upon what looked like a bunker complex. It looked abandoned, more likely blown apart. Lopes and the two new guys circled around and came in from behind. In a moment they signaled that all was clear. Sam had been right, it was blown apart, several dead NVA soldiers still in the complex attested to that.

Further up, Sam found a depression in the side of the hill that provided cover and shelter from the pounding rain. He stopped, signaling for the others to come up to his position.

"Sir, this might be a good spot take a break, recon from here."

The lieutenant nodded just as the sergeant arrived.

"Sergeant, let's break here for chow and rest. Send out a couple of recon teams from yours and Bob's squads see what's up ahead. Last report I had said the other company was about as high as we were, found the same things, destroyed bunkers. Arty doing its job."

"Right, sir."

The lieutenant left, Wilson motioned and his squad hunkered down to take a break, but before they could unload, the lieutenant came back.

"Sorry men, but we have to keep moving. The attack is set for tomorrow and we have to secure this hill today, to be ready for tomorrow. I already heard from the other company, they're still climbing, almost at the top. Heavy resistance at first, but not much since. Thinks they may have retreated back to the big hill to hold there, or better yet, di di maued out of here. Either way they said the resistance has been light so far."

Wilson started to speak, but the lieutenant put his hand up.

"Yeah, I know you're tired, wet, hungry and probably pretty pissed off by now, but I have my orders…"

Wilson smiled pointing.

"No sir, I was going to say the top is just up that ridge."

The lieutenant looked up surprised.

"Damn, we're that close?"

"No sir, we still have a tough climb, because we have to go around. And if arty did its job, we shouldn't hit anything. Three hours tops, we should be there."

The sergeant came up just then.

"Sir, I just heard we've been ordered to keep climbing?"

The lieutenant pointed.

"Wilson says it's right there."

The Sarge looked to where the lieutenant pointed.

"Fuckin' A. How long to get there?"

"Wilson says three hours, don't hit anything or anybody."

Five minutes later, Kensington was leading them around the ridge, climbing ever so gradually. They came upon another bunker complex, but again it was demolished. They wound past that and continued the climb.

Near the top, Sam halted the column. Wilson quickly joined him looking as Sam pointed.

"That one is still intact."

Wilson saw the bunker Sam was pointing at.

"Lopes, have the LT come up."

Moments later the lieutenant joined him and Kensington. Right behind him was the sergeant. Sam pointed.

"Anybody have any ideas?"

Wilson started to speak, but the sergeant cut him off.

"How about we put some thumper rounds in there, see if it stirs any reaction?"

"My thoughts exactly."

Wilson had already pulled his M79 out and fired off a round. Sam did the same with his. In tandem they fired off a couple of more rounds. When they received no response, Sarge spoke up.

"Okay, we send a couple of guys to recon the bunker, make sure."

The lieutenant nodded.

"Have Grite send…"

"We got this, sir."

Wilson was already making his way out of their spot, with Kensington behind him, Smooth following and Whitey on the radio. Wilson led them around as far as he could go without dropping down. They approached the bunker from the right side, stopping and waiting.

When they didn't hear anything they approached the bunker

straight on. It had been abandoned, but looked intact. Artillery had not penetrated this fortification. Wilson and his men returned.

"It was already abandoned, sir."

The lieutenant nodded.

"Sam, what say you get us to the top?"

"Roger that, sir."

A half hour later they made it to the top of Hill 900. The radio buzzed, the other company was also approaching the top. The platoon moved into position with the rest of their company and finally the other company.

A perimeter was established and ambushes were sent out for the night. Once again Wilson and his team spent a quiet night. In fact it was eerily quiet everywhere.

In the morning, the lieutenant came over and explained that now that they had control of this and the other hill, that they would make the final push today to drive the NVA off the big hill.

By mid morning all hell was breaking loose. Gunships pounded the top of the big hill, firing and explosions could be heard constantly. The ground shook as artillery rounds pounded the top prior to the assault. By mid day it was over, the good guys had taken the hill. The lieutenant gathered the men together.

"It's over. We took the hill. In fact we have all of Dong Ap Bia. Reports of escaping NVA are pouring in, but they are also sketchy. Scuttlebutt is that they left during the night last night. Must have known the final assault was coming, especially once we finally took this hill."

The lieutenant paused.

"Good news is we get to take it easy tonight. No ambushes.

We have the high ground now, so it's just a matter of defending it. But, I don't believe anything will happen, they're on the run right now, probably need to regroup before they try anything."

The lieutenant paused again. The men waited.

"We get a day or two of rest, resupply, hold the top for now. After that we'll probably run search and destroy missions to clean up anybody or anything left in the valley. At least that's what the CO said earlier."

The lieutenant started to walk away, but turned back.

"Sergeant, Wilson, Grite, have the men dig in. Spend the afternoon setting up a secure area. Have a detail work on clearing this area for an LZ. The other platoons will do that on this side, while the other company is going to do that on their side. Two bird LZ, I want this mountain top as strong as a fire base. It's our home next couple of days."

This time the lieutenant left. Wilson watched him leave before speaking.

"Listen up. We're gonna do this in two four man teams, one per hole. Four Seven, Hump and Whitey you're with me. Smooth, you Lopes, Big John and Body Man you're in the other hole. We each have a 60 in our hole. Let's get this done and we can take it easy rest of the day. No ambush tonight, just watches, one man per hole. Two hours on, two off. Okay, let's dig."

Several hours later, they were having night chow, sipping coffee and grabbing the last cigarette for the night and the mood was easy. The NVA were still out there and the chance of being attacked during the night was still very possible, but the odds were in their favor this evening. Wilson sat next to Kensington.

"Four Seven, what shift you want tonight?"

"Huh? What?"

"Tonight what shift you want? Early or late?"

"I dunno I was getting used to midnights."

"That what you want?"

"Sure why not."

"Alright then, you got it. See you then. I'll follow you. Rest up."

Wilson slapped him on the leg as he left.

Sam sat against his ruck, his eyes getting heavy as the sun disappeared. The last few days had afforded him and everybody else very little sleep. The tension somewhat subdued now, he let himself relax and in a moment he was fast asleep.

Nineteen

Everett Fremont and Jethro Longworth stood shaking in the morning chill. Samuel Kensington sat near by as the others stood with them anxiously waiting for the coffee to boil. Once again they were stirred before dawn, newly camped in a defensive position around Meadow Brook Ravine.

The sound of the Rebel cry coupled with the fire of muskets could be heard in the distance, but the morning chill and hunkering down with their morning coffee caused some complacency.

Within moments, officers barked orders, as men were formed into columns. Kensington, Fremont, Longworth and Alfred Lanning formed the first four, behind them stood Reginald Harrington, Edgar Fairchild, Rufus Meriweather and Edward Hutchens. Off to the side, as usual, stood Frenchy.

Activity was frenzied, as tents were flattened by a formed detail in preparation for movement of the camp. The dust was flying as troops were called to ranks and the process of packing was in full swing.

Less than a half hour after the explosion of musketry from the Confederates first sounded, the Brigade moved out of camp en echelon, marching toward the left flank, moving sharply eastward toward the sound of battle.

The early morning fog was thick and heavy, preventing any sort of rapid advancement. The column continued to move east, ever shifting to the sounds of other troops moving with them.

The storm of Minie balls fired by the Confederates in barrage after barrage rained down on the advancing soldiers. Men were being hit without knowing where the fire was coming from. Minie balls were flying in the air with such intensity that often a soldier had been hit by so many bullets that his body would actually fall apart. The chaos caused by this rain of Minie balls broke the ranks and scattered the line.

Kensington, Freemont and Lanning joined the others and took cover behind a berm, not more than a small build up of dirt and waited. There was no sense in firing back, at least not until they could see something. The sounds of soldiers moving about all around them brought a sense of anxiety. They could not know for sure who was out there.

Edward Hutchens stood up, straining to see beyond his position.

"Hey Frenchy, you see anything over there?"

Pierre LaSalle, Frenchy, could be counted on to be in a position other than where he would be expected to be. If anybody had a view it would be him.

"No."

"No? Where are you?"

In his usual heavy French accent, he responded somewhat melodically.

"On the left in the tree. The fog is still too thick. All I can see is more trees. Men are moving about, but I believe they belong to us. I'm going to try for a better place."

They could hear rustling as Frenchy moved through the tree. Edward Hutchens waited for a moment before yelling out.

"Anybody see anything?"

A faint chorus of no ran through the line leaving Hutchens frustrated.

"Kensington, is Fremont with you?"

"Yes. So is Jethro and Alfred. We're all over on the right."

"Fine, the others are with me on the left."

Edward Hutchens looked at the men around him.

"Are we just suppose to wait here?"

Before anyone could offer an answer, a blue clad soldier came upon them yelling above the whizzing of Minie balls flying through the air.

"Let's go. We've been ordered to move back, get out of this hell fire."

As quickly as he had come, he was gone. Slowly Hutchens moved his men from the berm toward the rear. Kensington and Fremont waited for Lanning and Longworth to move out before evacuating their position. Hutchens stopped and turned back.

"Frenchy. Frenchy, we're pulling back further."

"I heard, just one more look. I'll be right behind you."

Hutchens had already turned back and was moving with the rest of the men before Frenchy finished his sentence. Frenchy was not one to worry about, he would always find his way. Quietly, they left the berm and slowly moved in the direction the soldier had pointed. The firing had intensified and they were ducking from the sound of Minie balls whizzing by.

Falling in behind another column of men, they were moving back toward the hills adjacent to their campsite, joining up with the rest of the brigade.

Hidden in the fog, the Rebels had penetrated through the lines and were causing disruption in the ranks as the brigade retired to the hills. Shouts could be heard in the distance as men scrambled to make their way back into the ranks. More and more the line had to be opened to let soldiers back in behind their own defenses. The fog was so thick that often times the blue coats could only be identified when they were right upon other blue coats.

Kensington, Lanning, Fairchild and Fremont created one such defense, while Hutchens, Meriweather, Longworth and Harrington were just on the other side of a controlled opening. The sound of several men approaching unnerved them. As had been the norm, Hutchens took charge.

"Who's out there?"

When he didn't get an immediate response, he yelled louder.

"I said, who's out there? Speak up man or you'll be shot."

The movement stopped and voices could be heard whispering. Hutchens yelled again.

"Last chance. Identify yourself or we will commence firing."

When again they heard no response the soldiers pointed and aimed their muskets into the void toward where the commotion came from. Nervously they waited.

Samuel Kensington pulled the revolver from his waistband, drawing the hammer back. Fremont looked at him and nodded then turned back to face forward with his hands tight on his musket.

A voice came from the front where the commotion was.

"No, you identify yourselves, before we shoot you."

Hutchens looked at his men before answering.

"10th Vermont. Who be you?"

"14th New Jersey. We were on your flank, next to the 87th Pennsylvania. Got separated when the Rebels got between us. Took quite a few of those fellows out before we got here. Heard we were pulling back to reform. Been trying to find a way back. You gonna let us in or do we have to find another way?"

Both sides sat silent waiting for the other to make the first move.

"Come on then."

Edward Hutchens stood up, as did Longworth next to him, motioning with his hand to come forward. Kensington and Fremont stood on their side as well, watching and waiting. A steady stream of blue coated soldiers stepped forward. Kensington closed the hammer on the revolver and put the gun back into his waistband.

"Much obliged."

They watched the rest of the soldiers pass by, before getting back into their defensive position guarding that opening.

Federal soldiers were everywhere, resting, nervously waiting. Before long several officers rode through the scattered men and reformed ranks into new lines. The Confederates continued their attack toward the now newly formed blue line.

"Here they come."

Frenchy yelled from a tree branch, quickly lowering himself down to join the others.

Samuel Kensington tightened his grip on his musket, rubbing his hand across the butt of the revolver tucked firmly back into his waistband. Allowing himself a glance sideways he saw Everett Freemont facing forward his grip just as tight on his musket. Next to him Jethro Longworth held his musket in the air, waiting. Further along the line he could see the others in basically the same tense position. Nodding he turned his attention forward. Moments later the Rebels came toward the line.

His was just a small part of the line that put a terrible fire on those advancing Confederates, stopping and turning the Rebel advance. Reloading and firing as fast as he could, he continued to put shot into that gray line. As the Rebels retreated, Kensington looked at Freemont next to him.

"Everett, we stopped them."

"Samuel, I believe they'll be coming back afore we know it."

Edward Hutchens rose up waving his hand in the air.

"Here they come again."

The Confederates charged up the hillside, the Rebel yell preceding them as musket shot rang out from both sides. Kensington saw a gray clad soldier not more'n twenty feet in front of him. He aimed his musket, but the gray clad soldier fell, hit by someone else in the line.

"That was close."

Freemont raised his hand.

"I damn near could have touched him."

The two men reloaded their muskets and fired another Minie ball at the mass in front of them. As the sun broke through the fog, the formation of the Confederate assault could finally be seen. Their advantage now broken, the Rebels started to fall back, finally stopping the assault.

"Let's go."

A mounted officer stood astride his horse behind them ordering the men forward. Slowly the blue coats rose from their positions and marched forward, counterattacking the Confederates, driving them back. Finally the Rebels turned, their assault thwarted. Yells of victory went up as the blue coats celebrated their stand.

A regiment of Federal soldiers moved en echelon after the fleeing Rebels, while an officer on horseback held them back. Edward Hutchens stood by that officer.

"Kensington, you and Freemont get the others, lieutenant says to follow him back to our regiment."

Samuel looked at Everett, they both looked at Edward Hutchens. Kensington waved his hand in the air acknowledging the order. Fremont walked over to where Longworth, Lanning and Fairchild had positioned themselves and motioned for them to join the others.

"I think we got them boys on the run. Looks like we need to join up with the rest get our ranks back together."

Kensington stood next to Freemont.

"Everett, I sure could use some coffee right about now."

"Samuel, my friend I could use something a bit stronger than coffee."

"Yeah, Samuel, a little bark juice would do right about now."

The two men looked at Longworth, smiling. Samuel leaned

back against a tree, while they waited to move. The mass of soldiers milling about unformed was presenting its own problems. Officers astride their horses were trying to direct men into ranks.

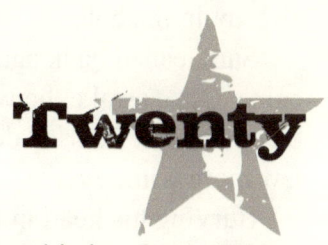

Twenty

Sam Kensington felt the tapping against his leg. In a moment he was awake focusing on the person tapping him. Hump, the new white guy, looked at him.

"You okay. You're up."

"Yeah, fine."

Kensington grabbed his sixteen, and placed the forty-five back in the shoulder holster that was still strapped on. He made his way to the hole, letting his eyes adjust to the dark in front of him. The outline of jungle came into focus.

He agreed with Wilson that the night should be pretty quiet. Once they were driven from the hill, the NVA had more than likely pulled back and would be pretty scarce for a while, at least until they could regroup.

The Americans had control of all the major hill tops and the reports were that the NVA were on the run for now. The night should pass quietly.

Sam hunkered down into a comfortable position, the poncho liner wrapped around his shoulders. For a country that was so fucking hot during the day, it sure could get chilly during the night.

He desperately wanted to light a smoke, but didn't want to drop down into the hole to do that, so he let the urge pass. Another urge was building, the desire to take a leak. He let that one pass as well.

After what seemed like forever, his shift finally ended. Quietly he made his way over to Whitey, tapping him on the leg as Hump had done to him. Whitey was awake immediately, nodding. Before Sam could get back to his ruck, Whitey was already in the hole.

Sam leaned back against his ruck, but sleep would not come. Once awake, he was awake. Determined to get another bit of shuteye, he tried desperately to clear his mind and grab a few more winks.

Burying his head in the poncho liner and crouching between his knees he lit a smoke, taking a few quick puffs, before putting it out in the ground. Pulling the poncho liner back off his head, he gathered the cloth around his shoulders and leaned back against his ruck. Checking his watch he saw it was two forty-five.

Sam Kensington woke with a start, still in the sitting position with his poncho liner wrapped around his shoulders. Daylight greeted him as he opened his eyes. Lopes was boiling water for coffee, while also working on a can of C-rats. Wilson was sipping his coffee already, pulling on a cigarette.

"Four Seven, getting your beauty sleep?"

Sam looked at Wilson and wiped his hand across his face. Without saying anything he reached for Wilson's canteen cup of coffee, took a strong sip, then handed it back.

"Yeah. Haven't slept in days, you know?"

Wilson nodded, pulling on his cigarette.

"Any word on what we're doing today?"

Wilson shook his head no.

"All I know is what I told you yesterday. Figure we'll stay on top for a day or so, maybe run some patrols. Same, same."

Sam nodded, working on his own coffee. Lighting and pulling heavily on a cigarette, Sam leaned toward Wilson.

"I had another dream last night, before my watch."

"Thought you fell asleep rather quick. Didn't even make it to dusk."

Sam nodded.

"Anything we need to know about?"

Sam shook his head no.

"Early morning, having coffee, Confederates attacked, we moved out in formation, something like a serious of steps, moving into the early morning fog. After a bit we pulled back into a defensive position. Troops scattered everywhere trying to get back behind our lines. Don't think it has anything to do with us."

Wilson nodded.

"I need to go meet with the LT, see what's up for the day."

Sam nodded as Wilson got up and walked away. Smooth came over and crouched down next to Sam.

"Hey, Four Seven. You got any skin left on your arms?"

Smooth stuck his arms out, both of which were lined with scratches from cutting through the elephant grass.

Sam nodded, sticking out his arms to show that they were just as cut up.

"Fuckin' A."

Wilson came back and sat down against his ruck. Smooth and Kensington waited for him to speak.

"Yeah, we're holding here for a day or two, maybe more. Going to clear the top, bring in some resupply, clean clothes, C-rats and more ammo."

Wilson paused.

"Word has it that we'll be conducting extensive search and

destroy missions from here back to the fire base, maybe some
RIF operations as well. Probably pull an ambush or two while
we're here."

Smooth and Kensington waited for Wilson to say more, but
when he didn't, Smooth asked first.

"Anything for today?"

Wilson nodded yes.

"LT says in an hour he wants two squads out. Work our way
down the far side of this fucking hill all the way down and back
up on the other side. Other squad down the way we came up
work around and back up."

Smooth nodded, Kensington raised his canteen cup in
the air.

Less than an hour later, they were lined up to go. Smooth walking point, Kensington at slack, Hump behind him, Whitey with
the radio, Body Man, Lopes and Wilson bringing up the rear.
Big John would stay behind, with his 60 in the hole, while they
were out.

Smooth walked them off the top, working his way down
the far side, cutting through elephant grass and some bamboo,
breaking through onto a plateau. Cautiously he worked around
the front, checking out the area. Wilson came up, as Lopes
fell back to pull rear guard. Kensington slid in next to them as
Smooth pointed.

"Beaucoup tracks through here. Lot of debris from arty.
Looks like pieces of equipment scattered about. Nothing looks
fresh, debris on the trail."

Wilson looked out into the open area.

"Yeah, sure looks that way."

Wilson looked over the area once more.

"Let's split up, work our way around, meet up on the other

side. Take it slow."

Smooth nodded. Kensington started to rise, but Wilson put his hand on Sam's shoulder.

"Four Seven, you take Hump, Whitey and Lopes. I got Smooth, and Body Man."

Sam nodded.

"All right, let's go."

Wilson dropped back and pointed each man in the direction they would go. Kensington put Hump on slack, Whitey in the middle and Lopes bringing up the rear. They started to the right of the open plateau, working their way around and staying inside the jungle growth.

They reached the path as it left the jungle into the open area. Again there were several tracks on that trail. Crouching, Kensington pointed and Lopes came around taking a spot just to the right of him, while the others moved up next to him. Pointing, Kensington led the men across the trail into the jungle on the other side.

Two steps in, two men turned back while the other two faced forward. When they were sure it was clear they started to move out and immediately came upon the bodies of three NVA soldiers, one still with his AK47 in his hands.

Lopes pulled the weapon from the dead man's hand, removed the banana clip and ejected the round in the chamber before slinging the weapon over his shoulder.

"Hump, check the bodies for intel."

Louis Humphries looked on, his face contorted in horror. Kensington walked over and put his hand on the new white guy's shoulder.

"Hey, we've all had to do it. You're the fucking new guy, so it's your turn."

Humphries nodded he understood and slowly approached the bodies. The flies scattered, as he got closer. The bodies had already started to bloat, dead for at least a day, probably more.

"Go through the pockets, we'll grab the gear."

Lopes and Sam started pulling the gear away from the dead men, while Humphries went through the pockets handing everything he found to Kensington.

"That's enough, let's get out of here."

Kensington pointed forward, leading the men in a circle around the opening. As he got closer to the other side, he saw Wilson giving him the come forward wave.

"We found three dead gooks, when we crossed the trail. Got an AK, some gear and this stuff."

Kensington showed him a pack of papers, personal effects. Wilson pointed. On the ground was some more gear.

"We found another two same way, other side of the trail. No weapons."

Kensington nodded.

"Shall we head back, drop this stuff off?"

"Negative. Ain't too much, we can carry this shit, finish what we started. Otherwise we have to go back up, then go out again."

Kensington nodded. Smooth walked up, slipping the AK off his shoulder.

"Looks like it will still fire."

Pulling the banana clip from his belt he held it in the air.

"Full clip."

Wilson nodded.

"You okay carrying that?"

Smooth nodded, putting the clip back in his belt and slinging the AK back over his shoulder.

"Let's go."

Wilson nodded.

"Saddle up, we're moving out."

Smooth took point again, with Kensington walking slack. The others fell into place behind him.

An hour later they reached the bottom without finding

anything else. Wilson motioned and they stopped for a break. Lighting a cigarette, Wilson waved his hand in the air and the men gathered around setting a defensive position for a break.

Wilson spoke softly, but knew everyone could hear.

"Okay, we're down. LT said to work our way around and come back up over there. I figure we'll walk the bottom for a bit and start to cut up over there."

The men nodded.

"Whitey, you call it in, tell the LT we're on the bottom, taking five, make our way around head back up. Should be back two to three hours."

Whitey nodded and started the call signs on his horn, relaying the message.

Fifteen minutes later, Wilson had everybody on their feet. Smooth slid into position, again with Kensington at slack. Slowly they made their way over to the area Wilson pointed out. Smooth stopped and waited until Wilson came up. Wilson stood beside him and looked the area over.

"Might be hard to go up there, let's go a little further, see if we can find something better."

Smooth nodded, starting the line moving. Finally he reached an area that looked like it had a more gradual rise that they could climb. He stopped, letting everyone catch up. Just as he was about to turn around he saw something in the distance. Dropping quickly, he raised his hand in a clenched fist and everyone else dropped as well. Wilson made his way to Smooth. Kensington stayed to the side facing out.

"What'cha got?"

Smooth pointed.

"Look over there, just past the rocks."

Wilson strained to see, but wasn't picking up anything.

"Look over the rocks, into that tree line."

Wilson saw it.

"Shit, we should probably check it out."

Smooth nodded.

"Better call it in first."

Wilson nodded and called Whitey up with the radio. After Whitey finished the call signs he handed the horn to Wilson.

"LT's on the horn."

Wilson nodded and took the handset from Whitey

"Sir, looks like we found a downed Huey. Think we should check it out."

Wilson waited, listening to the lieutenant on the horn.

"Roger that, sir. Will do. Out."

Wilson handed the handset back to Whitey.

"LT says go."

Smooth nodded and stood back up, working his way toward the downed bird. He made his way to the rocks and once there they could see it clearly. A Huey had crashed hard into the ground, the rotor blade had broken off and was now setting to the side. The tail boom was crushed and broken. The windshield had smashed out. The site looked deserted. Wilson motioned and the team moved forward from either side of the rocks.

The pilot and the peter pilot were still in their seats, dead. The crew chief lay outside and the door gunner was slumped over his gun still inside the slick. At first glance it looked like they were all killed in the crash, but closer examination showed the pilot and peter pilot had been shot several times. The crew chief had also been shot. The door gunner was the only one who appeared to have died in the crash.

Immediately the men took cover, just in case. After a bit of time, they fanned out and checked the area around the downed bird. Lopes came across two dead NVA, just inside the jungle grass. Weapons and gear were gone. Pulling the bodies into the opening, he yelled out.

"At least they got two of those mother fuckers."

Wilson nodded, looking up.

"Gonna be hard to get these guys out of here. Better call the LT, see what he wants us to do."

Whitey finished the call signs and handed the handset to Wilson.

"LT, we got four dead here and two dead gooks. Pretty tough terrain, to get them out…"

"Yes. Yes, will do. Roger, Out."

Wilson handed the handset back to Whitey.

"LT says to stay here until we get them out or we're relieved. Calling it in now."

Walking a ways from the Huey, Wilson pointed.

"Lopes, you and Hump, set up over there. Smooth, you and Body Man there and Four Seven and I right here. Whitey you stay by the bird with the radio, guide whoever is coming in."

Fifteen minutes later the buffeting of the air could be heard as a Huey arrived. They watched as it hovered just above them.

"Stick, pilot says he's going to drop a basket, get these guys out."

Wilson motioned to Whitey over the noise that he understood.

"Tell him keep an eye out while we load."

Whitey nodded and called it in. A moment later he raised his thumb in the air. Wilson and Kensington removed the door gunner from his gun and laid him out on the floor of the slick. Lopes and Hump put the crew chief in from the other side.

Wilson opened the pilot's door and dragged the pilot out. He still had his forty five in his hand. Wilson removed the gun and put the weapon back in the pilot's holster.

The hoist clanked against the mangled Huey as it lowered down. They put the pilot in the basket and motioned to raise it up. The basket returned and they loaded the peter pilot. Repeating the process for each of the other men, they completed the task of removing the bodies.

Wilson looked up as the last man was lifted out, grabbing Whitey's arm, he talked into Whitey's ear.

"Ask them about the bird, the guns and that stuff."

Whitey nodded speaking into the horn. He smiled and pointed. Just beyond the Huey hovering, was a shit hook, another larger helicopter. Wilson smiled.

They watched as three men repelled from the CH47 cargo helicopter down beside the crashed Huey. Right behind them dropped a set of straps.

"Who's in charge here?"

Wilson stepped up.

"That would be me."

The man released himself from the lines and walked toward Wilson, sticking out his hand.

"Thanks for the help. We're gonna take this thing out of here. Looks like the Jesus Nut broke off."

"The Jesus what?"

The man pointed to the top of the Huey.

"The main rotor retaining nut that holds the blade in place. Once that goes only Jesus can help you."

Wilson smiled.

"Looks like three of them were shot, might have survived the crash. We found a couple of gooks in the bush, might have taken them out first."

The man looked where Wilson was pointing and nodded.

"Didn't know, thought they were killed in the crash."

Wilson nodded.

"Listen, if you men don't mind holding for a bit, while we get this bird out of here, sure appreciate it."

Wilson stood with his sixteen resting on his hip.

"Fuckin' A."

Spreading his men around the Huey, Wilson motioned for them to take up a position protecting the area.

Less than an hour later the bird was hooked up and as the

three men climbed aboard, the Huey was extracted from the jungle. In a wind storm from the shit hook blades the Huey lifted and disappeared into the air. The man leaned out waving, as they were airborne. In a moment all was quiet.

Wilson gathered the men around.

"Look, if the gooks didn't try anything all the time we were here and while they were pulling that bird out, I gotta believe there ain't any around. "

He looked at each of the men before continuing.

"Four Seven, you got the mountain goat in you. How about you get us back up this fucking hill?"

Kensington smiled.

"Fuckin' A."

Sam made his way back to the point they had thought would be a good spot to start the assent. Climbing and shifting, Kensington worked the side of the hill as efficiently as he could. The team finally reached the top at sixteen hundred hours, hot and exhausted from the all day patrol.

Stopping at their position the men dropped down beside their rucks. Wilson dropped his gear and steel pot, but remained standing.

"I'd better go brief the LT."

Sam watched him leave, turning to Smooth.

"What'd you say about your arms this morning?"

Smooth smiled.

"What arms?"

Kensington raised his hand in the air.

Wilson was back before Sam finished his cigarette.

"LT says he heard several birds went down over the last couple of days. They're still looking for some of them. Crews been fifty-fifty on getting out. Might be a couple of more like we found, crew still inside."

Kensington lit another cigarette.

"Looks like we're here for another night at least. Pull out in the morning, in platoon strength, like before. Sweep the valley, make sure it's clear."

Kensington nodded, pointing with his cigarette.

"Same, same for tonight?"

Wilson nodded yes.

"You still want midnight?"

"Sure, why not?"

The two men sat silent for a bit.

"Hey, did we get the resupply today?"

Wilson nodded yes.

"Over there. Clothes, Cs and ammo if you need it."

Kensington looked to where Wilson was pointing. Lopes, Hump and Body Man were picking through the resupply.

"Well I better get mine before it's all gone."

"Fuckin' A."

Kensington got up from beside his ruck and made his way to the resupply pile, searching for a change of clothes. His were pretty rank and the desire for a shower, even a 55 shower would have to wait. At least a fresh set of clothes would help. Stripping out of his shirt and pants right there, he dropped the well used fatigues in a pile and quickly put on the fresh set. Grabbing some more C-rats and a couple of boxes of M16 ammo, he went back to his ruck, reloading the spent magazines.

As dusk approached, the men got quiet, talking in whispers. Evening chow, a set of fresh shirt, pants and socks made them feel a little better. Although a hot shower and a hot meal would be just the thing, they made do with what they had. Lopes had said it first.

"Even a little Tiger Piss would go down about now."

"Tiger Piss, that fucking Ba-Moi-Ba Vietnamese Beer?"

"Yeah, even that would taste good about now."

The others smiled. Big John spoke up.

"Hell, I wish I had some of my home grown right about now. I've been dry way too long."

Louis Humphries reached into his ruck. He had a container of something that he offered to the squad.

"It's a little of Big John's home grown mixed with some Kentucky Bourbon that I was saving for, you know, for when we might need it."

"Damn Hump, you had this all the time and didn't offer me none?"

Smooth was reaching for the container.

"I think Stick should have first sip. He got us here."

"Fuckin' A," went around as each man chimed in.

Wilson took a sip, handing it to Kensington, who handed it to Smooth, and on and on, until each man had a sip. Wilson waited until each man had his turn.

"That tasted so bad it was good. Four Seven, that what you got fucked up on when I took the new guys out?"

Kensington nodded.

"Big John, what the fuck is that shit?"

Big John explained how it was made.

"Thank Jesus there was some bourbon in it, kill that taste."

Big John smiled. Hump held the container out.

"There's a little left."

"You drink it, you earned it, carrying it all this time."

Louis Humphries downed the last of the liquid, his face contorting as he swallowed.

"Here's to us."

"Fuckin' A."

Hump tapped Sam's leg at midnight.

"You're up."

Kensington made his way to the hole, adjusting his focus to the dark of night, slowly taking in the same jungle features that had greeted him the night before.

Allowing himself the luxury of relaxing he settled into his shift, which seemed to pass quickly tonight. Before he realized it, his time was over. Making his way over to Whitey, he tapped his leg.

"You're up."

Whitey sat up, nodded, grabbed his gear and made his way to the hole. Sam settled down next to his ruck, covering himself with the poncho liner as he gathered inside the warmth. In a moment he was fast asleep.

Twenty-One

After stopping the Confederate advance, the lines were able to refresh their erratic front on the hills north of the hastily abandoned Federal camp. Once Colonel J. Warren Keifer's Brigade stopped the Rebel pursuit, he was able to regroup his men. Knowing the Confederates would return for another thrust, he braced for the next wave.

The Confederates, encompassing Kershaw's three Brigades, rose up from Meadow Brook Ravine, crossing the same ground they had earlier. Again they passed through the abandoned Federal campsite and drove toward the knolls occupied by Keifer's Brigade.

Samuel Kensington braced as the call went out. Looking over toward Everett Freemont on his left and Jethro Longworth on his right, he could see the rest of the men braced and ready.

"Samuel, you ready?"

"Let 'er rip."

"Everett?"

"Let 'er rip. Jethro, what about you?"

"Ready."

They waited as the Confederates broke from the ravine and

started toward them. A torrent of Minie balls poured from the blue line as the Federals unleashed a barrage of musket fire, followed close behind with cannon shot flying over their heads, dropping the Rebels and driving them back.

The order was given to advance.

Samuel Kensington, Everett Fremont and Jethro Longworth stood up and stepped from their defensive position. Alfred Lanning and Reginald Harrington came forth from their left. Edgar Fairchild and Rufus Meriweather came forth from their right. Edward Hutchens stepped between them.

"Let's go, men."

Raising his musket in the air, he led them forward toward the advancing Confederates. Before they could get very far the assault was called off and the men ordered back into position.

Edward Hutchens waved his hand in the air.

"We're advancing on our own men. Go back. Go back."

"What?"

"There's blue coats to the front of us, we've overlapped. Go back."

Samuel Kensington grabbed the sleeve of Everett Fremont, pulling him back. Jethro Longworth turned and looked at them falling back. He turned to Alfred Lanning next to him and did the same. Through the haze of smoke and lingering fog, they were able to reach out to each other and the men returned to their positions just as Rebel cannon shot fell all around where they had been. The dirt and debris flew through the air.

"If that don't beat the Dutch?"

Edward Hutchens was breathing hard standing between the two groups of men now back in their defensive positions.

"There was a whole line of blue coats on our left flank, marching right into us. Damned if that don't happen we would've been blown to pieces."

Another barrage of cannon shot hit the area they had just been in, followed by the Rebel yell.

"Here they come, boys."

Once again they let loose with a barrage of musket fire, shooting Minie balls into the advancing Confederates, again repelling their advance.

The retreat had left the advancing cannons exposed and now the Rebels were converging on them as they moved forward. Colonel William Emerson, commander of the First Brigade, made his way down the line ordering the men of the 10th Vermont to retake those cannon at once.

Samuel Kensington, Everett Fremont and Jethro Longworth rose from their position on the left, as did Alfred Lanning, Reginald Harrington and Edgar Fairchild who rose from their position on the right. Rufus Meriweather and Edward Hutchens joined from behind as they did the quick step forward toward the overrun cannon. Frenchy joined in from somewhere as he always did.

"Forward men. Follow the rest of our fine troops."

Samuel Kensington looked at the Colonel astride his horse riding alongside him. The first line of soldiers to reach the cannon were cut down in a barrage of Minie balls. The second line met with the same fate, but the third line broke through to the cannon before being cut down. Samuel Kensington and his men were in the fourth line. They followed the third line into position and, as the Confederates were doing battle with the men before them, they were able to penetrate through the Confederate line. The next two lines followed them in as well.

Too close to each other to fire a musket, the soldiers from both sides resorted to hand to hand combat.

Samuel Kensington was knocked to the ground from the blow of a Confederate musket. Bracing up on the ground he was able to avoid the next blow as the musket came crashing down. His own musket lay a short distance away. Without hesitating, he pulled the revolver from his waistband and fired a shot into the Rebel as he was raising his musket over his head to bring down on him. The Rebel staggered and dropped his musket harmlessly away. Falling to his knees, he clutched his gut.

Samuel Kensington looked away in time to see another Rebel about to smash his musket into the side of Everett Fremont's head. Pointing quickly he fired the revolver at the gray clad soldier, turning him.

"Everett."

Everett Fremont turned to see that Rebel soldier stagger away, clutching his gut. Walking over to where Kensington lay, he offered his hand and pulled Samuel to his feet.

"Much obliged."

Samuel Kensington nodded, the pistol at his side. Too hot to put back in his waistband, he held the gun in his right hand as he picked up his musket from the ground with his left.

A bloody hour later, the 10th Vermont was able to recapture the lost cannon, suffering heavy losses in the process.

Samuel Kensington looked around and thought he could see all of the men from his group. Although bloodied and battered they were all okay. He walked over to Fremont.

"Everybody accounted for?"

Fremont nodded yes.

"The line in front of us took the brunt of the assault. By the time we came through, they were on the run."

Kensington nodded. Longworth came over with Lanning and Hutchens and stood beside them, breathing heavily.

"I saw Fairchild and Meriweather over there. They looked okay. Haven't seen Harrington yet, but Edward Hutchens is by that cannon over there. He might have a broken wrist. Took a musket swung at him straight on."

The other men nodded they understood.

Frenchy walked up to them, with Harrington tagging along. Frenchy guided him to the ground and in his French accented broken English spoke softly.

"He'll be okay, just rattled a bit. Had his bell rung."

Frenchy pointed to his head.

Before the men had a chance to gather themselves and start rearward, they were ordered back, but the musketry was coming from the front and flank and they were forced to flee their position, once again abandoning the crest they were on.

"Let's go, we're moving. They're coming from the ravine. We need to fall back."

The men looked up. Edward Hutchens was pointing to the rear, further from the crest they had been driven off. Quickly they formed and started the quick step from their present location, marching further back. Other units around them were also streaming backward.

Finally the retreat was stopped and the remaining units regrouped. Behind trees and makeshift breastworks, they loaded and waited for the advancing Rebels. The cry of the Rebel yell sent a chill up each man's spine as the gray clad troops commenced their charge.

Samuel Kensington gripped his musket tightly waiting. He felt the pistol in his belt, ready to pull the weapon and use it again.

"Everett, they're coming."

"I hear them."

"Jethro?"

"Yeah, I hear them. Damned Rebel yell is unnerving."

"That's for sure."

"Hey Kensington, Fremont, move to your left a bit, we're too tight here."

Edward Hutchens stood behind the men waving his hand to spread them out further.

"Cannon shot will get you all."

Samuel Kensington shifted further to his left, as did Fremont, which caused Samuel to shift even more. Finally they were a good ways apart and again braced for the onslaught.

As the gray coated soldiers emerged from the ravine, the blue line unleashed a thunderous barrage of musket shot, sending the charging troopers reeling and dropping back down the slope. Amidst the wounded and dying, those gray clad soldiers tried once more to advance, but again were met with unrelenting musket shot.

Loading their muskets for another advance the men waited, but the Confederates were being flanked and driven from the ravine by other units closing in. One last burst of Minie ball crashed around them as the fleeing gray coats fired before retreating.

Dirt and debris flew up in front of Samuel Kensington as the Minie ball hit the ground where he lay. The sharp pain as it ricocheted into his shoulder caused him to cry out.

"Kensington, you okay?"

Samuel Kensington's face hit the ground as he tried to absorb the pain in his shoulder.

"Kensington? I think Kensington's been shot."

Everett Fremont was beside him first. Alfred Lanning came from behind sliding into place staying low behind the make shift breastwork. Jethro Longworth approached the same way. As they were about to turn Samuel over, he did it himself.

"I'm fine. Ball hit my shoulder on the ricochet. I'll be fine, soon as the pain subsides. Stung like hell, that's all. I'm fine."

Edward Hutchins was the next to arrive.

"Who's been shot?"

"Kensington."

"How bad?"

"I'm fine I tell you. Just a ricochet hit my shoulder, that's all. I'm fine."

Edward looked at the group of men for a moment, understanding.

"Well, then get back to your positions, this isn't over yet."

Slowly the others dispersed, moving back into their defensive positions, either behind a tree or makeshift breastwork. Edward knelt down next to Samuel Kensington.

"Hurts like hell, don't it?"

Kensington nodded yes.

"Doesn't look like it even broke skin. Probably hit solid on the bone, gonna sting for a while."

Kensington nodded again.

"Take a minute, just lay there. I think the Rebels have been repulsed, but we need to stay put until we're sure. Firing starts, you get back at it, otherwise lay there a bit."

Edward started to rise, but stopped and reached down touching Kensington's arm.

"Maybe rotate that a bit, might ease the stinging."

It was then that Samuel saw the blood on Edward's leg.

"You hit?"

Edward looked down to the blood on his leg.

"Naw, just scraped it against a tree branch when the Rebs first assaulted."

Smiling, Edward leaned in closer.

"After I fired my first volley, I slipped and caught the branch. But you tell anyone I'll deny it."

Edward Hutchens was up and gone before Samuel Kensington had a chance to respond. Letting himself lay there on his back, he started to rotate his arm to ease the stinging in his shoulder.

The musket fire grew distant as the Rebels were driven further back, away from where they were. Fremont called out.

"Kensington. How you doing?"

"I'm fine Everett, just fine."

"I think we got them boys on the run."

"I think you're right Everett. I think you're right."

A sudden surge of pain hit Samuel as he rotated his arm. Stopping quickly he rubbed his hand over the area and felt a lump growing there. Squeezing softly he tried to lessen the pain.

Twenty-Two

The sun was shining brightly in the sky overhead. It was obviously later in the morning than he usually woke. Sam Kensington sat up, squinting against the bright sun. Wilson handed him his canteen cup. The coffee was lukewarm, but he drank it anyway.

"Must have slept in."

"Fuckin' A, Four Seven. Need your beauty sleep, looking kinda ragged lately."

Sam looked at Wilson, finally smiling.

"Thought you were gonna keep me from sleeping?"

"Nothing going on would if I could."

Sam nodded as he rubbed his shoulder, the pain sharp, almost stinging. Wilson noticed.

"What's up with the shoulder?"

"I got shot with a Minie ball."

"A what?"

"A Minie ball, you know, fired from a musket."

"Need me to get the medic?"

"Huh? What? No."

Wilson nodded.

"How you get shot with a Minie ball?"

Kensington sat silent for a moment, still rubbing his shoulder, the stinging subsiding.

"Well, I wasn't actually shot, I was hit by a ricochet during the Confederate advance."

Wilson started to ask, but remained silent, waiting for Kensington to explain.

"We were attacking back and forth. We attacked them, they attacked us. After being driven from a crest we were forced back into a defensive position when the Confederates came up the ravine. As they were retreating they fired one last volley. A Minie ball struck the ground in front of me and must have ricocheted into my shoulder."

Wilson nodded.

"That's about it really.

"And you feeling that pain?"

Kensington looked at Wilson and stopped rubbing his shoulder.

"No. Of course not."

"Then why you keep rubbing your shoulder?"

Sam looked at Wilson rubbing his hand across the shoulder.

"Must have slept wrong, that's all. Shoulder's a little tight."

Wilson looked at him, but remained silent. Sam stopped rubbing the shoulder and shrugged to adjust his shoulders.

"Usual stuff. Don't think it means anything. But I will tell you this. When the Confederates overran our cannon, our Colonel rode down the line ordering us to retake the cannon and he followed us into the battle. Our brigade commander astride his horse right beside us. How about that shit?"

Wilson smiled.

"Ain't no officers in the field, riding into battle. Must be a fucking dream. Ain't never gonna happen here."

Sam smiled and shifted back against his ruck, his shoulder

gripped with a searing pain. He rode out the sharp pain, not letting on to Wilson that it was happening, not sure how he would explain it anyway.

"So what's on the agenda for today?"

Wilson shook his head no.

"Don't know anything yet. LT said that we were gonna move off this fucking hill today, start our RIF operation through the valley back toward the firebase. Probably break into platoon strength later and do some search and destroy along the way. Usual shit."

Sam nodded.

"I better get some coffee going, crab some Cs before it gets too late."

Wilson nodded. Smooth joined them.

"Just heard from a guy in the other platoon, said he heard we're moving off the hill late morning."

Wilson nodded. Sam looked up from his church key punched C-rat can, as the heat tab inside fired under his canteen cup, warming the liquid for his coffee.

"Have time for coffee?"

Smooth looked at him, Wilson smiled.

"Fuckin' A."

Wilson left with Smooth. They walked off toward the interior of the perimeter.

Watching as they got further away, Sam allowed himself a peek at his shoulder under his jungle fatigue shirt. The lump was small, but the skin had turned a nasty color of black and blue. The skin was tender to the touch and the pain was now a dull sting.

"Fuck me." He said it out loud, then quickly looked around, but no one was within earshot, or saw what he was doing.

The water boiling, he added the package of coffee and stirred the contents, then slowly sipped the hot liquid. Next, he placed a can of C-rats on the flame, pork stuff, another fine breakfast.

Just as Sam was finishing his can of pork stuff, Wilson was back, sliding in beside him, next to his ruck.

"I just confirmed with LT that we are moving out in a couple of hours."

Sam continued chewing his last bite.

"LT said we're leaving in company strength, down to the valley floor, stay together for another day, then we're gonna break into platoons and crisscross the valley back to the firebase, maybe five days, maybe a week to get there."

Kensington touched his heat can to see if it had cooled off enough to pack away. Taking the last sips of coffee he rinsed out the canteen cup and put that back on his ruck. Satisfied the heat can was cool enough, he packed that away as well. Wilson watched silently.

"Stick, who's leading the way out of here?"

"We are. You are. Since we're here, the CO said to have our platoon take us out. LT said we're coming off the hill by platoon. Us first, then the rest. We'll regroup on the valley floor, maybe spend a day or two together still, before we head out. Don't know until we get down there."

Sam sat back against his ruck and took a long pull on a freshly lit cigarette.

At eleven hundred, Kensington was standing at the edge, steel pot on backwards, the sixteen at his side, the forty-five shoulder holster cutting across the shoulder where the lump was. He had stuck some cardboard from a C-rat box in to buffer the area against the strap. The ruck sat firmly on his shoulders, but on top the shoulder holster. Shifting to adjust the weight load, the ruck rose up and actually alleviated the pain in his shoulder.

Grimacing, he turned around to see Smooth at slack, Wilson behind him, Body Man next, Big John with the 60, then Whitey with the radio, Hump and Lopes, the rest of the platoon behind them. Wilson waved his hand forward and Sam started the trek down the hill to the valley floor.

Following a staggered path, occasionally crossing over the well formed trail, Sam lead them off the mountain. Twice they came across NVA bodies on the trail, along with artillery debris and scattered equipment from the strikes. The bodies had been stripped of gear and weapons and were now just rotting in the intense jungle heat, the flies setting up shop on the decomposing flesh.

At the bottom they fanned out, forming a perimeter that grew as each platoon moved into a defensive position. By the time the last of the company was down it was already late afternoon and thoughts of running a patrol before dark were overshadowed by the efforts needed to setup a company size NDP.

Wilson set the watch and, as usual, Kensington had the midnight to two shift.

"Don't think there's much going on out there. Think we may have run the gooks out of the valley for now."

Sam nodded.

"What are you hearing?"

Wilson looked at him and smiled.

"Talked to a brother over in third platoon and he said he heard they were on the run. Once we took the big hill and ran them out, they di di maued back into Laos."

Sam smiled and lowered his head.

"And?"

"And what?"

"That all you have? I'm sure there's brothers all over this fucking valley that knows shit."

Wilson smiled, sticking out his hand. They did the white version of the black dap hand shake.

"Amen to that. Only way we can stay on top of you white redneck mother fuckers."

"I ain't no fucking redneck."

"Amen, brother."

Sam smiled, punching Wilson on the arm.

"I'd rather be called a brother, than no fucking redneck."

Wilson smiled, letting out a small chuckle.

"I'll tell Smooth you one of us now."

"Amen to that."

They sat in silence. Sam pulled and lit a cigarette from his pack, offering the pack to Wilson, who declined.

"You got any menthols? Throat dry as a mother fucker."

Sam reached into his ruck, removing a slightly crushed pack of menthol cigarettes. He handed the pack to Wilson who opened the pack and pulled a cigarette out then handed the pack back to Sam.

"Keep it, I got more."

Wilson put the pack inside his fatigue shirt pocket. Lighting the cigarette, he took a long pull before speaking.

"Four Seven, you want to tell me about that shoulder?"

Sam looked over at Wilson.

"Nothing to tell. Slept wrong. Got a knot won't break. You want to give me a rub down, make it all better?"

Wilson smiled.

"That the way you want to play it, okay by me."

Again, they sat silent, pulling on their cigarettes. Letting out the smoke deliberately, Sam spoke softly.

"Damndest thing. My shoulder has a lump and it's all black and blue, hurt like a mother fucker when I put the ruck on, but feels better now. I can't fucking explain it."

Wilson nodded.

"What you say hit you? A Minie ball? What the fuck is that anyway?"

Sam finished his cigarette and ground out the butt on the

ground in front of him.

"It's a round ball of lead fired from a musket, or a pistol. A little black powder, a percussion cap and boom, you have a single shot. Imagine having only that here. No auto. No rock 'n roll. Just think, if us grunts only had a musket to fight with, one shot at a time, reload…"

Sam saw Wilson staring at him.

"Sorry."

They sat silent for a spell. Finally Sam continued.

"I can't explain it. Dream about getting hit with a ricochet and wake up with a bruised shoulder. Has to be a coincidence. Somehow I hurt that shoulder. Hell, I'm not even sure it's the same shoulder. Can't remember."

Again they sat silent. Sam pulled another cigarette from his pack, pressing the flame from his lighter to the tip, pulling heavily, before releasing the smoke from his lips.

"You know the weird thing is that I'm dreaming again. Had a few days there, nothing."

"You didn't get a chance to do any real sleep."

"True, but still."

Wilson laid his head back against his ruck.

"Maybe we get back, talk to the XO some more, find out what that war, or maybe that battle has to do with anything. Might make some sense."

Kensington nodded.

"How about we get some chow and let it rest."

"Fuckin' A."

Wilson reached into his ruck and pulled out a can of C-rats.

"Maggots and brains. What'cha got?"

"More pork shit. All that was left when I got to the resupply. Trade you for that spaghetti?"

Wilson smiled.

"Four Seven, tell you what I'm gonna do. Let's cook up this shit and split it. You get half my maggots and brains and I'll take half your pork shit."

"Deal."

Sam Kensington sat against his ruck, watching the light fade away. Wilson slid in next to him against his ruck.

"Damn Four Seven, you usually asleep by now. You got watch in a few hours, might want to get some shut eye?"

"Slept in today remember. Didn't really do much today, all downhill. Not tired at all."

Wilson nodded.

"Remember that when Hump be waking you for your shift."

Sam nodded, but Wilson was already under his poncho liner, he sat there a while longer, not sure he wanted to sleep. No sleep, no dream. Besides his shoulder was still throbbing. What if something else happens? What then. This was getting just too fucking weird. One thing to dream, but to physically feel something was… well, just too fucking weird.

He pulled the poncho liner up around his shoulders, lying back against his ruck. Just when he thought he was dozing off, the tapping started on his leg. Hump was tapping him.

"Four Seven, you're up."

Kensington sat up, dropping the poncho liner from his chest. The sudden movement sent a sharp pain through his shoulder. Trying to ignore it, he made his way over to the hole and set up for watch. As usual, he waited for his eyes to adjust to the dark in front of him.

"I hope Stick is right, nothing happens tonight, not ready for action," he whispered to the open space in front of him. Absently, he rubbed his shoulder and once again whispered to the dark. "Just too fucking weird."

Once his watch was over, he made his way out of the hole and tapped Whitey on the leg.

"You're up, man."

Whitey sat up, then grabbed his weapon and steel pot before making his way to the hole. Sam hunkered down, resting his head on his ruck as a makeshift pillow. The poncho liner gathered over his head and chest. The steady hum of mosquitoes outside the covering lulled him to sleep. The throbbing in his shoulder started to rise up into a sharp pain, but quickly disappeared as he drifted off. In a moment he was fast asleep.

Twenty-Three

Everett Fremont sat next to Samuel Kensington watching as he rubbed his shoulder.

"How's the shoulder feel?"

"Not bad, a little sore that's all. I think Edward might be right, the Minie ball must of hit the bone."

Jethro Longworth came over and sat beside them.

"I think we're moving out. Heard them say, we're gonna attack before they come back and attack us."

The men sat silent, Kensington still rubbing his shoulder. Looking at Jethro he asked solemnly.

"Any of the other men hit?"

Jethro shook his head no.

"I was with Edward Hutchens, afore I came over. He's okay, hand a little swollen where he took the musket hit. Alfred Lanning and Edgar Fairchild said they took some debris, but no lead from that cannon shot that damn near got us earlier. Rufus Meriweather says nothing can get him."

The men chuckled. Jethro continued.

"Reginald Harrington, I think twisted his ankle jumping behind the breastworks, but he says he can go on, just a little sore."

"What about Frenchy?"

"Pierre. Good ole Pierre LaSalle. Hell, he's... hell he's Frenchy. Wouldn't know if anything was wrong anyway. I suppose he's okay. Haven't seen him since we repulsed that last assault by the Rebs."

Kensington nodded, as he rose from his position. He stood and wind milled his arm, trying to loosen the tightness in his shoulder.

The order finally came down to move out, the column was advancing. Now that the Rebels were on the run, it was time to finish the attack. As the men formed the lines, the order was given to advance. As the divisions moved forward, confusion caused the ranks to overlap and in one instance spread too far apart.

The confederates took advantage of this gap and fired their muskets and cannon into the breech, creating chaos among the troops, scattering them in all directions and eventually chasing them back into the woods. The loss of men, both dead and wounded was extremely heavy. The ranks broke and dispersed in disarray, fleeing as best they could. Being hit from an exposed flank prevented the advancing troops from forming any kind of defense and the reaction was to flee until they could reform.

Samuel Kensington, Everett Fremont, Jethro Longworth and Alfred Lanning made their way into a tree line before stopping and firing into the advancing Rebels. The other men stopped further down and prepared to fire before the cry came to halt. Several officers rode up, steadying the shaken men and ordering them back into ranks.

Slowly the men left their defensive positions forming back into the line and advancing forward. This time the breech was closed and the line moved forward en echelon toward the Confederate line. Gray coated skirmishers fired once before fleeing back to their lines.

Samuel Kensington, Everett Fremont, Jethro Longworth and Alfred Manning followed the pickets up to the wall. They could see Edgar Fairchild, Rufus Meriweather and Reginald Harrington next to them behind the pickets as well. The men nodded to each other. Edward Hutchens joined them at the wall. The Pickets fell back as the men took a position behind the rock wall, moments ago defended by those gray clad skirmishers.

"Fremont, Kensington, Longworth, Lanning, you boys set?"

They all nodded.

"Fairchild, Meriweather, Harrington, how you boys doing over there?"

"Fine," was the quick response from the men.

"Where the hell is Frenchy?"

"Edward, my good man, I'm right here."

Edward Hutchens looked over to see Frenchy set up on a tree branch giving him a look see over the wall, down a ways.

"And?"

"My dear Edward, I can see the gray line."

Edward Hutchens nodded, looking back and after receiving the signal shouted, "Now."

The roar of musketry sang out as every man on the line fired his musket toward that gray line. Quickly loading and firing again, they were met with a return volley, but most of the Minie balls aimed at them fell short. They were too far apart, which made everyone realize cannon shot was soon to follow.

"Hey, Samuel?"

"What, Everett?"

"I'm out of caps, got any you can spare?"

"Sure, I have quite a few left."

"Fine. Fine."

Samuel Kensington handed Everett a handful of percussion caps.

"Thought we were getting those Spencer repeaters. War will be over afore we get our hands on those."

"Samuel, I believe you're right. Edward, when do we get those Spencer repeaters we were promised? I'm still carrying cartridges."

Edward Hutchens looked at Everett Fremont, then turned his gaze to Samuel Kensington.

"Damned if I know. They told me we'd have them before the first battle."

"Hear that Samuel? We have them already."

Samuel Kensington smiled, waving his hand in the air.

"I'll remember that next time I have to load this thing after one shot."

"What you talking about? You still got that pistol, get six more off, before you have to reload."

Samuel Kensington felt the pistol tucked into his belt. He had only used it once so far and that was when they retook the captured cannon. He smiled.

"Now you know why I carry it, Everett."

"Still think it's too heavy to put up with, you use maybe once or twice."

"It only takes once."

"Maybe you're right, Samuel, maybe you're right."

The order was given to advance forward as the lines came back together, again moving out en echelon toward the gray line in front of them. The overall mass of blue coats moved toward the Rebels, this time they remained closed and tight as they advanced. Finally the gray line broke and began retreating and scattering in all directions.

This time the Federals bore down on the scrambling Confederates, breaking each of the defensives, further driving them out and finally pushing them from the captured Federal campsite taken during the morning's Rebel attack.

As the Federal troops moved back into their camp they

found the camp had been looted and plundered by the fleeing confederates. Gear, equipment and personal items left hastily when they were driven out were now scattered about or missing.

"Damn Everett, those damn Rebels like to take anything wasn't tied down."

"Samuel, our tent is still standing, but there's nothing left in it. Fortunately I had everything I needed with me."

"As did I, Everett."

The two men stood outside their leaning tent looking at the mess on the ground as items must have been dropped or just not able to be carried once the fleeing started.

The others stood outside their tents, experiencing the same feelings. Edward Hutchens walked about.

"We're back, that's all that matters. Quartermaster can replace anything missing. You boys need to gather up and see what you need, don't just stand around staring. We've been through the mill, but we're back in camp and those secessionists are on the run."

Edward Hutchens stood silent looking over the area trashed with dropped belongings and littered with items.

"Think of it this way boys, it's still better than bivouac, at least we have tents to work with for the night."

Edward Hutchens walked away. The men stood another moment before removing their haversack, gear and muskets. Fremont spoke.

"Well, it won't clean itself up. Let's get started."

Later that night word arrived that several Confederate wagons, including ambulances, cannon and several hundred Confederate prisoners had been captured on the road trying to flee the valley.

The men gathered around a campfire outside their tents, discussing the day's events.

"Sure wish we had some Bark Juice to take the edge off."

"Well Everett, I did have some stashed, but not no more. Rebs got it."

"Damn Rufus, couldn't you have hidden it better?"

The men chuckled.

"I did, but they took that too."

"Took what?"

"My long johns. I had an extra pair I was saving to change into. Five days in these is about all I can stand."

"Yeah, it's all we can stand, too."

The men chuckled.

"Wish we got something fresh to eat. That hardtack and salt horse we had sure left me with the fear of the Virginia quick step."

"Everett, whatever that meat was this time, mixed with those crackers that passes for bread will probably back you up anyway."

"Samuel, hardtack is not fit to eat, whether you call it crackers or not and I'd like to know what kind of salted meat we ate this time. All those horses killed today leaves me wondering."

"Pork."

"What?"

Alfred Lanning pointed to the campfire.

"I heard it was pork, salted pork. Captured a lot of the Rebel's stores and cattle."

Everett Fremont nodded.

"Just the same. If the damn secesh don't kill you the food just may."

The men laughed again.

"You're right, Everett. The secessionists may have started this, but we're damn sure gonna finish it."

The men looked at Edgar Fairchild, nodding their agreement. They sat silent around the campfire, basking in the heat of the flames. It had been a long day starting with being driven from the campsite, routed twice, overran, flanked, retreated and advanced, finally reclaiming their camp. It felt good to sit by the fire and rejoice in the day's victory.

One by one the men broke off and returned to their tent for the night. Everett Fremont, Samuel Kensington and Jethro Longworth remained by the fire late into the night, sitting silently for long spells.

"Samuel, what you say about that pistol? That's your good luck piece?"

Samuel Kensington nodded, his hands folded in his lap, the butt of the pistol inside the left palm, looking over at Everett Fremont.

"Well, we sure were lucky today. Been lucky all the way, but today?"

Pointing, Everett swept his hand in the air.

"That cannon shot just missed us, would have left most of us in pieces. I ain't no religious man, but I gotta think God was looking over us. A minute. Just a minute and we would have been fodder for the animals. How you figure we dodge that?"

Samuel started to answer, but Jethro spoke first.

"Fate. It wasn't our time, that's all."

"Then how do you explain our surviving the assault on the cannon? When the Rebels captured our cannon and we were ordered to retake them, we lost a good part of our unit. It surely was a remarkable day for us."

Everett turned toward the tents behind him.

"For them, for us. We're all still here, no one badly wounded… or worse, killed."

He looked at Samuel.

"Begging your pardon Samuel, I know that shoulder must hurt something terrible, but you know what I mean."

Samuel Kensington nodded, waiting to see if anymore would be said before he spoke. Satisfied, he could, he spoke softly, just above a whisper.

"I ain't no religious man either, and I do believe God had a hand in today's fate, we sure saw the elephant today. And I will agree we sure were fortunate on many occasions, but beyond that I'm not sure luck had anything to do with it."

Everett Fremont looked at his friend and fellow soldier. Jethro Longworth kept his focus on Samuel as well, waiting for him to continue. Kensington looked up from the fire.

"I mean, sure everything involves a little luck, we all know that."

He paused as he gathered his words.

"Let's just leave at we had a good, victorious day and that we're still here to talk about it. I don't think we need to make any more of it."

Jethro nodded his agreement. Everett smiled.

"Samuel, I believe you're right. Now if you boys will excuse me, I think it's time to turn in."

Jethro tossed his stick into the fire.

"Same for me. See you boys in the morning."

Samuel Kensington nodded goodbye as the two men left, leaving him alone in front of the fire, now starting to burn down, the light fading. His left palm still resting on the butt of the pistol in his waistband, he pulled the weapon free and held the pistol in the air. Softly he whispered to the fire.

"Everett, you may be right, we sure were lucky today."

Sticking the gun back into his waistband, he stood and stared at the fire for another moment before turning and heading toward his tent, the throbbing in his shoulder starting to subside. The lump was almost gone, only the discolored skin remained of his encounter with an errant, but gratefully deflected Minie ball.

Sure, luck had nothing to do with anything. He smiled at the thought.

Twenty-Four

Wilson reached over and tapped Kensington on the leg.

"Hey Four Seven, wake up."

Sam Kensington opened his eyes and looked up at Wilson.

"You fidgeting something fierce."

Kensington sat up and wiped his hand over his eyes. Looking outward first, then back over to Wilson, he stretched.

"What did you say?"

Wilson looked up from cleaning his weapon.

"I said you be fidgeting. Figured you were dreaming again, thought I'd put you out of your misery."

Kensington nodded, sitting up against his ruck.

"Yeah."

Wilson nodded.

"Thought so."

Wilson handed him his canteen cup filled with coffee.

"Fresh cup, thought you might need it."

Kensington nodded.

"Thanks."

Wilson offered the pack of smokes. Sam took one and waited for Wilson to flame his lighter, then leaned forward to get a light. Pulling heavily on the cigarette, Sam fell back against his ruck. He took a sip of the coffee before speaking. Wilson sat silent focused on his weapon.

"Heavy day of battle. Confederates drove us from our camp, ran us back a ways, until we regrouped. We attacked back, got flanked and fled again. Finally got it together and routed them from the camp and drove them back. Sat around the campfire with the men in the unit. Went to sleep."

Wilson looked up and over at Kensington, smiling.

"Just like that?"

"Just like that."

Sam took another pull on his cigarette, letting the smoke drift out.

"And yes, my shoulder still hurts."

Wilson nodded.

"What you think that means?"

"The shoulder or the battle?"

"Both."

Sam nodded, taking a sip of coffee and another pull on the cigarette.

"The shoulder is what it is, can't do anything about that."

He took a pull on the cigarette, the smoke drifting as he talked.

"The battle seems important, maybe significant, the way everyone is acting. Said something about capturing the Rebels fleeing with wagons and equipment. Don't know much more that that, but the mood around the camp is relaxed. Maybe we accomplished something. Just a feeling I get."

Wilson looked up at Kensington.

"What you think?"

Sam ground his cigarette after taking the last pull.

"Seems like it was a big deal we got back in our camps. Damn Confederates plundered the camp, trying to take everything we left."

Wilson smiled.

"You thing the gooks wouldn't do that they had a chance?"

Sam smiled as he waved his hand in the air.

"Of course they would, but this seemed different, more like an act of desperation. They took things like clothes and blankets, stuff like that. I don't think the gooks would give a shit about our poncho or poncho liners."

Sam reached for his cigarettes and removed and lit another, drawing heavily before continuing.

"It just seemed all so desperate is all I'm saying."

"And you got all that from a dream?"

Sam sat silently pulling on his cigarette.

"Not sure, just something I feel."

Wilson nodded as he finished putting his weapon back together, thoroughly cleaned.

"Well Four Seven, as much as I'd like to continue, time we got going."

"Going? Going where?"

"Need to go see the LT, find out what we're doing today."

Sam smiled, raising his hand in the air. Wilson walked away. He thought about what he had just told Wilson about the dream, more importantly what he thought was the feeling. Was it all just the dream, or could it be more?

"Hey, Four Seven?"

Smooth stood over him.

"Stick go see the LT?"

"Yeah, wants to find out what we're doing today."

Smooth sat down next to him.

"Heard something from a guy in second platoon that we might be getting resupplied here before we move out."

Sam nodded, pointing.

"You know, you and me been doing all the point and slack work."

Smooth nodded.

"Fuckin' A."

"What I mean is that maybe it's time one of the new guys takes point and one of us walks slack."

Smooth smiled.

"You think they ready?"

"No one is ever ready, but they got to do it sometime."

Smooth nodded, looking over their area.

"Hey Hump, Body Man."

Smooth waved his hand in the air to motion them over. The two new guys came over and stood by Smooth and Kensington.

"Four Seven thinks you're ready to walk point. What you think about that?"

The two new guys looked at each other, then the new black guy, Body Man spoke first.

"We're ready. Been watching you two, last week or so, think we can handle it."

Hump nodded his agreement.

"There you go, Four Seven."

Smiling broadly, he continued.

"Now all we got to do is convince Stick."

Smooth waved his hand and the two new guys left.

"What's really on your mind, Four Seven?"

Sam looked at Smooth. Pulling out his pack of cigarettes again, he offered one to Smooth who accepted. Lighting both, he pulled heavily.

"Not so much what I'm thinking, but they gotta get experience, we won't be here as long as they will. They don't walk soon, it will be harder later. You know how it is, we both went through it. Besides now that we've conquered the fucking A Shau Valley, what better place for them to do it? Get time in."

Smooth nodded, smiling.

"Fuckin' A."

Wilson walked up and sat down hard against his ruck.

"Smooth, Four Seven."

The two men nodded, waiting for Wilson to speak.

"LT says we got a 'bush tonight, get the day off, no patrols, but we gonna get resupplied here, we got chopper duty, do the unloading, shit like that."

Smooth smiled, Kensington nodded. Wilson looked at both of them questioning. Sam pointed to Smooth.

"A guy in second told me we'd probably be here another day to get resupply."

"Must have been a brother."

Sam raised his eyes in the air.

"Of course it was."

Smooth nodded.

"Fuckin' A."

The three men sat in silence. A soldier unknown to them walked up.

"Wilson?"

"Yeah?"

"LT said to bring your men up. Need to cut the LZ for the resupply birds."

Wilson looked at the soldier with his "who the fuck are you" look. The soldier knelt down closer.

"CO's been up everybody's ass this morning, afraid we might be sitting around, wants to make sure everybody is doing something. He's sending out extra patrols and those of us have ambush tonight need to be working. My squad has a 'bush tonight so we're on LZ detail, thought I'd give you a heads up. Don't let the CO catch you sitting, at least not today. Don't know what hair is up his ass, but he's being a real prick today. LT said stay sharp."

The soldier rose and left as quickly as he came.

"Well you heard the man, let's go cut some fucking jungle, look busy."

Sam raised his hand into the air.

"Yes sir, boss."

Smooth broke a smile.

"Fuckin' A."

Fifteen minutes later, the men were standing with their machetes in hand ready to cut jungle. Wilson led them to the center of the perimeter where another squad of soldiers was gathering. Wilson saw the man that had come over earlier and nodded. The man tapped his machete to his forehead.

Chopping and cutting, they created a flat LZ for the Huey to come in and drop off the resupply. Before long they heard the buffeting of the blades as the Huey approached. Popping smoke, the bird made its way into the freshly cut LZ. Wilson directed the bird down, crossing his arms as the skids hit the ground. In an instant men were at the sides pulling supplies off the bird. Moments later the Huey was airborne and gone, the sound of the blades fading in the distance.

Boxes of ammo, C-rations, fresh uniforms and a couple of sundry packs, containing cigarettes, toilet paper and other items lay strewn on the ground. The men worked to gather up and organize them for distribution.

Soldiers headed over to get theirs. Men stripped on the spot, putting on the fresh uniforms and dumping the discarded clothes into a pile for pickup. Wilson and his squad did the same and took what they needed before departing the area.

Quietly, Wilson gathered his team for the night's ambush position. As usual, Kensington, Smooth, Whitey on the radio, Big John with his 60, Body Man and Lopes made up the team. Hump stayed back with his 60 and one of the thumpers.

Wilson took point leading the team to a position roughly 150 meters from the perimeter, up a slight rise. They could see the perimeter from their position. Fairly confident the night would be quiet, they settled in.

"Stick, what you think?"

Wilson looked at Smooth on the ground next to him. The others looked at him as well, waiting.

"Patrols said they saw nothing, area looks deserted. No fresh tracks, no activity, even bunkers looked long deserted. Think it will be an easy night."

Wilson raised his hand in the air.

"Don't mean we slack off. Don't mean Charlie ain't there, just laying low, maybe waiting for an opportunity. Stay sharp. Make sure we have good fields of fire."

The men sat quietly. Wilson motioned and each man took up his position. Ambushes produced mostly sleepless nights, with everyone ever watchful. Tonight would be no different.

"Cat naps, fifteen each. Figure it out amongst your selves."

"Stick, you and me together?"

"Roger that, Four Seven. No way you sleeping tonight."

"Fuckin' A."

Sam Kensington leaned against a tree. Wilson was against a rock next to him. The others took up similar positions.

"You first."

"What?"

Wilson pointed.

"You watch, I'll sleep. Get me in fifteen."

Sam nodded. That was the routine throughout the night. As Wilson had surmised, the night passed without incident.

"Whitey, call in, tell them we're coming back. Make sure they pulled the trips and claymores. Don't want to walk up on nobody."

Whitey nodded, already running through the call signs. He raised his hand in the air.

"All clear. Said to come on home."

Wilson nodded.

"Saddle up, we're heading home."

After gathering up their weapons and gear, the team fell in

line behind Wilson who led them back into the perimeter.

Sam Kensington sat heavily down against his ruck, putting a cigarette to his lips and the tip to the flame of his lighter. He took a long pull. He wanted to put some coffee on but was too tired to make the move, deciding instead to just sit there for now.

Twenty-Five

"**L**T says we're moving out in sixty, splitting into platoons, make our way to the firebase that way."

Sam Kensington opened his eyes with a start, his catnap interrupted.

"Damn Stick, we don't get no rest first?"

Wilson looked at Sam, then Smooth, then the rest of the squad, waiting for his answer.

"Well, that's what I asked."

Wilson paused.

"LT said let's get away from here first, move a ways, then maybe we can stop, run a patrol or two. Said be better once we get away, CO still has that hair up his ass, wants to continue the chase."

"Chase? Chase who?"

Wilson looked at Smooth, but knew everyone was thinking the same thing.

"Any stragglers might be hanging around, still in the Valley. LT thinks they already be back in Laos, wait for us to move out before they come back."

Wilson paused and the squad remained silent.

"I think the LT is right, let's get away from the rest of the company. CO is staying with second platoon like before. Once we're away we can take a break."

Wilson stepped over to his ruck.

"Six zero mikes, we move."

Forty-five minutes later the squad was packed, loaded and ready to move. Wilson nodded.

"Four Seven, you lead the way, same formation. Whitey?"

"Yeah Stick, on your six with the radio."

Wilson nodded.

"Smooth, you behind me this time, I'll walk slack till we get out of here. Second squad with LT is walking drag, Sarge in the middle."

Wilson looked around, motioning with his head. Lopes called out.

"We're ready back here, everyone's in place."

Wilson nodded.

"Four Seven?"

Kensington led the platoon out of the perimeter, passing through a small open area they had cleared for a better field of fire. Pulling his machete from the back of his ruck, he cut into the jungle in front of him. Passing through flowing elephant grass, he angled around a bamboo patch. Coming upon another clearing he stopped and knelt down. Wilson joined him.

"What you see, Four Seven?"

"Nothing. I see nothing but more jungle."

Wilson nodded.

"Let's go."

Kensington nodded and led them through the opening, no more than two men in the opening at the same time. Sam kept the long green line moving. Approaching a small plateau, he halted the platoon and motioned to Wilson.

"Think maybe the LT let us set up here for a break?"

Wilson looked into the opening. The plateau rose up a bit,

giving them some high ground to defend if needed. Wilson motioned using his fingers in a phone position. Whitey came forward and stood while Wilson took the horn.

"LT's coming up. We wait."

Kensington dropped his ruck and sat down, keeping his glance forward watching for movement.

The lieutenant joined Kensington and Wilson looking out over the area. He nodded his approval.

"Yeah, looks good. Let's get into position, run a patrol or two, keep up radio activity, let them know we're humping our asses off and take a nice long break. Maybe even make this our NDP."

Wilson smiled.

"Roger that, sir. Four Seven, you heard the man, let's go."

Sam slipped back into his ruck. Wilson helped him up. Slowly they moved into the area, each squad finding a spot to set up in. He sat down heavily against his ruck, lighting a ciga-rette. Wilson sat down beside him.

"LT says take a half hour, then we do a patrol, take the rest of the afternoon off."

Sam nodded.

Forty minutes later, Wilson, Kensington, Smooth, Whitey with the radio, Body Man and Lopes were ready to move out. Big John and Hump stayed back with their sixties. They got to dig the hole for the night.

Smooth took point, again Wilson was on slack and Kensington right behind him, Body Man, then Whitey and Lopes bringing up the rear. Smooth wound around the area, staying behind the plateau. He hadn't gone very far when he suddenly stopped, raising his hand in the air. Wilson joined him, kneeling. Smooth pointed to his ear. Wilson heard it. Voices could be heard speaking Vietnamese, but slowly, delib-erately, no apparent sense of urgency.

Smooth and Wilson crawled forward. Through the elephant

grass they saw a downed Huey, pretty beat up lying slightly to the side. What appeared to be villagers were standing around inside and out of the downed Huey.

Wilson brought the others forward. Using his hands he pointed to both sides. Lopes and Whitey went to the right. Kensington and Body Man went to the left. Slowly they put the downed Huey in a horseshoe block. Wilson nodded to Smooth, together they made their way to the opening.

"Dung Lai. Dung Lai."

The villagers turned and saw the soldiers pointing their weapons at them. They started to move out in confusion, but Wilson hollered again.

"Dung Lai. Dung Lai."

Body Man tapped Sam.

"Means stop, halt something like that."

Body Man nodded. Wilson moved forward toward the now terrified villagers, his sixteen up and pointed at them. Smooth was to his right moving with him, also with his sixteen up and pointed right at the villagers.

"Dung Lai. Caca Dau VC, Caca Dau."

"No VC. No VC."

The villagers gathered together. An old man stood off to the side. Two younger looking women, dressed in the traditional Ao Dai, flowing slit skirt and trousers, their conical hats low covering their faces stood in the center. Finally three children came out of the Huey they had been playing in. An old woman came around the side, all now huddling together.

Wilson kept his weapon pointed at them. Sam turned to Body Man.

"Said to stop or he'll kill them, kill all VC."

The villagers stood motionless as Wilson and Smooth approached. Wilson faced the villagers as he spoke.

"Bo Doi?"

The villagers shook their head no.

Wilson looked at the group of people in front of him and spoke with authority, keeping his sixteen pointed directly at the huddled villagers.

"Four Seven, Lopes work around the Huey, let me know. Smooth anybody moves… Caca Dau."

The villagers stood terrified, barely moving, the women crying, the children clinging to one of the younger woman's legs. No one moved, Finally Kensington, then Lopes emerged from the jungle.

"Nothing Stick, all clear."

"Same here."

Wilson lowered his weapon. He motioned to Smooth, who did the same. The villagers stared at the soldiers not moving much and looked frantically from one soldier to another.

"Doesn't look like anything, probably trying to salvage what they can."

Wilson walked up to the villagers. They tensed up, but he kept his weapon down at his side, as did the rest of the team.

"Di di mau… go… di di mau."

The villagers waited a moment before moving, but Wilson waved his hand in the air as he spoke softly.

"It's okay… di di… di di."

Slowly the villagers left the area back into the jungle. The team watched them leave. Wilson waited until they were gone before speaking.

"Looks like the crew was extracted. The guns are gone, radio pulled out and…"

Suddenly he turned, seeing one of the younger women reappear from the bushes. Pointing his weapon at her, he watched and waited.

His sixteen pointed at the ready, Wilson's focus was centered directly on her, but he let his eyes dart from side to side and finally behind her, ever vigilant of any movement. Letting his focus turn back to the woman, her face now visible under the conical hat she wore, he was struck by the elegant contours of her face, so beautiful in the middle of all this ugliness. Smiling, but keeping his weapon pointed at her, he knew the others did as well. Slowly he raised one hand in the air and waited letting his sixteen lower slightly.

"Stick?"

Smooth called out, but Wilson waved his hand.

"I got this."

Still watching the woman, she motioned for them to follow her.

"What the fuck is this all about?"

Wilson looked around.

"Four Seven, you and Lopes come with me. The rest of you wait here. Stay sharp."

Smooth grabbed Wilson's arm.

"Sure you want to do that?"

"No."

Smooth nodded.

"She either wants to give us some boom boom, lead us into a trap or show us something."

Wilson smiled.

"Personally, I'd opt for the boom boom, but I believe she wants to show us something. Gut says it isn't a trap. Could be wrong. If I am, you're in charge."

Smooth smiled.

"Keep your shit together."

Wilson nodded and motioned. Kensington and Lopes flanked him as they followed the young woman into the jungle overgrowth. Ever watchful as they moved, they didn't go very far before she stopped and parted the elephant grass, pointing.

"Bo Doi. Bo Doi."

Wilson looked to where she was pointing. Beyond the elephant grass were five dead uniformed NVA soldiers. He motioned and Kensington had a look see, as did Lopes. Wilson

turned to the young Vietnamese woman and bowed. The
woman smiled and bowed back. Backing away, she left them
and disappeared back into the jungle.

"Damn, I really was hoping it was boom boom. Do you
know how long it's been?"

"Just as long for me."

Kensington pushed past him toward the dead soldiers.
Lopes smiled, grabbing his crotch. Wilson smiled back at him.

"What we got, Four Seven?"

"Five bodies. Weapons and gear gone. Pockets turned inside
out. Could have been the villagers did that, looking for money.
Look here."

Sam pointed to two of the men propped against a tree.

"Looks like they were hit and moved here, but these three
were raked with bullets. Maybe a gunship put up fire to cover
the escape. These three got a lot of holes in them. Lotta blood
was spilled here. Might be others wounded tried to get away.
Should we go look for them?"

Wilson looked over the scene, finally meeting Sam's gaze.

"Two, three days ago, I would have said yes, but they been
here a while. Maggots already inside the bodies. Anything out
there is already gone or rotting like these. Let's get back."

Just inside the jungle at the opening, Wilson called out.

"Coming in."

Walking up to the others he explained what they found.
Smooth pointed to the downed Huey.

"No blood inside, looks like they got away clean. Had
enough time to take what's important. Looks like they left the
bird here this time."

Wilson nodded.

"Let's head back, tell the LT what we found."

He pointed and Kensington went back to point, following a
different way back to the perimeter.

After he briefed the lieutenant, Wilson came back and sat

down against his ruck. Sam offered a cigarette, which Wilson took. Lighting both, Sam sat back, letting the smoke drift out. Wilson pointed with the cigarette toward the jungle in front of them.

"LT said he wasn't surprised we found the Huey. Said several went down during the ten day battle for that fucking hill. Probably find more before we get to the firebase."

Sam nodded.

"Got anything going this afternoon?"

Wilson took a pull shaking his head no.

"LT said to take it easy, get set up for the night."

"Ambush?"

"Nope. Said we'll all stay in tonight, rest."

"Okay, why's he being so kind to us?"

Wilson smiled, taking another pull on the cigarette.

"Also said we're going to hump our asses off tomorrow, get to the firebase fast. Wants to be done fucking around out here. Gooks are gone. Won't come back until we leave."

Sam looked out in front of him, drawing heavily on his cigarette.

"Amen brother. Amen."

The two men sat in silence for a spell, finishing their cigarettes. Finally Sam ground his into the red dirt.

"And tonight?"

"Midnight 'till two."

"Fuckin' A."

Wilson got up and walked over to the rest of the squad, bringing them up to speed. Sam let his eyes close briefly, and enjoyed a quick catnap.

Hump tapped Kensington on the leg.

"Four Seven, you're up."

Sam sat up, wiping his hand across his eyes. He had been sleeping solidly, but he barely remembered closing his eyes. Making his way to the hole, he got into position, eyes focusing, adjusting to the dark.

Wilson had told them before the watches began that it would be a boring night. All was clear, but that is when you'll get your dick shot off, so to stay sharp, still could be something out there, maybe trying to get out and straggling about, separated, shit like that.

Sam smiled, remembering Wilson's speech, but he did agree with him. Could be anything out there. He directed his focus into the night, his eyes gaining a clearer vision in the dark.

Finishing his shift, he went back and tapped Whitey.

"You're up."

Whitey sat up, taking a moment before making his way to the hole. Sam crawled up against his ruck and barely got into position before he was fast asleep.

Morning came quickly. He awoke with a start, obviously the first one awake. Sitting up, he leaned back against his ruck. After pulling out the cooking can and removing a canteen from his ruck, he filled the cup with water, lit a heat tab and placed the water on the fire. Sitting back waiting for the water to heat up, he lit a cigarette.

Wilson stirred next to him.

"Two over medium, hash browns, bacon crisp, toast and coffee."

Sam smiled as Wilson pulled the poncho liner off his head.

"Coffee brewing?"

Sam nodded yes. Wilson sat up against his ruck.

"I'm with the LT, ready for this shit to be over."

Sam poured the packet of coffee into the bubbling water, using his spoon to mix it up. After taking the first sip of the hot liquid, he passed the cup to Wilson.

"Thanks."

Wilson took a couple of sips before handing the cup back. Sam took the cup and slowly sipped the hot liquid. Wilson sat against his ruck. Sam handed him the pack of smokes. Wilson took one and handed the pack back.

Smooth came over and sat down next to them.

"Hey Stick, what the LT got in mind for us today?"

"Wants us to get our asses to the firebase. Lot of humping today."

Smooth nodded.

"Why can't we get lifted out, forget this bullshit?"

Wilson looked at Smooth, waving the cigarette in the air.

"We ain't going that far. Firebase we going to, still in the valley. We suppose to sweep, make sure the trash has been taken out."

"Say what?"

Wilson looked out into the jungle.

"Couple of firebases built before we got here, as support. We going to one of them. For now, the fucking A Shau Valley is still our home."

Kensington and Smooth sat silent. Sam finished his coffee, using a drop of water to rinse it out.

"How long 'till we get there?"

Sam looked at Wilson.

"Might get there today, depending on how fast we move. Sounds like LT wants that to happen, otherwise we spend another night out here. Said he picked the direct route, left second and third platoons to work around, take longer to get in."

Smooth nodded.

"How soon we getting started?"

"Soon as we pack up. You got point today. I'll walk slack again. That okay with you, Four Seven?"

Sam nodded. Smooth reached over and did the white version of the black dap handshake with Kensington.

"But it don't mean nothing."

"But it don't mean nothing."

Smooth left them returning to his ruck. Sam looked over at Wilson.

"What else you heard?"

Wilson looked at Kensington.

"About what?"

"Anything."

Wilson looked straight ahead.

"Lot of guys got killed on that fucking hill. We got lucky we weren't in the middle of that."

Kensington sat quietly, letting that last statement pass. Sarge appeared in front of them.

"You boys ready to move out?"

"Fuckin' A."

"Good, LT wants us there today. Think we can do that?"

Wilson stood up.

"Depends."

"On what?"

"He want us to get there, or check things out on the way? We find something, might hold us up for a while."

The sergeant looked at Wilson, then at Kensington sitting up against his ruck.

"Let's just say we don't find anything on the way that might slow us down."

"Roger that."

The sergeant walked away.

"Smooth."

Smooth turned and walked toward Wilson. Sam remained propped against his ruck.

"Change of plans. Four Seven going to walk point, I'll still be slack."

Smooth looked at Wilson, then over at Kensington.

"Sarge say something about me?"

"No. Fuck no. He wanted to make sure we got the LTs message loud and clear that he wants us at the firebase today. Thought I'd put Four Seven out, since he got the mountain goat in him, get us there quick."

Smooth smiled.

"Four Seven, you do got that mountain goat shit in you. Fine with me. Sooner we get there the sooner we get out of this shit."

Sam raised his hand in the air. Smooth slapped it.

"Fuckin' A."

Wilson waited for Smooth to leave.

"Think he believe that shit?"

"No."

"Neither do I."

Sam stood up.

"Let's just stick with the story."

Wilson nodded.

"Well, you heard Sarge. Let's get there make sure you don't find nothing."

Kensington nodded.

After an hour of humping, Kensington paused. Wilson was beside him immediately. Sam pointed.

"We're gonna have to go up for a ways to get over that rise."

Wilson nodded, waiting, as he knew Sam had another reason for stopping.

"But, if we go that way, we can make better time."

Wilson looked to where Kensington was pointing, starting to understand what Sam was getting at.

"We go down that way, more exposed, not the best idea."

Kensington nodded.

"What you thinking, Four Seven?"

Sam looked at the route again, then at Wilson.

"Well if what we been hearing and seeing for ourselves is true that we did in fact ran those fuckers out of the valley, then it shouldn't be no problem to go that way."

"But?"

"But, we go that way we got no place to react. We'd be sitting ducks they have something set up. Wouldn't even give it a thought, things were different."

Wilson nodded. He could hear rustling behind him somebody was coming up. In the next moment, Sarge was next to him.

"What's the holdup?"

Wilson pointed.

"Smart move be go up and over that rise."

"And?"

"We go that way we save maybe an hour, maybe more."

Sarge looked to where Wilson was pointing and immediately saw the problem.

"Not real smart, we go that way."

Wilson nodded, as did Kensington.

"What you thinking?"

Wilson pointed to Kensington. He nodded.

"Like I told Stick, if that shit is true that we ran those fuckers out of the valley, we should be fine, but if that's bullshit, then..."

Sarge looked at Kensington, then at Wilson.

"What you think?"

"I'm with Four Seven. Can we believe the intel, or do what we know best?"

Sarge stayed silent, looking out over the two options.

"When's the last time you believed the intel?"

Wilson smiled.

"Right?"

Sarge left. Wilson pointed and Kensington nodded. Sam led them up and over the rise, stopping at the top. Once again

Wilson joined him. Sam pointed.

"Over there."

Wilson looked to where Sam was pointing, nodding. He motioned for Smooth to come up. Lopes joined them. Wilson led Smooth and Lopes toward the bunker that, Sam had spotted on the top of the rise. As suspected they were deserted, but provided a perfect place to pour fire down on anyone that might have been walking below. Wilson smiled, motioning for them to head back.

"Four Seven, could have been ugly, we went the other way and somebody be sitting up here."

"Fuckin' A."

Over the rise they could see the outline of the firebase in the distance, maybe another klick or so. Kensington led them over and down, stopping when they reached the cleared area. Whitey called in their presence and was given the clearance to come in. Kensington led them in.

Inside the firebase, the platoon was directed to an area they could set up, with only one hole to guard. Wilson started to ask, but the lieutenant was already motioning everyone together.

"Listen up men. Now that we're here, we get to take a break. No patrols, no 'bushes, no guard duty for the next twenty-four, a complete stand down. Get settled in. I've been told we can get a shower, fresh uniforms and chow. No duties tonight. Get a good night's sleep. I'll know more tomorrow, when the CO gets here with second."

He started to walk away, but turned back.

"Don't know what tomorrow brings, so enjoy tonight."

Again, he turned and walked away.

Sarge moved into the position the LT had been.

"You boys need directions on how to take a break?"

With that he was gone.

Wilson dropped his ruck down in what he thought would be a good spot. Kensington dropped his next to him and Smooth dropped his on the other side. The three men sat down against their rucks. Kensington removed the pack of smokes from his shirt, offering one to Wilson, then Smooth. Lighting and enjoying the first pulls before speaking, the men started to relax. Finally Wilson spoke up.

"Now we know why the LT was so hell bent on getting here. He wanted to beat the CO in, get a break before he got here."

Smooth nodded.

"So why'd you put Four Seven out instead of me?"

Wilson smiled. Sam stared straight ahead.

"Smooth, I don't know what you're talking about."

"Damn, Stick. Thought you could level with me?"

Wilson raised his hand.

"Okay. Okay. Sarge told us make sure we didn't find anything might hold us up, prevent us from getting here today. Figured the less that knew that the better. Four Seven heard, thought it best let him lead, put blinders on. Besides, he's the mountain goat. Got us over that rise pretty quick."

Smooth leaned forward, looking past Wilson at Sam, finally breaking out in a smile.

"Four Seven, you are a mother fucking goat. Got us up and over, 'fore I knew we were climbing. Stick, next time, tell me."

"Fuckin' A."

The three men sat in silence watching the activity around them as the rest of the squad settled in to a comfortable spot. Finally, Sam stood up.

"I'm gonna go find that shower."

As dusk settled in, Wilson, Kensington and Smooth sat against their rucks. A 55 shower, fresh clothes, a relaxing meal, of C-rats, sure, but slow and easy had put the men at ease. Wilson took a cigarette from his pack then offered the pack both ways.

Smooth took one, but Kensington already had one lit.

"Heard from a brother here, that we suppose to get hot chow tomorrow. Choppers be bringing it in midday. Also said he heard might be mail on that bird. Said he heard we'd be here a couple of days at least."

Smooth and Kensington sat silent.

"Anyway, that's what I heard."

Wilson took a long pull on his cigarette. The night started to move in.

"Four Seven, want me to wake you at midnight?"

"Fuck no. I'm sleeping through the night, dream or not. I don't give a shit anymore. Looking forward to not having Hump tapping my fucking leg at midnight, even if it is only one night."

"Roger that, Four Seven. You do need your beauty sleep."

"Fuckin' A."

"Four Seven, you still dreaming that Civil War shit?"

Sam looked past Wilson at Smooth.

"Off and on Smooth, bunch of shit going on, can't make sense of it."

Smooth nodded and leaned back. They sat silent. Sam tapped Wilson on the arm.

"So Stick, that brother you know have any home grown?"

Wilson smiled, reaching into his ruck.

"I got better. Got me some of Kentucky's finest, I got from one of you rednecks."

"I told you I ain't no fucking redneck."

"That's right, sorry. Smooth, I forgot to tell you he one of us now, wants to be called a brother."

Smooth leaned forward looking past Wilson, holding his fist in the air.

Wilson passed the container around as they each took a strong sip of the bourbon. There was enough for each of them to take a second sip.

"Well you boys do what you want, but I'm with Four Seven, a full night's sleep sounds pretty fucking good to me."

Wilson slid down on his ruck, pulling his poncho liner over his head. Smooth nodded to Kensington, doing the same. Sam looked out over the compound for a moment before joining them.

Gathered under the poncho liner, Sam felt the bourbon kick in, feeling relaxed. The thought of not having Hump tap him on the leg at midnight was relief enough, but the bourbon sure helped smooth the way. His eyes closed and before he realized it, he was fast asleep.

Twenty-Six

Nathan DeLacroix staggered back into camp, his head bandaged, his wrist taped up and most of his blue clad uniform torn to shreds. Making his way slowly over to the street that housed his tent he observed the other streets. After the Confederate's had plundered the camp, some streets were still left in disarray, but others had already been cleaned up, the tents tightened and the debris cleared from the area. However, some tents stood silent where men did not return.

"Hey, Vermont?"

Samuel Kensington looked around to see Nathan DeLacroix approaching him.

"Jesus, Nathan, what the hell happened to you?"

DeLacroix walked over to where Samuel stood, and took a seat. Kensington sat down next to him. Nathan held his bandaged hand out.

"Oh this, it's nothing."

Samuel Kensington looked at his new found friend, the near total destruction of his clothes and the many injuries to his body.

"Looks like you've been through the mill."

Nathan looked up, smiling.

"Well, I've had a time, that's for sure."

The two men sat in silence for a moment before Nathan finally continued.

"On that last drive, we were climbing a small rise and a cannon shot exploded in front of us. Some men went down immediately and just when I thought we would get over, something, I believe now was a piece of shrapnel, grazed across my forehead."

Nathan paused, wiping his face with a handkerchief.

"Well, the force must have knocked me backwards, because I fell into a bunch of bushes, sharp as knives."

Nathan held out his hand.

"Trying to break my fall, I grabbed on to something that tore my hand apart. After that, I figured I should just lay there."

He wiped his face again, Samuel waited for him to continue.

"Finally, a couple of men from my regiment pulled me out, but in doing so, ripped my clothes to shreds. The bushes cut so deep they actually cut my skin underneath."

Samuel Kensington looked at his friend and he wasn't kidding. Blood spots could be seen all over his body, through the shredded blue coat and pants. He waited for him to continue.

"That shrapnel not only left me bloodied, but a bit dazed. I vaguely remember being led away. Next I recollect I was sitting on a stump and a feller from the hospital gang was wrapping a bandage around my noggin."

Nathan held up his hand again.

"Told him I didn't need anything for my hand, but one of the cuts was pretty deep. He wrapped it up, said to keep it tight."

Nathan continued to turn the hand in the air. Kensington continued to stare at him.

"I went over to Quartermaster to see if I could get a new uniform, but the place was in shambles. Damn Rebels tried to take everything, thoroughly trashed the wagons, even pillaged the Robber's Row. Sutlers in a frenzy, all their stuff gone and they didn't get no money for their goods."

Nathan let out a hearty laugh.

"Here those boys try to charge us for every little thing we can't get otherwise and now they the ones who saw the elephant on this day."

Samuel smiled with him. It was a sort of poetic justice.

"So when I couldn't get nothing from Quartermaster, I figured I'd jut come back to my regiment."

Samuel Kensington nodded. Nathan let out a big sigh.

"That ain't all my friend. I heard some stuff while I was with the hospital gang, make your hair stand on end. The cries of pain was overwhelming. The tent across from the one I was in is where the sawbones was doing his work non-stop. Feller told me there was a pile of limbs on the other side of that tent, growing by the minute."

Nathan DeLacroix took a breath, before continuing.

"Not to mention those that won't live out the day. Some too shocked to even realize they be dying. Tent I was in was for fixing and patching men up, didn't have to see any of that, but you couldn't help but hear it."

Nathan DeLacroix took a deep breath before continuing.

"Doctors working non stop patching men up. Wagons rolling in with more medical staff and supplies as the wounded continued to come into those tents. Men all around... We sure were fortunate they were there. Finest care, I tell you."

The two men sat silently digesting what he had just said. Nathan turned his bandaged hand over and over.

"You know we lost a lot of men today, last couple of days?"

Samuel nodded.

"We lost our commander couple of days ago."

Nathan nodded pointing with his bandaged hand.

"The 87th Pennsylvania lost every one of their officers over the last couple of days. Every one of them."

Nathan leaned in closer. Samuel did the same.

"I'm sure you know by now that Brigadier General Ricketts also fell some time back. We even lost our Division Commander."

Kensington nodded.

"Yes, I did hear that this morning. Heard something yesterday, but it was confirmed this morning."

Nathan nodded. The two men sat silent. Nathan tapped Samuel on the arm.

"How you boys doing?"

Samuel looked at Nathan, shaking his head up and down.

"Still here. Boys I been with last few days all still here. Lost a lot of the regiment when we tried to retake those cannon. Got flanked and run over. Almost stepped on another unit crossing our path. Rebels took advantage of that, run us off. But, we regrouped and advanced, made it back here."

Nathan nodded.

"About the same with us."

The two men sat silent for a bit. Nathan pointed in the direction of a big house off in the distance.

"That's Belle Grove over there."

Samuel nodded, not understanding the significance of the mansion he was pointing at. Nathan continued.

"You'll never believe who's in there, well besides the Federal officers that took it over."

Samuel Kensington shook his head no.

"When I was waiting in the field hospital, I heard some officers talking. I asked one of the hospital gang what they meant and he explained it."

Nathan paused while Samuel waited, wondering what he was going to say. Finally Nathan leaned in again, as did Samuel.

"Boys told me they have Major General Stephen Dodson Ramseur himself. Seems he was wounded pretty bad and when we overran the Rebels trying to escape, he was in one of the ambulance wagons."

Nathan nodded.

"Told me out of courtesy they brought him over there. Officers been going in and out all day. Even Custer himself went by to pay his respects. Can you beat that? The general leading the Confederates we been up against since we entered the valley, is in there, a federal headquarters, dying."

Samuel Kensington nodded, turning his head to look at the mansion in the distance.

"War don't play no favorite that's for sure. General or private, Minie ball gonna get you."

Samuel turned back to face his friend.

"Ramseur is in there. I had heard other Confederate officers had fallen, but Ramseur? He's…"

Nathan nodded.

"He sure is."

Samuel turned again to look at the mansion in the distance. Nathan continued.

"Boys from the hospital gang said they're not treating him as a prisoner, but as a friend and compatriot. Hell, most of them generals, blue and gray, went to West Point together. That's why most of the Federal officers are going by to pay their respects. They all know each other."

Samuel turned back, nodding.

"I heard one more thing while I was there. Heard this from an officer in the tent getting patched up for a shot in the thigh. Let me tell you he was one happy feller, ball went right through the muscle. Felt sure he would keep the leg."

Nathan paused, wiping his face with the handkerchief.

"Said the Rebels had been driven from the Shenandoah Valley and that some of the Federals would be leaving, going back. Said last he heard the VI Corps would rejoin the Army of the Potomac, while XIX Corps would go into winter camp here. So it looks like we are done here. You and me be heading back."

Kensington nodded.

"Yeah, heard something like that earlier this morning. Makes sense. You say they got Ramseur in there."

Samuel pointed to the mansion in the distance.

"What else that officer say?"

Nathan shook his head no.

"That was it really."

Samuel nodded, turning back to face the mansion, hardly believing this was over. He turned back to DeLacroix.

"Any idea on how soon?"

"Well Vermont, that I don't know, but I do know this. I know Joe Buxton has his Faro game going and if I know Joe, and I do, I'm sure he already has some more Bark Juice, some good ole home grown already. The Rebels might have gotten his stash, but knowing Joe like I do, he found a way to get some more. What say we go pay him a visit?"

Samuel Kensington smiled broadly.

"Sure could use a taste of something."

The two men rose up. Samuel followed Nathan DeLacroix back to his street. Following Nathan into the tent, they were greeted with friendly hellos and back slaps.

"Damn Nathan, what happened to you?"

"Long story, tell you all later. Joe, you got any?"

"Over there."

Nathan turned to Samuel.

"Told you he'd have something."

"Nathan, look in that bag over there. Should be a jacket and pants might fit you."

DeLacroix turned to face Joe Buxton smiling. Inside the bag was a blue coat and pair of pants that appeared to be just the right size. Samuel Kensington was already placing a bet on the Faro cloth when Nathan sat down beside him. He offered the jug, which Samuel took, pulling the cork and taking a healthy gulp. His face contorted and he choked momentarily.

"Damn Joe, what's in that?"

Joe Buxton smiled, pointing to the Faro cloth.

"Place your bets."

DeLacroix patted Samuel Kensington on the back.

"Well Vermont, we got through this one. Now let's see if we can get past Joe Buxton. If he don't kill us with that Bark Juice, he'll probably take all our money."

Joe Buxton smiled. Samuel Kensington took another gulp of the home grown. Nathan DeLacroix let out a hearty yelp.

Joe Buxton turned the card, more yelps and hollers as men lost and won their wagers. Several hours later, Samuel Kensington and Nathan DeLacroix staggered out of Joe Buxton's tent, shaking hands they parted company. Samuel made his way back to his tent.

Sitting down heavily, the Bark Juice having its effect on his coordination, he looked up at the sky, finally letting his gaze turn toward the mansion in the distance. Although he couldn't make it out, the night being punctuated by the many campfires burning, he knew where it was. The totality of the days events coupled with the information he now knew somewhat overwhelmed him at the moment.

The fall of their division commander, Brigadier General James Ricketts as well as the many other officers who had also fallen during the various battles to take this valley. That coupled with the news that Major General Stephen Ramseur, the Confederate leader, had also fallen really brought home what Nathan had said. Minie ball doesn't care if you're a general or private.

Quite sure the Bark Juice was affecting his thinking, Samuel Kensington shook his head trying to clear the cobwebs forming. Looking out into the night, he knew how lucky he had been. If the mighty can fall, how did he survive? How did anyone survive the carnage of the last few days on either side. The totality of losing at the very least, these two powerful generals on the field of battle only strengthened his resolve. The thought of leaving this valley, this Shenandoah Valley that once had been a Confederate stronghold, but was now clearly controlled by the Federals, with no intention of giving it back, gave him pause.

Everett Fremont walked up, stopping next to Samuel Kensington sitting on the stump outside his tent.

"Samuel."

Kensington looked up at his fellow soldier and friend.

"Everett."

"Well Samuel, we made it through another day."

"That we did Everett. That we did. Did you know?"

Samuel gathered himself and pointed to the mansion in the dark.

"Did you know that Confederate General Ramseur lies dying over there?"

Everett Fremont looked to where Samuel was pointing, but only saw the glare of the campfires in the night.

"No Samuel, I did not know that."

Kensington nodded, the Bark Juice taking its toll.

"Heard that this afternoon from Nathan."

"Who?"

"Nathan DeLacroix, friend of mine from the 87th Pennsylvania, who was wounded. While he was getting fixed up he heard that very thing."

Everett nodded.

"You don't say?"

"Everett, do you think it's over?"

"Do I think what's over?"

"This?"

Samuel waved his hands in the air. Everett looked at his friend and fellow soldier.

"It is here. That's for sure. We're done with this valley. It's ours now and I dare say we intend to keep it."

Kensington waved his hands in the air again.

"That's what I believe too."

Everett nodded.

"Well Samuel, I believe I'll turn in. Let's see what tomorrow brings."

Kensington nodded.

"Good night Everett."

Everett Fremont disappeared into his tent. Samuel Kensington sat on the stump looking into the night, trying to make out the mansion through the smoke and glare of the campfires. Belle Grove, where the great Confederate general lay dying, or maybe even already dead. Somehow, in his Bark Juice influenced mind that fact meant so much more to him than he could explain.

Slowly he rose up and staggered into his tent. Plopping down on the ground, Samuel Kensington fell fast asleep. Whatever else might be over, this night was certainly over for him.

Twenty-Seven

Sam Kensington sat up with a start, letting the poncho liner slip from his face. Daylight had started, but just barely. Sleeping through the night was a luxury he hadn't experienced in, well, he couldn't remember when.

Wilson still lay under his poncho liner. Smooth was the same. Looked like nobody was awake but him. Not wanting to disturb either of them, he walked a ways away before lighting his morning cigarette. Standing against a sand bag wall, he flipped his lighter open, struck a flame and placed it to the tip of the cigarette, drawing deep. Slowly letting the smoke from his lungs, the white cloud gathered around his face, the coolness of the morning engulfed him.

As he tried to remember the aspects of last night's dream he was distracted enough to not hear Wilson walk up.

"Four Seven, you okay?"

Sam Kensington turned with a start, surprised to see Wilson standing next to him.

"Huh? What? Yeah, sure. Didn't want to disturb anyone. Sorry if I woke you."

"At ease, Four Seven. Bad night? Another dream?"

Sam Kensington looked out over the compound. Signs of activity started to come into view as the sun rose in the sky.

"Yeah."

Wilson nodded, placing a cigarette in his lips, flipping his lighter open and striking a flame to the tip. Pulling and releasing the smoke he pointed.

"Nice to be inside for a while. Whole night's sleep. What you make of that?"

Wilson was trying to keep him talking. Sam nodded, waving his hands in the air.

"Can't remember when I've had it this luxurious."

Wilson smiled.

"Fuckin' A."

The two men stood silent, enjoying their cigarettes. Wilson prodded.

"Want to talk about it?"

Sam turned, fully knowing what Wilson meant.

"Talk about what?"

Wilson smiled.

"All that pussy we been getting last couple of days, I think my dick is about to fall off, we had…"

Sam raised his hand in the air stopping him.

"Okay, I deserve that. How about we get some coffee first?"

"Works for me."

Dropping the cigarette butts on the ground and grinding them out, the two men turned and walked back to their rucks. Smooth was awake and already had three C-rat can fires going with canteen cups on top, water boiling.

"Thought you wouldn't mind my getting your cups out. Looked like you two fine gentlemen could use some coffee."

Wilson smiled, Sam nodded.

"One thing though, I get to listen in this time."

"Listen in?"

Smooth pointed at Sam.

"Four Seven, I want to hear about the latest dream, got me interested. Curious as to what you're up to. You know, I mean back there."

Sam smiled this time. Wilson punched him on the shoulder. They sat down next to Smooth, fixing their coffee. Sam looked at Wilson first then Smooth.

"Want to eat first?"

"Fuck no. Pork shit, maggots and brains or ham and mother fuckers ain't my idea of breakfast no way. Shit can wait."

Wilson and Sam looked at Smooth, who seemed anxious to hear about this latest dream. Sam shrugged his shoulders.

"Okay then."

He paused to take a sip of hot coffee.

"Damn that's good in the morning. Doesn't matter it's instant and stale canteen water. Sure hits the spot."

Wilson and Smooth stared at him.

"Okay, okay. Where shall I start?"

Before either man could answer, Sam went into the details of the dream.

"Apparently we routed the Rebels, you know the Confederates, from our camp and the surrounding hills. Not without cost mind you. My regiment, the 10th Vermont, got decimated trying to retake captured Federal cannon back, then got flanked and run out. Just about the time we had our act together and started our advance, we stepped on another regiment and had to pull back, with the Rebels taking full advantage of that blunder."

Sam took another sip of coffee. Smooth wanted to ask, but Wilson stopped him.

"Let him finish first."

Smooth nodded. Sam looked at both men. Taking another sip of the hot liquid, he continued.

"So anyway, we're back in our camp. Heard several wagons, cannon and such was captured as the Rebels tried to flee the valley…"

"Valley? What valley you in?"

Sam looked at Smooth, Wilson interjected.

"Smooth ain't been privy, don't know the basics."

Sam nodded.

"Of course."

He took another sip of the hot liquid, finishing the last of the coffee. Smooth took his canteen, filled it with fresh water and put it back on the fire can.

"Probably need a couple of cups this morning."

Wilson looked at Smooth, then handed him his cup as well. Smooth nodded, adding fresh water and placing it on one of the can fires. Sam smiled.

"We're in the Shenandoah Valley in Virginia. It was part of a major push to drive the Confederates from their stronghold, basically stop them from running operations and providing stores to the other Confederate units. You know stop them from moving men and supplies in and out of the valley."

Sam paused and waited. Smooth looked up from the canteen cup he was fixing with a coffee packet, looking first at Sam, then Wilson. Wilson waited for him to digest that last statement as well. Smooth's eyes darted back and forth as he processed the information.

"Holy fuck. Ain't that what we be doing here?"

Wilson smiled, looking over at Sam, who just nodded. Smooth pointed at him.

"And what the fuck does that mean?"

Sam started to answer, but Wilson held up his hand.

"Smooth my man, Four Seven here has been fighting two wars, one on the ground and one in his head. Well, actually in his dreams. Some kind of parallel war fucking thing."

Wilson looked at Kensington. Sam shrugged his shoulders. Smooth handed each of them a fresh cup of coffee. Wilson held his, Sam took a long sip, slowly swallowing the hot liquid.

"Still don't understand any of it. Gonna talk to the XO when we get back to camp, see if he has anymore to offer."

Smooth stared at Sam, watching as he took another sip.

"Yeah, okay. Go on. Tell the rest."

Sam nodded, taking one more sip before continuing.

"Well, I met up with Nathan."

"Nathan?"

Sam looked at Smooth. Wilson raised his hand to stop Smooth.

"Let him roll. Questions later."

Smooth nodded. Sam looked at them both, taking another sip of the hot liquid before continuing.

"Nathan DeLacroix from the 87th."

Before Smooth could ask, Sam explained.

"The 87th Pennsylvania. We set up on streets next to each other."

Smooth was ready to jump, but Wilson kept his hand up.

"In camp our tents were set up along streets. We met the first day we moved into camp before marching into the Shenandoah Valley."

Sam took another sip. Smooth sat silent, chomping at the bit to ask more.

"Nathan staggered in all bandaged up. He had been hit in the forehead with a piece of cannon shot, then had fallen into a scrub bush or something, cut him to pieces. We got to talking. He confirmed what I had already heard that Third Division Commander, Brigadier General Ricketts had fallen. We had lost our general. Days earlier we lost the commander of the 10th Vermont, a major, name escapes me now."

While Sam paused to take a sip of coffee, Wilson couldn't resist.

"That's how I know it's all a dream. Ain't no fucking generals, colonels, majors out in the field, only us fucking grunts and a couple of first line officers. Shit, general be killed in battle, ain't no fucking way, unless his air conditioner breaks and he dies of heat stroke, shit."

Sam let Wilson ramble on, smiling at his usual tirade. Smooth sat wide eyed, alternately looking at both of them. Sam continued.

"Anyway, Nathan told me the 87th Pennsylvania had lost all of their officers."

Sam took a sip, the liquid cooling quickly. Wilson remained quiet. Smooth looked on, totally absorbed in the retelling of the dream.

"But the real news was that the main confederate leader, the one we been fighting last few days, Major General Stephen Ramseur was laying mortally wounded in some captured mansion the Federals were using for their headquarters. All the Federal officers in the area went by to pay their respects. Imagine that, officers from one side paying respects to a general from the other side. One they had been fighting against all this time."

Sam paused and took another sip. Smooth was busting to ask questions, but Wilson held him back. Sam noticed and continued.

"Nathan said even Custer, George Armstrong himself went by to see Ramseur."

Smooth couldn't wait, interrupting.

"Custer, you mean that guy got slaughtered by Indians?"

Sam smiled.

"That be him."

Smooth wanted to ask more, but Sam pressed on.

"Hell, if you know the history, they all went to West Point together, knew each other. Didn't pick sides. Sides were picked for them."

Wilson looked at Sam, asking with his hands.

"Hell, I don't know, sounded good, it's what Nathan said."

Wilson nodded, Smooth jumped in.

"Okay, who's this guy? Ram?"

"Ramseur, Major General Stephen Ramseur."

"Yeah, him. Who is he?"

"Ramseur was the Confederate General who led the regiments against us that we battled back and forth with. According to Nathan, or what he heard, Ramseur was wounded and captured as the Rebels tried to escape the valley. But instead of treating him like a prisoner, they brought him to this mansion that the Federals… ah, Union officers were using as a headquarters."

Sam took a sip. Smooth pointed to Sam.

"Yeah, but what does it mean?"

Sam shrugged his shoulders.

"That's just it Smooth, I don't have a fucking idea what it means, or what any of it means. I gotta tell you though, just like I told Stick. These fucking dreams are so vivid. I feel like I am actually there. Not some fuzzy thing that you are in some other dimension kinda shit. I can taste the dust, smell the horses, feel the heat and all."

Sam finished the coffee and rinsed the cup out before placing it back into the canteen pouch. Smooth sat back, not sure what to ask next.

"Stick's the one thought it had some parallels with what we were doing here. Only thing that's made sense of any of it. You know, enter some God forsaken valley, to drive the enemy out, keep them from using the valley to run men and supplies. Otherwise, I don't have a fucking clue as to what it all means, or why I'm having the dreams at all. But they do seem to be mirroring what we are doing here. Gotta think Stick is right about the parallel."

Wilson nodded, pointing at him. Sam sat back against his ruck, pulling a cigarette from the pack. He offered the pack to Wilson and Smooth, who both declined. Flipping the lighter open he struck the flame and placed the fire against the tip.

Drawing heavily, he closed the lighter and let the smoke drift from his lips.

"Somehow the wounding and impending death of this Confederate Major General, this Stephen Ramseur has some major significance to the overall campaign. I truly don't know, but the magnitude of it all seems to be a big thing. Maybe when we get back, I can talk to the XO again. He might know what that means, or meant at the time, or something."

Sam pointed to Wilson, trying to change the subject.

"So Stick, what's on the agenda for today."

Wilson shrugged his shoulders.

"Don't know any different, than what we knew yesterday. For now we're on stand down. Let some other fuckers do the work, while we rest."

Sam nodded, taking a long pull on his cigarette. Smooth opened a can of C-rats. Wilson and Kensington looked at him.

"What? Still gotta eat, whatever this shit is, it's all we got."

"Fuckin' A."

Sam looked at Wilson, who was rummaging in his ruck for a can of something. He was content to just sit there and finish his cigarette.

The rest of the day passed uneventfully. No one bothered them or even came over to their area. The lieutenant was meeting with the other officers and left them alone. Sergeant Owen Hubbard sat with them, getting his gear updated and cleaned up, suggesting they do the same while they had a chance. Word had it that resupply would be coming later in the day and if they needed anything now was the time to request it.

The afternoon resupply birds flew in and let the slicks rest on the ground, instead of at full hover. Supplies could be off loaded with ease for once instead of with the usual intensity.

Taking turns at the resupply, Wilson's squad stocked up on more C-rats, replenished their ammo stores, picked up fresh uniforms and picked through the Sundry packs for cigarettes and toiletries.

Word had spread that they would be getting hot chow later in the afternoon, but that rumor never materialized and C-rats were the only dinner fare.

Another quiet evening was on the agenda. Someone suggested playing some Tonk to pass the time and various groups partook of the game at different intervals.

Wilson was on a mission to secure some hooch, whether home grown, Kentucky's finest or even rotgut if he had to, but he was determined to get something. An hour later, he returned with an unmarked bottle.

Kensington and Smooth were engaged in a game of five-card stud with Big John, Whitey and Hump when Wilson walked up carrying the bottle. The game stopped and each of the men looked up at him. Holding the bottle in the air, Wilson spoke softly.

"Mostly bourbon, but some home grown mixed in. Has a kick, but won't kill ya."

He removed the cap, taking a sip before passing it around. Each of the men at the game took a sip, before Wilson took the bottle and walked to the other men in his squad. Kensington, Smooth, Big John, Whitey and Hump went back to their stud game.

Later that night as the sun dropped below the horizon, Wilson, Smooth and Kensington sat against their rucks.

"Four Seven, want me to get you at midnight?"

"Fuck no. If I dream, I dream, but I want my full night's sleep."

"Fuckin' A."

Wilson removed the bottle from his ruck.

"Got me three sips left."

He handed the bottle to Sam, who took a sip, passing it back. Wilson handed the bottle to Smooth, who did likewise. Wilson, retrieving the bottle from Smooth, tilted the bottle up, taking the last gulp.

"Well, that's it for me. Feel all warm and fuzzy inside, time to hit the rack."

Sam looked at Smooth. They both watched Wilson pull the poncho liner over his head, getting into a comfortable position against his ruck.

Sam reached across and Smooth slapped his hand. A short time later they both did the same.

Sam Kensington woke to the buzz of activity going on around him. Smooth sat up, letting the poncho liner drop around him. Wilson was sitting up against his ruck, pulling on a cigarette.

"What the fuck?"

"Don't know, Four Seven. Mother fuckers been jumping since early morning. Something must be going down."

Sam nodded. Smooth pulled his poncho liner off.

"They gotta do it so fucking early?"

"Looks like they bringing in some heavy shit. Like they gonna reinforce this firebase, for future use. No longer temporary."

Before they could continue their bitching about the early morning noise, Sarge walked over, motioning with his arms.

"Listen up."

The men in Wilson's squad gathered around him.

"We're being lifted out this morning back to camp. We're done here. The A Shau will be just another bad fucking memory."

Controlled smiles spread across the men's faces.

"LT says to get your shit together. Even the CO is tolerable today."

Sarge pointed with his hand.

"Our lift area is over there. We leave by platoons. Five Hueys for each platoon. We're first. Don't know why, but LT said don't look a gift horse in the mouth, just get on the fucking bird, get the fuck out of here."

Sarge looked at the men before him.

"Personally, I think they want us out of here sooner rather than later. Heard they're building up this firebase to hold, rather than support and want to bring fresh troops in to do the work. We're just in the way."

Sarge paused, turning to look behind him.

"You guys should know that the LT pushed for us to be on the first Hueys. Said since we had to do point the whole time we were here, it was only fair we'd be the first to leave. Didn't go over too well with the CO, but the other platoon lieutenants said they agreed."

Sarge looked around at the men.

"Wilson, get your men ready now, don't know when those first birds will be in, but I don't want to take a chance. Pack up and move to the lift point. Don't care if we have to sit there for hours, just be there. Bird lands you get on it. Got it?"

"Roger that, Sarge."

The men watched as Sarge walked away. Wilson turned to the men.

"Don't know about the rest of you, but don't have to tell me twice."

The men of Wilson's squad, Kensington, Smooth, Lopes, Big John, Whitey, Hump and Body Man had their rucks packed in moments. Ten minutes after Sarge had left they were on their way to the pickup point.

An hour and a half later the Hueys started arriving. Wilson and Kensington climbed in on the left side, Smooth and Whitey on the right side with Body Man sitting inside. The bird lifted off, taking them out of the A Shau Valley. The lush vegetation of the jungle below became nothing more than another patch of ground as the bird climbed higher and turned.

Lopes, Big John climbed on the left, Hump on the inside and two men from Bob Grite's second squad climbed on the right slick. The rest of Bob Grite's second squad climbed aboard the next bird. Third squad with the lieutenant and Sarge took the next two birds. Twenty minutes after that first bird landed the platoon was airborne out of the A Shau Valley.

Twenty-Eight

The first four Hueys landed, with the men exiting from both sides, then waiting on the tarmac as the next four landed. Once the whole platoon was down, the men from the far side crossed over and joined the others. The lieutenant gathered the platoon together.

"Head back to your tents. Grab a shower, fresh clothes, whatever you need."

He looked the men over.

"Should be here for a couple of days. Don't have any other orders yet, so let's enjoy the break."

He started to say more, but stopped. Nothing more needed to be said. The lieutenant turned and walked away. Sergeant Own Hubbard motioned with his hands.

"You heard the man, let's go. Get off the fucking tarmac. This extremely fucking hot tarmac."

Slowly the men dispersed. Wilson and his squad made their way back to their tent, finding it pretty much as they had left it.

Wilson dropped his gear next to his bunk, removing the shoulder holster with the forty-five as well, dropping that on the bed. He lay down on top pushing the holster to the side.

Kensington did basically the same, dropping his ruck on the ground, pulling the shoulder holster off and placing it on top his ruck. Plopping down on the bunk he let out a sigh.

"Not sure I like this. Got used to sleeping on the ground and what have you. This too fucking soft for my taste."

"Fuckin' A."

Smooth, Lopes, Big John, Whitey and the two new guys standing behind them waited. Wilson looked at them standing there.

"What?"

"Just thought you should know there's a big fucking rat living under your bunk."

Wilson was up in an instant, the forty-five in his hand. He stepped back looking to where they were pointing. Kensington was off his rack as well. If Wilson was about to blast away, he wanted to be on the other side of where the pistol was pointed.

They all stood staring. Finally, Wilson moved toward the critter, but it didn't move. Getting even closer, he nudged the rat with the barrel of the forty-five, but still no movement.

"Fucking thing is dead."

Wilson stepped back.

"Somebody got a broom or something?"

No one answered. Wilson turned to face the men, but all he got was shrugs of shoulders and head shakes. Wilson looked around the tent, but seeing nothing he could use he considered other options.

Lopes stepped up with the C-ration case backing from his ruck removed.

"Here use this. I was going to put a new one in anyway." Wilson nodded taking the cardboard from him. Again moving in slowly, he wedged the cardboard under the critter, finally getting the carcass out from under his bunk.

Lifting the cardboard with both hands, he walked toward the opening. Hump pulled the tent flaps back so he could exit freely. Outside, Wilson looked around, finally spotting a trash can set up a few yards away. Quickly walking toward that he deposited the critter, cardboard and all into the receptacle.

Back inside, Kensington was already back on his rack. The rest of the men were either laying or sitting on theirs. Nodding to no one in particular, he went over to his bunk. For good measure, he looked underneath. Satisfied, he was alone this time, he plopped back down on top, pushing the holster out of the way, but keeping the forty-five in his hand for another moment.

"Anybody you know?"

Wilson looked over at Sam, but his focus was on the top of the tent.

"Think it was one of the sergeants I had in AIT."

Sam looked over, smiling.

"I think I had the same guy."

Sam swung his legs over sitting up facing Wilson.

"Well, I'm going to find me one of those 55 showers, get some of this red dirt off my skin. Get me some new fatigues."

Wilson nodded.

"Wake me when you get back."

"Roger that."

After a long shower, and a new set of clothes, Sam made his way across the compound, stopping at what he thought was the right Quonset hut. Quickly stepping inside, he saw that he had guessed right. Spotting the man he was looking for, he crossed over and stood next to him, waiting for him to finish the conversation with another officer. That officer looked Sam up and down, no doubt wondering who he was and what he was doing in here. The XO noticed and quickly diffused the situation.

"This is one of the field grunts I told you about. Information from them is invaluable. Asked him to update me when he got back in. Just came from that mission in the A Shau Valley, you know?"

The other officer, nodded and looked Sam up and down again, his contempt barely masked as he turned and walked away.

"Still using that same bullshit, sir?"

"Yeah, why not? Bullshit still works."

The XO looked at Sam for a moment, then around the hut they were standing in.

"How about we go get a cup of coffee?"

Sam nodded and followed the XO out of the hut. The light outside seemed brighter as they emerged from the filtered light inside the hut. They walked in silence to the mess tent. Getting coffee from a large, beat up, well used urn, they made their way to a table off to the side. Adding cream and lots of sugar, Sam stirred his coffee.

"Where do you want me to start, sir?"

The XO looked at Sam for a moment.

"Why don't you just tell me what you remember?"

Sam nodded, sipping his coffee. He told the XO about the battles, the captured cannon, the flanking, being run out of their encampment, finally routing the rebels, getting back into their camp and everything else he could remember. The XO sat patiently and listened to the details.

"Well, that all sounds like you're still in the Shenandoah Valley campaign. Basically what we originally thought."

Sam nodded.

"Something else that you remember?"

Sam sat back in his chair palming his coffee cup.

"Well, there is one thing that I don't quite understand."

The XO nodded, waiting. Sam leaned forward.

"I have a buddy."

Sam stopped and smiled.

"I mean in the dream. I have a buddy, another soldier named

Nathan DeLacroix that I meet up with periodically."

Sam looked at the XO, but when he didn't get a reaction, he continued.

"Anyway, right after we got back into our camp, I mean the Federal camp that the Rebels had overrun earlier in the day…"

Sam stopped, wiping his hand across his face.

"Sir, I gotta tell you these are not those hazy, fuzzy kind of dreams, like you know when you dream you're running through a field or falling… or…shit."

The XO didn't speak waiting for Sam to continue.

"I mean these are so fucking real, so vivid. It's really like I'm there, you know? Hell, I can taste the dust, smell the horses, feel the heat…"

Again the XO remained silent, not interrupting. Finally, Sam continued.

"So anyway, this Nathan fellow, he's with the 87th Pennsylvania by the way, so this Nathan DeLacroix comes by, he's all bandaged, caught a piece of cannon shot across the forehead, but then fell into some kind of sharp bush, cut him to pieces, but a… anyway he comes over."

Sam paused, taking a sip of coffee. He looked up at the XO, unsure for a moment, but believing that the XO was generally interested, he continued.

"So Nathan is giving me, I mean the guy in the dream, which I guess is me?"

Sam pauses, shaking his head, finishing the last of the coffee. Taking the XO's cup as well, he walks over and fills them both back up. Adding cream and lots of sugar to his, he stirs longer than he needs too. Finally, returning to the table and looking up at the XO, he continues.

"Well, Nathan is giving me an update on what he heard while he was with the hospital gang, you know, getting patched up. Basically, we are discussing the officers we lost. Tells me, but I already knew, that we lost General Ricketts, I knew we lost our commander, the 10th Vermont commander. I had heard that other officers had fallen. Anyway, he says they lost all of the officers in the 87th."

Sam paused, smiling.

"Stick, I mean Wilson, my friend here, you know, present day war?"

Sam stopped, looking up.

"This is just too fucking weird."

The XO smiled, waving his hand in the air.

"Tell me anyway."

Sam nodded, setting the coffee cup down on the table.

"Stick says it has to be a dream, ain't no fucking generals in the field, certainly not ones got killed. Says I must be dreaming, if I think there are officers in battle, shit. Only us grunts are expendable. He says."

Sam paused, smiling. Even the XO smiled. Sam looked at him for a long time.

"Well sir, what I was about to tell you is that, Nathan, you know the guy from... anyway, he said he heard that they had captured the Confederate commander, at least the guy we've been up against this whole time, they captured him as the Rebels were trying to escape, but they didn't take him prisoner, they brought him over to some mansion the Federals were using for their HQ."

Sam paused, noticing the XO's interest was peaked.

"Who'd they capture Sam?"

"I believe his name was Ramseur, Major General Stephen Ramseur. Nathan said the hospital gang said even the Federal officers were stopping by to pay their respects. Even Custer went there."

Sam paused, the XO's face lit up in obvious elation.

"Ramseur? Do you know who that is?"

Sam shook his head no.

"Other than being the Confederate general that we were

apparently up against, I don't know anymore about him."

The XO leaned in closer to Sam, talking just above a whisper.

"He was probably one of the finest fighting officers Lee had. Fought in several major battles. A highly regarded and well respected officer in the Confederate, or any, army for that matter. I'm pretty sure Custer and others were probably in the academy with him. Losing him was a big loss to the Confederate Army. Hell, the Confederate cause."

Sam sat silent, just listening.

"A terrible loss for the Confederacy, but more importantly, that as much as anything signaled the end of Confederate control of the Shenandoah Valley. As I recall, after that the Confederates were driven from the valley, their stores were captured or destroyed and a means of support to Lee's army in Richmond was cut off. A major victory for the Union forces to say the least. Quite possibly a turning point in that war."

Sam nodded, not sure he cared one way or another, but felt compelled to listen, as maybe this would help explain why he was having the dreams in the first place. The XO continued with the history lesson.

"Once the conquest for the valley was completed, I'm pretty sure the VI Corps rejoined the Army of the Potomac and the XIX Corps went into winter camp there in the valley."

"Winter camp?"

The XO looked at Sam, then continued.

"In the northern states, when winter set in, the armies from both sides went into winter camp, basically stopping the fighting until the weather got better."

"No shit?"

The XO smiled.

"Basically the Union Forces, Federals as you keep calling them, took control of the Shenandoah Valley, routing the Confederates and held it from that point on until the end of the war, putting further pressure on Lee from Grant to take Richmond and the seize of Petersburg, eventually leading to Lee's surrender in April, 1865."

The XO noticed Sam sat there with a blank stare.

"Anyway, that's basically what happened after the valley campaign."

Sam nodded, pointing.

"So you're saying this Ramseur was an important guy?"

The XO nodded yes.

"Because for some reason it stuck as important in the dream that he was captured, but more importantly that he was treated with such respect."

The XO nodded again.

"He was widely respected. A very fine general regardless of what side he was on.

Sam nodded, finishing his coffee.

"Well sir, we come back to the original question, which is, why?"

The XO looked at Sam.

"Still don't think I can answer that to your satisfaction. I can tell you that it appears you have reached the end of that campaign. The Shenandoah Valley Campaign of 1864. For all intents and purposes it's over."

Sam nodded.

"Just like it is here."

The XO smiled, waving his hand in the air.

"Anything in your dreams might tell you different?"

Sam shook his head no.

"What was your latest dream about?"

"Haven't had one. No dreams since we left the firebase. Last dream was what I told you. Nathan DeLacroix told me what he heard. We went off to play some Faro and drink some home grown."

The XO smiled.

"Same there as it is here?"

"Yeah, sure looks that way."

Sam smiled.

"Nothing like some gambling and some home grown to pass the night."

The XO nodded.

"Ain't that the truth?"

Sam raised his hand in the air.

"What the hell is Faro anyway?"

The XO looked at Sam, not speaking for a moment.

"Let me see, as I recollect, it is a card game, a banking game. That is to say all the players play against the bank or the house, like black jack. One man, or the house fronts all the bets."

Sam nodded, the XO continued.

"There is a green cloth painted with one suit of cards, usually spades, but that really doesn't matter. Each player places a bet on a particular card, after which the dealer pulls a card. The first card drawn is the loser, if you placed your bet on that card the house wins. The second drawn is the winner, if you placed your bet on that card you are a winner. Even money bets, one for one. You bet a buck you win a buck or lose."

The XO paused.

"There were other bet combinations which I don't remember specifically right now, but I do remember if your bet was on a different card, nothing happened, basically a push."

Sam stared at the XO.

"It would be easier to understand if you were looking at the game. It was the most played game of the nineteenth century, bar none and was certainly played widely during the Civil War. All you needed was the cloth and a deck of cards."

Sam nodded.

"And this game was played over stud poker?"

"Absolutely. Much like you guys play Tonk all the time. It

was their game back then."

"So a little down time, a little home grown and some gambling?"

The XO smiled looking at his watch.

"Well Sam, sorry I couldn't be more help. That's what I remember about that time of the war. 1864 was a vital year for the Union Army. That was one of the many campaigns they launched."

The XO noticed Sam was staring off.

"Anyway, hopefully that can clear some things up for you. Help you make some sense of the dreams."

The XO paused.

"Although it does seem curious that of all the battles and campaigns waged during the Civil War that would be the one you focused in on, you know, I mean dreamt about. I think somehow that has some significance."

Sam turned and looked at the XO.

"Yes sir, I appreciate all you've told me. At least I understand the battle I'm dreaming about. Don't know what the fuck it means, but at least I know. Thanks for the info. Still think Stick has the right idea, it's some kind of parallel war fucking thing. Only thing makes any sense."

The XO nodded.

"You might be right, Sam. Somehow you're dreaming about a campaign similar to the one you just went through."

The XO paused.

"Still, I find it curious that your dreams focused on that campaign, with all the others the Civil War had to offer."

Sam nodded.

"Pretty fucked up, huh?"

The two men stood, shaking hands. Sam watched as the XO left the mess tent. Stepping outside into the bright sun, he made his way back to his own tent.

"So you had your meet with the XO?"

Wilson sat on his bunk cleaning his sixteen. The forty-five lay next to him, obviously already cleaned.

"Yeah."

"And?"

Sam sat down on his bunk facing Wilson.

"Looks like I've reached, I mean the guy in my dreams, reached the end of that battle. We won. The Federals drove the Confederates out of the valley and are setting up a winter camp to hold it."

Wilson looked at him.

"It's okay, I didn't understand it either."

They sat silent for a moment.

"So at least I know what happened and all about that battle in the Shenandoah Valley. Still don't know what the fuck it means, but at least I know."

Wilson looked up from his weapon.

"Well Four Seven, I got some news for you. You may have won that battle, but we lost ours."

"Huh?"

"Heard from a brother this morning. The NVA already moved back into the A Shau. Gooks already reestablished on that godforsaken hill, was so fucking important. Brother said, Intel reports they already back in full operation as if we were never there. So again we took it, then gave it back. Same same."

Wilson began putting his weapon back together.

"Maybe we should go fight your war. Keep what you take."

Sam smiled.

"What else the XO say?"

"Nothing more really. Seems this Confederate General, this

Ramseur, was pretty important. Too bad he had to die in battle."

Sam looked at Wilson waiting for his usual rant about generals in battle, but he didn't give it a go this time. Wilson finished, putting his weapon back together, setting it on the bed next to him. He leaned over to Sam.

"Tell you what Four Seven, maybe put some general's ass on that fucking hill, maybe we don't give it back so easy."

Sam smiled reaching out with his hand. They did the white version of the black dap handshake.

"But it don't mean nothing."

"But it don't mean nothing."

Twenty-Nine

Sitting around late one morning after a couple of days in camp, Wilson, Kensington, Big John, Whitey and Body Man were playing Tonk, passing the time, when Wilson dropped his bomb shell.

"Hey mother fuckers, I broke 60 this morning. Hit 59 this morning's wake up."

Kensington nodded.

"Well, I'm right behind you, 86 as of this morning."

Wilson looked at him.

"Damn Four Seven, that's like a whole 'nother month."

Sam nodded.

"Yeah, but I'm still right behind you."

He looked at Body Man, pointing. Wilson nodded.

"Yeah, we won't even ask."

Body Man nodded.

"Me and Hump can't count that high."

Wilson smiled, Sam chuckled, Big John laid down his cards. The others tossed their cards in. Wilson stood up and walked back to his bunk.

"That's enough for me."

Body Man got up. Sam followed him walking back to his bunk. Whitey shrugged and Big John dealt another hand.

"Well Stick, I'm not complaining mind you, but this sitting around has its good and bad points."

Wilson looked at Sam.

"What, you'd rather be out there in the bush?"

"I'm not saying that. I'm just saying."

"Uh huh."

"What I mean is that, after that, sitting around wears on you."

Wilson nodded. Smooth called out from his bunk.

"Four Seven is right. Humping the bush gets the heart going, sitting around here, worrying about some officer or lifer ready to hassle you about some bullshit, wears on the nerves."

Sam pointed toward Smooth. Wilson nodded.

"Shit!"

They all looked over at Whitey.

"God damn, Big John, you can't lose today. I'm done."

They watched as Whitey made his way back to his bunk.

Before anyone could say anything else, Sarge came into the tent, with Bob Grite behind him. Wilson looked up.

"You come to play or this a BOHICA?"

"Neither."

Wilson continued to stare at Sarge, until he noticed it.

"God Damn, Sarge. God Damn, you made it."

"Fuckin' A."

Sam looked at Wilson, then at the Sarge, not getting it.

"Four Seven look at the man's collar."

Sam honed on the collar and spotted it immediately.

"Damn Sarge, another stripe, no shit?"

"That's a rocker for you peons, but yes, I made E6, staff sergeant."

Wilson and Sam both stood, reaching for and shaking his hand. The sergeant waved them off.

"It gets worse."

Wilson's smile faded, Sam stood silent.

"You two made E5, not that specialist crap but buck sergeant."

"What?"

"Yeah, what?"

Wilson and Sam stood silent as Sergeant Own Hubbard smiled.

"That's right you two and Bob made E5. How do you like that shit?"

Before either of them could answer, the sergeant continued, waving for the rest of the men to come closer.

"The LT put you guys up and me of course, some time ago, but you know how long it takes to get things done."

The Sarge paused, the men waited.

"Well, I gotta tell you, when he came in as a butter bar, I didn't have much hope, but once he made silver, he grew a pair, turned out to be okay."

Sarge wiped his brow.

"Anyway, said he was putting us up for promotion. Top didn't like the idea and probably would have blocked it or at the very least sat on it, but LT went to battalion direct. Since we lost so many men on that fucking hill, they were all too happy to get some more cadre."

Wilson looked at Sarge, then Bob Grite and finally at Sam.

"Son-of-a-bitch. What that mean?"

Sarge waved his hand in the air.

"Well, the good news is you're all too short."

"Fuckin' A."

Sarge looked at Wilson.

"As I said, you're all too short to get reassigned, so you'll stay with the platoon, at least for now."

Wilson nodded, Sam looked at Sarge.

"And?"

"Well, one of you will have to be platoon sergeant."

"Grite."

"Grite."

Sarge looked at Wilson and Kensington, before turning to Bob.

"Well, Bob looks like you got their vote. Besides I think you have the most time left."

Bob Grite nodded.

"So one of you have first squad, Wilson's squad and the other has Grite's squad. Bob will have third squad as I did."

"Why, where are you going?"

Sarge looked at Sam.

"Boys, I'm done. Time is up. I'm being reassigned to admin until I can process out of here. Got an instructor job back in the world."

"A DI?"

"No, hell no. But, I'll be providing training of some sort."

"What's the LT think about all this?"

Sarge looked at Wilson, a smile forming on his face.

"Don't know. He's already been reassigned. You'll be getting a new butter bar any day now. So, I suggest you rest up, you know how gung ho those new lieutenants are when they get here."

The smile grew bigger on his face.

"Well, gentlemen, I'll leave you to work things out."

The Sarge started to leave, then turned back.

"I just want to say, we did good out there. Only one man killed and six wounded, pretty fucking amazing considering all the shit we were in. Outstanding job. Talked to the helicopter squad that supported us. Said they were grateful we found that bird with the men still in it. Appreciate getting their men back. Said you need anything let them know."

Sarge paused looking at the men.

"Well, I just want to say thank you all."

The Sarge turned again and started to leave but turned back one final time, offering a salute that was returned by Wilson and Kensington.

"AMF."

The Sarge left this time. Hump stood next to Kensington.

"AMF?"

"Adios mother fuckers."

"Butter Bar?"

Sam looked at Hump.

"When an officer starts out he's a second louie, second lieutenant, gold bar on his collar, butter bar, then makes silver, first lieutenant."

Hump nodded.

"B... O..., what was that?"

Sam smiled.

"BOHICA, Bend over here it comes again. Usually when an officer or sergeant comes in, someway, somehow we are about to be fucked."

Wilson smiled.

"No usually about it."

Hump nodded, still standing.

"Damn when you guys leave, I'll need to find me a grunt to English dictionary, so I know what the fuck you're talking about."

Wilson smiled, starting a small laugh, Kensington did the same, Smooth joined them, and finally the rest of the men started a laugh that wouldn't stop. Not that it was particularly funny, but more of a release. Even Hump laughed, caught up in the moment.

Wilson sat back on his bunk.

"Four Seven, ah excuse me, Sergeant Kensington."

"You call me that again and I'll call you Sergeant Wilson."

"Fair enough."

Sam smiled.

"So Four Seven, what you think about that?"

"Well, I like the money and it'll be better when we get back to the states, but here, it could only mean trouble. Think we might know something."

Wilson looked at him.

"Yeah, could be a problem short term. You okay with my squad, I'll take second?"

Sam nodded.

"Yeah, that works for me. You're good with second?"

"Yeah, I know a brother in second, couple of other guys, it'll be fine."

The two men sat silent on their bunks. Smooth walked over standing in front of both of then.

"Tell me I don't have to call you sergeant."

Wilson looked at him, waving his hand in the air.

"Might have to hurt you, if you did."

Smooth smiled.

"Did I hear Sarge say we're getting a new LT?"

Wilson nodded.

"Say when?"

"A day or so."

Smooth nodded, turned and walked back to his bunk. Wilson and Sam sat in silence.

Early the next morning, a spit and polish clerk summoned Wilson and Kensington. Bob Grite already stood outside their tent.

"What's up?"

Grite pointed to the center of the compound.

"New LT is here, wants to meet with us."

Wilson nodded. Sam looked to where he was pointing. Standing in the center were two men, talking. One of the men was the first sergeant, Top to the men. As they approached, Top nodded and left.

"Gentlemen, I'm Lieutenant John Summers, I'm your new platoon leader."

Wilson and Sam looked at the shiny new butter bar still on his collar glistening in the sun. The LT noticed.

"Sorry, haven't had a chance to change yet, just got here an hour ago."

Wilson looked at him, Sam shifted his weight to the other foot.

"I understand from Top that I'm a little top heavy in sergeants, which could work to our advantage. I also understand that a couple of you are counting down."

The lieutenant paused looking the three sergeants over.

"Who's who?"

"Bob Grite, platoon sergeant. That's Wilson, second squad and Kensington, first squad."

The lieutenant nodded.

"Understood."

The three freshly new sergeants stood silently waiting for the lieutenant to continue.

"As I was saying, I think this can work to our advantage, having three experienced men still attached to the platoon. Top says he'll see to it that you stay put, even though the other platoons are in need of men with leadership."

Wilson fought hard not to roll his eyes. The lieutenant continued.

"Take a day to get your gear in order."

The lieutenant looked at Wilson and Kensington with forty-fives hanging in shoulder holsters.

"Are those personal guns?"

Kensington looked at his forty-five, Wilson just stared at the lieutenant.

"I don't believe you're authorized to carry those, but if they are personal guns, I won't object to your keeping them."

"Begging your pardon sir, but what the fuck are you talking about?"

The lieutenant looked at Wilson, smiling.

"I'm only wondering why enlisted men have forty-fives and I have to fill out a shit load of paperwork to be considered."

Wilson smiled.

"Would you like me to get you one?"

"That would be great."

"Roger that, sir."

Bob Grite interjected.

"Sir, Wilson and Kensington also carry a thumper. Sarge… ah, Sergeant Owen Hubbard, our former platoon sergeant wanted us well armed going back into the A Shau."

The lieutenant nodded.

"That's fine, sergeant."

"My next line would be I want the men to stand for inspection, but even I understand the absurdity of that, so here's what I want you to do. Get your gear updated, pack for a five day patrol. Yes, we'll get resupplied while we're out, but I expect to be out five to seven days."

"Out, sir?"

The lieutenant looked at Grite.

"Yes, we're going on a five day patrol that could stretch to seven days."

The lieutenant waited, but none of the three men spoke.

"I understand that you all just came back from the A Shau, but while everyone was out there, it seems we have neglected our own backyard."

The lieutenant paused.

"The CO says you guys have been laying around, thinks you need to get back to work, so he's volunteered our company to run patrols for the next week."

The lieutenant paused.

"Besides, if the reports are right, it should be pretty quiet out there. Battalion wants to make sure it is."

The lieutenant looked at the three men, half expecting some resistance but when none came, he continued.

"Look, here's the plan. No question, I need seasoning, so what better way than to have a taste with what should be a relatively easy assignment to get my feet wet. I promise you I will listen, observe and learn from your experience."

Wilson looked at the lieutenant almost in disbelief.

"Okay, that's a load of crap, but you know what I mean."

Wilson smiled.

"Sir, one question."

"Yes?"

"You want the deluxe package or the basic, get you by, show and tell?"

The lieutenant smiled.

"How about a little of both?"

"Roger that, sir."

The lieutenant stood silent for a moment.

"One thing though, I don't mind, in fact, I welcome your input on all levels, but remember I'm still in charge. The men have to understand that. Hopefully, you understand that."

"Sir, that won't be a problem, we know how to handle butter bars."

The lieutenant looked at Bob Grite, even Wilson looked at him, Sam covered his mouth shielding a smile.

"Well then Sergeant Grite, I think we'll get along fine."

"Sir, I meant no disrespect."

"None taken."

The men stood silent for a long moment. Finally the lieutenant raised his hand in the air.

"Well gentlemen, I think that's it. I'll be by later to meet the rest of the men, performing that ah… inspection we talked about."

Wilson smiled.

"Whatever you need, sir."

The lieutenant nodded, turned and walked away. The three men stood there for a bit, before starting back.

"Well Bob, what you think?"

"Wilson, he just might be okay. Time will tell. Time will tell."

Wilson nodded.

Back in the tent sitting on their bunks, Wilson looked over.

"Well Four Seven, you got your wish. We're going back to the bush."

Sam nodded.

"It wasn't exactly what I wished for, but you gotta admit, it's better than sitting around here all day, waiting to have some officer or lifer climb up your ass, for something. Shit I've shaved more regularly in the last week than the whole time I've been in country."

Wilson nodded, Sam continued.

"You know I was wondering what the CO was up to. He's been pretty quiet since we got back to camp. Figured he'd have us out doing drills and shit like that."

Wilson smiled. Sam sat silent. Smooth came over and sat on Sam's bunk. Wilson sat up on his.

"Four Seven, I was wondering, you been having those dreams, maybe… you know, might be something we about to do?"

"Smooth, no I haven't had a dream since we got back. According to what the XO told me, looks like that battle is over, just like the A Shau is over for us. Maybe we get out there, something new comes up, but so far nothing."

Smooth nodded.

"So, what you guys think about the new LT?"

Wilson looked at Sam, but he pointed back at him.

"Hard to say yet. Trying too hard to be one of us, but I like some of the things he says, which reminds me I have something to do."

Wilson was off his bunk and heading out of the tent. Smooth and Kensington watched him leave.

"What the hell was that all about?"

Sam shrugged his shoulders.

"Four Seven, how you and Stick gonna play this?"

Sam looked at Smooth for a moment then, realizing what he meant, he smiled.

"Stick's taking over second and I'll lead first for now."

"Sounds right. Stick knows a brother in second."

"Of course he does."

"Huh?"

"Nothing, never mind."

"We getting any FNGs you know of?"

Sam shook his head no.

"Haven't heard any such thing, but we probably will. Always do."

"Four Seven, you have a dream, will you let me know?"

"Will do Smooth, will do."

Smooth got up from Sam's bunk and half ass saluted as he left. Kensington watched him leave, remembering that he hadn't had any dreams in a while, wondering if it really was over and what that meant.

An hour and a half later, Wilson walked in with the new lieutenant next to him.

"At ease, men."

Wilson walked over and sat on his bunk. Sam finally saw it and punched Wilson on the arm. The new lieutenant was wearing a shoulder holster with a forty-five hanging at his side.

"I just wanted to stop by and introduce myself. I'm Lieutenant John Summers, your new platoon leader. Any questions?"

No one spoke up. Wilson and Kensington had brought them up to date, on what they knew about the new guy and they were satisfied for now. The lieutenant nodded.

"Okay then, but if you do have a question feel free that you can come to me with anything."

The men nodded, watching the new guy.

"Well, if there is nothing else, I'll leave you men be. Remember, day after tomorrow we'll be heading out for a five to seven day patrol. So, if you need anything get it now, new gear, ammo, supplies. If you can't get something, let me know and I'll see what I can do."

The lieutenant paused.

"Men."

The lieutenant walked out of the tent.

"Hey Stick, hope he's not that nervous in the bush."

"Smooth, he'll be fine. If not we'll leave him out there."

The laughs started slow but quickly rallied into an all out hysteria, with hand slapping and pounding on the bunks.

"Nice move."

"Four Seven, I don't know what you're talking about."

"A forty-five and a shoulder holster, in what, like an hour and a half."

Wilson smiled.

"Some colonel will have a lot of explaining to do, his forty-five gone missing. All the paper work clean, he's out, LT's in."

Sam shook his head.

"Fuckin' A."

Wilson sat up on his bunk.

"Let's get some chow."

Sam looked at his watch.

"Little early, isn't it?"

Wilson looked at him.

"We walk slow."

Sam understood and got up from his bunk. Together they left the tent, walking slowly toward the mess tent. Wilson pulled and lit a cigarette, offering one to Sam, who took it.

"Well Four Seven, still can't believe we be sergeants. All I wanted to do was get by, finish my tour and get the fuck out of here, now I gotta think and make decisions, not sure I like that."

"Damn Stick, it don't change nothing. We'll still do the same, just get more money for doing it, that's all."

"That's true."

They walked in silence.

"Well Sergeant Kensington, think we get better chow, now that we're important?"

"Well Sergeant Wilson, I believe it's the same shit, don't matter you more important now."

"Fuckin' A."

Tossing the cigarette butts into the butt can, they entered the mess tent.

Thirty

Standing on the tarmac, they waited while the Hueys powered up. The signal was given and the men boarded the helicopters to take them out to their rendezvous point.

The plan was for them to be choppered out and then make their way back to camp on foot, hopefully catching anything that might be between them and the camp, rather than walking out from camp and giving anyone out there a chance to escape. Looked good on paper anyway.

Kensington, Smooth, Big John, Whitey with the radio and Hump on the inside boarded the first bird. Lopes, Body Man, Wilson, the lieutenant and another guy from second boarded the second bird and so on.

The Hueys lifted off together, getting into formation in the sky and flying low out to the predetermined LZ. Gunships were circling the area, already having laid down covering fire. They parted as the Hueys approached, landing two at a time.

Kensington and the others were off the first bird, Wilson and his group were off the second. Two more birds landed and the men disembarked. The last bird carrying the rest of the platoon landed, dropping off those remaining soldiers.

Before the dust cleared, the men were on the ground and the Hueys were gone. A minute later the gunships left, the noise from the blades buffeting the wind gone.

Kensington, Wilson and Grite stood next to the lieutenant, reviewing the map. Determining a route to take, the lieutenant turned to Kensington.

"I understand your squad is point."

Sam nodded.

"Well then, let's go."

Sam walked back to his squad.

"Smooth you okay with point, we can take turns like before."

"Negative Four Seven, you be the man now. I'll take point, put Hump at slack, time he get accustomed. Tomorrow him and I can switch off. Maybe put Body Man at slack next day."

"Roger that."

Sam looked at his squad.

"Okay, listen up. Smooth on point, Hump slack, then me, Whitey with the radio, Big John with the 60, Body Man, then Lopes bring up the rear. Wilson's gonna keep the distance between squads, just like before. Lopes, you keep your eyes on the drag."

Lopes nodded, his M16 resting on his hip, the steel pot tilted slightly on his head.

"Right."

Sam looked at the men moving into position.

"Alright let's go."

Smooth lead the squad off the LZ, dropping down a bit before climbing a slight rise. Over the rise he halted the movement. Sam came up. Smooth pointed.

"We got beaucoup tracks, but they be old. Lot of men came through here some time ago. My guess they were moving through didn't want to make contact, kept their distance from the camp. Direction is back toward the A Shau. Might have been reinforcements."

Before Smooth could say any more, Wilson, Grite and the lieutenant were next to them. The lieutenant looked to where Smooth was pointing.

"Sir, we got beaucoup tracks, but old. Lot of men passed through heading that way. Think they might have been reinforcements for the A Shau. Stayed out here far enough to avoid the camp. Don't think they wanted anything to do with the camp."

The lieutenant nodded.

"Can you tell where they were coming from?"

Smooth looked up, and then stood up.

"Could have been from anywhere. One of the Villes around here, or maybe from another location, moved here for support. Hard to say."

The lieutenant nodded.

"Of course. Of course."

"Smooth, give us a minute."

Smooth looked at Wilson.

"Sure."

Smooth left the three sergeants and the lieutenant.

"Smooth, have the men take five."

"Got it, Four Seven."

The lieutenant looked at Sam and wanted to ask, but left the question for another time. Wilson squeezed past Sam and Grite.

"Sir, it probably holds what the report says that the area is quiet. Tracks been here awhile, no movement recently. What Smooth says, probably was reinforcements, moving to that fucking hill in the A Shau."

The lieutenant wanted to ask, but Wilson beat him to it.

"Tracks been rained on, the dust is dry. I make it a week, maybe more."

The lieutenant nodded.

"Thanks."

"My orders are to proceed on this course."

The lieutenant pointed in a sweeping motion.

"Any reason we should deviate."

Wilson shook his head no.

"Bob?"

"Sir, I think we'd be okay to continue on course, but might I suggest we take a break in place and send out a team up the trail a bit, see if anything looks different, maybe one down the trail as well."

The lieutenant looked at Grite.

"Wilson, you go up and Kensington, you go down, maybe ten minutes then back. I don't want to be here too long."

"Roger that, sir."

The four men pulled back.

"Grite, see if you can put together some kind of perimeter for now."

Grite nodded. Wilson got four men from second, one of them with a radio. Sam did virtually the same from his squad. Together they stepped out onto the trail. Wilson headed up the trail in the directions of the tracks. Kensington headed down in the direction the tracks came from.

Fifteen minutes later they were standing next to the lieutenant.

"All clear, sir."

Wilson nodded the same.

"Alright then, let's get back on the move."

Smooth led them across the trail, back into the jungle. Humping into the early afternoon, Smooth came upon a small plateau that could serve as a nice perimeter for a break. He summoned the lieutenant up, pointing.

"Sir, that might be a good spot take a break, get some chow."

The lieutenant nodded, looking the area over.

"Kensington take a couple of men, work your way around the far side, come up the back. I'll take a couple of men this way meet you there."

Sam looked at him.

"I'll be fine, I'll have…"

The lieutenant looked at Hump in the slack position.

"Son, what's your name?"

"Louis Humphries, but they call me Hump."

"Well Hump, how about you me and a couple of guys do what I just said?"

Hump looked at Sam long enough to get a nod of approval.

"Sure thing, sir. Four Seven, see you on the back side."

The lieutenant turned to Big John.

"Tell the others what we're doing."

Big John nodded. Hump led the way, with the lieutenant right behind him. Sam took his guys around the far side. The two teams met up in the back of the plateau.

"All clear, sir."

The lieutenant looked at Sam.

"Same here. Let's get the platoon in place. Hump, you and the others go back and tell them to come forward."

Hump nodded. The lieutenant and Kensington walked onto the top of the plateau, looking out.

"Sir, this might make for a good NDP."

The lieutenant nodded, pulling his map from the protective plastic.

"Well sergeant, I would agree with you except that we need to be here by night fall."

Sam looked at the lieutenant, but remained silent.

"However, everything looks good on paper. Fetch the others and we'll discuss."

"Roger that sir."

Kensington went off to get Wilson and Grite. The lieutenant stood on the plateau, looking out in the direction they were suppose to go. The three sergeants stood beside him, waiting.

"Kensington thinks this might make a good NDP, but we need to be over there by nightfall."

The men looked to where he was pointing.

"Any thoughts, before I make my decision?"

Grite pointed.

"Sir, we could send out a team forward, see what's up ahead. If the terrain is in our favor, we could make good time tomorrow, catch up. But if it looks rough, which I suspect it will be, we might want to consider moving further tonight."

The lieutenant nodded.

"How about we do this? Take a break, fifteen at the most, mount up and push on. I'm sure we can find another spot for our NDP."

Wilson and Kensington stood silent. Grite started to speak, but held it in, waiting for the Lieutenant.

"Gentlemen, I respect your input, speak up."

Wilson looked at Grite, then Sam.

"Sir, I believe you're right, that we can find another spot, might I suggest that we give it another hour, but then take the first spot we find, so as not to be stumbling at dusk. I have no problem with moving on, but when we find something, that's it, we stop and set up."

"Good point, Wilson. I'll accept that."

The lieutenant looked at Kensington.

"We good, Kensington?"

"Absolutely, sir."

Smooth led the long green line through the jungle, chopping and cutting his way through the elephant grass, bamboo fields and hold me back vines for the next hour and a half without finding anything suitable to setup in. Stopping at a clearing he called Sam up.

"Might have been a good spot but look."

He pointed to either side. The opening gave way to a slight rise on each side. Sam nodded.

"Let's continue on."

Smooth nodded, standing and working around the clearing, Hump on slack right behind him. The procession moved on. Forty-five minutes later Smooth came upon another plateau, rising up from the floor to the side of a small hill. Three sides were high ground, but the backside protruded from the hill. He stopped. Once again Sam joined him.

"Four Seven, that could work. Might have to put a team on top the hill, make sure nobody flanks us."

Sam nodded, motioning for the others to come up.

"Sir, we got a plateau gives us three sides high ground, but we have to deal with a back side rise. Smooth says put a team on top, cover our ass."

The lieutenant nodded.

"Let's do it."

The platoon moved onto the plateau, promptly setting up a perimeter defense. The lieutenant, Grite, Wilson and Kensington sat in the middle, working out the arrangements.

"Have third squad set up an ambush on top, secure that area. First and second squad cover the base right and left."

"Should I have the men dig holes?"

The lieutenant looked at Grite.

"No. I think a small defensive position will be okay for one night. Just have them dig in. Standard watch intervals."

Grite nodded. The lieutenant continued to look at his map.

"We covered a lot of ground. I appreciate that. Thanks."

He looked at Wilson.

"I know it's later that we wanted to set up, but I believe we still got time for chow and a smoke, you know, before quiet time."

"Quiet time?"

"Isn't that what you call it before dark?"

Wilson smiled.

"Oh that? Yes, of course. I just thought maybe that was some weird officer thing."

The lieutenant looked at Wilson, starting a smile.

"No slack, huh? You're gonna fuck with me all the way aren't you?"

"Who me, sir?"

"Go on, get out of here."

The lieutenant continued to smile as they walked away, finally folding his map back into the protective plastic.

Wilson came over to Kensington's position and sat down next to him.

"Well, Four Seven, how's your first day in the field?"

"Fuck you mean, first day?"

"Easy Four Seven, I meant as a newly minted sergeant."

"Same as yours. I feel out of place, putting Smooth on point, Hump on slack. Don't see why I can't walk point no more."

Wilson smiled.

"Yeah, right."

Sam removed the pack of cigarettes from his shirt and offered one to Wilson. Firing his lighter he lit both. Taking a long pull, he let the smoke drift out, using the cigarette to point.

"Good thing we found this spot."

Wilson nodded.

"You pissed he didn't listen to you back there?"

"Huh? No, fuck no. Just meant we got lucky to find something, before the day got too long, that's all."

Wilson nodded.

"Don't matter, ain't nothing out here anyway. The only way they'd be here is if they was planning to attack the camp. They all back in the mother fucking A Shau, waiting for us to be stupid enough to go in again."

Sam nodded.

"Besides, this way we get the best of both. Out of the camp so as not to be hassled and in the bush when we know it's relatively safe. Can't be fucking around now that we're short timers."

Sam looked at Wilson and stuck out his hand.

"Fuckin' A."

They did the white version of the black dap handshake.

"But it don't mean nothing."

"But it don't mean nothing."

Three more days of humping resulted in no new discoveries. The area was quiet. The lieutenant asked for and was granted permission to go back to camp. Another three days of taking it easy was met with another patrol assignment.

Once again Hueys lifted them out, to an area to search for signs of activity. Another five days of humping, with no new results, brought them back to camp. This time they had four days of rest, before another assignment.

The new area took them much further out to an area that had been suspected as a route into or out of the A Shau. The Hueys landed on the makeshift LZ, depositing the troops as before.

The lieutenant gathered his three sergeants around, using the map to explain the mission.

"We're here, we need to get there, set up a perimeter and run small patrols, maybe an ambush or two. Stay there for two days, then pack up move to a new location and do the same. CO wants us to operate in small teams this time, maybe catch something that could evade a platoon moving, something like that."

The men stood silently waiting for the lieutenant to continue.

"My feeling is that by putting us so far out, they think we might run into elements moving through the area, far enough away from camp to feel safe."

"Kensington, your squad has point, get us here."

Sam looked to where the lieutenant was pointing on the map.

"Affirmative, sir."

Once again Smooth led the way moving the long green line toward the position. Finding a good spot to set up he stopped the column and motioned for Sam to come forward.

"How's this work?"

Sam nodded.

"Yeah, should be good for a couple of days."

The platoon moved into position setting up a defensive perimeter. Spending the rest of the day running patrols, the men settled in for the night. Wilson joined Sam by his position, this time he offered the cigarettes.

"Stick, you find anything out there today?"

Wilson shook his head no.

"You?"

"Nothing, not even old stuff. Area's clear. Nobody been here."

Wilson nodded.

"This is fucked up. I'm too short to be in the bush. White guy this short, wouldn't be out here."

"I'm short and I'm a white guy and I'm out here."

"Not that short."

"What's the count?"

"40."

Sam nodded.

"Probably last patrol. Won't send you out after this."

"After this. Shouldn't even be out here now."

Sam nodded, not having an answer.

"I'm gonna ask the LT if I can take the resupply bird back in."

"We're getting resupplied already? We just got here."

"I mean when it comes in a couple of days. See what he says."

They sat silent, pulling on their cigarettes. Finishing, Wilson stood up.

"See you in the morning, we can do this shit all over again."

Wilson started to walk away, but came back kneeling down leaning close to Sam.

"I been meaning to ask. Any dreams?"

Sam shook his head no.

"Probably because we're not doing anything. Maybe a good sign, won't hit nothing before I can get out of these fucking boonies."

Sam smiled.

"Glad I could help."

Wilson smiled.

Another day of patrols netted nothing. The lieutenant decided to stay another night and take resupply in the morning before finding a new location. For good measure he sent out two ambushes.

Resupply was scheduled for late morning, after which they were to pack up and move out. Two early morning patrols had come up negative. The lieutenant was eager to move to a new location and was on the horn requesting resupply come out earlier, but was informed that the schedule had been set. They would try to be out as early as possible.

Handing the horn back to his RTO, the lieutenant started to walk away, but the RTO called him back.

"Another call, sir."

The lieutenant took the handset and listened for a few moments, nodding, finally handing the handset back to his RTO. Just as quickly he walked away, heading for the other side of the perimeter.

"Wilson."

"Here, sir."

"Wilson, I've just been informed that you're to be on that

resupply bird out of here. I guess somebody finally did the math, realized how short you were. Pack up your shit, you're done."

The smile on Wilson's face continued to grow.

"Wilson, you should have enough time to say goodbye. Who do you want to take over the squad?"

"Calvin Weathers, he's my second."

"Very good. I'll give him the good news. You get ready."

Wilson nodded. Packing his gear, he set the ruck sack on the ground. All he needed to do was pick it up. Walking over to where first squad was set up he couldn't contain his smile. Kensington saw him first.

"Well?"

"Fini boonies."

"That's it, you're outta here?"

"What the LT say when you asked?"

"Didn't have too. Somebody in the rear instructed him to send me in. Gonna be on that resupply bird soon as it gets here."

The rest of the men gathered around him. Smooth and him did the black dap handshake. Whitey and Big John shook his hand. Lopes did the abbreviated version of the dap. Hump and Body Man patted him on the back. They drifted away leaving only Wilson and Kensington standing together.

"Stick, it's been a pleasure."

Wilson nodded reaching out to do the white version of the black dap handshake they always did.

"I'll see you back in camp. Got some processing to do, should be there for a couple of days, you know."

Sam looked at him as they finished their handshake.

"We're supposed to be out here another four, five days, think you'll be there that long?"

Wilson looked at Sam, his smile shortening for a moment.

"Sure I will, you know how long paper work takes."

Sam nodded. Wilson turned to walk away, but turned back

hugging Sam, who returned the embrace.

"You alright for a white guy."

"Yeah, you're not so bad for a black guy."

Wilson nodded, then turned and walked briskly back to his ruck on the ground. Grabbing it up he made his way to where the Huey would be landing on their makeshift LZ.

The buffeting of the blades announced the arrival of the resupply bird. Sam Kensington watched the Huey land, the supplies being pulled off and caught a glimpse of Wilson getting on. He watched the bird take off and disappear into the distance.

Nodding to no one in particular, he saluted the disappearing bird.

After six more days of patrol they finally went back to camp. Wilson's bunk was empty. All of his gear and personal stuff was gone. The bed was stripped and the mattress rolled up.

Sam Kensington dropped his ruck next to his bunk, sitting down hard, staring at the empty bunk next to his. Smooth walked over.

"Looks like Stick di di maued already."

Sam nodded

"Hey, a bunch of us going to get some hot chow. You want to join us?"

Sam looked at Smooth.

"Yeah, that'd be great. I'm right behind you."

Smooth nodded. Sam watched him and the others walk out of the tent. Before the tent flap had a chance to close, a spit and polish clerk entered. Sam watched him.

"I'm looking for a Sergeant Kensington."

"That would be me, but call me Sam."

"Yes, sir."

"Sam or sergeant or Kensington or… but not sir, okay?"

"Yes, sir."

Sam just shook his head.

"So what can I do for you?"

"Stick, I mean Sergeant Wilson gave me this envelope to give to you."

Sam motioned for him to come over, taking the envelope from him.

"Sit."

The clerk sat on the empty bunk across from Kensington as Sam tore open the envelope. Pulling the single sheet of paper out, he read and broke into a smile.

Thought you should know a brother.
Thanks for the magic.
Wilson.

Sam handed the sheet of paper to the clerk.

"You a brother?"

"Yes, sir."

"A brother I should know?"

"Yes, sir."

"I see. What else did Wilson tell you?"

"He said to never call you no redneck."

Sam smiled.

"What else?"

"He said to keep you informed as long as you are here, tell you I hear anything about the platoon or whatever, think it might be important you should know. And if you needed anything to get it or find out for you."

Sam smiled, sitting back against his bunk.

"Did he tell you I'm a brother?"

"Yes sir, he did. Said you might look otherwise, but no doubt you were a brother."

Sam sat smiling.

"Sir?"

Sam looked at the clerk sitting on Wilson's empty bunk.

"What did he mean by thanks for the magic?"

Sam smiled, sitting up and leaning in closer to the clerk, knowing full well what Wilson meant.

"Nothing really, just the bond that forms between the men in the field, something you REMFs wouldn't understand."

Sam paused looking at the clerk.

"Do you know what a REMF is?"

"Yes sir, its what you grunts call us in support."

"Yeah, right. Anyway promise me you won't be a REMF. Grunt needs anything treat him fairly. Don't get no attitude, like you're better than him."

The clerk nodded.

"Anything else Wilson say?"

"Told me I didn't treat you right, he'd make my life miserable, might even get me transferred to the bush. Can he do that, sir?"

Sam smiled.

"What you think?"

"Sir, I gotta believe he could. Stuff he knows, told me stuff even I didn't know. How he know that stuff?"

"He knows a brother."

"Huh? Beg pardon, sir?"

Sam smiled waving his hand in the air.

"Let's just say he knows a lot of people."

The two men sat silent. Sam looked up.

"How long is he gone? How much did I miss him by?"

"Wilson left a couple of days ago. Got orders to Cam Rahn Bay, to finish up, some admin job. Said there was a nurse over there that needed his attention. I'm not sure…"

Sam put his hand up stopping the clerk.

"Say no more, I understand."

The clerk sat silent. Finally Sam looked up.

"Anything happening, I should know about?"

"No, sir. Best I know your CO wants to keep running patrols. I heard him say too many of his company were short and that he would have to start over before all the experienced men were gone."

Sam nodded.

"That right?"

"Yes, sir."

Sam looked at him.

"I got a little more than two months left. What's next?"

The clerk smiled broadly, reaching into his breast pocket.

"Well sir, I saved the best for last."

Sam watched as he unfolded the paper.

"These are your orders. You leave here in ten days to go to Cam Rahn Bay. You need to be below sixty to get reassigned, so I had to delay the execution date. They're already in transit. What I did was post that you would be on patrol until then and couldn't leave before that date. Otherwise someone might get suspicious. Think you can stand another patrol?"

Sam looked at the clerk reaching for the paper.

"These are legit. Just like that?"

"Yes sir, but not yet, won't exist for another seven days."

"How? How did you get these cut?"

"I didn't. They came from a first lieutenant back there requesting you be reassigned to his unit for field Intel. You might know him sir, he was the XO here."

Sam sat back on his bunk laughing out loud.

"Boy, I sure do know him. Always pumping me for Intel on the bush."

The devilish smile growing on his face.

"Did Wilson have anything to do with this?"

The clerk sat up.

"Whatever do you mean, sir?"

"I mean that Wilson is in Cam Rahn Bay and the XO, Lieutenant Orville Smith I worked with here, is in Cam Rahn Bay and here are orders assigning me there…"

Sam looked at the clerk, who smiled.

"I'm sure it's all a coincidence, sir."

"Right."

"Will there be anything else, sir?"

"No, that has been quite enough."

The clerk rose up and started to walk away, before turning back.

"Remember sir, those orders don't officially exist yet."

Sam held the paper in the air.

"Got it."

Sam watched the clerk leave through the tent flap. He had forgotten all about eating. He sat back on his bunk holding the sheet of paper in front of him, rereading the transfer order to Cam Rahn Bay.

Sam Kensington finished the last patrol getting back in camp in time to officially receive his transfer orders to Cam Rahn Bay. Unfortunately he was too late to catch up with Wilson who had already boarded the freedom bird home.

Meeting up with the XO, he actually had an assignment to brief the former XO on the details of their patrols over the last few weeks. They spent most days together and nights discussing the dreams. The former XO was still intrigued how Sam knew such vivid details about the battle for the Shenandoah Valley. Lieutenant Orville Smith had some information sent from home on the battle and was able to give Sam a few more details that didn't matter much.

The lieutenant was even more intrigued that Sam hadn't had any more dreams since they left the A Shau Valley. After

several sessions, when it was obvious that Sam was growing weary from talking about dream sequences, the lieutenant
finally gave in and accepted the theory Sam had said Wilson
proposed that it was some kind of parallel war thing and let it be.

Sam did bring him up to speed on their patrols outside the
camp and that they were finding nothing to speak of. Their vis-
its dropped off after that.

Finally the day arrived and Sam Kensington boarded the
freedom bird home. Vietnam, the A Shau Valley and even the
Shenandoah Valley would be just another memory.

He sat back in his seat as the plane took off. Allowing himself a glance out the window, the sight of an army installation
gave way to lush green meadows, growing ever smaller as the
plane rose in the air.

Sitting back into the seat, he waited for the sign to go off
and reached for the pack in his fatigue shirt. Striking a flame,
he lit the tip pulling heavily, letting the smoke drift out. The
quiet roar of the plane soothed him.

Was it really over?

The cigarette ash dropped to the floor. Realizing he wasn't
out in the field, he sat up opening the ashtray and putting the
cigarette out. Using his foot he spread the fallen ash on the
floor.

The stewardess asked if he wanted a drink. The site of a
round eyed woman caused him to smile. He ordered vodka
rocks.

Yeah, it really was over.

Thirty-One

Sam Kensington sat dozing on his front porch, slipping in and out. Waking with a jolt he was surprised to see other men sitting around him. He was even more surprised when his eyes began to focus and the outline of men in uniform appeared before him.

To his left sat a Federal Soldier in his Union blue clad jacket and pants. Immediately next to him sits what appears to be a cavalry soldier, also dressed in Union blue, with a wide brimmed cavalry hat. Next to him is a man dressed in a uniform he doesn't recognize. Next to that man is a world war one soldier and finally next to him is a world war two soldier.

Sam Kensington fought hard to focus in and clear his vision. The aspect of what is in front of him is just too fantastic to believe. It has been over twenty years since he left Vietnam, and all of that behind him. Not even a dream since, nothing. Now what the hell was this in front of him?

A voice spoke out.

"Just give him a minute, he'll come around."

Sam looked at the man speaking, the man on his far left in the Federal uniform. Shaking his head one more time, Sam tried to clear the vision, but it would not go away.

"Who are you? What the hell do you want?"

"Now he's got it. Focus in son, we'll only do this once."

"Huh? Do what?"

"Give him another minute."

The men sat in silence as Sam tried desperately to focus in, hoping the whole thing would fade away. Finally, when the vision didn't fade, he gave in.

"Okay, I'm listening."

Sam looked at the men from right to left and was struck by their uniforms. Obviously this had some kind of military con-notation. The men continued to sit silent. Finally the man on the far left, the man in the Federal uniform spoke up.

"Your head clear yet? Don't want to repeat myself."

Sam Kensington nodded.

"Yeah. Yeah, I'm ready. What is this?"

Sam looked at the men from left to right, stopping at the man on the far right. It was his father, a much younger version of his father in his world war two uniform. Unfortunately, his father had passed away ten years ago.

"Dad?"

The man on the far right just waved his hand in the air and pointed to the man on the far left, the Federal.

"Alright then, I'll start."

Sam looked back at the man in the Federal uniform, barely able to take his eyes off his somewhat younger looking father.

"You listening?"

Sam nodded and turned slightly to face him directly.

"I'm Samuel Kensington of the 10th Vermont. The one who started all this, purely by accident I can assure you. This here is Samuel Kensington as well, fought with the Union Cavalry in the Indian wars of the 1880s. Next to him is Albert Kensington fought in the Spanish American War, still don't know what he did, but that's where he fought. Next to him is Albert

Kensington Jr., fought in the great one WW One. The last man you know, of course, Joseph Kensington, fought in the next great one WW Two."

Sam looked at each man as he was introduced.

"What has it been, twenty years now since your war? Had the dream, while you were there, I 'spect?"

Sam nodded yes wanting to say more, ask any number of questions, but held back. The Federal soldier nodded, pointing his finger.

"They all have had the dream, or so they say."

The Spanish American Soldier, Albert Kensington interrupted.

"Did anyone else have the headaches? How come I'm the only one who had the headaches?"

The Federal soldier interrupted him.

"Will you shut up with the headaches? No one else had the headaches. Only you. You ask that every time."

Gathering himself, the Federal soldier continued.

"We're all back in the Shenandoah Valley fighting Jubal Early and his Confederates. Of course I was the only one who was actually there. Didn't understand any of it when my son Samuel told me, thought he was nuts. Still do."

The union cavalry soldier looked at him, waving his hand in the air.

"I never said they was no dreams. I only said it felt like I was fighting alongside you when you was there. Must have been the stories you told me as a child, made me think I was there. Filled my head with that nonsense."

They all sat silent for a moment. The Federal stared at him.

"Are you through?"

The union cavalry soldier nodded yes.

"How come we have to have these interruptions every time we do this?"

The other four men sat silent not answering.

"Okay, where was I?"

He cleared his throat, waiting to see if anyone else would chime in, but when they didn't he continued.

"Like I said we, I mean all of you seemed to have dreamt about being in the Shenandoah Valley fighting that war as I actually did. Anything else comes to mind?"

The other four men nodding, all spoke at the same time.

"The gun."

"That's right, the pistol I carried, even though everyone thought I was crazy for carrying it into battle."

He nodded, pointing his finger.

"Well, let me tell you how crazy I was."

The Federal looked hard at Sam.

"Boy, you still have that gun?"

Sam perked up, looking back at him.

"Yes, of course. My dad gave it to me before I left for Vietnam, said it would protect me. Said it was the family good luck charm. I didn't pay much attention to that. Put it in a drawer for safe keeping. Yes, I still have it."

"Good. What do you know about it?"

"Nothing. It's an old Civil War Pistol, that's all I know."

Samuel Kensington looked at him brushing at his blue coat.

"What's your full name, boy?"

"Albert Samuel Kensington, Sam to my friends."

"Right. How do you think you got your name?"

Sam looked at the men around him.

"Well, now it's obvious that I was named after you fellows. I did know my grandfather was Albert and that I had a Samuel in the line. Thought it was funny that my dad was named Joseph."

"I did that to get away from the cadence of Samuel and Albert, thought we were finished with those. Your father obviously has a sense of humor."

They all looked at the man in the WW One uniform.

"Are we through?"

They turned their attention back to the Federal soldier.

"If you boys are through with the small talk I'd like to continue."

He looked at each of the men, then back to Sam.

"So your old Civil War pistol as you call it, mean anything to you?"

Sam shook his head no.

"Well, let me tell you about that gun."

Sam sat up, turning to face Samuel Kensington.

"It's an 1860 Army Colt Revolver. Fine weapon. Black powder, fires a Minie ball. We could actually get paper cartridges for it from Quartermaster, so we didn't have to load the ball, the powder... "

He stopped.

"Except for my son, you boys don't have any idea what I'm talking about do ya?"

The Spanish American Soldier, the first Albert Kensington raised his hand.

"I actually carried it, but never used it. I think I was the last one to actually carry it into battle."

Samuel Kensington stared at him until he was uncomfortable.

"Anyway, it was a fine weapon. Came in handy on more than one occasion. We had those single shot muskets..."

Samuel looked at the men.

"What's the use? It not the pistol so much it's what happened to me when I got that gun that's important."

He sat silently measuring his thoughts, finally looking directly at Sam.

"Boy, you gotta understand, I don't take to that stuff, and wouldn't have given it another thought if not for the fact I was there."

He paused again.

"It was at Cold Harbor. I was out walking the battlefield, for no particular reason. The Negroes were out clearing the field as they do, putting the discarded weapons in the wagons, stacking the bodies. Removing the Federal boys and loading the Rebels into wagons for them to claim."

He paused for a moment, looking down, but then quickly looking up.

"Strange thing happened. I came upon a horse had been shot dead and still had that double pommel holster on the saddle. Well one of those holsters still had that very pistol tucked in it. The other side was missing. Always figured the feller riding it probably abandoned the horse when it went down and didn't get a chance to get his other pistol."

He paused, looking down the line of men before turning back to Sam.

"Anyway, I pulled it from the holster. It was still new looking, all shiny. I checked and it was fully loaded. Thought I'd hang onto it. About the time I was set to put in my belt, I heard a Negro yell to stop. Wondering what that was all about, I waited for him to come towards me, but keeping my hand on the hammer, in case he was about to try something."

Nodding and pointing, he continued.

"You couldn't be too careful with them Negroes. Lot of them freed slaves running wild, never know what you're up against."

He paused again. Sam waited for him to continue. The other men sat silent. Sam wondered if they had heard this story before, but then assumed they had to have heard it. He was about ask, when the Federal Soldier continued.

"Turned out to be a young boy, no more'n fifteen, sixteen maybe, came up beside me and said: 'Massuh suh, you don't want to be holding no dead man's gun, bring you bad luck.' I said how you know that man who owns this gun dead? He said he didn't, but I shouldn't take no chances."

The Federal soldier paused, nodding.

"Not sure what he was getting at, I asked him again. Again he said he didn't know, but had a way to fix it for me. I followed him over to an old Negro lady leaning against a tree. Negro boy said it was his grandmother's mother and she could fix it for me."

The old Federal paused and smiled.

"Boy I gotta tell you eyes like to look right through you. She gave me this big toothless grin and motioned for me to sit down next to her. Once I did she reached for the gun. Now mind you that gun was loaded and I was hesitant to give it to her, but the boy said it would be okay, she just wanted to make it better. By this time I thought they both were nuts."

He paused.

"Well, I finally handed it over to her and she placed it on her lap. Next thing I know she's got some things look like charms or something and she's waving them across the pistol, chanting, I don't know what. Her eyes roll back and she starts mumbling some stuff. I tell you I was fixing to get the hell out of there, but the boy pushed on my shoulder, holding me down. Kept saying she'll make it better."

Pausing, he looked around for a moment before fixing his eyes back on Sam.

"I gotta tell you boy, I about had enough. Finally her eyes come back into the sockets and she looks directly at me. Placing the gun in my hands, I thought it was over, but she grabs both wrists and holds them tight keeping the pistol in them. She starts rocking back and forth, chanting again. Again her eyes roll back and she starts shaking, sweating something fierce, she goes through this again and again. Finally she lets go, looking totally exhausted from all the rocking about. Her hands drop to her sides and she appears to be fast asleep. Well, now I'm starting to get mad."

Stopping for a moment, he leans forward as he continues.

"Well boy, this is when it gets even stranger. The young Negro boy tells me that she removed the bad spell from the gun, so nothing bad will happen to me while I have it, sort of like a good luck charm. I thought he was as crazy as the old lady. But then he tells me that when she laid hands on me, she gave me a protection spell, so nothing bad will happen to me, or my family. Said as long as the pistol was in the family, the family would be protected from harm."

He paused shaking his head.

"You understand, boy?"

Sam nodded yes.

"As long as it is in the family, nothing bad will happen."

Sam continued to nod yes.

"I thought it best to accept what he said and high tail it out of there, before I pressed my luck."

He paused then looked directly at Sam.

"I asked this old Negro doing the cooking what that might have been about. He said the older Negroes practiced the old religion from their country. Probably came over, wasn't from here. They all had strong beliefs in their ways back there. Said the woman worked one of the spells they believed in, removed the bad spirits and summoned the good spirits to protect me. It was what they did and I should pay no mind to it... but if I felt different."

The Federal paused again pointing.

"I though he was nuts as well."

He paused again.

"But I did know the Negroes had their own religion they practiced. Knew they strongly believed, much like the Baptists, or those damn Methodists... Saw them Negroes on many occasions doing just that huddled together. Figured it must be no more than that and let it be. Didn't pay it no more mind."

Once again he paused gathering his words.

"Like I told you I don't take to that stuff. It wasn't until a few years after the Shenandoah Valley that I realized just how close I came to... well, how it all worked out. And left it at that."

Pointing to the man next to him, he continued.

"Well when Samuel here, my son, went off to fight the Indian Wars out west, chased Geronimo for as long as we fought the damn war."

The old Federal looked at his son, the cavalry soldier, who waved his hand in the air. Finally he continued.

"Anyway I insisted he take the gun with him, even though they was using them new six shooters."

The second Samuel Kensington interrupted this time.

"I did use if for a spell, but after, I just kept in my saddlebag. It was always with me."

The cavalry soldier, the second Samuel Kensington shrugged his shoulders.

"Had a few scrapes, might have gone either way."

The Spanish American Soldier, the first Albert Kensington chimed in.

"Well I actually did carry it into battle. Why I..."

The first Samuel Kensington raised his hand in the air.

"It's probably why you got the headaches, because you're giving me one now."

Samuel the first, motioned to Albert the second the WW One soldier who spoke softly.

"I left it at home, here in the states while I was over there, but I did carry one of those new .45 automatic pistols they issued us, so maybe..."

Joseph Kensington raised his hand in the air and also responded.

"As did I. We also had those .45 pistols. And son as you know you left that colt at home while you were in Vietnam, so it appears..."

Sam nodded yes, and was about to mention that

Wilson gave him a .45 as well, before they went into the
A Shau, but was interrupted before he had a chance to say
anything.

The old Federal waved his finger in the air, speaking over
everyone.

"Point is, it appears it just has to be in the possession of the
one who needs protecting. Look I still don't know what that old
Negro lady did, but we all made it through, don't know if it was
the spell she put on the pistol or the spell she put on me. I never
tried to figure it out. As long as the revolver was passed down
to the next generation, that gun protected the current holder
and that's all you need to know."

They all sat silent. Finally, Sam spoke up.

"What about the dreams?"

The old Federal looked at him.

"You'll have to ask them. I didn't have any damn dreams, I
was there."

Sam smiled.

"Of course. Dad?"

Joseph Kensington looked at the rest of the men then turned
back to his son.

"Whenever I was about to go into battle, I would have a
dream about Samuel in the Shenandoah Valley campaign, same
dream always the same dream, no matter what. Never could
figure it out. Did a little research when I got back home, but
nothing seemed to make sense or mean anything so I let it be.
Albert?"

Joseph Kensington turned to his father, the WW One
soldier.

"Nothing here either had a dream before a battle. Once I got
home they stopped, I never thought about them again until you
fellows came to visit."

The Spanish American soldier nodded.

"Never thought much about the dream, too busy with the

headaches…"

"Again with the headaches?"

"You don't understand, the headaches were as real as the dreams, why…"

The old Federal raised his hand stopping him from speaking.

"Son, what you think?'

The union cavalry soldier, Samuel the second looked at his father.

"I already told you what I thought."

The Federal nodded looking directly at Sam.

"Boy, what you think?"

Sam looked at him, then the rest, then his father.

"In my case, I was actually in a valley fighting, the A Shau Valley in Vietnam that was paralleling your battle in the Shenandoah Valley. Just thought the dreams mirrored that battle which was why I was having the dream, some kind of parallel thing. Any of you fight in a valley campaign like his?"

The other men sat silent. Sam continued.

"I tried to figure it out, but kept coming back to the fact both battles were fought in a valley for the same reasons, to rid them of enemy and supplies. It seemed logical at the time. One valley campaign to another."

The old Federal sat back in his chair.

"That what you figure, boy?"

"Yeah, it made sense at the time."

"Pure coincidence that's all. Do you want to know what I think?"

Sam nodded yes.

"First battle after that old Negro lady put the spell on the gun, and me for that matter, that's all. Since all you boys have the same dream, it stands to reason it has to do with that foolish spell somehow, no more than that. I 'spect since the dream always focuses on the time I had close calls, could have gone either way, it has something to do with that spell that old Negro lady put on me or the gun, or both, that's all. Still don't cotton to that stuff, but maybe there's something to it. Don't know and don't care either way."

Sam nodded. The rest sat silent. The Federal leaned forward and continued

"Besides boy, when was the first time you had the dream?"

Sam looked at him, trying to remember.

"I'd have to say, the first time we met the enemy?"

"Were you in that valley then?"

Sam looked at him shaking his head.

"No. No, we weren't."

The old Federal raised his hand in the air as if to say see I told you so. Sam sat silent, digesting that concept for now. Wanting to ask so much more, but thinking better of it, instead looking at each of the men before him.

"So why are you all here?"

Joseph Kensington spoke softly.

"How old is Carroll now?"

"She's eighteen. She was only eight when you…"

Sam stopped looking at his father, putting his head down.

"And is it true what she's about to do?"

Sam looked back up at his father, nodding.

"Yes, she's decided to join the military."

"If that don't beat the Dutch?"

Sam looked hard at the old Federal, but he just pointed back at Sam. For effect, he spoke with authority.

"Then you know what you have to do now, boy."

Sam continued to stare at the old Federal, but he continued in that authoritative voice.

"You have to give her the gun, make sure she's safe. Won't do us no good anymore… you neither."

Sam nodded, clearing his throat, somewhat intimidated by the old Federal raising his voice.

"So that's why you're here, to make sure I pass the gun on?"

"That's right boy, has to pass to your... kin."

The old Federal couldn't say it. Sam stared at him, waiting for him to continue. Finally, after looking at the rest of the men, he did.

"Still don't get why they let women in the military. Doesn't make sense, they wanting to go off and get killed. Should be in the home where..."

The old Federal looked at Sam glaring back at him.

"Well, that's my opinion."

Sam nodded.

"So I need to give her the pistol now? What if she hadn't gone in the military? Then what?"

The old Federal pointed waving his hand in the air.

"Every generation has its war. Simple as that. No question you would need to pass the gun on, just didn't think..."

Sam looked at the old Federal, waiting, but he looked away this time. Finally turning, he glanced at the other men in front of him, then turning back to the old Federal, he nodded, he understood.

The world war one soldier, Sam's grandfather spoke softly.

"That's the way it's always been."

The old Federal nodded and waved his hand at the rest of the men.

"Besides if that was the case boy, we wouldn't be here."

Pointing again at Sam, the old Federal continued.

"Remember what your father said when he gave you the gun?"

Sam nodded.

"Yes, he said to make sure the gun got passed down to the next generation, never to sell it or lose it, it has to stay in the family."

"Correct. Make sure your... daughter understands that. She'll need to pass it on when it is her time."

The old Federal looked at Sam, leaning forward in his chair, but spoke softer this time.

"Do you understand that?"

Sam nodded.

"Then I believe our work here is done."

The rest of the men sitting there in their uniforms nodded in agreement.

Sam Kensington woke with a start. The day was growing long and he was getting a chill out on the porch. Looking out onto the street, he tried to visualize the men sitting around him just a moment ago, but realized they wouldn't have fit on his little area. As he focused in on that scene, he realized the street had been dirt and the porch was a big white wraparound. Certainly not his porch. He could only imagine that he must have been on Samuel's porch as if he had been summoned, just like the others must have been summoned.

Digesting what he remembered from the latest dream, or vision, or whatever the hell that was, he was sure of two things. His daughter was going into the military and the gun was still in his drawer, which he apparently needed to pass down before she went into the service.

Getting up from his chair he felt the cramps of having fallen asleep in an awkward position on that old chair, as he had come to do quite often lately. Stretching, he made his way into the house, back toward his bedroom. Inside the bottom drawer, wrapped in a protective cloth was the 1860 Army Colt Revolver.

Sitting on the bed he laid the cloth on his lap. Moving the cloth away the pistol came into view, still in the same pristine condition as when his father gave it to him. Gripping the handle he raised the gun up, looking the pistol over. The revolver was certainly something to behold.

Back when Samuel used it in battle it was just another gun, but now it was something special, something too special to ever use again. Sam turned the gun over in his hands once more before placing it back on the cloth.

He removed the receiver from the cradle, punching in his daughter's number. She answered on the third ring.

"Carroll, hi it's dad."

"Yes, yes, I'm fine."

"Listen, I need to see you, what's your schedule like? Will you be home tomorrow?"

"In the evening then. I can come by then."

"No. No, nothing 's wrong, really. I promise."

"Alright I'll see you then, say around six thirty?"

"Great, see you then."

Sam hung the phone back up. He looked at the gun on the bed next to him. Carefully he wrapped the revolver back in the protective cloth, setting it back down beside him on the bed. He felt a chill pass over him.

Thirty-Two

Sam Kensington took a deep breath before he rang the bell. The gun, wrapped in the protective cloth, held tightly in his left hand, tucked into his side. Waiting as the door unlocked he took another deep breath.

Married shortly after he returned home, but divorced five years later, the last person he wanted to see when the door opened was his ex wife. Their relationship was tenuous at best, confrontational at the worst. His fears were relieved when he saw his daughter standing there.

"Hi, dad."

"Carroll."

They gave each other a hug.

"Com'on in, what's up?"

Sam stepped inside as she closed the door behind him.

"Come in. Come in."

Sam walked into the living room taking a seat on the couch. She sat down across from him turning, tucking her leg under her. He took another deep breath.

"So, you're really going through with this?"

"I believe so."

Sam nodded.

"You're sure that's what you want to do? I mean there are other options."

"Like what?"

"College, for one."

Carroll smiled.

"This will give me the opportunity to do both."

Sam nodded looking away for a moment.

"One last question."

She nodded okay.

"I know you're doing this just to piss off your mother, and actually I'm okay with that aspect, but I want to make sure this is really what you want to do, not something concocted for any other reason."

"Dad, I'm sure. Really I am. I thought this through and I believe it is the best option for me at this time. I almost think I want to make a career out of the military."

Sam nodded again reaching for the cloth.

"Then you're going to need this."

He handed her the cloth-covered pistol.

"What is this?"

He motioned she opened the cloth.

"A gun. You got me an old pistol. I don't think I can use this."

She stared at her dad, smiling at him, then noticed the seriousness on his face. Sam pointed to the gun.

"It's not just a gun. It's an 1860 Army Colt Revolver, used primarily during the Civil War."

"The what?"

Sam waved his hand in the air.

"That's really not important. That gun has been in the family for a long time."

"I bet it has."

Carroll turned the gun in her hands looking the weapon over.

"Anyway, it is a family tradition that when a son…"

"Screwed that up didn't I?"

Sam smiled, waving her off.

"It is a family tradition to pass the gun down to the next generation, especially if one of that generation is going into the military."

Carroll sat silent watching her father squirm a bit, not sure why he was so nervous.

"My dad gave it to me just before I left for Vietnam. He called it our family good luck charm. Somehow it's suppose to protect you from harm."

Carroll let out a laugh.

"Really?"

Sam waved his hand in the air.

"Never mind. Just know his father gave it him and his father gave it to him… it has been passed down for several generations. Like I said it's known as the family's good luck charm. It's family stuff, don't try to analyze it."

Sam sat silent, Carroll waited for him to continue. She set the gun back in the cloth but left it unwrapped. Sam looked at the revolver lying on the couch.

"Listen, I never told anyone this before and I'm only telling you this one time, so you'll understand, okay."

Carroll nodded.

"Back in Vietnam, we had a mission into the A Shau Valley, a well fortified enemy base of operations."

Sam hesitated taking a deep breath.

"I can't believe I'm about to tell you this."

Sam took another deep breath, sweat forming on his forehead. He removed his jacket. Carroll moved closer, taking his hand.

"It's okay, you can tell me anything."

Sam looked at her, nodding.

"We were on patrol and a mortar shell exploded right in

front of us, myself and two other guys. No way we could have avoided it, but instead of exploding completely, the shell blew out sideways, to the right and left of us and behind where the shell hit. In other words, nothing came our way. It was totally bizarre. We chalked it up to a defective shell, but we all knew something happened that day, we just didn't know what."

Sam put his head down. A quick flash of the incident, with Wilson at his side saying as much, passed. Sam looked back at his daughter.

"Do you understand what I'm saying?"

Carroll nodded yes, still rubbing his hand.

"You know me well enough to know I don't go into that kind of stuff and all kinds of weird shit happens in a war. Just know something happened that day, or more specifically didn't happen, that can't quite be explained."

Carroll nodded.

"Thanks for telling me."

Sam nodded.

"Listen I don't know from nothing about that gun, but... look, all I'm asking is for you to take possession, put it some-place safe and keep up the family tradition of the good luck charm. Okay?"

Carroll smiled. Sam waved his hand in the air.

"Jesus, my dad just handed it to me and said: 'Here for good luck, put it away, it's the family good luck charm.' I took the gun from him stashed it in a drawer and forgot about it."

Carroll patted his hand.

"Okay, I got it. I'll take that pistol, put it somewhere safe and like that."

Sam nodded.

"That's all I ask."

"You know I'm going in the Air Force. We don't do war like you grunts did."

"Doesn't matter, you could wind up in a war zone. War

doesn't discriminate between services, you know?"

"Yes daddy, I know."

Sam nodded pointing.

"Listen, you'll be in the military, chances are you'll wind up somewhere dangerous…"

"Okay, I got it. You sold me. I'll take the revolver and put it somewhere safe as my good luck charm."

Sam nodded.

"How soon you leaving?"

"Right after I graduate. I get a month off then head to basic training."

Sam nodded.

"Well, you need anything you let me know."

"Yes, daddy. I'll be fine."

Carroll picked the gun up.

"So tell me about this thing."

"That thing, as you call it is an 1860 Army Colt Revolver, mostly used by the cavalry. They had this special holster that held two guns mounted on their saddles. Because of the weight, most infantry didn't carry one. They had single shot muskets."

"Uh huh."

She put the gun back in the protective cloth and wrapped it back up.

"I do have one question."

Sam looked at her.

"Since I still live with mom and once I go in, I really won't have a place, what do I do with this?"

Sam looked at her, thinking.

"You still have your room here, don't you?"

"Well yes, but once I leave, I'm sure mom will take that over, put my stuff in the storage shed or knowing her in the trash. I wouldn't want her to find this, do something stupid with it."

Sam nodded.

"You're right, that is a problem."

He sat silent thinking. Finally he looked up at her.

"You do understand she doesn't know anything about this or anything I just told you?"

Carroll nodded yes.

"I assumed that."

Sam nodded, pointing to her.

"So, how about we do this. You put your stuff at my place and you can stick the gun in with that. I'll keep it safe, until you get back or send for it. That way we'll both know the gun is safe."

"Works for me. I have two boxes ready to go, shall I just put it in there."

Sam put his hand in the air.

"No, you keep it until you leave, put it in that last box you bring over. Make sure it's your stuff in that box."

Carroll nodded.

"Okay, I can do that. You really think it is that important?"

"Yes I do."

Sam looked at her, then reached over to take her hand.

"Listen, I know you don't take any of this seriously, but if for no other reason just do it for me?"

"Okay. Okay, I said I'll do it."

Sam patted her hand.

"Any other stories you want to tell me?"

"Huh? What?"

"About your time in Vietnam?"

"Maybe some day, not yet."

"Ah, you're no fun."

Sam waved his hand in the air.

"Well, I better get going. Don't want to run into your mother, if I don't have to."

Carroll smiled.

"And you ask me why I'm leaving?"

Sam smiled, they hugged and walked arm and arm to the door.

"Remember what I told you."

"Yes daddy."

"Call me, you need anything."

"I will."

They kissed and Sam walked out the door hearing it close and lock behind him. He turned to face the door, nodding. Quickly walking down the driveway he got in his car, taking one last look at the house his daughter lived in. He fired up the engine and drove off.

Thirty-Three

The sound of a passing car caught his attention for a moment. Subconsciously he pulled his collar tighter around his neck. With the sun lower in the sky, the late day chill was starting to engulf him as he sat there on the porch of his house.

Two days ago he had given his daughter the family good luck charm, the fabled 1860 Army Colt Revolver that his father had given him and for the first time since he went off to Vietnam the pistol was not in his possession. The chill he was feeling wasn't totally from the day growing later.

Looking up and out to the street, focusing on nothing, Sam Kensington let his mind drift. Starting with the encounter on the porch, somebody's porch, with those five soldiers, which still rattled him. Seeing a much younger version of his father in his uniform, both unnerved him as well as haunted him, not to mention actually speaking to him.

Sam Kensington shook his head as if to clear the cobwebs, trying to refocus to the present. The passing traffic on the street came into view for a moment, but his mind quickly went back to the vision of those five uniformed soldiers sitting in front of him.

Focusing on his father first, he panned left to the man in uniform next to his father, his grandfather, to the man in the uniform he didn't recognize, his father's grandfather, to the man in the union cavalry uniform, and finally to the old Federal, actually a very young striking man in the Union Blue uniform. They sat there staring back at him as if waiting for him to speak.

From the story of the old Negro woman casting a spell on the gun, to cleanse the bad spirits and then the spell on the old Federal to protect him and his family. Did he really believe any of it? Could he believe any of it? All he knew was that just before he went off to Vietnam, his father brought the gun to him and told him to hang on to it, put it in a safe place he had said. Said it was the family good luck charm.

After stashing it in a closet, he gave it no more thought and went off to war. Yes, war, Vietnam, the A Shau Valley. What did Wilson say? "Thanks for the magic." Had there been magic at work? The story he told his daughter about the mortar shell exploding sideways. How about the fire fight where several rounds were fired at point blank range and not a bullet hit? There were other incidents, or course, but those two were most notable, because even Wilson had noticed and made sure to point them out.

What about Wilson, why did he never make contact when he got back? How could he get so close to a person, then just forget him? He had been told war does that to people. Adapt, hang on, do what you need to survive, then just forget it. Sounded like a lot of bullshit now.

Remembering boarding that freedom bird back to the world, the mind had forgotten so many things. Leaving a war to return to normal life caused that. You can't hang on. You can't relive the past. Moving forward is the only survival. To dwell on the past, relive those experiences only tends to throw you off balance. Contact with anyone from that time would mean a rehash, would only bring back those memories. A clean split is the only solution. Again, that sounded like so much bullshit…

Sam Kensington looked at the street again, a passing car caught his attention if for no other reason than it was driving by. He watched until he could see it no more.

Twenty plus years had passed since that time now so long ago. Once that freedom bird landed back in the states, he had thought no more about the war, Vietnam, the A Shau Valley and most importantly those dreams of another war, during another time. Wilson said it best, it's one thing to actually be fighting a war, but to be dreaming you in another war at the same time is just fucked up. Sam smiled, remembering that exchange.

A truck passing caught his attention for a moment as the sound of the diesel motor engulfed the air, making a rather loud noise. He waited for the truck to move on before focusing back on his little memory trip.

All those meetings with the XO, Lieutenant Orville Smith, had only served to tell him where he was in the dream, and basically what that battle was all about. He was sure Wilson's assessment that he was in some fucking parallel war was really still the best answer. Fighting a war in two valley campaigns sounded logical to him, which had made it interesting to hear from the old Federal that that had nothing to do with anything.

Well Samuel Kensington, you old Federal, I beg to differ with you, it had everything to do with everything. The causes were the same, the idea was the same and the results were… well never mind, the ending was far from the same.

He had made the effort to research that Shenandoah Valley Campaign of 1864, while he was attending college on the GI bill and much to his amazement, the campaigns, more than one hundred years apart, were eerily similar in every respect. On both counts the campaign was performed to drive the enemy from their stronghold, disrupt their movement and destroy their

stores of supplies, basically to prevent the enemy from supporting other regiments, thereby disrupting the flow of men and
supplies to other… Damn Samuel, how can you say it didn't
matter? It was exactly the same. Why, you could put both of
them on a piece of paper and draw lines to, well between them
and… Ah fuck it, what does it matter anyway?

He watched another car pass, pulling the collar tighter
around his neck. Even though the chill was getting colder, he
wasn't ready to go inside yet. Two kids on their bikes passed,
waving as they did. He waved back, keeping his hand in the
air a bit longer than necessary. As they disappeared down the
street he slowly dropped his hand down, resting it in his lap.

He thought about his daughter. Was she really going off to
war? She's certain about joining the military that was for sure.
And maybe being in the Air Force, gave her some advantage,
she wouldn't be some low life grunt as he was. Still there are
situations that can be quite dangerous even for the Air Force.
Well, she's got the gun now, that will protect her, or so the old
Federal said.

"Thanks for the magic." That's what Wilson had written in
the note. The gun sure protected him, as well as me and apparently everyone around us, in that godforsaken A Shau Valley in
South Vietnam so many years ago.

The sound of a horn caught his attention. He watched as a
rather attractive young woman came running out of a house
and jumped in a car with a boy driving. Damn, they still do
that, honk, rather than going to the door? He watched the car
drive away.

And what about those dreams? They were so vivid. Why
was he reliving the old Federal's battles? That was never really
explained even with what that old Federal thought about the
spells and such. Apparently the others had their dream as well.
Can't just be because it was the first battle after the spell was
cast. And to what degree did the others dream? Was it just one

battle? Two? And no one else was in a valley at the same time as the dream. I still gotta believe that was more than coincidence. No, doesn't matter what the old Federal says, there was more to it than that, so much more.

Sam Kensington again looked toward the street, but nothing was passing by this time, all was quiet. He stared for a long time, the chill growing colder, and the sun just about gone. He noticed the street lights were on already.

No those dreams were so much more, the campaign too damn similar, the parallels too rich. No, so much more was going on in his dreams and real world at the time that couldn't be easily explained away.

The one thing no one had mentioned, and he certainly wasn't going to bring up, was that time when Samuel Kensington, that old Federal, took the ricochet in the shoulder, how his own shoulder hurt, turned black and blue. Yeah, how do you explain that? He wondered how the old Federal would have responded to that question.

Sam Kensington sat for a long time on his porch staring out to the street. Darkness had completely set in and the cold had completely engulfed his body by now. Slowly rising from the porch chair, he stood and stretched before going inside.

Pouring vodka over ice, he added some cranberry juice. Shaking the glass to mix the contents he took a sip. Having quit quite a few years ago, this was one of the few times he wished he had a cigarette. Boy, they sure smoked a lot over there. He remembered back to Big John's rotgut and smiled as he took a sip of the drink in his hand.

Sinking heavily into the chair, he took another sip. Not ready to let go, he gave it all one more pass in his mind. Something Wilson had said came back to him, something about ain't no generals in the bush, hell ain't no officers in the bush. How that contrasted with the Civil War battles, where many officers and quite a few generals on both sides died in battle.

In fact, if he remembered right, they lost their division commander, Brigadier General Ricketts and oh yeah, that general from the Confederate side, what was his name again, oh yeah, Major General Stephen Ramseur. That seemed to be a big deal, losing him.

Sam Kensington took another sip of his drink, and realizing he had finished, got up to make another. As he swished the contents around to mix it, he had a thought.

What if there had been generals killed on that fucking hill in the A Shau in Vietnam, instead of just lowly grunts that were obviously expendable. What did Wilson say, the only way a general gets killed over here is if his air conditioner breaks and he dies of heat stroke.

Sam smiled and held his glass in the air in a mock salute.

Okay, back to that thought. What if a general or two, or even a colonel got killed on that fucking hill in the A Shau, would that have changed anything? Would that have mattered in the grander scheme of things? And what did that XO say, once the Union forces captured the Shenandoah Valley, the Federals held it, not giving the Confederates the opportunity to just take it back. How would that have changed things in the A Shau?

What was it Wilson heard from a brother, the NVA had already moved back onto that hill, before we had even actually left that fucking valley?

Sam Kensington finished the drink and set the empty glass on the counter, the ice cubes clinking.

Yeah, how would that have played out in the A Shau, if a general or two had been killed taking a worthless hill, but more importantly, if once we had taken that fucking hill, we held it? What a fucking novelty. We take the hill and we keep it?

Don't tell me there's no correlation between the two. The battle for the Shenandoah Valley was a matter of pride and sacrifice on the highest level, where as the battle for the A Shau was a waist of time and too many good men for apparently no good reason.

Sam Kensington reached for the vodka bottle, removing the cap and pouring the liquid over the ice. Adding a splash of cranberry, he swirled the glass around before raising it in the air.

"Here's to you Old Federal, for what you did, so many years ago and here's to you Stick, wherever you may be, I thank you man."

Sam Kensington downed the drink in one gulp, setting the glass down heavily on the counter bouncing the ice out of it.

"But it don't mean nothing."

acknowledgement

Many thanks to Ralph Kimball, my editor extraordinaire, whose attention to detail keeps me grounded. As a "storyteller," I tend to "pound it out," but Ralph's ever-watchful eye brings me back into focus. I cannot adequately express my appreciation for his incredible efforts to add the finishing touch to my storytelling.

www.ingramcontent.com/pod-product-compliance
Lightning Source LLC
Chambersburg PA
CBHW032143010726
47494CB00002B/334